9/10

THE LADY AND THE OFFICER

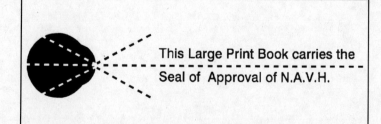

This Large Print Book carries the
Seal of Approval of N.A.V.H.

CIVIL WAR HEROINE SERIES

THE LADY AND THE OFFICER

MARY ELLIS

THORNDIKE PRESS

A part of Gale, Cengage Learning

GALE
CENGAGE Learning·

Farmington Hills, Mich • San Francisco • New York • Waterville, Maine
Meriden, Conn • Mason, Ohio • Chicago

Copyright © 2014 by Mary Ellis.
Civil War Heroine Series #2.
Scripture quotations are taken from the King James Version of the Bible.
Thorndike Press, a part of Gale, Cengage Learning.

LIBRARY OF CONGRESS CATALOGING-IN-PUBLICATION DATA

Ellis, Mary, 1951–
    The lady and the officer / by Mary Ellis. — Large print edition.
        pages ; cm. — (Civil War heroine series ; #2) (Thorndike Press large print Christian romance)
    ISBN 978-1-4104-7233-5 (hardcover) — ISBN 1-4104-7233-7 (hardcover)
    1. United States—History—Civil War, 1861–1865—Fiction. 2. Large type books. I. Title.
PS3626.E36L33 2014b
813'.6—dc23   2014025654

Published in 2014 by arrangement with Harvest House Publishers

Printed in Mexico
1 2 3 4 5 6 7 18 17 16 15 14

This book is dedicated to my husband, Ken, who stomped around an inordinate number of battlefields, museums, monuments, cemeteries, historical inns, and bed-and-breakfasts for years in the name of research.

The man also patiently slammed on the brakes at a countless number of roadside historical markers.

ACKNOWLEDGMENTS

- Thanks to Mary Elizabeth Massey's book *Women in the Civil War,* Phoebe Yates Pember's *A Southern Woman's Story — Life in Confederate Richmond,* and Bell Irvin Wiley's *Confederate Women* for inspiration for my fictional characters. Thanks also to Harold Elk Straubing's *In Hospital and Camp* and Louisa May Alcott's *Hospital Sketches.*
- Thanks to the Virginia Civil War Trails of Richmond and the U.S. Department of the Interior — National Park Service for a plethora of maps and research information, and fabulous vacations.
- Thanks to the countless authors of history that I have pored over for years, including Shelby Foote, Bruce Catton, Edwin Bearss, James M. McPherson, and Brian Pohanka.
- Thanks to Philip LeRoy, who loaned me his copy of *Killer Angels* by Michael

Shaara. The Pulitzer Prize-winning novel opened the eyes of this history lover to the wonders of historical fiction.

- Thanks to Donna Taylor and Peggy Svoboda, who read the rough draft of this novel years ago and encouraged me to keep at it.
- Thanks to the Western Reserve Historical Society, Cuyahoga Valley Civil War Roundtable and the Peninsula Valley Foundation of Ohio and GAR Hall, whose appreciation for Civil War history has kept my passion alive locally.
- Thanks to my agent, Mary Sue Seymour; my lovely proofreader, Joycelyn Sullivan; my publicist, Jeane Wynn; my editor, Kim Moore; and the wonderful staff at Harvest House Publishers. Where would I be without your hard work?

ONE

Cashtown, Pennsylvania
Late June 1863

"Gentlemen, please take heed to what your horses are doing to my flowers!" Madeline Howard spoke with the indignation that simmered after two long years of war.

Four blue-clad officers paused in their conversation to gaze down on her wilted ageratums and hollyhocks. The flowers were trampled almost beyond recognition beneath their horses' hooves. The soldiers offered faint smiles of regret and then resumed their postulating and pointing, affording her as much attention as they would to a gnat.

Except for one officer, who straightened in his saddle. Tugging gently on his reins, the man guided his mount out of the flower bed toward the road. "Good afternoon, miss. General James Downing, at your service. I apologize for the damage." He

11

tipped his hat and then turned his attention back to the others.

"Madeline Howard, General. *Mrs.* Howard." She marched down the porch steps. "If you would kindly move your meeting to someone else's yard, I shall be forever in your debt."

A thin, gangly officer mounted on a sorrel mare was quick to retort before the general could reply. "See here, madam. In case you're unaware, the war has come to the fine Commonwealth of Pennsylvania with the arrival of Robert E. Lee's infantry. Unfortunately, your posies are of no importance to the Union Army —"

"I'm well aware of the war, sir. My husband died on the banks of Bull Run Creek, leaving me alone to run this farm." Madeline settled her hands on her hips with growing indignation. "Those Rebs you're chasing marched through last week, stripping every ear of corn from my fields and every apple from my orchard. They stole my chickens, killed my hogs, and led my milk cow away on a tether. They took every bit of food from my kitchen and larder. So if I request that you not trample my flowers for no apparent reason, I would think you could oblige me!" Madeline completed her diatribe with a flushed face and sweating palms. After months of privation, she had finally lost her temper.

Silence reigned for several moments as the officers stared at her in disbelief. Then General Downing addressed the wiry, haughty officer. "Major Henry, you will order the troops to remain within the confines of the road so as to not needlessly damage civilian property." Along the highway, enlisted soldiers trudged in formation toward town, raising a cloud of dust that would linger for days.

Saluting, the major and the other officers spurred their horses and rode off, leaving Madeline's garden empty but ruined.

"Please accept my apologies, madam. And I thank you for your husband's sacrifice to our country." General Downing pulled off his leather glove and extended his hand to her.

"Thank you." Temporarily flummoxed, Madeline reached up and gave his callused fingers a quick shake.

"I will do my best to protect your town from further harm." He held her fingers and gaze far longer than necessary . . . or proper.

Tugging her hand free, she retreated backward so quickly she trampled the few remaining blooms missed by the horses. She felt a flush climb her neck as she picked up her skirt and ascended the steps. Pausing in the shelter of her porch, she looked back at the man who still sat watching. He bowed a second time, replaced his glove, and galloped away, adding another cloud of dust to the heavy air.

Madeline retreated inside and slammed the door, not pleased with her behavior. She wasn't a woman who normally became flustered in the company of men. Remembering the trampled flowers under her feet, she shook her head. At twenty-six years old and widowed for the last two, she had no time for silly flirtations or coquetry. When her wits returned, Madeline went out to her stable to check the animals. The din of artillery shelling all morning had made her mares skittish. If it hadn't been for quick thinking last week, her beloved horse stock — Tobias's pride and joy — would now be in the hands of the enemy. She stroked their sweaty flanks and scratched their noses, trying to calm them with soft words and a gentle touch.

Her own fears were another matter. Widowhood had inspired a determination to keep her husband's livelihood flourishing. War had created a constant demand for the horses she had bred and raised from brood mares. Although she would never become wealthy, the bills were paid. Tobias would have been proud of her.

Tobias. It seemed so long ago when he marched off proudly with the Sixth Pennsylvania Volunteers. He died at a battle the papers were calling First Manassas — first because a second unsuccessful battle was fought at the same loathsome place. He died before she'd grown used to the idea that he was a soldier. Madeline had missed him fiercely during the first year. Now, with the responsibilities of a farm, endless chores filled her hours, allowing no time for grief. She couldn't remember a day she hadn't fallen into bed exhausted. Usually, though, a sense of satisfaction accompanied her fatigue, so she persevered.

The marauding Confederates had taken everything she had, all but her beloved horses. The moment she spotted ragged butternut uniforms on the road, she had hidden her horses in a nearby cave — a place known only to her and the neighborhood children. Today, while her mares munched hay from their bins, Madeline stood in the barn doorway and watched wave after wave of boys in blue march toward the center of Cashtown. The war had come to Pennsylvania soil. What would happen to her sleepy little community?

■ ■ ■ ■

June 30

"Reverend Bennett?" Madeline called the man's name through an open window because no one had answered her knock on the door. From every indication, her preacher and his wife were both home. Laundry fluttered on the line, the barn door was open, and the back door stood ajar to catch the breeze. As she'd ridden her mare through the town square and down cobblestone streets, she'd seen very few people — nothing like the way things usually were, with friendly neighbors hanging over picket fences or milling on the church steps Sunday mornings. "Reverend Bennett!" This time she hollered his name in an unladylike fashion.

The middle-aged preacher's face appeared in the doorway. "Mrs. Howard. Come in, come in. Why are you out and about on a day like today?"

"I hoped to hear something of what is going on. Because it's been so hot, I rode my mare instead of driving the carriage. I tied Bo to your water trough in the shade. I hope you don't mind."

The reverend lowered himself onto an

upholstered chair. "Of course not. Please sit and make yourself comfortable. I was referring to the commotion on the roads, not the heat. With so many soldiers afoot, my wife insists we remain below in the cellar. So you haven't heard the news?"

Madeline sat on the edge of the couch and shook her head. "All I know is that I've seen troops on both sides moving for several days. First the Rebs stripped my farm, and now our boys in blue are stirring up the dust."

"Everyone appears to be headed to Gettysburg. Entire brigades of cavalry have been spotted, along with long caravans of wagons. And all those poor boys marching in this heat." He fanned himself with a folded newspaper. "Many of my neighbors are scared. They packed up their possessions and left."

"Where were they going?" Madeline asked, sounding childish. The fact she had no nearby relatives to offer shelter undermined her confidence in her ability to wait out the war on her farm.

"North, east — anywhere away from what's about to happen. But the time to leave is long past. It's no longer safe to travel. Rabble-rousers follow every army. You must stay with us until this ordeal is over. There most certainly will be a great battle."

"No, Reverend. I couldn't possibly stay. I need to tend Tobias's horses. If I'm not home, who knows what will happen to them?" She rose to her feet, regretting her decision to ride to town for news.

"All right, but at least come below and share a bite with Mrs. Bennett. She worries about you alone on your farm."

Madeline loved the preacher's wife like a dear aunt, so she followed him down the rickety steps to the cellar.

Later, after arriving home safely that evening, she relaxed and rocked serenely on her front porch. Lamplight from the kitchen window illuminated the handiwork of a spider. The thin gossamer strands weren't organized into a web, but were tiny trapezes strung between porch rails. Madeline stared, mesmerized by the insect's artistry. As she waited for the spider to reappear, the glittering yellow eyes of some creature peeked from the shrubbery. She felt no fear, only mild curiosity. The opossum issued a high-pitched squeak and then crept off toward home.

Heat lightning danced and shimmered over dark hills. The faint report of gunfire miles away was soon drowned out by peepers and cicadas. The frog-and-insect summer symphony soothed Madeline's nerves with its familiarity. The war, although close at hand, was far from her mind that night. Her thoughts drifted to a tall Union officer with silver glints in his hair and sparkling white teeth beneath a black mustache. Strength and power seemed to emanate from him. For the life of her, Madeline couldn't remember why the situation in the garden had so vexed her. They were *silly flowers.* She had lost much more just days ago. She'd lost her entire world a mere two years ago. For the first time, Tobias's face was replaced by that of another man. General Downing was on her mind as she replayed their conversation over and over.

"Foolish woman," she muttered. Rising to her feet, she peered up at a sky studded with bright stars. The moon had already finished its nightly path when she climbed the stairs to her room. She undressed without lighting a lamp, donned her long cotton gown, and slipped beneath cool sheets. Forcing away thoughts of the general, she quickly fell asleep and slumbered fitfully . . . until the scrape of a rusty latch roused her senses.

With her heart pounding in her chest, Madeline bolted upright. The sound of a whinny lifted the tiny hairs on her neck.

Someone was in her horse barn! She ran to the window and drew back gauzy curtains. Peering into the darkness, she could see nothing until the moon broke free from the clouds. Speechless, she watched as her prize-winning mares and new colts were led from the barn by several men.

What should I do? Grab Tobias's squirrel rifle from above the fireplace? Race outside and open fire on those who would pillage in the dead of night? Clad in my nightgown?

Instead, she did nothing. This time the thieves weren't the same marauding enemy who had stolen her chickens and milk cow. The men riding away with her beloved horse stock tethered to their mounts wore the blue uniforms and gold emblems of the U.S. Cavalry.

July 1

The next morning dawned hot and hazy, with acrid smoke hanging heavily in the air. Soldiers in every shade of blue, from the recently conscripted recruits to sage veterans, marched in both directions on the road. Horses pulled limbers of artillery and caches of ammunition, while farm wagons hauled food to a hungry army. White Conestoga wagons with red painted crosses carried the wounded from an early skirmish or

20

boxes of medical supplies. Young couriers galloped down Taneytown Road at break-neck speed, perhaps with vital dispatches.

In the hectic fervor, few soldiers took notice of a woman heading toward town on the side of the road. Walking in ninety-degree heat through clouds of dust didn't put Madeline in the best of moods. She arrived at the parsonage on Hemlock Street three hours later perspiring and thirsty. No one answered her knock until she finally pounded relentlessly on the door.

"Mrs. Howard!" said an astonished Reverend Bennett. "What brings you back so soon? I told you to stay indoors today —"

"May I come in, sir? And perhaps trouble you for a glass of water?" Madeline leaned wearily against the door frame.

"Forgive me, my dear. Come in. Rest in the parlor while I get you something to drink."

Madeline slumped onto a dainty embroidered chair and closed her eyes. The minister returned a few minutes later with a glass, a pitcher of chilled well water, and a plate of gingerbread cookies.

"Thank you." She filled the glass, drank it down, and refilled it. "This isn't a social call. If I may, I would like to borrow one of your horses. I have urgent business in

21

Gettysburg." She pressed the glass to her forehead.

"Of course you may. But why not ride one of your fine Morgans?" Reverend Bennett asked, pushing the plate of cookies a bit closer to her.

"They were stolen. That is my business down the road."

His face blanched with anxiety. "Goodness! That's awful, but you must not endanger your life because of horses. Soldiers are fighting down the road. There is a battle right here in Adams County." He whispered as though the enemy might lurk nearby.

Madeline straightened in the chair. "Those Morgans are all I have left. Please, Reverend, I've never asked you for anything before. I promise to return your horse safely."

"I cannot refuse you, Mrs. Howard, although I strongly advise against pursuing this matter. I will saddle my gelding once the sound of artillery ceases." He lifted his hand to forestall argument. "But I won't permit you to blunder into the fray. Rest for a few hours and refresh yourself. You can leave when it's quiet. It should be cooler by then too." He pointed at the settee and left the room before she could object.

Madeline sat for several minutes. Then

she devoured the plate of cookies and reclined on the couch. She'd intended to close her eyes just to rest them, but she awoke from a deep sleep to someone shaking her arm.

"My horse is saddled. Go with God, Mrs. Howard. I will pray for your safe return."

Mumbling her thanks, Madeline left by the back door and easily swung up into the saddle. The sun was already low in the western sky. She reached the Chambersburg Pike within minutes at a gallop and then slowed her pace. At the outskirts of Gettysburg, she had no difficulty locating the headquarters of the Union Army's Fourth Corps. Her spirits lifted when she spotted a beehive of activity surrounding the vacated farmhouse. Confusion might allow her to enter unnoticed. Madeline sucked in a breath, set her jaw, and rode into the fenced yard, stopping at the hitching post.

A stout lieutenant shouldered his rifle and grabbed the gelding's bridle. "Hold up, miss. The Martins no longer live here. This house is army property now."

"I'm well aware of that. I have business with General Downing. He's expecting me," she lied. Madeline slid from the horse and marched up the front walk, leaving the lieutenant still holding the bridle. Determination got her as far as the open doorway.

Then the same wiry, arrogant major she'd met in her flower garden blocked her path. "I cannot allow you to enter, madam. You may state your business to me." He spoke with obvious disdain for the intrusion.

"My business is that someone in this corps is a horse thief. My brood mares were stolen last night, and I expect redress from your commander."

"If it's financial restitution you seek, that is a matter for the quartermaster. You'll not be troubling the general with —"

"It is not money I'm interested in, sir. I want my property returned." Madeline fought to control her voice even as her courage flagged. Suddenly the partially open door swung further, startling woman and aide alike.

General Downing appeared as shocked to see her as the minister had been earlier. "Mrs. Howard, come in. I consider your visit a propitious omen." He turned toward the other officer. "It's all right, Major. I will spare a moment to settle a civilian injustice." He stepped to the side so that she could enter. Then he closed the door in the astonished major's face.

In an austere room smelling faintly of tobacco, Madeline's confidence vanished in a heartbeat. "You may not be pleased to see me once you hear me out." She tucked several loose wisps of hair behind her ear. "General, all of my horses were stolen from my barn last night while *Union* troops were moving through Cashtown." She paused to moisten her dry lips. "From my window I saw blue uniforms on the thieves. I can only surmise they were your soldiers." Surreptitiously she glanced at the maps and drawings spread across the desk.

General Downing appeared to choose his words carefully. " 'Thief' is a harsh word that some may consider treasonous. Considering that your husband died fighting for this great nation, would you deny the army desperately needed replacement mounts? Our officers and cavalry require horses." He dropped his voice to a murmur. "Today, there was a cavalry battle east of Gettysburg. Many good men died on the field. Many horses were lost as well. Everyone must make sacrifices in times of war."

Madeline's stomach churned, but she forced herself to meet his gaze and swallowed hard. Then she continued with far less zeal. "I understand your predicament, General, but those horses are my only source of livelihood. Without them, I will be at the mercy of friends and neighbors this winter. But beyond my selfish desire to survive, I respectfully request that at least *one* of those horses be returned. Bo is a medium-sized, brown Morgan with a distinctive white blaze down her face. She was bred from the best bloodlines in Pennsylvania. I hand-raised and trained her myself. You may keep the others as my contribution to the war, but please not Bo." Her voice trailed off as she willed herself not to cry.

He reflected on her words for a long moment. Then, "If you would make yourself comfortable, madam, I will be only a minute." He pointed at a chair and closed the office door behind him.

Madeline strained to hear what was being said through the solid maple, but the commotion outdoors masked all but the intensity of the general's discussion with the irritable major. She inhaled a breath to steady her nerves and perched on the edge of the straight-backed chair.

What an effect this man had on her. She felt as skittish as she had during her brief courtship with Tobias. She had never been one to be affected by a man's looks, yet her attraction to the officer was undeniable. Tall and broad shouldered, General Downing had thick dark hair that curled over his jacket collar. So dark they were almost black, his eyes transfixed a person with their intensity. He wore a meticulously neat uniform, distinguished, but with none of the flashy gold tassels seen in daguerreotypes. Yes, he was handsome, but his appeal stretched beyond physical attributes. He possessed some unseen quality — a magnetism that drew her like bees to nectar.

And she didn't like that one bit.

Madeline's woolgathering was abruptly curtailed by the door swinging open.

The general crossed the room in a few strides and then turned to face her. "I've sent word to the cavalry commander with Major Henry, my chief of staff. When the situation and time permits, he is to look into last night's *unauthorized acquisition* of civilian livestock, specifically for the horse you described. I cannot promise, but you have my word I will do my best to find Bo." He bowed from the waist as though they had just been introduced socially.

Madeline leaned back from his close proximity. "Thank you, General. I'm sure your *best* will be more than adequate. It's truly more than I expected. Good day." In her haste to leave, she knocked over the chair she'd been sitting in. If she had paused to pick it up, she might have recovered enough composure to make a graceful exit. But when she noticed the deep wrinkles around his eyes and the smile tugging at his lips, she fled from the room like a startled rabbit.

He is laughing at my clumsiness!

She saw that the young lieutenant was still holding Reverend Bennett's horse when she reached the porch. Madeline swiftly crossed the dusty yard, mounted, and rode home as though the entire Rebel cavalry was breathing down her neck.

James Downing had seen pain and suffering without measure during the past two years. He had witnessed deprivations of every sort in both civilians and soldiers alike. Yet something in Mrs. Howard's tender plea for a beloved horse tore at his soul. From his window he'd watched her disappear into a cloud of dust on the road with her bonnet ribbons streaming behind her. His intrigue with the perplexing woman went beyond a pretty face and comely figure. Was it small-town living that had preserved her sincerity and innocence? Why else would she worry about ruined flowers when the eastern theater of war had arrived at her doorstep? Yet she possessed enough spunk to ride into chaos to rectify an injustice.

He allowed himself one long, delicious moment to stare after her before turning back to his duties. *Great Scott, did I just agree to find a blasted horse in the middle of an engagement?* But before he slept that night, he would endeavor to keep his promise. If he had it to do over, he would agree to that and more. And the realization that Mrs. Howard had such power over him didn't sit well. Closing his eyes, his brain etched a picture of her face to carry into battle tomorrow. With creamy skin dusted with freckles, wavy hair the color of ripe wheat, and blue eyes that flashed in amusement or pique, Madeline Howard would be a hard woman to forget. He'd been smitten the first time he saw her on the road to Cashtown, and he would remember her long after he moved his corps to the next battlefront.

Her long limbs had moved gracefully beneath the cotton dress in her woebegone garden. Considering the fierce look on her face, his staff thought they had met the enemy sooner than anticipated. Never in his life had an upbraiding been so pleasurable. The moment she marched from her house, he lost his entire train of thought, having no idea what they had been discussing. And when he glanced back over his shoulder, he thought the window curtains had parted an inch. Had Mrs. Howard been peeking from between the lace panels? If he thought so enchanting a woman could be interested in him, he had indeed gone mad.

There was a surreal quality in the air before a battle. The din of the afternoon had mercifully yielded to an unholy quiet that evening. The common sounds of crickets and tree frogs not only failed to calm her, but also added to her trepidation of what the morrow would bring. Madeline had barely touched her dinner. She'd completed her chores in a dreamlike state and headed to the porch to read her Bible. Tobias's squirrel rifle, leaning against the post, offered little security. She had just settled into her favorite rocker when the distinctive sound of a sliding latch gripped her heart.

What on earth? There is nothing left in the barn to steal!

"Who's there?" she called into the dark. "Identify yourself or I'll shoot." She lifted the single-shot musket to her shoulder. Moments passed interminably until a familiar face stepped into the circle of light from the kitchen window.

"Please don't shoot. It is I, Mrs. Howard." General Downing pulled off his hat. "I

30

returned your horse to the barn. You'll not be troubled by future procurements." Fumbling with his hat brim, he looked more like a schoolboy instead of the highest commander of an army corps.

"Thank you, General. I'm deeply grateful for Bo's return, but I've been realizing I was selfish to make such a demand on a day like this. Please forgive me." Setting down the gun, she extended her hand over the porch rail.

He walked up the steps and shook briefly. "You are welcome. Truth be told, my adjutant thought me mad to trifle with such an errand, but if the horse was to be found, it had to be tonight. Tomorrow will bring a different world than the one we know today." He walked to the end of the porch and peered into her trampled flower garden.

A frisson of fear snaked up her spine. "Did the battle go well? Did your soldiers prevail?"

"My troops were only marginally involved today. We are still awaiting final casualty numbers from the cavalry commander, but it would seem they did *not* prevail. We have entrenched and established our lines around Gettysburg, positioning our artillery on high ground. We are prepared to meet the enemy." He turned to face her, leaning back against the rail. "Tomorrow my infantry will yield nothing. They won't be pushed back, but I'm afraid the outcome is far from decided."

"You must think me very foolish to ride to Gettysburg about a horse."

"I thought you were very brave to pursue what you wanted." Two or three moments passed before he added, "Your husband must have been very proud of your fearlessness."

She struggled to keep her voice steady. "I had little chance to be brave during the brief time we were married, sir. He signed up at Mr. Lincoln's first call for volunteers."

"My sympathies, madam, for your loss."

Madeline shook away her painful memories. "I have coffee left from supper. Would you like a cup before you return to camp? Inside — away from these infernal mosquitos?" She pulled open the screened door and gestured inside invitingly.

His laughter was an unanticipated response as he followed her into the warm room. "Forgive me, but your question took me by surprise. On my ride here, I racked my mind for some excuse that would allow me to sit at your table, even for a brief while."

"Why would you be eager to sit in my

kitchen? I have nothing to offer you except black coffee." With a flutter of nerves, she reached for the china cups above the stove.

General Downing gripped the back of the chair she had offered him but didn't sit. "Because I'm far from home, and this war has stretched beyond anyone's early estimations. Your kitchen is like a desert oasis." He gestured at the low-burning lamp sitting on the delicate lace tablecloth. "But mainly because I yearned to gaze again on the loveliest woman I've ever seen." He spoke the words as though they were painful.

Madeline silently stared at him, dumbfounded, and then she resumed filling two cups with the tepid brew. "Goodness, General. This war has certainly dragged on if that description fits me. My feet are blistered, my hair needs washing, and I could use a new dress." She laughed to ease his discomfort.

Blushing, he averted his eyes as he accepted the cup. His confession, hanging in the humid air, had embarrassed him.

"Please sit and enjoy your coffee after an eventful day." She slipped onto the opposite chair.

For a few moments he stared into the dark liquid. "Do not leave your house tomorrow," he said. "There will be heavy fighting.

A young woman was killed today by a stray bullet through her kitchen door. I understand she was engaged to be married, and she was only twenty years old. Spend the day in your root cellar, where you will be safe."

"But I can't possibly. I need to return my minister's horse —"

"*Please,* Mrs. Howard. I have a better idea of what's coming than you."

"Very well." She nodded in agreement as her chest constricted. The air seemed to have left the room. Who was this man who could so affect her? His brash compliment had pleased her, stirring emotions long dormant. Yet at the same time, she felt disloyal to Tobias's memory.

General Downing drained his cup in one long swallow and set down the cup. His hypnotic gaze held her transfixed. When he lifted his hand, she feared he might reach for her face. Madeline held her breath, unable to move. He was a stranger — a man she had met only two days ago.

Suddenly they heard horses in the stable yard, followed by the clatter of boot heels on her porch steps. She pushed up from the table as someone rapped insistently on her door. She opened it to find the irritable major on the other side.

"General Downing, couriers have brought word that General Buford is on his way to headquarters and wishes to confer with you."

The general faced her again. "Thank you for the coffee, Mrs. Howard. I'm afraid the demands of war have returned. Remember what I said about tomorrow." He donned his hat and swept from the room without a backward glance.

She heard the sound of horses' hooves thundering down the road before she could reach the window. The war had returned indeed.

July 2

Madeline awoke coughing in the hazy dawn. Her sleep had been dream filled and restless. The window she'd left open to catch the nighttime breezes admitted the acrid smell of smoke. Her eyes burned and began to water as she struggled to close the sash. A thick fog hung over the grassy paddocks and stripped cornfields, but at least for now it was blissfully quiet. She bathed and dressed in her coolest frock, anticipating another hot day.

After braiding her long hair in a loose plait, she donned a full-length apron and headed to the barn. Chores would occupy her hands and keep her mind off the general's warning. How could she cower in the cellar when she had two hungry horses to feed? Physical labor would relieve the anxiety building inside her. She sought relief from her restless thoughts of James Downing too.

How on earth did he find Bo among hundreds of cavalry horses?

After filling the grain bins with the last of her oats, she brushed Bo until her coat gleamed and her mane was free of tangles. Later she would return the Bennetts' gelding and buy horse feed with her dwindling cash. At the well she hauled up enough water to fill the troughs and last throughout the day.

The incessant sound of gunfire and cannon fire had begun shortly after first light.

Carrying two more buckets of water, Madeline retreated to the barn to crosstie and calm the horses. Both the gelding and her mare had turned skittish with the increasing cacophony. With her chores complete, she slumped down on a bale of straw in between the stalls. This was as good a place as any to wait out the bombardment. But two hours later, Madeline returned to the shelter of her house. She'd grown jumpier than her equine companions. After sponging off with cool water, she changed her dress and rummaged in the pantry for something to eat. Yet before she finished her meal, deafening roars of artillery began in relentless succession. Blast after blast shook her house to its stone foundation.

Madeline threw herself into a frenzy of activity to keep from going mad. In her room, she filled her largest valise with her favorite garments, personal mementoes, and framed daguerreotypes. She emptied her small horde of cash into her reticule as if embarking on a pleasant shopping trip instead of retreating from bedlam. She wasn't sure why she packed a bag, but when smoke began filtering under the door, she grabbed a jug of water, her Bible, and her valise and then headed to the root cellar.

The general's plaintive words flowed through her mind as she batted away cobwebs in the cellar's driest corner. Settling onto a rickety bench, she tried to collect her wits as the clamor increased outside her home. For an undeterminable length of time, she labored to read in the light from a streaky window while waiting for the battle to cease. Cramped and exhausted, she finally closed her Bible and leaned her head against the cool stones of the cellar wall. Heedless of spiders that might be lurking nearby, Madeline fell asleep in the dank confines as darkness fell across the blighted land.

Hours later, stiff and clammy, she awoke to discover that the shelling had stopped. She fumbled around for a match to light the kerosene lamp. As she struggled to ignite the wick, there was a new assault on her senses. Wood smoke. Not the sulfurous fumes from cannons but the definitive smell of burning wood. It took several moments for her eyes to adjust to the dark, and then she saw with chilling certainty smoke drifting through the floorboards of the kitchen above her head.

Fire! Her beloved home passed down from Tobias's parents was on fire. For several seconds she sat paralyzed until panic cut through her stupor. The cellar, her refuge during the battle, was rapidly filling with smoke.

Stuffing her Bible into her bag, she crawled on hands and knees in the direction of the steps. Not the wooden treads leading to her kitchen but the stone steps leading up and out to the backyard. Her parched throat and seared lungs ached, but she kept her watery eyes clenched shut against the smoke. On she crawled, dragging her reticule and valise over the uneven river rocks that made up the cellar floor. Something repulsive skittered over her fingers, while sparks and embers drifted down between the cracks overhead.

Coughing and choking with lungs desperate for air, Madeline at last bumped into the hard bottom step. She pressed her cheek against the cold stone and prayed that she wouldn't die in such a loathsome place. With almost no strength left, she pulled herself up toward air and light and life, but before she reached the third step, she sank into black oblivion.

■ ■ ■ ■

Two

■ ■ ■ ■

"Mrs. Howard!" Once James had broken a hole through the cellar door, he spotted a limp form at the bottom of the stone steps. Despite their brief acquaintance, the sight of her lying motionless filled him with terror. He yanked what remained of the door from its hinges and sprinted down the steps. With a new escape route, smoke billowed from the subterranean hole as fresh oxygen fanned the burning floorboards above her head. Shaking her by the shoulders, James tried to rouse her to consciousness.

"Breathe, Mrs. Howard!" He lifted her into his arms and carried her from the fiery tomb as a shower of sparks rained down from above. Several embers had already burned holes in her dress, and soot coated her face and hands. Just as they reached level ground, the kitchen floor gave way with a thunderous clatter of splitting wood and a belch of smoke. If he'd tarried another minute, she would have been buried under debris.

James laid her in the grass at the picket fence. "Madeline," he said next to her ear.

Suddenly she coughed and sputtered, fighting against his restraint.

"Rest easy. We're far from the fire. You're safe." He helped her to sit up and rest against a fence post.

A coughing fit racked her thin frame as she struggled to clear her lungs. It took her several long moments to regain her senses. "General Downing? I'm . . . I'm rather glad to see you," she said hoarsely.

"And I, you. I feared the worst when I spotted flames from the road. I prayed you'd taken my advice and sought shelter."

She straightened her back against the post. "I went below when the shelling began. If you hadn't come along, that cellar would have become my grave."

He flinched. "I've witnessed death all day, Mrs. Howard. Let's not speak of yours. God has shown mercy."

"Still, I'm in your debt, sir." Rising to her knees, she attempted to stand.

"Please rest here for a while."

"I cannot sit while my house burns to the ground."

With little choice James helped her to her

feet. "Major Henry, bring Mrs. Howard some water." His adjutant saluted but strolled off in no particular hurry. As they watched helplessly, the roof and walls collapsed, quickly turning to ash and embers.

"My home, along with everything I own," she said.

"Not quite everything. One of my aides retrieved your satchel from the stairwell." James pointed at the scorched bag.

"Thank you for that." Suddenly, her head snapped up. "The horses — mine and Reverend Bennett's!" She began stumbling toward the barn until he took hold of her shoulders.

"Your barn stands upwind of the fire. The horses will be fine where they are." He tried to restrain her without undue familiarity.

For a brief moment Mrs. Howard slumped against his shoulder. "I owe you my life and my beloved Bo."

James realized his soldiers were studying them with keen interest. "You men check on her horses. Tie them up across the street if it appears that the fire will spread."

After a quick salute the men left to follow his orders.

"General Downing?" Major Henry held a dripping canteen, keeping his gaze fixed on him. "The water is fresh from the well."

45

"Thank you, Major." James accepted the canteen without returning his salute. "Drink slowly," he said, pressing it into Mrs. Howard's hand.

"I'm obliged." She drank deeply, alternating gulps with choking coughs as her throat rebelled. "This was my husband's family home. His grandfather crafted all the furniture. Tobias brought me here as a bride." As she spoke, tears streamed down her face, leaving streaks in the soot.

"I'm sorry, but we cannot tarry here. There's still danger from artillery shells." As the heat from the burning house increased, James retrieved her valise, gently clasped her arm, and drew her to a grove of trees across the street

"I'll be forever in your debt for saving my life."

James Downing, a man who confidently issued orders from dawn until dark, didn't know how to respond. A woman with a smudged face and torn dress succeeded in doing what thousands of enemy troops couldn't — render him speechless.

He said the first thing that came to mind. "Keep drinking, Mrs. Howard. The water will do you good." After she took another long swallow from the canteen, he turned her chin away from the smoldering ruins

46

with one finger. "There is nothing left here."

"But this is all I have. Maybe I can fix a place to sleep in the barn until I'm able to rebuild." She sounded resolute, but a quivering lip betrayed her emotions.

"Impossible. There will be more fighting tomorrow. Allow me to offer you protection until this engagement has been decided."

Shaking her head, she pressed her fingertips to her temples. "How could I possibly come with you? I barely know you, sir. We are in the middle of a war."

"I'm well aware of that, madam, which is all the more reason to let me help until you can make other arrangements." James felt his back stiffen and his face flush even though they stood far from the blaze. "Today's battle was a mere taste of what's to come." As though to hone his point, an artillery shell burst over the trees, showering them with twigs and leaves.

She wiped her palms down her skirt. "Very well. I'll accompany you, providing I can bring the horses. One of them needs to be returned to the preacher." She crossed her arms over her chest as though chilled by thoughts of a bleak future.

James nodded and turned to his adjutant. "Major Henry, saddle Mrs. Howard's mare and tether the gelding to my saddle. Have the men take whatever tack and saddles remain from the barn to prevent them from falling into enemy hands."

Despite the direct order, his adjutant remained motionless. "Mrs. Howard is coming with us, sir?"

"Yes. We'll provide temporary shelter for her," James answered while placing a steadying hand on her back. She seemed ready to faint into the sunbaked weeds.

"Yes, sir." His chief of staff offered a frown with his salute and left him alone with a widow on the verge of hysteria.

James racked his brain for something to say, to provide some distraction, but he came up empty. Instead, they silently stared at the flames leaping toward the sky, the fire's smoke mingling with artillery haze, until an aide returned with Bo.

Mrs. Howard mounted with the grace of one born to the saddle. She stroked the horse's flank and murmured soothing words to calm the mare.

"Thank you, Corporal," he said. But the young man couldn't take his eyes off her. James could practically read his thoughts: *Who is this woman who made an otherwise sane, middle-aged officer dash off as soon as the Rebs were in retreat?*

Who indeed? Settling his hat firmly on his

head, James swung onto his own mount. The corporal handed up Mrs. Howard's valise, and James set it securely in front of him. "Are you ready, Mrs. Howard?"

She lifted her chin and nodded.

He looked at his men. "Mount up. We'll not stop until we reach headquarters." They took off at a breakneck pace, yet she seemed to have no difficulty staying astride. Despite her torn dress, soot-streaked face, and hair in a wild tangle down her back, Madeline Howard held her head high. She rode away from the smoking embers of her home as though she'd already put the fire into her distant past.

Who indeed? I have met my match for the second time today.

Madeline rode with the group of Union soldiers down Chambersburg Pike in silence. Although darkness had nearly fallen, she saw hundreds of dead and wounded men dotting the fields in grotesque shapes. In death some had raised their arms toward heaven as though pleading for mercy. It might have been a common sight for the veterans of the Fourth Corps, but she was aghast. She stared with morbid curiosity until bile rose in the back of her throat. Then she could look no more. By the time they arrived at federal headquarters, emotional and physical exhaustion had taken its toll. She nearly fell from the saddle. The general led her through the parlor that looked exactly as it had when she'd pleaded for Bo's return — a visit that seemed years ago.

He opened the door to a spacious, brightly painted bedroom. "You may rest here for the night." He set her valise on the floor next to a wall.

Madeline gazed around the room. "Isn't this someone's home?"

"Yes, but they won't be returning soon."

It took little time to consider her options. "This will be fine. Thank you, General."

He pointed at a marble-topped table in the corner. "There is water and clean towels so you may refresh yourself." He didn't take his eyes off her.

They were awkwardly alone for the first time since her rescue. Yet despite the fact he'd risked his life for her, she couldn't think of a single thing to say. Madeline lifted the bag containing her few remaining possessions from the floor.

"I'm sure you're hungry. I will see that a plate is brought in."

Nodding her head, she clutched her valise to her chest like a shield.

"Madeline." He spoke sharply as though trying to get her attention.

His familiarity snapped her from her stupor. "You've not been granted leave to use my given name, sir." She strode across the room away from him like an angry schoolmarm.

"Begging your pardon, Mrs. Howard, but I feared you'd taken leave of your senses."

"I'm in full control of my wits and prefer that you will take no undue liberties. I've heard tales of Union generals who tried to wield their power, and of women who threw themselves shamelessly at their feet."

"Where would a lady hear such things?"

"The newspapers are full of such stories."

"Yes, of course. I will post a guard to ensure your privacy." Bowing deeply, General Downing backed from the room.

"Wait! Where are you going?" Her voice contained none of the spunk from moments ago.

"To my troops camped in the field. Good night, Mrs. Howard." He closed the door behind him with a clatter.

She gazed out a window grimy from smoke and soot like everything else in town. Pushing up the sash, she found no relief in a gentle breeze from the west. She was alone in a stranger's house, in a world turned

51

upside down.

Madeline awoke in a comfortable bed in a cheery room to the soothing sound of rain on a metal roof. Slowly, as the details of the previous day returned, her gut twisted into knots. Kicking off the quilt, she perused her accommodations. A fire had been laid on the hearth for the next cool evening behind an ornate metal screen. Along with the four-poster bed, a bentwood rocker and a chest of drawers furnished the former owner's domain. She bathed at the basin for the second time since arriving, yet she couldn't rid the scent of smoke from her hair. She hastily dressed in a fresh dress from her valise, fearful that a soldier would walk in unannounced. Voices drifted through the walls, but she couldn't distinguish anything being said.

Her rumbling stomach reminded her that it had been a long time since her last meal. She'd sampled the food provided last night, but the cold, indistinguishable meat had held little appeal. Dark specks peppering the coarse bread looked suspiciously like dead insects. So instead she had drank the weak tea and crawled into bed, achy with fatigue. Madeline pressed her ear to the door and then ventured forth when she no longer heard voices, but the parlor was far from empty. The general's adjutant was leaning over the massive table.

"Good morning, Mrs. Howard. I trust you slept well." His tone contained none of the cordiality that usually accompanied such a greeting.

"Very well, sir." She smiled, clasping her hands behind her.

"We haven't been properly introduced. I'm Major Justin Henry, General Downing's senior staff officer." His gaze raked her from head to toe before refocusing on the red-marked map on the table.

Madeline walked to the window to peer out on the street, where soldiers on horse-back galloped in both directions. Wagons and ambulances bumped over potholes created by heavy artillery caissons.

A young man of no more than seventeen ran up the walkway to the house. "From General Sickles of the Third Corps," he said. Saluting his superior officer, he held out a sheaf of papers.

Major Henry pulled them from his grasp. "Wait for my orders on the porch," he snapped. The boy flew from the room as quickly as he'd entered. "General Downing requested that you remain here where you will be safe." The major spoke while scanning the newly delivered documents.

It took Madeline a moment to realize he was addressing her. "And where might General Downing be?"

"On the battlefield, madam, where we have engaged the enemy not a mile away."

"I was confused, sir, because you are still here." She met and held his scornful gaze.

"As the general's chief of staff, I assist maneuvers from headquarters based on dispatches from other commanders. But none of this concerns you, Mrs. Howard. Your breakfast is in the kitchen under a linen cloth. Your horses have been cared for, and the privy is out back. General Downing's orders were to protect you, but I have no time for further interruptions. I respectfully request that you stay in your room, out of my way." He pointed at the bedroom door with a gloved finger.

Incensed, Madeline strode to the kitchen as a minor act of defiance. Slumping onto a chair, she pulled off the linen napkin on the plate and devoured two flapjacks, a piece of dried bacon, and a shriveled apple. Today she chose not to inspect the food too closely. On the stove she found a pot of coffee, strong and still warm. Savoring a cup, Madeline assessed the kitchen — one wobbly table, five chairs, and a poorly made pine corner hutch that held the previous owner's treasures — chipped and mismatched china. She felt a pang of sorrow for the unknown lady of the house. Such a pitiful collection of goods that undoubtedly represented years of hard work. But when she remembered that everything she owned was packed in a cloth satchel, her glumness deepened.

On her way back to her room, she noticed that Major Henry and his aides never lifted their focus from their maps and drawings. Once she was behind a closed door again, she found a book on the bedside table to occupy her time, one certainly not left behind by the farmer.

Trying not to think about her cherished possessions lost in the fire, Madeline settled in the rocking chair to read *Medical Procedures for Regimental Surgeons and Nurses from the Office of the Medical Director of the Army.* Despite the monstrous title, the volume contained interesting recipes for soups and stews to build strength in convalescing patients. She pored over the application of tourniquets and field dressings until her back grew stiff. Outside, the rain had ceased, leaving behind a mist hanging dismally over the streets. Dropping her head into her hands, Madeline began to sob. At first she cried for herself and everything she lost. Then she mourned for the countless men who lay dead or dying on the battlefields in the distance . . .

Suddenly, she jarred awake with a crick in her neck and a sour taste in her mouth. She'd fallen asleep trying to distinguish the types of blood poisoning following limb amputations. The grisly descriptions had failed to hold her attention. Rising, she drew back the curtain on an eerily silent street. A white canvas medical wagon rattled down the thoroughfare, jostling its inhabitants mercilessly.

Madeline squeezed her eyes closed and pressed fingertips to her ears. She neither wished to see nor hear anything that would haunt the rest of her days. She returned to the chair, uncertain what to do. Should she wait for a man who had promised to protect her? What if General Downing had perished or been grievously wounded? If so, how would she explain her presence at federal headquarters to whomever arrived to take command? Despite the fact she'd known him only a few days, she couldn't bear the thought of him lying lifeless on the battlefield. Uttering a hasty prayer for his safety, Madeline hoped God wouldn't consider her plea shamelessly selfish.

Hours later, after the moon had risen over

the horizon, she heard the sound of voices and the stomp of boot heels on the porch. Madeline held her breath until a sharp knock was heard at her door. She swiftly went to it and swung it open. "Goodness," she gasped, wide eyed. "What has happened?"

General Downing entered her room dusty and haggard, not the same distinguished officer whose horse had trampled daisies in her garden. Stubble darkened his jawline, and his boots were caked with mud and blood. "Mrs. Howard, I am relieved to find you here."

"I share your relief in that you're still alive, sir." Then she spotted a dirty bandage tied over his uniform sleeve. "Have you been wounded?" She quickly closed the distance between them.

"It's nothing," he said, running a hand through his hair.

Madeline plucked at the knot that held the rag in place. "Not according to the medical journal I just read. That wound needs to be cleaned thoroughly or poison could spread through your body."

"Please don't concern yourself. The bullet has been removed, and the wound was dressed by a surgeon." He walked to the window overlooking the yard. "How did you fare today? You weren't troubled unnecessarily by my aides?"

"What an odd question, considering what you endured." Madeline shifted her weight, growing uneasy. "What of your soldiers? Did they prevail on the field?"

"Indeed, my men covered themselves in glory. But great losses have been suffered on both sides. The wounded have overwhelmed the town of Gettysburg. I must move my headquarters to a tent so this house can serve as a hospital."

His grim expression galvanized Madeline to action. She began stuffing her soiled dress, hairbrush, and Bible inside her valise. "I won't take up more of your time. If you would have Bo saddled, I will return to Cashtown. Reverend Bennett probably wonders what happened to his gelding." Finishing her task as she spoke, Madeline picked up the valise and turned to exit the room.

The general blocked her path in the doorway. "I didn't mean you had to leave this minute. Do you have any idea what the Chambersburg Pike will be like?"

She tried to step around him. "I believe so after reading that gruesome medical manual."

"Then you know it's no place for a lady."

58

"How can I stay here if this house will soon become a hospital? I must return to the Bennetts' at once."

The lady and the officer stared at one another for several moments.

He was the first to give in. "Very well," he said with a sigh, stepping aside. "I will accompany you to the preacher's."

"That won't be necessary." With her path clear, Madeline marched out the front door.

General Downing trailed on her heels. "Stragglers from both armies are desperate to get away from the battlefield, Mrs. Howard. Someone will steal those horses within the first half mile. We should cut through the back country, and you simply must have an escort."

She hesitated, finally hearing the wisdom of his words. Over her shoulder she said, "As you wish. Once again, I find myself in your debt, sir."

As soon as the horses were saddled, she tied her valise to the saddle horn and mounted Bo. Two of General Downing's aides prepared to accompany them, one on each side. Madeline prayed none of their horses would stumble in gopher holes or become lost in the dark. Fortunately, they came across nothing to cause concern, and within the hour they rode up the lane to the

Bennetts', creating a clatter that brought the minister and his wife to the porch.

"Thank goodness, Mrs. Howard," called Reverend Bennett. "You have been spared by God's grace."

Before she could respond, General Downing addressed the preacher. "My soldiers will secure the two horses in the barn, Reverend, and I will check on Mrs. Howard's welfare as soon as possible." He touched his hat brim and then disappeared into the darkness without another word.

Madeline slid from her mare and handed the waiting soldier the reins without a chance to express her gratitude or even warn the general about the dangers of dirty bandages. She walked toward her lifelong friends feeling bereft . . . and strangely disappointed to be once again separated from him.

THREE

James washed the dust from his face and hands and dressed in the cleanest uniform he owned. With his decimated corps to reorganize — forming regiments into new brigades, brigades into new divisions, and combining divisions to fortify his weakened Fourth Corps — his laundry and personal appearance hadn't been foremost on his mind. But now, with a pleasant errand before him, he tried to not look as disheveled as he felt. Even after thirteen hours in the saddle, he eagerly anticipated the hour ride to the preacher's house. He'd dismissed his staff for an evening of rest and recuperation. Frankly, he could do without Major Henry's sneers and thinly veiled questions about Mrs. Howard.

Attempting to court a widow in the aftermath of a battle might indeed be folly, but James had a right to be a fool at this point in his career. He'd been a soldier since leaving West Point as a young man. After serving in the Mexican War under Winfield Scott, he'd risen quickly through the ranks. When the army splintered after the secession of South Carolina from the Union, there had been no question of his allegiance. Born and raised in a small town east of Philadelphia, he'd been promoted to the rank of major general with the outbreak of war.

Now the conflict held duty, but no glory; responsibility, but little honor. After two long years, James had seen men commit acts repugnant to his Christian upbringing. Yet the interminable war dragged on, and he had no choice but to see it through. Tomorrow, or the next day, or the one after that, the new Commander of the Union Army would order him to follow General Lee through Maryland back into Virginia, perhaps finally bringing this juggernaut to a conclusion.

At thirty-eight, James was no longer young. But unlike twenty thousand other unlucky souls, he also wasn't dead. He intended to gaze on the lovely face of Madeline Howard for as long as possible, at least until she insisted he stop interfering in her life and go about his business. Tonight he rode alone to Cashtown, refusing offers to accompany him. If Mrs. Howard dressed him down at the front door, he would have no staff guards for an audience.

However, it was Reverend Bennett who answered his knock fifty minutes later. "General Downing, I'm indebted to you, sir. Madeline said you provided shelter and saved my horse from certain procurement by the cavalry."

"You're welcome, Reverend." James stepped across the threshold. "I wondered if I might have a word with Mrs. Howard if she is still your guest."

"Yes, of course. I'll see if she's —"

"Good evening, General Downing." Mrs. Howard appeared on the stairs. "I'm pleased beyond measure you traveled to Cashtown again. I have much to say to you as well."

Reverend Bennett clapped his hands. "Why don't you two make yourselves comfortable in the parlor? I'll see if Mrs. Bennett has a pot of tea handy and some of those shortbread cookies left from dinner." He gestured toward the small formal room.

She spoke before James could collect his thoughts. "Thank you, Reverend, but I'm eager to stretch my legs after being confined indoors today. I thought the general and I could take a stroll if he doesn't mind. I would like to show him your heartbreak."

"If he feels it's safe on the road, then by all means." Bennett's gaze fixed on James.

He rested his hand on his holstered side-arm. "I can assure you of Mrs. Howard's safety, sir."

"I'll just get my shawl." She turned and moved gracefully up the stairs.

While waiting for her return, James pondered the foolishness of his statement after what he had witnessed the past three days. Groups of men cut down by artillery shells, while one man was left unscathed. Bullets instantly killing a line of seven soldiers, leaving the eighth to drop to his knees in shock. There was no rhyme or reason in war. He couldn't possibly guarantee he could protect Mrs. Howard from harm. Although, without a doubt, he would die trying.

When she joined him at the bottom of the steps, she didn't seem to notice his false bravado. She began chatting the moment they reached the street. "Mrs. Bennett and I tore bed linens into bandages all day. Then we packed up canned goods to be delivered to Gettysburg. With so many wounded soldiers taken to town, they'll need extra food for weeks to come."

"You have a kind heart, Mrs. Howard, in light of your own troubles." They walked inches apart on the narrow sidewalk. The lemony scent of her toilet water filled his head like an elixir.

"I would imagine your hands are full after three days of battle."

"We're still tending wounded in the field and reorganizing the troops," he said, glad the evening shadows hid his expression. "But if it's the same to you, let's not talk about the war."

"All right, but I must thank you for accompanying me last night. I hope I didn't seem ungrateful for your kindness."

"Fatigue often circumvents our best intentions. I'm heartened to see you again. Have you given any thought to your plans? Will you live with the Bennetts until you are able to rebuild your home?"

She remained silent so long that he thought she wouldn't reply. Then she said, "I foolishly spoke in vain the other night. I have no money to replace my house. And the Bennetts have no reason to remain in Cashtown much longer." She came to a halt on the sidewalk.

James peered around, looking for anything that would indicate danger. But he could see nothing until the moon broke free from the clouds. Then a burned-out shell of a building appeared before them on a narrow lot. "I gather that is what's left of the preacher's church."

"The First Reformed Church and Cashtown school are no more." She crossed her arms and shivered. "Stray shells hit both buildings, the same as my home."

Silently, they watched a curl of smoke trail toward the clouds. "I'm sorry, Mrs. Howard. Your townspeople suffered much through no fault of their own."

She turned her back on the wreckage. "The minister and his wife will leave soon for Gettysburg. There's nothing for them here. They'll live at the Lutheran parsonage and assist with the wounded."

"Will you join them? Perhaps yesterday's reading may serve you after all."

She shook her head. "Only one room is available at the parsonage. I can't inconvenience the Lutherans or the Bennetts more than I already have. Besides, considering my queasiness with seeing your wound, I doubt I would make a good nurse."

"If I could . . . if you would allow it . . ." He struggled for the proper words, while his one opportunity was about to slip away.

Mrs. Howard turned her face toward him. "State your mind, General. We must return soon so Reverend Bennett doesn't worry."

"I wondered if I might write to you once you're settled. And may I hope for an occasional letter in return?" He blurted out the two sentences in quick succession.

"Yes, I would like that, but I'm not sure what I'll say with little to keep me busy." She began walking briskly in the direction they had come.

"The weather, the local harvest, perhaps an interesting tidbit you heard from a neighbor — I would relish any news from you."

Laughing, she cocked her head to one side. "At the very least, my letters will make for a good sleeping tonic, considering your worrisome career."

James tried to think of a witty retort or a way to express his delight, but one banality after another came to mind. They reached the preacher's front yard without exchanging another word. Then fate looked kindly on the hapless officer.

"General Downing," Reverend Bennett called from the porch. "If your troops aren't leaving town at daybreak, please come to supper tomorrow night. You may also bring your staff. We have food to cook and eat that won't travel well." The minister beamed at Mrs. Howard and then at him.

James spoke without a moment's hesitation. "Yes, I accept. Thank you."

Climbing the steps, she angled a smile

over her shoulder. "Before tomorrow night, I'll assess the weather, observe the harvest, and eavesdrop on the neighbors. I shall be ready for you, sir." She entered the house and let the screen door slam behind her.

James was left speechless in Cashtown once again.

Madeline awoke with an odd sense of confusion for the third morning in a row. She glanced around the austere furnishings of the Bennett guest room trying to regain her bearings. The memory of her home burning to the ground returned with a bit less pain than the previous two days.

When God closes one door, He opens another.

She wondered about her mother's favorite saying in light of her recent acquaintance with General Downing. Would *he* be her newly opened door? How could he be? The Union Army would only be in Pennsylvania as long as Confederate troops remained on Northern soil. Then the general and his corps would undoubtedly go to where the war took them, while she remained in Adams County where she'd lived her entire life.

But where exactly would she live? Certainly not in her cobwebby, mice-infested barn. And she couldn't live here when the Bennetts moved to Gettysburg. Not for the first time in life Madeline yearned for brothers and sisters. A large family provided a place to go when disaster struck, or at least someone to lend a sympathetic ear with well-intentioned advice. Her parents' untimely deaths had left her bereft of close relatives. Madeline thought back to happy childhood summers when her mother took her to visit her sister in Virginia. How she'd enjoyed playing hide-and-seek with her younger cousin, Eugenia. But angry words between the two brothers-in-law had put an end to their yearly visit.

Shaking off pointless reminiscences, Madeline washed, dressed, and headed downstairs to be useful. After all, with any luck she would see General Downing again tonight.

"Good morning, my dear." Mrs. Bennett's smile couldn't get any brighter. "Did you sleep well?"

"Like a lamb. What can I help you with, ma'am?"

"There will be plenty of time for work. Sit. Try my cornbread and tell me your plans," Mrs. Bennett said invitingly as she filled two porcelain cups with coffee.

Madeline laughed with little humor. "I

was just pondering my limited options while getting dressed."

Mrs. Bennett set a plate of cornbread in front of her along with her coffee. "Don't think you wouldn't be welcome with us. Every able pair of hands can be put to good use at the hospital. Mr. Bennett has already ridden there to work, but he'll return in time for supper."

"When will you join him in Gettysburg?" Madeline asked as she slathered her bread with warm butter.

"Day after the morrow. But he'll seek permanent accommodations for us and apply for a position at the seminary. Cashtown residents won't have money to rebuild their church for many years. You may live with us once we find a house."

Madeline knew this poor woman in a faded dress with one cloak to her name didn't need another mouth to feed. "You are so kind, ma'am, but I decided to write to my favorite aunt. I've always been fond of her and she of me. I know that under the circumstances she will insist I make my home with them."

"Your aunt?" Mrs. Bennett sounded skeptical. "You haven't spoken of her in many years."

"Aunt Clarisa and Uncle John live in Richmond."

Mrs. Bennett's disbelief changed to shock. "Richmond is the capital of the Confederacy! You would be moving to the heart of Dixie."

Madeline cut another piece of cornbread with her fork. "Hardly the geographic heart, ma'am, considering Richmond is a scant hundred miles from Washington."

The older woman clucked her tongue. "The number of miles makes little difference." Suddenly, she gripped the table as though dizzy. "Your uncle isn't a slave owner, is he? That is such ghastly business."

Madeline considered fibbing but dismissed the notion. A person shouldn't lie to the wife of her preacher. "If my memory serves, the Duncans own a few slaves who work in the house. But they live in town, not on a plantation. My uncle makes his living as some sort of treasurer."

"Slavery is slavery. It's an abomination."

After an uncomfortable moment, Madeline replied in a soft voice. "Then we must both pray for a swift resolution of the war and slavery's abolishment. But their lifestyle doesn't alter my current circumstances."

"Amen!" Mrs. Bennett rose to her feet to refill their coffee cups. Changing the subject, she asked, "Are you eager to see General Downing this evening? I thought we could serve fried chicken, succotash, fresh corn, and cucumbers. What say you?"

"That sounds delicious, but I thought we were using leftovers that won't travel or keep well."

Mrs. Bennett *tsk'ed* rather primly. "We can't serve dried bread, deer jerky, and two-year-old preserves when a general and his staff come to call, especially not considering . . ." The rest of her sentence hung in the air like laundry on the line.

Madeline nearly choked on her food. "Considering what, exactly?"

Mrs. Bennett picked up her empty plate and bustled to the sink. "Considering the fact the gentleman checked on your welfare two days in a row and then made a third trip here last night. Surely you don't believe that's ordinary behavior for a military man." She dropped her voice to a whisper. "Scores of people have been uprooted and rendered homeless after a battle. An officer keeps his focus on the task at hand, unless . . ."

"Unless what?" Madeline's back stiffened at the suggestion of impropriety.

"I mean no offense, my dear, but I think the man is sweet on you. And I saw *your* eyes glow like stars when he arrived. Beggin' your pardon, of course."

She shook her head. "Nobody courts during wartime."

"Quite the contrary. Many a young man proposes on the eve of his enlistment and then marries the gal the next time he's home."

Madeline stood and went to the sink. She began washing the dishes for something to do. How could she balk at Mrs. Bennett's conjectures when James Downing had crossed her mind no less than a dozen times? "We'll just see if he drops to one knee and pledges his undying love after dessert."

"He might if you play your cards right."

"Mrs. Bennett! Our sect doesn't allow card playing, as you well know. Your husband would be aghast to hear you say that."

"You know very well what I mean," she said with a wink.

A few minutes later, Madeline left the room to get her laundry. She planned to stay busy helping Mrs. Bennett prepare for the move, and also to keep her mind from fixating on the woman's preposterous ideas.

That evening Reverend Bennett was pacing the front hallway, anxious for his supper, while his wife paced the kitchen, hoping her chicken wouldn't dry out in the oven. Madeline rearranged a vase of wildflowers for the third time.

"Why don't we feed your poor husband?" she asked Mrs. Bennett. "He must be famished."

"Let's give our guests another fifteen minutes. A corps commander has plenty of responsibility."

Madeline opened her mouth to protest when the sound of hooves cut her short. She nervously patted down her hair and wiped a drop of sweat from her lip.

The minister greeted the officers at the front door, ushering them into the parlor amid a flurry of handshaking and introductions. Madeline stuck to the wall like new wallpaper. General Downing had brought two lieutenants along with the insufferable Major Henry.

"Good evening, Mrs. Howard," the general said. "I apologize for our tardiness." He removed his hat and closed the distance between them. "We received last-minute dispatches that required our attention."

"Think nothing of it. I'm . . . we're pleased you were able to join us."

"Shall we be seated?" Mrs. Bennett said as she bustled past with the platter of chicken. "I know you gentlemen must be hungry."

General Downing offered his elbow for

the short walk to the dining room. When Madeline took his arm, the officers nodded respectfully as she walked by. All except for Major Henry.

"Mrs. Howard, you sit there, between the lieutenants — a rose between thorns." Mrs. Bennett pointed at the opposite chair. "General Downing can sit here, across from you and next to me. The major and my husband will take the foot and head and shall be in charge of passing bowls." She hurried out for the rest of the meal.

When Madeline followed her to help, Mrs. Bennett ordered her back to the dining room. With five pairs of eyes on her, she sat down at the table feeling like a child. She noticed the table had been set with the Bennetts' finest china and an Irish handmade cloth. The lace had been repaired several times, but in the flickering candlelight the room looked lovely.

"Don't be shy, boys," said Reverend Bennett. "Let's start on these biscuits." He took one for himself and handed the basket to his left.

Madeline spent the next few minutes buttering every nook and cranny of her biscuit, not daring to meet the general's eye. When Mrs. Bennett returned with a tray of side dishes, the conversation turned to compliments about the fare as bowls changed hands and plates were filled.

"Thank you, Mrs. Bennett, for your hospitality," said General Downing. "It's been a long time since we dined at such a bounteous table."

"Hear, hear," chimed two of the soldiers. Mrs. Bennett blushed like a schoolgirl with the praise. "It's our duty and pleasure to feed our soldiers in blue."

"Is there any word when the army will move out?" asked Reverend Bennett. "You still have much to do in town, I would imagine." He placed a second piece of chicken on his plate.

"We're awaiting orders from the commander," General Downing said, glancing in Madeline's direction.

Major Henry slid three pieces of chicken from the platter and announced, "General Meade seems to suffer from the same malady as General McClelland — a bad case of hesitancy. Let's hope it's not terminal."

The lieutenants chuckled even as the general cleared his throat.

Ignoring the subtle warning, the major attacked a chicken leg as though the enemy had arrived. "We could have ended this war if we had been allowed to follow Lee. We could have struck while his divisions were disorganized."

With a fork paused midway to his mouth, General Downing glared at his chief of staff. "Perhaps the commander has information you are not privy to, Major. And regardless of the situation at headquarters, let's not spoil the evening for Reverend and Mrs. Bennett and Mrs. Howard with talk of the war."

"Begging the pardon of the ladies," Major Henry said, nodding solely in the direction of the minister's wife.

To fulfill his request for local news, Madeline had come up with several witty comments about the July weather and discovered news about a parishioner who just bore twins. But Major Henry's thinly veiled scorn eroded her confidence. Instead, she nodded politely while passing bowls and focused on her food. Throughout the meal she could feel General Downing's gaze on her.

After dinner, Mrs. Bennett rose gracefully to her feet like a society matron. "Why don't you gentlemen retire to the porch? I'll send Mrs. Howard out with a pot of coffee in just a few minutes."

As the dining room emptied, Madeline stacked the dirty plates onto a tray.

"Go to the kitchen for the coffee and pie, my dear." Mrs. Bennett bumped her with a well-rounded hip. "I can handle this. Make sure you pick out the best small plates."

"I'm happy to deliver the dessert, ma'am, but I insist on helping you with dishes."

"Nothing doing," Mrs. Bennett hissed under her breath. "Those officers spend all their time with one another. How they must long for polite female company." She pushed Madeline out of the room. "Go. I'll make sure Reverend Bennett remains with you outside."

A short while later, Madeline carried a tray out to the narrow porch filled with cigar smoke. "Pie, gentlemen?" she asked. Passing around the plates, she tried not to choke on the fumes.

"I cannot eat another bite." General Downing set his slice down on a table. "But I would appreciate your company in the garden." He gestured down the steps.

"I must serve the coffee." Madeline held up the carafe as though proof of her assertion.

"My men are capable of pouring their own. Come, Mrs. Howard." He led the way down the steps.

Once she was away from the other soldiers, her courage returned. "Goodness. I'd forgotten who was in charge for a moment."

"Tell me how goes the harvest." He barked the order as if she were one of his men.

"What?"

"The harvest," he said in a tone more suitable for a man courting a woman. "I know you asked nearby farmers." Chuckling, he turned his gaze toward the panoply of stars.

"Let's see," she said, stopping at his side. "You just ate two ears of the first local sweet corn, and hay is ready for the second cutting."

"And the weather? What say you about that?"

"It's still too hot for my taste, but the breeze from the west may bring a shower or two."

"What about Cashtown news?" He turned his focus from the sky to her.

Madeline felt as though her heart stopped for a moment. "Mrs. John Price gave birth to twin sons this week. Mr. Price is said to be overcome with joy."

"Overjoyed . . . as I am in your presence. Thank you for your forbearance with my staff tonight. They are often blustery following a battle." General Downing reached for her hand, pressed it to his lips, and lightly kissed the backs of her fingers. "Good night, Mrs. Howard."

Before she could react or think of a single clever reply, he disappeared around the corner of the house. Madeline stood thunderstruck on the Bennetts' parched lawn. *But you haven't touched your pie yet.* She remained in the garden until the sound of hooves faded in the distance. Then she wordlessly climbed the stairs to her room and closed the door.

She'd never felt more confused in her life.

■ ■ ■ ■

FOUR

■ ■ ■ ■

July 15

Unable to sleep, James stood at the flap of his tent at headquarters waiting for dawn to break on a wet, dreary world. Heavy rains during the night had turned the roads into a sloppy mess. If new orders arrived today, moving his troops a considerable distance would be downright nightmarish, if not impossible.

"Coffee, sir?" Major Henry appeared with two steaming mugs in hand.

James gratefully accepted one and let the hot liquid scorch his throat on the way down. Something needed to break him free of this tedium. Time spent waiting for General Meade to make a decision had been unbearable. Each day the Union Army hesitated, General Lee moved deeper into Virginia into areas he was not only familiar with, but could depend on townsfolk to feed and reoutfit his troops.

Not that his soldiers didn't have anything to do. The battlefield had to be combed for cartridge boxes and abandoned weapons. Horses running loose after riders had been wounded or killed had to be corralled and reassigned. Quartermasters required time to forage and procure available food for man and beast. And the dead? What a loathsome task to bury ten thousand men in blood-soaked, unhallowed ground. Civilians arrived daily to pick through a grisly array of corpses in vain hopes of finding a son, husband, or brother. That horrific sight would linger in his mind until he moldered in his own grave.

"Breakfast, sir?" Major Henry placed two plates on a low table. "Fried eggs and ham, biscuits and gravy, fresh berries."

"I'm not hungry, Major. More coffee will suffice." James stared at the street where wounded prisoners moved through town under regimental guards.

"It might be awhile before we see food like this again, unless General Meade decides to remain here for the rest of summer. Perhaps he plans to wait till next spring to mount an offensive on the Rebs." He refilled the general's cup from the pot.

"Leave the food, Major. That will be all."

"Tarnation, sir. President Lincoln replaced

George McClelland because he was too cautious. And now our new commander is dragging his boots through the dirt too."

James finished his cup of coffee, reluctant to chastise his aide for speaking frankly. Hadn't he been thinking along the same lines? "Be that as it may, we must —"

Without warning, a breathless courier stepped inside and snapped a salute. "General Downing, a dispatch from General Meade with his compliments, sir."

James grabbed the rolled parchment and scanned the contents. "I have been summoned to federal headquarters for a meeting of corps and division commanders. Major, alert the officers to ready the men to move out."

"Yes, sir!" Major Henry sprinted out the door on the heels of the courier.

James picked up the plate of food and devoured half. His body would need strength, but his resolve needed no fortification. The sooner they pursued the Confederate Army, the sooner this conflict would be over. If they thwarted the enemy at their next encounter, he would waste no time in returning to this lovely valley. He would seek out Madeline Howard in Cashtown. If she had moved elsewhere, he would follow. This would be his plan, his course of action to see him through whatever lay in his path.

His meeting with the Commander of the Army of the Potomac held few surprises. They were to form ranks at first light and then head south — several corps on the Emmitsburg Road toward Turner's Gap and two corps toward Frederick by way of Taneytown. According to cavalry reports, the enemy was moving toward Thurmont. For the remainder of the day, James packed his ledgers, maps, and personal effects and then conferred with his staff. Every officer under his command knew what to do to prepare thousands of men, wagons, artillery, and horseflesh to travel dozens of miles each day.

However, he had one more errand before he slept for the final night in Gettysburg. He rode the familiar back trail through fields and woodlots toward Cashtown, arriving at the Bennetts' home long after the preacher and his wife had retired for the evening. A sinking feeling filled his gut that he'd squandered his last chance to meet with Mrs. Howard.

Reining his horse to a walk, James rode around the overgrown flower beds into the backyard. In the kitchen window burned a kerosene lamp, offering a glimmer of hope. He crept toward the light and peeped through the window like a mischievous schoolboy.

Mrs. Howard sat close by reading a tattered book. With her face in repose, she looked much younger than she had after the fire. When his horse issued an impatient snort, her head snapped up.

"General Downing, what on earth are you doing in the shrubbery?" she demanded, recognizing him.

Stepping into the pool of light, he climbed the back steps without a logical answer.

She opened the door and stepped onto the porch. "Why didn't you knock at the front door, sir?"

"Because I feared the Bennetts wouldn't receive me at this hour."

"You are most likely correct. What is so urgent that it wouldn't keep until morning?" She pressed the book to the bodice of her dress.

"Could we sit, Mrs. Howard?" He gestured toward the swing.

Frowning, she glanced between him and the swing. "Just for a moment. This is no time to entertain callers." She sat and covered her ankles with her skirt.

"Tomorrow my men march south in pursuit of General Lee into Maryland, at long last."

"I shall pray for God's mercy on you," she murmured.

"Thank you, but I've come to ask about your plans for the future. May I know where you are headed?"

"I have written to an aunt in Richmond, asking for shelter for the remainder of the war. Confederate territory or not, I cannot rely on the Bennetts' charity forever."

James stroked his beard while choosing his words carefully. "May I offer you an alternative? Richmond may soon become a hotbed of action, a dangerous place for a Northerner."

"What do you suggest?"

Even in dim light, he could see her forehead furrow. "That you come with me . . . or rather my corps. We have many civilians who accompany us as laundresses and seamstresses."

"Become a camp follower? How dare you ask such a thing? We've had this conversation before. I know the true vocation of most ladies who call themselves *laundresses.*"

He recoiled as though slapped, yet he couldn't deny her assertion. "Again, I meant no disrespect. Your virtue would not be tested by my behavior."

"But an incorrect assumption would be

drawn nonetheless." She rose to her feet.

"Perhaps if I —"

"No, General. I trust that your offer was made with honorable intentions, but I must decline. I will leave for Richmond by train, by way of Washington. I will write to you in care of the U.S. Army, Fourth Corps, once I reach my destination. I hope my letter will eventually find its way into your hands."

General Downing clutched his hat brim with a death grip. "Do you know the address of your destination? If letters can get through, truly I wish to correspond."

She hesitated a few moments before tearing a blank page from her book. "Clarisa and John Duncan, 17 Forsythia Lane." She scribbled down the information with a scrap of pencil she pulled from her apron pocket. "I have no idea how long my trip will take, or if Yankee mail will be delivered, but I will hope for the best." She handed him the slip and pulled open the door.

"Another minute, please."

Halfway inside, she paused.

"I beg you not to forget me. I will think of you often during the coming weeks. While this war drags on, I have nothing to offer." He held up his palms. "But one day I will offer you everything I have, everything within my power."

Madeline gasped at his bold statement before a sudden smile bloomed on her face. "*Everything* sounds sufficient, sir. I will pray nightly for your safe return." She hurried into the house, letting the door slam behind her without a thought for her slumbering hosts.

General Downing left the Bennett homestead, the village of Cashtown, and soon the commonwealth of Pennsylvania with a small flame glowing inside his heart.

After mailing her letter to the Duncans, Madeline kept busy at the Bennetts. While the minister and his wife nursed the Gettysburg wounded, she packed their remaining possessions and tended their vegetable garden. In the evening, Mr. Bennett returned with a borrowed wagon, and together they loaded up furniture, cooking implements, and linens. Household goods were in short supply, so the Bennetts donated what they could to those in need.

"God will provide when the time is right." The preacher repeated his mantra not less than a half dozen times. Soon, like their guest, he and his wife owned only one suitcase of clothes. But at least they had a place to stay at the end of the week.

With a heavy heart, Madeline sold Bo to a

federal procurement officer for a fair price. A lady couldn't ride all the way to Richmond on horseback, and a carriage would quickly bog down on roads ruined by both armies. After kissing her beloved mare on her white forehead, Madeline sobbed as she was led away. But how could she cry about a horse when countless men lay in unmarked graves a few miles away?

Madeline wiped her face and packed the last of the garden produce into a small basket for her and a larger one for the Bennetts. Waiting on the porch provided plenty of time to ponder the general's offer. Her back still stiffened with indignation at his cavalier invitation to join an army caravan, and yet the possibility of never seeing him again saddened her as much as losing her home. In the last two years, Madeline hadn't given much thought to men, assuming she would spend the rest of her life as a widow. James Downing had swept into her life in a cloud of dust and then vanished almost as quickly.

Reverend Bennett drove the borrowed team up his lane promptly at five o'clock. "All set, Mrs. Howard? Climb on up." He slapped the seat of the rickety wagon.

"Whatever for?" she asked in surprise.

"To join us for the night, of course.

There's nothing left in the house. You can't sleep on bare floors."

"I planned to walk to Gettysburg tomorrow to catch my train." She clutched her basket handle with both hands. "Thank you, sir, but I can't impose on your kindness any longer."

"You can't walk that far in this heat. Besides, Violet found a room for you, free of charge. A widow in town was so grateful to get our furniture, she said you may stay as long as you like. Hers was carried right out of her house while she searched the battlefield for her son." He shook his head with dismay.

Madeline shuffled her feet in the dirt, unsure what to say. "She's willing to open her home to a stranger?"

"She is. Please, Mrs. Howard. Violet will shake her wooden spoon at me if I don't bring you back." He offered Madeline his hand.

"All right, sir, but only for one night." Placing her valise and the baskets in the back of the wagon, she climbed up beside him.

Madeline recalled the afternoon she had accompanied Mrs. Bennett to the seminary hospital. Though she had been eager to put her newfound knowledge to use, she couldn't stop retching in the slop bucket after her first dressing change. Although she forced herself to stay a full day, she realized she had no stomach for nursing. The sight and sound of men in agony, the foul odors — she would have to find another way to serve her country.

Soon she and Mr. Bennett were bumping down a road devoid of traffic. Since the federal army had left Adams County, the constant hubbub had drawn to a close except at the makeshift hospitals. It would be weeks before soldiers recovered enough to return to their regiments, travel home as invalids, or join their comrades in the ground. Madeline turned to Reverend Bennett as they reached the outskirts of Gettysburg. "What will they do with the dead?"

Her forthright question took him by surprise. "The local cemetery is too small. Some official from Washington purchased a large pasture south of town on Washington Street. A detail of soldiers remained behind to handle the gruesome task of burying most of the fallen. Officers will be sent home for burial."

"And the Rebels? Surely they won't let them lie where they fell."

"Certainly not. If officers can be identified, their families will be notified to claim the remains. Otherwise, they will be buried with the enlisted men in a separate section of the new cemetery. Nasty business, war. I pray to never see the likes of this again."

Madeline nodded, gazing to the east. The reflected sun burnished low hills that had swarmed with cavalry days before.

That evening the widow Buckley served supper on the Bennetts' heirloom table. The reverend and his wife joined Madeline for her last night in Pennsylvania. She was given a quick tour of the house and then hustled into the dining room.

"I'm glad to have your company, Mrs. Howard. I'm not accustomed to an empty house at night," said Mrs. Buckley, handing Madeline a bowl of turnips.

"I'm relieved to have a bed tonight. Thank you." She took a small portion before passing it back.

"You may stay for as long as you like. I'm sure they can use another cook in the seminary kitchen. I know for a fact they're shorthanded." She smiled at her guest from across the table.

Madeline shook her head. "I am grateful for your generosity, Mrs. Buckley, but tomorrow I'm catching the train to Frederick. From there I will go to the war department in Washington, where I hope to obtain a pass to cross into Virginia."

Mrs. Bennett's lips pulled into a frown. "We can't dissuade you? Truly, my dear, you should remain with your own kind."

The Bennetts, as well as Mrs. Buckley, were poor as church mice. Inviting someone equally as destitute meant they would have to do with less. Madeline's aunt and uncle might not share her political views, but at least they were wealthy. Another mouth at their table wouldn't present a hardship. "I'm afraid I cannot," she said, locking eyes with her benefactress. "The Duncans are my kinfolk, so that makes them my kind."

Several seconds spun out before Reverent Bennett broke the silence. "Smoked ham, Mrs. Howard?" He passed her the platter. "I read a Baltimore newspaper today at the seminary. I have no idea who brought it in, but we were all eager for news."

"Shouldn't this matter wait until after supper?" Mrs. Bennett asked, looking uneasy.

"I don't see why it should. As Americans we're obligated to stay informed." The minister lowered his voice. "Recent immigrants are rioting in the slums of New York City. People are lying dead in the street."

"Goodness gracious." Mrs. Buckley fanned herself with a napkin. "Because of food shortages?"

"I dare say not. They're rioting because of President Lincoln's conscription decree. The army is desperate for more troops, especially after the heavy losses here and out West, yet the immigrants refuse to be drafted."

His wife cocked her head to one side. "They are willing to die fighting conscriptors, but not with valor on the battlefield?"

"So it would appear," Reverend Bennett replied before bowing his head in prayer.

That night, Madeline slept soundly on a feather mattress. During dinner she had eaten two slices of meat, a hearty portion of vegetables, and a slice of blueberry pie, not knowing when her next meal would be. Her meager finances wouldn't permit eating in fancy hotels.

When she entered the kitchen the next morning, her hostess was already sipping coffee at the table.

"Good morning, Mrs. Buckley."

"Good morning, Mrs. Howard. The Bennetts left a note for you on their way to the hospital." Mrs. Buckley handed her an envelope.

With trembling fingers, Madeline extracted a single sheet and began to read.

Dear Mrs. Howard, please don't forget that Cashtown is your home. Our door will always be open to you. And you'll remain in our prayers until we see your lovely smile again.

Even though they had signed with formal names, their sentiments filled Madeline with sorrow. Would Cashtown ever be home again? "Thank you, Mrs. Buckley." Fighting back tears, she ate breakfast and left the widow's home as soon as possible. Carrying her tattered valise and a sack of biscuits, she walked to the depot with an odd sense of relief. Gettysburg had become a loathsome place — homes and businesses were scarred by artillery shells, and every one of them were filled with wounded. Nothing would ever be the same. After boarding her train that afternoon, she became wedged between a cigar-smoking newspaperman and a young mother with a crying infant. Everyone was in a hurry to get somewhere, but Madeline was only eager to leave behind a world gone mad.

She spent a sleepless night on a bench in Frederick, not daring to leave the depot. Trains ran at all hours, well off schedule.

Had the next train to Washington pulled into the station while she rested in a boarding house, who knew when the next train would arrive? The following day, she bought her ticket from a harried stationmaster and climbed aboard another crowded train. This one carried Union soldiers on their way back to the front line. Once she arrived in Washington, Madeline obtained directions to the war department. Tired and in need of a bath, she stopped at every rooming house she came across along the way. None had rooms to rent . . . at least, not to her.

Desperate and hungry, she jammed her boot in the next door before it could close in her face. "Please, ma'am. I need somewhere to spend the night. I have money to pay. Perhaps you have space in your attic if nothing else?"

After a sidelong glance, the woman let her in. "For two dollars you can sleep on the cot in the pantry. My former kitchen maid slept there before she ran off." Without fanfare, the woman showed her to the small cubby, handed her a clean towel and blanket, and pointed out the location of the privy. "Breakfast at eight. Fifty cents. No smoking pipes in the house." The woman turned on her heel and left her alone.

Smoking pipes? Wasn't this a boarding

house for ladies?

Madeline had little time to ponder the odd rule. She washed outdoors at the pump, ate a supper of cold biscuits and raw carrots, and slept as though on a bed of roses. Tomorrow she would call on the war department and return each day until someone gave her a pass into the Confederacy. She couldn't wait to see Aunt Clarisa and Uncle John. After all, wasn't blood thicker than water?

■ ■ ■ ■

FIVE

■ ■ ■ ■

Richmond, Virginia

"Kathleen, where are you?" Clarisa Duncan called up the steps for the third time.

"I'm here, ma'am." Kathleen O'Toole sauntered down the hallway as though on a Sunday afternoon stroll.

"What took you so long to answer?"

The maid shrugged negligently. "I s'pose I didn't hear you the first two times. I was helping Esther peel potatoes like you told me to."

Then how did you know I called you thrice? Clarisa thought, but she didn't voice her petulance. Kathleen would only invent another excuse, further delaying the tasks at hand.

"What did you want me to do?" the maid asked, crossing her arms over her starched white apron.

At least she was paying better attention to her personal appearance. When Clarisa had hired the new maid at the riverfront docks, she looked as though she'd neither bathed nor washed her hair since leaving Dublin. Many recent immigrants applying for service positions didn't aspire to the American custom of daily baths. *But I sat in a tub last week, and I haven't fallen in the mud since.* Kathleen's answer to the cleanliness question had triggered a fit of giggles from Eugenia, but Clarisa hadn't seen the humor. But now that Kathleen maintained a presentable appearance, Clarisa had other goals in mind.

"Please set out the pitcher of lemonade and the decanter of wine on the sideboard."

"I thought I would bring 'em in once Mr. Duncan gets home. That way the ice won't melt so fast," Kathleen said, slouching against the newel post.

"I would like you to set them out now and every day at this time. Mr. Duncan prefers a cool drink as soon as he arrives." Clarisa struggled to contain her exasperation as Kathleen dropped a half curtsey and strolled slowly to the kitchen.

"What's wrong, Mama?"

Her daughter's voice startled the wits out of Clarisa. "Eugenia, please don't listen from the steps. Polite people make their presence known when entering a room."

"Yes, ma'am." Coming down the steps, Eugenia wrapped her arms around her mother. "I hadn't meant to. I was waiting for Papa. But it's so entertaining to listen to Kathleen's excuses." She dropped her voice to a whisper. "Some days I think you should fire her."

"More amusing for you than me." Clarisa guided her daughter into the parlor with an arm around her waist. "Almost every day I also think I should fire her, but domestic help is impossible to find. All the slaves have run off, and many families can't afford to pay freemen enough to keep them. Just last week Mrs. Martin said she sometimes washes her own clothes because her laundress works for three families. Each must wait their turn." Together they sat on the settee, sweeping their hooped skirts out of the way.

Eugenia's expression indicated that the girl didn't appreciate such difficulties, but her mother knew that the first time she had to iron a ball gown, she would understand.

"What do you need to talk to your father about?"

"I've been invited to a tea at the ladies' academy, the one I hope to enroll in next year. All my friends will be there, so I must have a new dress. Everyone has already seen every one of mine no less than a million times."

Clarisa smiled at her daughter's exaggeration. "You haven't lived a million days yet. When you have, we'll order you a new frock."

Eugenia frowned but didn't argue as Kathleen carried in a pitcher, a decanter of claret, and a plate of shortbread cookies.

"Thank you, Kathleen, but where are the glasses?" asked Clarisa.

"You didn't say nothing 'bout glasses, just drinks."

"Miss O'Toole, do you expect Mr. Duncan to tip the decanter up to his mouth?" Clarisa felt a flush climb her throat.

"No, ma'am, 'spect not. I'm just used to folks tellin' me what they want."

The butler appeared in the doorway with glassware on a silver tray. "Shall I pour you and Miss Eugenia a glass of lemonade, madam?" He spoke with the cultured accent of a free man of color, one who had been trained in Louisiana.

"Yes, Micah, thank you. That will be all, Kathleen."

After both servants left, Eugenia whispered behind her raised fan. "I won't trouble Papa with a request for a new frock. Then we can afford to give Micah a raise. What would this family do without him?"

"I quake at the thought." Hearing the familiar crunch of wheels on cobblestones in their *porte cochere,* Clarisa breathed a sigh of relief. Although her husband's job merely entailed writing checks to purchase war accoutrements abroad, she still worried about him until he returned home each night.

"Papa!" Eugenia sprang to her feet, spilling cookie crumbs caught in her skirt across the floor.

"Sit down, daughter," Clarisa scolded. "You're eighteen years old, not eight. Wait to greet your father properly."

"Nonsense." John Duncan strode into the room. Although he looked more haggard than usual, he managed a warm smile for his family. "A girl is never too old for her father."

Eugenia giggled as he pecked her forehead with a kiss. "I feel the same. Shall I pour you some lemonade?"

"A small glass of claret will suit better, thank you." John buzzed Clarisa's cheek with another kiss and then settled in a comfortable chair. Lines around his mouth seemed to have deepened the short time he was gone.

"How goes the war?" His wife asked the

same question each day and received the same answer she always did.

"It goes as well as expected, dear heart." Accepting the glass from Eugenia, he drank half the contents in one long swallow. "Ah, that's better. Now it's time for a surprise." He pulled a wrinkled envelope from inside his waistcoat pocket. He smoothed it against his thigh before passing it to Clarisa.

"Pennsylvania?" she said, staring at the smudged envelope with a frisson of unease. "Mail from the North? Who do you suppose this is from?"

"I believe I can guess, but we'll know for certain if you open it," John said as he stretched out his long legs.

Tearing open the envelope, Clarisa scanned the single sheet. Then she reread the letter a second time as though the contents might change. "Pour me a drop of claret, Eugenia."

"Please, Mama, don't keep us in suspense. Who has written?"

Clarisa leaned forward to relay snippets of information. "It's from your cousin — my sister's daughter. Madeline must be twenty-five . . . no, twenty-six now. She married and has been widowed." Clarisa hastily crossed herself with the reference to death. "She's been alone for two years, trying to continue her late husband's vocation — breeding and selling horses. Her house was hit by an artillary shell earlier this month and burned to the ground."

Clarisa paused and met her husband's gaze. He nodded with comprehension without mentioning the battle by name. No one in Virginia wished to speak of the horrible loss of Confederate soldiers at Gettysburg.

"Cousin Maddy? Wasn't I still wearing skirts above my knees the last time she visited?" Eugenia handed her mother a small glass of wine and then began skipping around the room.

"Do you want to hear the rest or not?" Clarisa offered her daughter a stern expression. "If so, I suggest you comport yourself."

"I beg your pardon, ma'am. Please continue." Eugenia sat primly as instructed by governesses long ago with her ankles tucked beneath her skirt.

"Was your niece hurt in the fire?" asked John.

Clarisa refocused on the paper. "Apparently not, thank the Lord. But she lost everything she owned that hadn't already been —" She tilted the letter toward the lamplight. "Appropriated."

"Appropriated by whom?" John demanded.

"My dear, I can only impart details contained within. Madeline wrote something else but scribbled it out." Clarisa smiled patiently at him.

"Please continue." He leaned back in his chair. "I'm setting a poor example of proper comportment."

"Madeline was left with only a single mare, but she was forced to sell the horse for traveling money." Clarisa lowered the paper to her lap.

"What an adventure! Where is she taking a trip to, Mama?"

"Your cousin is coming here and requests shelter for the remainder of the conflict."

Conventions of comportment could no longer confine Eugenia to her chair. She jumped to her feet and applauded as though attending the theater. "At long last I will have company! It's been dreadfully dull in town with people too poor to throw parties."

Clarisa swallowed her remonstrance. Sacrifices of war affected the young more than others.

"She's coming to Richmond? But she's a Yankee." A voice spoke from behind them.

All three Duncans turned with a start. Their maid stood in the doorway, the butler bobbing in the shadows behind her. "Do not eavesdrop on our conversation, Kathleen. And should you accidentally overhear family discussions, kindly keep your opinion to yourself." This time Clarisa didn't make an effort to mask her petulance.

"Yes, ma'am," the maid said with little enthusiasm.

"Micah, please ask Esther to expect a guest. Let's make sure dinners will be special after Mrs. Howard arrives, even if it means reserving this and that from our meals now."

"Everything will be ready for her arrival." Micah bowed from the waist and vanished down the hallway.

The smile Clarisa had for the butler faded as she turned to Kathleen. "Prepare the yellow guest room with fresh linens and place a bouquet on the mantle."

The maid nodded, her face now expressionless.

"And regarding our guest's politics or state of residence? Those aren't your business, Kathleen. Mrs. Howard is my beloved sister's daughter. She will be afforded every respect and courtesy while she's in our home. This household shall make her feel welcome. Have I made myself clear?"

"Yes, ma'am. If that's all, I'll see to that room now."

"It is." Clarisa picked up her glass of claret and downed it in two swallows — something she'd never done before in her life.

Kathleen marched from the room without bothering with her usual poorly executed curtsey.

Madeline knocked on the carved door of the imposing mansion too timidly to be heard. She waited, clutching her bag like a refugee from the docks. To her right stood a trellis of riotous yellow roses. On her left loomed a boxwood hedge taller than her. The flagstone walk from the street had been swept clean, while not a weed intruded upon the perfection of the flower beds.

Much unlike my trampled beds buried beneath a mound of ash and soot.

Shaking off the painful memory, she lifted her hand and rapped again. Within another minute the door swung open, and she peered into the face of a tall, dignified black man in full livery.

"Good afternoon, madam. May I be of assistance?" He spoke perfect Queen's English with a slight drawl.

"I'm Madeline Howard. Is Mrs. Duncan at home? I'm her niece from Pennsylvania."

"Come in, ma'am. The Duncans have been expecting you. Both ladies are in the back garden. I would be happy to show you the way." He stepped aside so she could enter.

As he reached for her valise, Madeline saw his nostrils flare. "I apologize for the bag. The cloth still retains the smell of smoke."

"No apology necessary, madam. I'll see that it is properly cleaned. My name is Micah if I may be of assistance to you."

Madeline didn't hear him as she peered around the two-story center hall with a gaping mouth. A round table held a porcelain urn with an enormous arrangement of flowers. Below her feet was a highly-polished marble floor covered with a fringed Persian rug. Every item in the foyer seemed oversized and ornate, including the multifaceted crystal chandelier overhead.

Micah cleared his throat. "Shall I show you to the garden, or would you prefer to rest in your room?"

She briefly contemplated the coward's choice. "Please take me to my aunt."

"Very good, madam." The butler led her through a long corridor lined with portraits of ancestors, long dead judging by their garments. At the far end, a set of French doors opened onto a terrace of wrought iron tables and padded chaise lounges. Huge potted palms and hibiscus lent a tropical feel to the garden.

Spotting her aunt doing needlework in the shade, Madeline quickly wiped her palms down her skirt. The years had been kind to Clarisa Duncan, her skin remarkably unlined at forty-two. "Mrs. Duncan?" Suddenly self-conscious of her appearance, she trilled like a canary.

"Madeline! How wonderful to see you." Aunt Clarisa dropped her embroidery hoop into the wicker basket.

The pretty young woman sitting beside her sprang to her feet. "Do you remember me, Cousin Madeline? I'm Eugenia." She extended a delicate hand.

Madeline crossed the flagstones toward the two women. "I recall playing with a sweet child years ago. I'm pleased to see what a lovely woman you've turned into." She clasped the girl's fingers and squeezed.

As Eugenia blushed demurely, Madeline turned to her aunt. "Mrs. Duncan, forgive my intrusion on your afternoon. I pray my visit was not wholly unannounced." She bobbed her head in deference.

Her aunt's face warmed in the dappled light. "*Mrs. Duncan?* Please call me Aunt Clarisa the way you did years ago. And you are intruding on nothing at all. We were

116

heartbroken to hear of your loss in your letter."

"It came just yesterday," Eugenia interjected. "I could barely sleep a wink last night wondering how long your journey would take."

A wave of embarrassment washed over Madeline. "Oh, dear me. You've had but a day's notice?"

"Little notice was needed, my dear. We relish guests and always maintain preparedness in hopes of one." Aunt Clarisa's encouragement couldn't have been more effusive. "Please, sit. You must be exhausted." She gestured toward a chintz-covered chaise.

Madeline perched on the edge of her seat nervously, even though plump pink and green pillows beckoned her weary body to recline in comfort.

Aunt Clarisa shook a small silver bell next to her chair. "Your uncle and I were truly sorry to hear about the fire, Madeline. Couldn't anything be done to save your home?"

"Nothing. And had I not been rescued by a passing soldier, I would have died. I had taken refuge from the artillery fire in the cellar, but once the house caught fire, smoke filled the cellar so quickly I couldn't breathe."

"Saints be praised," Aunt Clarisa said softly, pressing a hand to her throat.

"You were saved by a soldier? Was he riding a white horse like a knight in Merry Olde England?" Eugenia pulled her footstool nearer the chaise. "How romantic, Cousin Maddy."

Aunt Clarisa clucked her tongue at her daughter. "Why do you insist on reading dime novels when we have a library filled with Shakespeare and Dickens? And you are fixating on her rescue instead of the terrible loss of her home."

"I beg your pardon, Cousin Maddy." Chastised, Eugenia cast her eyes downward.

"What about your barn and horses? I remember from your mother's last letter that you had married a horse farmer."

"It's all right, Eugenia," Madeline said. "And no, Aunt, the barn was spared, but it had already been picked clean by one army and then the other. I did have one horse left . . . after a fortuitous twist of fate." Madeline chose not to mention meeting General Downing in her garden, calling on his headquarters to plead for Bo's return, and then being pulled from the inferno by him. Young Eugenia would believe every single fantastic tale inside dime romances.

Aunt Clarisa placed a delicate hand on her arm. "Well, you are safe here with us. All of that misfortune is behind you."

"Thank you, ma'am, and I will work for my keep. I don't wish to be a financial burden on you."

Her aunt's eyes grew as round as an owl's. "You'll do nothing of the sort. We have paid staff to handle our household needs. No family member of mine will lift a finger to earn her grits and ham." She laughed merrily. "Ah, here's our tea now."

The imposing butler carried a silver tray with delicious-looking things to eat. He set it down on a filigree table, straightened, and waited, clasping his gloved hands behind his back.

"Thank you, Micah. Have you met Mrs. Howard?"

"I'm pleased to make your acquaintance, madam." He bowed in her direction.

"And I, yours, sir," murmured Madeline.

"His wife, Esther, is our cook. You will have a chance to taste how blessed we are to have her this evening," Aunt Clarisa said, smiling graciously at him.

"Thank you, madam. Shall I serve?"

"No, no, we will be fine on our own. That will be all." Aunt Clarisa tilted a sandwich tray toward her niece. "Would you like something to eat? We have both salmon pâte and watercress. How about you, Eugenia?"

"I'll have one of each, Mama." She fluttered a linen napkin across her lap.

Madeline stared at the crustless triangles surrounded by seasonal vegetables of every variety. Someone had arranged the crudités by color. "Salmon, please."

As her aunt handed her a plate, a tall thin girl delivered a tea service to the opposite table. "Tea, ma'am." The girl spoke with a heavy Irish brogue.

"Please pour, Kathleen. You know how Miss Eugenia and I prefer ours. How do you take your tea, Madeline?" Aunt Clarisa handed a cup and saucer to the maid.

"Just plain will be fine." At the moment, she didn't dare admit she vastly preferred coffee over tea.

"Kathleen, this is Mrs. Howard, my niece and our guest. Please see that she's made comfortable in every way."

Kathleen filled all three cups before responding. "How do, ma'am." She bobbed her head while handing her the tea.

"Very well, thank you." Madeline shifted uneasily on the chaise, unaccustomed to being waited on. "Do you have many servants, Aunt Clarisa?"

"In addition to Micah, Esther, and Kathleen, we hire a laundress and gardener for piecemeal work. Micah also drives Mr. Duncan to and from the office because our former chauffeur . . . moved north recently along with the other maids."

"We don't have to worry about any more slaves running off because we have none left," Eugenia added between bites of her sandwich.

"Yes," Aunt Clarisa intoned almost melodically. "Micah and Esther have been paid staff for quite some time, but Kathleen moved here from Ireland less than a year ago. She booked passage on a cotton factor's ship on its way to Wilmington. When she came to work for us, we could barely understand a word she said."

The maid refilled teacups and left the garden without acknowledging the conversation had centered on her.

Madeline ate her first sandwich in three bites. Then without a thought to decorum, she devoured the second as quickly, not realizing how hungry she had been.

Aunt Clarisa discretely placed two more sandwiches on her china plate. "Was your journey tedious, my dear?"

"The trip by train wasn't bad, but I didn't care for our nation's capital. The muddy streets were teaming with panhandlers. I had difficulty finding a room with so many people in town."

"It's not our capital anymore, Cousin Maddy," Eugenia said matter-of-factly, without a hint of pique. "Richmond is our capital now."

Aunt Clarisa angled her daughter a wry expression. Then she turned her attention back to her niece. "Were you forced to spend much time in Washington?"

Her hunger somewhat abated, Madeline nibbled her third sandwich. "Four nights. I found a ladies' boarding house willing to take me in the first night. It proved a blessing because I had to call on the war department four days in a row. Finally, an aide wrote me a pass allowing me to cross the Potomac into Arlington County."

"You waited that long?" Aunt Clarisa set her cup in the saucer. "Where, on a hard wooden bench in the hallway?"

She nodded. "My name was put on the appointment list, but I daresay others took precedence over me."

"Where did you eat your meals?" Eugenia scooted her stool closer.

"A woman sold sandwiches from a pushcart. They were twenty cents for jam and bread, forty-five for smoked ham."

"Dear me, you've suffered greatly to come

here." Aunt Clarisa stood with the bearing of a queen. "You must be exhausted. Eugenia, please show Madeline to her room. I'll have more tea sent upstairs."

"But she hasn't seen the rose garden or had a tour of the house —"

"There will be plenty of time for that tomorrow."

Madeline stood. "I would like a brief rest before dinner."

Eugenia reached for her hand and whispered, "We'll take the long way to your room."

"We usually dine at half past seven. You needn't wear anything fancy tonight because it will be just the family," Aunt Clarisa said, smiling warmly at her tired niece.

"I'm relieved to hear that. I'm afraid a farmer's wife has no need for ball gowns. I own day frocks and two good dresses for Sundays."

"Not a single gown?" Eugenia fluttered her dark lashes with dismay.

"There were few parties in the small town where I lived."

"Have no worries," said Aunt Clarisa. "We're overdue for a trip to the dressmaker. It's almost August. The social season is just around the corner. You must let me treat you to a few new gowns, my dear. It's the

least I can do for my sister's only child."
With the matter already settled in her mind,
she walked through the French doors, leaving the younger women alone.

Madeline looked into Eugenia's sweet
young face and swallowed hard. *Ball gowns?
Aren't these privileged Virginians aware that a
war is going on?*

"Come with me and I'll give you a quick
tour of your new home." Eugenia dragged
her up the outdoor staircase to the second-
floor gallery.

With her traveling money exhausted,
Madeline had no alternative but to smile at
the daughter of her new benefactor.

■ ■ ■ ■

SIX

■ ■ ■ ■

Late August

"What are you thinking, sir?" Major Henry asked, reining in his horse beside General Downing.

James studied the lay of the land with his field glasses. From his vantage point on a grassy hillock, he could see nothing but unfenced pastures and scrub vegetation. "I think this is as good a spot as any. The higher elevation will allow our scouts to spot any movement of troops. We don't want any surprise attacks from General Lee."

"Do you think he would try that, sir, after the whooping we gave him at Gettysburg?"

"I think we would do well to not underestimate General Lee or General Longstreet."

"But they lost Pender, Barksdale, Garnett, and Armistead. Four generals moldering in their graves should make our job easier."

"Hold your tongue, Major! Some of those

men were my friends at the academy." James clamped down on his back teeth, never able to abide with disrespect.

"Begging your pardon, sir, but the Rebs surely must need to bolster their regiments. More graycoats are lying in the grave in Adams County than our boys."

"Both armies are on Virginia soil now. Lee will have an easier time of filling ranks than us."

"True enough, but he had to send troops down to the Tennessee River to Braxton Bragg's corps. He wouldn't dare attack us now."

"General Meade had to send three divisions west as well. Nevertheless, I would welcome an attack by General Lee. Then we could finish this bloody business once and for all."

"We'll be ready for him, sir."

James focused his field glasses on a cut in the western hills. "That tree line to the west is a good spot to place our picket line. We'll make camp here east of the Rappahannock. The grazing is good, and we're close enough to Warrenton to get supplies. As long as we maintain control of the rail line, we won't be cut off from Washington. Keep a full regiment posted as guards at all times. War department dispatches and telegraph messages must be maintained."

"Yes, sir." The major surveyed the area with his own glasses. "You think we'll be stuck here all winter, out in the middle of nowhere?"

"We'll make camp, but I don't think we're finished with engagements for the season. General Lee may have slipped our noose in Pennsylvania, but General Meade won't let the grass grow beneath our boots for long." James shoved his field glasses back into his saddlebag. "See to my orders, Major."

"Yes, sir." He snapped a salute and rode off in a cloud of dust.

James pulled a cigar from his breast pocket. He only indulged in the nasty habit on rare occasions, usually when he found himself in a foul mood. Now happened to be one of those times. Nothing but headaches had followed his corps through Maryland into Loudoun and Fauquier Counties of Virginia. At least daily marches kept him too busy to fixate on the enigmatic Mrs. Howard. But when he closed his eyes for a few hours of sleep, it was her face he saw, and the scent of lemon verbena filled his head.

He'd written her several letters, posting one each in Frederick, Purcellville, and then Middleburg. He prayed each night that one would find its way to Forsythia Lane in Richmond. *Was her journey fraught with danger? Was she greeted with hostility in Jefferson Davis's capital?*

He should have insisted that she stay with his parents in Philadelphia, but there had been little time to make the arrangements. And they had spent too little time together for such presumption on his part.

If the Army of the Potomac stayed in this lush part of Virginia for a while, surely any reply she wrote would reach him. If only he knew her heart. If only she didn't lose patience and faith in him after months of separation. Because he planned to do everything in his power to see his troops prevail. Then nothing . . . and no one . . . would stand in the way of his finding her again.

Madeline slept for ten straight hours her first night in Richmond. Marching bands or exploding artillery shells couldn't have woken her. Not that there were either of those on Forsythia Lane. The side street the Duncans lived on was blissfully quiet. Neighbors went about their business mindful of people's privacy, as they did elsewhere in the country.

Yet Madeline no longer resided in the United States. Virginia and eleven other states had withdrawn from the nation as they might have from a club whose rules they could no longer abide. Still, her aunt, uncle, and cousin, along with their staff, not only welcomed her but treated her like an honored guest. Aunt Clarisa insisted that Madeline treat the mansion as her home. But no house she ever lived in contained fourteen rooms, with servants' quarters, galleries, terraces, and two formal gardens. The Howards of Cashtown had never dined on china, crystal, and silver, or spent two hours at the table. She and Tobias sat down, said grace, and ate their food. Then they returned to chores after a brief exchange of news, such as ripening tomatoes or the foaling of a mare.

That was not the case in the Duncan dining room. They discussed all sorts of matters, such as which bills were being debated in the state legislature or which candidates might run in the fall elections. Blessedly, the topic of war had been avoided during her first evening. After dinner Eugenia took her on a tour of all three floors, including the subterranean winter kitchen. The younger woman explained that two of the five staircases were reserved for servants. When Madeline asked if she ever just used the closest steps, Eugenia had replied:

"Why, no. That never occurred to me."

After Madeline bid her cousin good night, she'd fallen into bed exhausted. However, her fatigue had nothing to do with the train ride from Washington. She wasn't accustomed to being polite for hours. Two years of widowhood had turned her into a semi-recluse. Now that she was part of a family again, that had to change. For the next two weeks, Madeline studied the Duncans' routines so she would no longer ask naive questions about the conventions of proper — and decidedly Southern — society.

Aunt Clarisa's excursions to the dressmaker consumed the better part of three days. First, they selected patterns and fabric from an impressive array. Next, they were measured down to the circumference of their wrists. Finally, Madeline had to try on every ready-made garment in the shop because her new gowns wouldn't be finished for several weeks. Even the two she selected took a week to be altered.

Each afternoon when they returned from shopping, after being poked, prodded, and stuck with pins, Madeline collapsed onto a chaise, grateful for a few hours to nap or read in the garden. Had she been home in Pennsylvania, she would have chopped, peeled, and cooked in a never-ending cycle of meal preparation. Here, the Duncans had servants for the tedious chores.

Home . . . would she ever see Cashtown again?

More importantly, would she see James Downing again? Each night she struggled to remember details of his handsome face, the sound of his voice, and the touch of his hand. And each night it grew more difficult. She'd written three letters since arriving, but how did someone correspond with a corps commander of the Union Army?

Excuse me, Uncle John. Could you post these tomorrow on your way to President Davis's headquarters — the so-called White House of the Confederacy?

Dinner conversation often veered abruptly onto other subjects whenever her uncle or aunt realized she might be embarrassed or angered. Two sisters had grown up in the same household and ended up on different sides of a war. Aunt Clarisa's simple Pennsylvania childhood was buried under years of wealth and social position. She was as Southern as her penchant for grits instead of oatmeal, cornbread over sourdough, and the addition of sugar to every beverage. On afternoons she and Eugenia weren't shopping or attending church activities, they waited to entertain callers in their opulent parlor. And ladies arrived most afternoons, wearing cumbersome hoops beneath their voluminous skirts. Huge hats shielded their faces from the sun, with brims festooned with feathers and odd types of ornamentation. Aunt Clarisa's guests treated Madeline politely and were never intrusive with their questions, not even when they heard her Northern accent.

Despite her aunt's pretentions, Madeline fell in love with her after two short weeks. Aunt Clarisa was patient and kind to everyone, including the sullen maid who didn't deserve indulgent treatment. Aunt Clarisa fussed over her daughter and husband, and now she fussed over Madeline too. Even at the supper table, her aunt made sure everyone had loaded their plate before taking no more than a thimbleful for herself.

Despite the lavishly appointed home, Madeline realized the Duncans were not as wealthy as they once had been. Curtains with tears in them were repaired, not replaced. Every scrap of leftovers from a meal was reused in a soup, stew, or casserole. And despite the dressmaker having consumed three mornings of their lives, mother and daughter ordered only one gown each. And neither had chosen the expensive fabrics shown last during the presentation. Aunt

Clarisa was more concerned that Madeline had a suitable wardrobe during her visit to Richmond, however long it might be.

This morning Madeline entered the sunny dining room wearing one of the tailored-to-fit dresses. Although never overly concerned with appearances before, this down-to-earth farm girl adored her new clothes. The soft blue frock, with its white collar and cuffs and deep-V neckline, revealed more skin than Madeline had ever showed to anyone other than her husband. Aunt Clarisa assured her that this amount of décolletage was quite proper for daytime.

"You're up!" Eugenia greeted enthusiastically, pouring coffee from a silver urn. "I'm delighted you didn't sleep in."

"Am I late, Aunt Clarisa?" Madeline felt a flush climb her neck on her way to the table.

"Not at all, my dear. Eugenia has planned a full day for you and can't wait to get started. Your uncle had to leave for work earlier than usual." Clarisa rang the silver bell next to her plate. Micah appeared almost immediately with a platter of fried eggs and crisp bacon.

Madeline inhaled the aroma and fluffed a linen napkin across her lap. "I will undoubtedly gain weight while your guest. Everything has been delicious."

"You were too thin. Now you have color in your cheeks."

"That's because Maddy usually forgets her hat when we walk in the garden, Mama," Eugenia said as she scooped up a modest portion of eggs.

Aunt Clarisa's brows kitted above her nose. "Did you ask permission before assigning your cousin such a familiar moniker?"

"Yes, ma'am, she asked," Madeline injected before Eugenia had a chance. "I like the name. That was what my mother called me when she wasn't perturbed with me."

"I can't imagine my sister being angry with you. She was such an easygoing, gentle soul. You are very much like her."

"Indeed, she was. Thank you for the compliment." Madeline tried to swallow the lump in her throat. If she squinted, she could see her mother in Aunt Clarisa's features.

"I'm sorry we didn't attend your mother's funeral. Your father didn't inform us of her passing until after the fact. Had I known she was ailing, I would have come to nurse her back to health . . . or at least stayed until the Lord called her home."

Madeline's eyes filled with tears. She hadn't realized anyone mourned her mother's death besides herself, her father, and Tobias. "He forbade me from contacting you."

Setting down her coffee cup, Clarisa shook her head. "It wasn't your fault. Forgive me for bringing it up. When I heard of your father's passing from a mutual acquaintance, I grieved again for you, Madeline." They locked gazes for a long moment. Then Aunt Clarisa turned toward her daughter. "What adventures do you have planned?"

"Wednesday is Esther's marketing day. We'll ride in the carriage with her to the riverfront. Because Papa walked to the office, we can get an early start." Eugenia turned toward Madeline. "Along the way Micah will drive past Richmond's most famous sites. Finally, you will receive an official tour of your new home."

No matter how long I stay, Richmond will never be my home, no matter how lovely the city. "Will you join us, Aunt Clarisa?"

"Goodness, no. I will sew uniforms with the parish auxiliary and pack canned goods to be sent to our soldiers." She picked up her cup and sipped her sweetened coffee.

"It'll just be the two of us, Maddy, along with Micah and Esther, of course. Since my pitiful debut last winter, I've had few outings without Mama." Eugenia looked dolefully at her bacon as she cut it up into small pieces.

Madeline had folded her bacon and eaten it whole. She must remember to sip, not swallow; nibble, not devour; and most of all, slow down. The Pennsylvania blood running in her veins made her hurry through everything she did. "Why do you describe your debut as pitiful?" she asked. "I thought 'coming out' was an exciting season for young women of society."

Forcing a smile, Eugenia looked to her mother to respond.

"Since the start of the war, there have been few balls and parties. People simply don't have resources to spend on frivolity while our soldiers' needs go unmet."

"There's privation on both sides," Madeline replied.

"True enough. Yet I cannot impress on Eugenia that sacrifices must be made during times like these."

Eugenia stared now at her lap. "You must think me horribly vain and selfish, Cousin Maddy. Forgive me."

Madeline swallowed her last bite of fried egg and pushed away her empty plate. "I think nothing of the sort, Eugenia. A woman is young only once. It's normal to have expectations about the future and feel a loss if they aren't met."

"Thank you. I'm so glad you came to visit!" Eugenia jumped up and wrapped her arms around Madeline's neck. "Let's get our hats and parasols so we can be off." Bobbing her head in her mother's direction, she hurried from the room.

"Good luck today, niece," Aunt Clarisa said, winking as Madeline followed the dynamo out the door.

Micah's tour took them past the gates of Hollywood Cemetery, St. Charles Hotel, and St. John's Church, where Patrick Henry had delivered his famous "Give me liberty or give me death" speech. Madeline ooh'd and aahed at every architectural or botanical landmark. Micah seemed to know more about his adopted city than Eugenia. However, the youngest Duncan knew the name of every family that lived in the palatial mansions on Broad Street . . . and how many of the sons were still eligible bachelors.

At long last they arrived at the open-air market along the waterfront of the James River. Normally, the docks would be no place for a lady, but according to Eugenia, even respectable people crowded the narrow lanes on Wednesdays. Flatboats and packets of all shapes and sizes came down-river to sell freshly caught seafood in addition to the fruit, vegetables, and smoked meats available other days.

Madeline stood on tiptoe to scan the lively scene. "My word, what a selection."

"This isn't half the normal amount of merchants. The federal blockade keeps out bananas, coconuts, and coffee from the tropics. We're lucky to get fruit, rice, and tea grown in the Carolinas, Georgia, or here in Virginia. Begging your pardon, cousin." Eugenia raised her fan to hide her face.

Madeline patted her arm. "You needn't apologize every single time you mention the war. Otherwise, our conversation will become downright cumbersome."

The Duncans' cook stepped in between them with her huge basket. "I know Miss Eugenia will want some callas but don't go wandering too far. Stay where I can keep an eye on y'all."

"Of course, Esther. This way to the sweets." Eugenia grabbed Madeline by the arm.

"What are callas?"

"Rice and brown sugar formed into a ball and then fried. You will absolutely fall in love."

Love — a word never far from Eugenia's

mind — or Madeline's either, lately. How she yearned for a letter from General Downing. They each bought two rice cakes, one for now and one to save for tomorrow. Madeline tried not to get powdered sugar down the front of her dress while nibbling hers.

Esther, however, was all business inside the market. She paused at each stand to poke and sniff, and she wouldn't buy unless confident of freshness. Madeline studied the foods not sold in Pennsylvania, while her cousin studied the crowd. Eugenia watched the ladies to see what they wore and the gentlemen to see if anyone was watching *her*. As they slowly worked their way to the waterfront, Esther filled her basket with bargains.

"Mercy," moaned Eugenia. "We're getting close to the fishmongers. That smell isn't something I want clinging to my clothes." She took hold of her cousin's arm.

Madeline gently shrugged off her hand. "I want to see the seafood. We get little from the ocean in Cashtown, just river trout."

"You go ahead, Maddy. I'll wait for you in the carriage. My feet are beginning to hurt."

Esther looked from one to the other and frowned. "Don't know 'bout you two separatin'."

"It's all right, Esther. I'm twenty-six and a

matron. I'm allowed to shop without a chaperone." Madeline tried not to grin at the older black woman.

The cook wasn't convinced, but in the end Esther followed Eugenia toward the street.

Madeline continued to browse the stalls with interest. Some of the fish didn't smell "caught yesterday" as the sign proclaimed, but nevertheless the array was impressive. "What do you call that creature, sir?" she asked, peering at a monstrosity with tentacles.

"Squid, ma'am." The vendor doffed his cap, releasing a bounty of white hair.

"And those?" Madeline pointed at critters resembling cockroaches.

"Crayfish or crawdaddies, however you prefer."

"Hmm, some things should remain exactly where God put them," she said, smiling at the burley fisherman.

"Definitely not a delicacy for everyone, that's to be sure. Your accent says you're not from around here. Where are you from, ma'am?"

"I'm Mrs. Howard from Pennsylvania," Madeline said, holding her handkerchief to her nose.

"Name's Captain George. I hail from

Boston, as you might have figur'd out by now."

"You are farther from home than I, Captain."

"Truth be told, but here's where the money's to be made." Captain George lowered his voice. "I can run up the Chesapeake because I know most of them navy ships in the harbor." He hooked a thumb toward the river. "I can sell things the local boys can't get their hands on."

Madeline blinked, shocked that a stranger would share such confidences. "I wish you good sailing, Captain, but I must be going." She backed away from his unnerving presence.

"I'm here most Wednesdays should you be needin' a friendly face to talk to, seeing we're both Yankees and all." He grinned before hastily adding, "Meaning no disrespect, ma'am."

"I have a houseful of kinfolk should I wish to chat," Madeline said coolly, miffed at his boldness. She marched away but didn't get far before an idea occurred. Hurrying back, she leaned precariously over the squid. In a much warmer tone, she said, "Actually, could you could get a letter into the hands of someone in the Union army? I would like to write to my . . . brother." She regretted lying, yet she dared not trust this swarthy sea captain.

Captain's George's grin revealed a gold tooth. "That I can, ma'am. I'm here most Wednesdays. Don't take your business to nobody but me." He resettled his cap on his head and turned toward crates stacked on the ground.

Madeline practically ran through the crowd to the Duncan carriage. She was eager to lock herself in her room, write one more letter, and then bind them all together with string. But when she and her cousin had entered the foyer, Aunt Clarisa asked them to come to the parlor before Madeline could escape upstairs.

"I'm glad you're finally home, Eugenia. Colonel Haywood had business with your father and has graciously agreed to stay for dinner." She waved her hand toward the tall, distinguished officer who had risen to greet them. "Colonel Haywood, you've met my daughter, Eugenia. And this is my niece, Mrs. Madeline Howard."

"Good afternoon, Colonel." Eugenia curtsied charmingly and extended her hand.

"Miss Eugenia, how lovely you look in pink." He gripped her fingers briefly before turning his attention on Madeline. He stared at her briefly, and then his smile doubled in size. "Mrs. Howard, a pleasure to make your acquaintance." The colonel bowed deeply from the waist.

Madeline didn't know how to respond. She wasn't wearing gloves, had just been in a public market, and feared she would fall if she attempted to curtsy. "The pleasure is mine, Colonel, but you must excuse me. I seem to have misplaced my gloves during our outing." She clasped her hands behind her back, regretting her second lie of the day.

Yet if this Confederate colonel would be staying for dinner, she suspected it wouldn't be her last.

■ ■ ■ ■

SEVEN

■ ■ ■ ■

At thirty-eight years of age, Colonel Elliott Haywood had known more than his fair share of lovely belles. In the past, some had vied for his attention because of his father's money and social position as a Virginia planter. However, in recent years their slaves had run off and the crops were picked clean by a hungry army. His family would be fortunate to raise enough for the next tax bill. Some women were attracted to the pressed and polished uniform of a Confederate officer, yet with only one functioning arm, his reassignment to Richmond's home guard no longer carried the same prestige as a member of J.E.B. Stuart's cavalry. Frankly, Elliott had grown weary of vapid young women who clung to an old way of life. He was neither sentimental nor particularly attached to the trappings of polite society.

He had fought bravely in battle for the

South. Shot from the saddle, he had lain for a full day in mud and blood, fully expecting to die on Northern soil. When Yankee soldiers carried him to the crowded yard of a field hospital, he fully expected to die from neglect under a blistering sun. So many wounded men lay in rows like forks in a drawer with so few doctors to attend to them. But when a sweet-faced angel appeared above him, he thought he'd woken in the Promised Land. Elliott was stripped of his jacket and hat and carried into the surgeon's tent. Each morning thereafter he'd fully expected to be hauled off to a Union prison. But he neither died nor was marched away under guard. Then one day, after he recovered sufficient strength, he walked out of that gruesome hospital and chaotic little town and came home . . . home to Richmond.

Elliott rather liked his new assignment. Certainly, ensuring the safety of Jefferson Davis and members of his staff shouldn't prove too taxing. His shoulder still ached where the bullet had been dislodged. And although he still possessed two arms, one hung limply like wet laundry on a clothesline. Tonight he had been invited to dinner at the home of John Duncan — one of the president's most trusted staff members. Unlike his own family, the Duncans apparently still possessed the wherewithal to entertain. John Duncan's daughter had always seemed immature for her age, even though she'd officially come out. Elliott didn't need another reminder he was almost forty and still unwed. What he hadn't expected was to recognize the face of his saving angel when introduced to Mrs. Duncan's niece . . . and a very pretty face, at that.

An hour had passed since he had been introduced to her. With murmured excuses, the young women had left them to freshen up after their morning out. Eventually, Elliott followed his host and hostess into the dining room, and while Elliott tried to keep his attention on his conversation with the Duncans, he couldn't help internally anticipating the return of their niece.

"What news do you hear of the navy's plans to destroy the blockade, Colonel Haywood? We simply must get regular shipments from England and the continent —" Mrs. Duncan's question to him hung in midair as she suddenly turned toward the doorway. "Ah, there you two are. Please join us. Dinner is about to be served."

Elliott and Mr. Duncan had risen to their feet with the appearance of Eugenia and Mrs. Howard.

"Please forgive my tardiness, ma'am," Mrs. Howard murmured deferentially, while Eugenia flounced to her chair.

"Not at all, my dear. We were enjoying an aperitif, knowing you two had a tiresome day."

"Good evening, Mrs. Howard." Elliott lifted his glass in salute. "I'm delighted to see you again after all this time."

She looked puzzled as she lowered herself to her chair. "I beg your pardon, sir. We were introduced but an hour ago." Mrs. Howard angled her head toward the parlor as the Duncans stared in confusion.

Elliott held up his glass for the butler to refill. "I'm not surprised you don't make the connection. My appearance was less than presentable at the time. But I will never forget you, no matter how long I live."

Mrs. Howard waved away the offer of a glass of wine. "Again, sir, you have me at a disadvantage." She placed a goblet of water to her rosy lips.

He nodded with the deference she showed Mrs. Duncan. "You graciously intervened on my behalf in Gettysburg. Had you not spoken to the surgeon in the field hospital, I certainly would have bled to death far from home. I am and will forevermore remain in your debt." Gazing around the table, he lifted his glass in toast. Hastily Mr. and Mrs. Duncan raised their wine stems.

"You knew Cousin Maddy in Pennsylvania?" asked Eugenia, wide eyed.

"Indeed, Miss Eugenia." Elliott didn't take his eyes off the flummoxed Mrs. Howard. "She was working as a nurse and stopped at my bedside. Actually, I was lying on the hard ground, but I won't insult the ladies with unnecessary details. After Mrs. Howard convinced the good doctor my wound wasn't mortal as originally assumed, I was moved to the surgery. I had been left outdoors with the other . . . hopeless cases."

"My word, what a fortuitous coincidence," Mr. Duncan said before taking a hearty swallow of his drink.

"It was the hand of God." Mrs. Duncan took a small sip, eyeing her niece.

"Mrs. Howard offered me a ladle of water, which tasted sweeter than wine or brandy, and noticed that my wound had stopped hemorrhaging. Upon her intervention on my behalf, the doctor extracted a bullet and sewed me up without fanfare, perhaps still expecting me to die."

Madeline drained her water glass. "Now I remember you, sir," she said with a warm smile. "It is a joy to see that you recovered."

The Duncans gaped from one to the

other, bewildered, until Mr. Duncan finally spoke. "You fooled them all, Haywood, and here you are — a grand turn of events! Micah, I believe we are ready to eat."

Mrs. Howard leaned back in her chair as platters were presented at table. "Lest you give my aunt and uncle a false impression of my heroism, sir, I should admit that you were the only soldier I . . . saved. For me, the things I experienced at that field hospital were unbearable, and I never returned. I volunteered only that one day."

"Be that as it may, I was the fortunate recipient of your foray into nursing. Your face will remain etched in my memory always."

"Please don't be so dramatic regarding my involvement, sir. God decreed your time wasn't done." Mrs. Howard took a hearty scoop of mashed potatoes. "Have you recovered full health and vitality?"

He watched her mannerisms and gestures, intrigued by her every movement. "Healthy with all four limbs accounted for, even though one does not function." He touched the sleeve of his useless arm.

Mrs. Howard blanched and averted her gaze. "I hadn't noticed, sir. Excuse my boldness. Your return to the Confederacy is extraordinary in itself, Colonel Haywood.

You might have ended up in a federal prison."

"That's a long story better saved for another day. I shall share it on a different occasion." Elliott pivoted toward his hostess, suddenly aware Mrs. Duncan was studying him curiously. "This ham tastes delicious, madam. The honey glaze reminds me of home." He thumped his chest with a clenched fist.

Mrs. Duncan smiled and nodded to the butler. Micah made a second trip around the table with the ham platter. "Our butcher is the best in town, Colonel."

"I'm surprised to find you in Richmond, Colonel," asked Mrs. Howard. "Has your arm prevented your return to the army?"

"Unfortunately, yes. I'm in command of the Richmond home guard. My responsibility is to keep the city secure at all costs. It's my honor to protect men such as your uncle, who offer immeasurable service to the Cause." Elliott nodded at his host.

"Our invalid soldiers have stepped into valuable roles in the war department," Mr. Duncan said, taking another slice of ham from the platter.

"How about you, Mrs. Howard?" asked Elliott. "What made you abandon your hometown and take up residence in our fair city?"

She set down her fork. "I never would have left, sir, but my town was almost destroyed by the battle — our church, the school, my home. With my brood mares stolen, I had no choice but to throw myself on the mercy of my aunt and uncle. They have graciously taken me in." She lifted her chin with sorrowful dignity.

Elliott almost choked on his food. "Forgive me, madam. I had no knowledge of your loss."

"No harm done, Colonel, but might I trouble you for a slice of ham? I prefer not to make poor Micah walk around the table a third time." Mrs. Howard held out her plate to him.

His discomfort vanished with one flash of her magnificent smile. "It would be my pleasure." He speared the juiciest slice on the platter for her.

September 1863
Madeline awoke from her afternoon nap to a face looming above her, barely a foot away. "Goodness, Genie! You startled me." She straightened to an upright position in the chaise.

"Is my face that frightening?" Her cousin

feigned a childlike pout.

"Your face is fine, but why are you watching me sleep?"

Eugenia hurried toward the bed where three gowns had been laid out. "Mama said I shouldn't wake you, but I feared you would sleep until tomorrow morning."

Madeline scrubbed her face with both hands. "This Virginia humidity makes me drowsy in the afternoon. Back home, summer would be waning by now."

"No more tedious talk of the weather, cousin. Although I daresay, it's your favorite topic. Help me select my gown for the festivities tonight." One by one, Eugenia held up a soft blue, pale peach, and sunny yellow dress beneath her chin.

"All are lovely, but the peach makes your eyes sparkle and complements your blond hair." Madeline poured a glass of cool water to regain her senses. "Why are you deciding between ball gowns?" she asked after her first hearty swallow. "I thought tonight was to be a simple dinner for Uncle John's friends."

Eugenia rolled her eyes. "There's nothing *simple* about dinner for thirty at seven o'clock. This might be the closest we come to a social occasion for the entire month. I begged Mama to let me wear something

157

special, and she finally agreed." The girl waltzed around Madeline's room with the peach dress for a partner. "I'm surprised these gowns haven't deteriorated from neglect."

Madeline pressed a wet cloth to her neck. "Should you wish to pursue a career, I strongly recommend the theater."

Eugenia looked scandalized. "A *lady* thespian? Mama would faint and then lock me away in the attic."

"There won't be dancing at a Thursday dinner party, will there?" Madeline had her own reasons to be scandalized. "The conventions of Virginia society never cease to confound me."

"Of course not, but there will be at least a dozen officers in their fancy uniforms at the table." Eugenia opened her fan with a flutter. "Colonel Haywood and General Rhodes, Major Penrod and Major Lewis — so many I can't keep them all straight."

"Will there will be other females besides those of this household?"

Eugenia's initial response was a giggle. "Yes. Mama invited a few ladies from her auxiliary and their daughters. She also invited President and Mrs. Davis, but they sent their regrets. Varina is suffering one of her headaches." Her mouth formed a perfect

O. "Don't tell Mama I used Mrs. Davis's given name. She would scold me."

"I promise I won't. You mentioned Colonel Haywood's name first in your list, prior even to a general. Are you sweet on him? I must say he's a handsome man."

Eugenia stopped preening in front of the mirror. "Heavens, no. He's so old. I heard he's practically forty. At that rate he'll catch up to Papa. Plus there's the matter of his poor crippled arm. How dreadful. Since *you* find him handsome, perhaps you should plan to catch his attention. Now, you must ring for the maid for your bath and get ready. Mama borrowed staff from the neighbors to ensure this party will be perfect." She gathered all three gowns in her arms and headed for the door.

Madeline was glad to be alone with her thoughts. *Catch the Colonel's attention?* How could she explain to an eighteen-year-old that she was in love with someone else? A Union general, no less. In the short time she'd been with the Duncans, they seemed to have forgotten her Yankee birthright. It was as though they expected her to adopt their drawl and the stars-and-bars flag. But she hadn't forgotten. Each night she prayed for an end to the conflict . . . an end with a resounding Union victory. How could she make polite conversation with these men who were the sworn enemies of her beloved?

All men are equal in God's eyes. He loves not one over another. One of her mother's favorite expressions, no doubt a paraphrase from Scripture, would keep her polite and respectful, behaving with grace as long as she lived under the Duncans' roof.

"Madeline, my dear. The guests have grown restless, waiting for the honor of your presence." Her uncle bowed when she reached the bottom of the stairs, as did his three companions.

"But the other ladies have only just arrived, Uncle. We felt you gentlemen required time to discuss important matters." Opening her fan, Madeline used it to cover her bosom. The idea of exposing so much flesh at a Thursday night supper was altogether uncomfortable, even though Aunt Clarisa insisted her dress was modest by their standards.

"We talk important matters all day. We yearn for witty banter," Uncle John replied, winking at her.

"Mrs. Howard, a pleasure to see you again." Colonel Haywood took her hand and kissed her gloved fingers. "May I present my comrades in the home guard?"

One by one, each man smiled and bowed when introduced.

"How do you do, gentlemen?" said Madeline, choking back a chuckle. One of the officers had a mustache so outrageously large, he reminded her of a walrus from a childhood storybook.

"Ah, there you are, Major Penrod." Eugenia slipped her hand into the crook of the man's elbow as she joined the group. "I do hope you're being kind to my cousin. Madeline isn't from here and doesn't know a soul in town other than us, her loving family." She batted her thick eyelashes at the tall, gangly soldier.

At least this man is young and not an ancient forty, despite his huge mustache, thought Madeline.

"That's not altogether true, Miss Duncan." Colonel Haywood spoke softly so that only those nearby could hear. "Remember that I met this saving angel in that forsaken town that shall remain unnamed." He lifted his glass of champagne in salute.

"Is that true, Mrs. Howard? You worked in a hospital up north?" asked Major Lewis.

"My career lasted one short day. I discovered the stomach doesn't always follow where a compassionate heart may lead. I have but one feather in my nurse's cap."

She lifted her glass of punch to return the toast.

The colonel's grin filled his entire aristocratic face.

But it was Major Lewis who responded. "My stomach leads me straight to supper. I just heard the butler's summons. Shall we, Mrs. Howard?" He extended his arm to her.

Madeline glanced at her uncle, who looked pleased, and then to Colonel Haywood, who did not. "Thank you, sir. I don't wish to delay events for a second time this evening."

She accompanied Lewis into the candlelit dining room. The table, extended with several leaves, stretched onto the terrace through the open French doors. Illuminated by dozens of tapers and a gas chandelier turned low, the effect was elegant beyond compare.

The number of male guests outnumbered females two-to-one, yet Aunt Clarisa had orchestrated the seating arrangements with the expedience of a seasoned hostess. "Madeline, I would like you there in between Colonel Haywood and Major Lewis." Aunt Clarisa tapped a chair with her fan. "Eugenia, you are here, in between Major Penrod and our distinguished guest, General Rhodes." She guided the sixtyish officer to his intended seat.

If Genie thinks forty is ancient, I pity the at-tention the elderly general will receive from his supper companion. Madeline grinned at her inner musings.

"Does your smile indicate pleasure with the table arrangement, Mrs. Howard?" Colonel Haywood spoke softly next to her ear. "I pray it does."

Madeline looked more than a little sur-prised. "Forgive me, but I'm unaccustomed to gentlemen being so direct with their ques-tions."

Using his right hand, he shifted his left arm to a more comfortable position. "If I learned anything during the last two years, it is that life is brief. We all should be forthright and stand in good stead with our Maker, because no one knows the number of his days." The colonel took a sip of wine. "I see no wineglass at your place setting. Is that an oversight I could remedy?"

"No, sir. The staff is aware that I don't imbibe alcohol. However, I impose no judg-ment on those who do." She nodded po-litely. "My small Protestant sect frowned on it."

Colonel Haywood cocked his head to one side. "I believe the Duncans are Roman Catholics, are they not?" he whispered. "May I have the honor of escorting you to

St. Paul's Episcopal on Sunday? The Haywoods have held a pew there since it opened."

Madeline tasted her soup while pondering the question.

"It's merely to church and straight home, Mrs. Howard. You have my word as a gentleman. Have no fear." His blue eyes twinkled.

"I'm not afraid of you, Colonel. *If* I decide that the church is too far away to walk to, I shall send word to you. In the meantime, your soup grows cold."

For the next two hours, they dined on fresh oysters, crisp salad, roast beef with fresh peas, and buttery croissants. Fortuitously, General Rhodes entertained the table for the majority of time with tales of valor exhibited by his men. Madeline didn't feel up to personal conversation with either Major Lewis or the colonel. It wasn't hard to figure out why. Her heart belonged to another man — mere miles but another world away.

Contrary to custom, the women and men didn't go in separate directions after dinner. The ladies sipped lemon tea, while gentlemen enjoyed brandy on the terrace. Neither sex seemed to want the evening to end. Madeline wandered over to where General Rhodes held court, surrounded by his staff officers and men of the home guard. They were so immersed in conversation that no one noticed her next to a potted palm.

"We plan to turn Meade's flank, driving him north from Prince William County once and for all," General Rhodes said, blustering with an increasingly florid complexion. "We'll get them on the run to Fairfax County and then, with the grace of God, back into Maryland. We need to take control of Bristow and the other stations along the Orange and Alexandria rail line. To sever this serpent in half, we must cut off the Yankees' access to Washington."

"An interesting bit of information, don't you think, Mrs. Howard?" Major Lewis suddenly appeared at her side, close enough for her to smell his hair pomade.

Madeline was temporarily taken aback until she noticed that his deep drawl had vanished. In its place was the clipped accent of a New Englander. "I try not to involve myself in the politics of war," she said, unsure how to process her realization.

Major Lewis took her arm and drew her away from the conversation. "But are you not a Northerner — a lover of the Union — determined to see it fully restored?" He spoke in a soft whisper. "Or have your rich relatives already swayed your opinion?"

Madeline's spine stiffened. "I love my aunt and uncle truly, sir, but I was born and will die a Yankee. I gather by your altered accent that the same is true of you."

Major Lewis pulled on his mustache. "I am treading dangerously by admitting this, but yes, Mrs. Howard, my allegiance is not to Jefferson Davis and his dreams for a new South."

"You are a traitor?" Madeline touched the stripes on his sleeve with her fan.

"Not to my God and country — to them I am true." He stared down at her. For several moments they assessed one another like foxes eyeing the same rabbit. "What we've learned tonight will be of great use to General Meade and his army encamped west of Fredericksburg. But alas, my usefulness in Richmond is drawing to a close." The major patted his leg. "My wound has healed. I'm about to be transferred from the home guard back to Longstreet's corps at the front lines."

"You will fight against the Union?" Madeline didn't try to hide her shock.

He released a wry laugh. "Of course not. I will cross the Potomac and head north long before anyone realizes I'm gone. But you will still be here, Mrs. Howard. Perhaps you could mull over your duty as an American.

Good evening." He bowed deeply and strode away.

Madeline remained shivering in her embroidered slippers for several minutes on an unusually warm evening.

■ ■ ■ ■

EIGHT

■ ■ ■ ■

After the dinner party, Madeline spent plenty of time alone. She walked the manicured paths of the rose garden, stared out her bedroom window while presumed to be napping, and counted cracks in the plaster ceiling when sleep refused to come. But no matter how long she brooded, she couldn't get Major Lewis's startling revelation out of her mind. He was a spy for the Union Army, working right under President Davis's nose. If the officers at the dinner party knew that, they would consider him a traitor and hang him.

How did she feel about his duplicitous nature? Madeline believed that the states' rights argument masked the South's true intention to preserve slavery. But many men fighting for the Confederacy lived in homes that had never owned slaves. A child grew up adopting the customs and standards of a region as well as those of their family. Yet

Madeline wasn't sure she could act a role solely to obtain military information — secrets that could change a battle's outcome or perhaps the course of the war.

Because of his desire to preserve the Union, Major Lewis placed himself in great personal danger. Had the information they overheard at the party already been conveyed to the Union commanders? Had James received the dispatch? Was he already organizing his men to thwart General Lee's best-laid plans? If so, would Lewis's information bring a more expeditious end to the bloodshed? What would the end of the war bode for her and James?

Madeline had begun to fixate on his given name like a schoolgirl suffering her first infatuation. Had her letters been able to cross battle lines? Nary a word from him found its way to Richmond. With a possible end to the conflict in sight, Madeline needed a letter to reach him — one that made her feelings clear.

Her affection for him had not diminished.

Her anticipation of their reunion grew more poignant each day.

And if it was still his intention to court her, he would find she was of an agreeable mind. Madeline left her well-trodden path in the garden and hurried to her room. Not bothering to walk around the house, she used the back outdoor steps, those reserved for servants. With a sense of purpose heating her blood, she couldn't wait to put pen to paper in her private quarters.

In her letter to James, she described the kindness shown by the Duncans. She explained their attempt to maintain a lavish lifestyle despite dwindling finances and the restriction of goods from the seacoast blockade. Finally, she detailed her difficult struggle to emulate the family's dress, customs, and indolent habits. Would he be amused by her vignettes or find her ungrateful for the Duncans' largesse? All she could do was write what came to mind and pray her words would be well-received . . . if the letter was received at all.

An hour later, she went downstairs and entered the kitchen dressed in a new day frock and her wide-brimmed hat. "Good afternoon, Esther. Where is everyone?"

The cook glanced up from a chopping board of colorful vegetables. "The missus and miss are napping in their rooms. Master Duncan is still at his office. Micah's in the stable, I am here, and Lord knows where that Kathleen be."

"Today is market day. Could I trouble Micah to drive me to the waterfront?"

Esther's eyes turned very round. "You wanna go to market at this hour?" Her tone would have been appropriate had it been close to midnight. "The time to go to the docks is after breakfast, when the fish is fresh, not after it be baking in the hot sun all day." She returned to chopping green peppers, the matter settled in her mind.

"Please, Esther? I so wish to buy peaches before they are gone for the season. I've had a hankering for a cobbler my mother used to make."

"You're too late. Peaches are done."

"Pears, then. Some sweet Bartletts will work. Let's be inventive with the recipe."

The cook's brows lifted with suspicion, yet she was too well-mannered to question Madeline's motives outright. "Nobody does a cobbler with pears, but I 'spose we could make a compote. Will that satisfy this hankering of your'n?"

"Indeed it will!" Madeline flashed her a sincere smile.

"Go find Micah in the stable or garden." She resumed chopping.

"Thank you, Esther." Madeline caught herself before hugging the woman around the midsection, something highly inappropriate between servant and houseguest.

"You're welcome, but you gotta pick up

Master Duncan on your way home. No time for Micah to go back and forth." Esther scraped a mountain of peppers, onions, and diced tomatoes into the soup pot. "So you best have some fruit to show for your trouble." She pointed at a large basket hanging on the wall.

Grabbing it from the hook, Madeline ran outside.

Fortunately, Micah took little exception to her odd request for a Wednesday afternoon. "Why don't you wait on the shady bench in front, ma'am. I'll hitch the carriage and pick you up there. Too many flies are buzzing around the stable yard."

Filled with anticipation, Madeline was afraid she couldn't sit still. But pacing might draw the attention of her aunt and cousin, so she perched on the stone bench and waited. Tucked inside her bag was an envelope for General James Downing, Fourth Corps Commander of the Army of the Potomac. If it were discovered, her letter contained no planned military maneuvers and no estimates of troop strength. It was merely the chaste confession of a woman's heart. Just the same, the outing filled her with a sense of purpose long absent in her life.

At the riverfront, Micah parked in his

usual spot under shady elms. Then he climbed down with his slow, arthritic gait.

"Micah, why not wait for me here?" she said sweetly.

"No, ma'am. It is my job to carry the basket." He lifted it from behind the seat.

Madeline practically yanked it from his hands. "With only one item to purchase, I prefer to shop alone. Remember, I'm a Yankee, accustomed to doing things for myself." She hoped she didn't sound overly rude.

The dignified man frowned but released his grip on the handle. "All right, ma'am, but don't tarry too long. We mustn't forget Master Duncan." Micah patted his vest where he kept his prized possession — a pocket watch.

"I won't," Madeline called over her shoulder.

Loiterers crowded the narrow aisles, still hoping to nab a late day bargain. Using her basket as a shield, Madeline cleared a path through the fruit and vegetable merchants toward the waterfront. She paused long enough to buy some pears without bothering to sort through them. However, when she reached the spot she had met the Yankee fisherman, his table was empty.

"Where's Captain George?" she asked

breathlessly.

"Gone." The woman at the next table spoke without lifting her focus from her dwindling supply of soft shell crabs.

"Yes, ma'am, I can see that, but to where?" Madeline offered what she hoped was a pleasant expression.

Looking up, the woman wrinkled her sunburned nose. "Not to Paree or Rome. Back to the *Bonnie Bess,* I reckon. George sold out early and has probably hauled anchor by now."

"Thank you," Madeline said before running down the dock behind the stalls. The wharf stretched well past the market area into a loathsome row of decrepit warehouses. She tried holding her breath until she spotted the twin masts of a schooner with *Bonnie Bess* across the stern.

"Captain George!" Madeline hollered in an unladylike fashion. "Are you there, Captain?"

After a moment, a wooden hatch scraped open and a white-haired head appeared. "Mrs. Howard!" he boomed. "I'm just getting ready to run down the river. Another five minutes and I woulda been gone."

"May I come aboard, sir? I have an important matter to discuss with you." Madeline lifted her skirts a few inches in preparation

177

to jump the gap between land and sea.

"No, no. I'll join you there. Can't let a lady fall into the James River wearin' a hoop. You would get tangled up and drown for sure." The seafarer punctuated his conjecture with a belly laugh.

Madeline arched an eyebrow. "I learned to swim years ago in our farm pond."

"I don't doubt it." Reaching her side, Captain George loomed half a foot taller. "Now what brings a fair Northern matron down to the docks? So late in the day, no less. A tad earlier and you could have had the shrimp I just tossed in the drink."

Blanching at the thought of rancid, oily shrimp, Madeline glanced around to be certain no one stood within earshot. "I'm not here for seafood. Could you take a letter for me, Captain? I wish this to reach the commander of the Fourth Corps, infantry." She extracted the envelope from her reticule along with one of her few remaining coins.

He stared at her for a long moment. "I can take it to Fort Monroe on the peninsula. They'll know how to get it into the hands of —" He read her slanted script. "General Downing. Keep your coin, Mrs. Howard. This one is compliments of the *Bonnie Bess.*" He bowed and swept his cap from his bushy head.

"I'm in your debt, Captain." Madeline attempted a half curtsey.

"Yes, ma'am, you are." He tucked the envelope inside his coat. "Now be off with you 'fore somebody sees ya talking to an old sailor."

Madeline didn't have to be told twice. She picked up her skirts and ran until she reached the last shoppers pawing through shriveled produce.

Her relief was soon matched by Micah's. "I was just about to start looking for you, Mrs. Howard." The butler slapped the reins on the horse's back the moment she stepped into the carriage. Soon they were rattling down the cobblestones toward the center of town without a moment to spare.

Growing impatient in the heat, Clarisa rang her silver bell for the second time. Not a breath of air stirred the leafy branches overhead. If it became any more humid, a person could wring the air like a wet dishrag.

Eugenia lifted her skirts to cover her legs on the chaise and snapped open her fan. "Tell me again where Cousin Maddy went in the carriage."

"As I said five minutes ago, Esther said Madeline remembered a recipe for peach cobbler that she favored and went to the market with Micah." Clarisa picked up her needlepoint for the third time with little interest.

"I don't understand why she didn't mention this cobbler at luncheon. She knows I love haunting the aisles and stalls on market day." Eugenia's lower lip trembled.

"Don't pout, dear. It's very unbecoming in a lady. And don't use the word 'haunt.' You know I don't care for references to ghosts or phantoms." Clarisa glared over her half-moon spectacles.

"Sorry, Mama. I'm truly out of sorts since Maddy left me behind." Eugenia tried to drink from an already empty glass.

"Esther mentioned that Madeline asked about you but was told you were resting. She knew how poorly you've been sleeping lately and probably considered her actions merciful."

"I would be happy to sleep through supper for a chance to break our monotonous routine. If I spend another afternoon listening to the auxiliary ladies bragging about their sons and grandsons' heroism, I will go mad. You know their tales cannot possibly be true or we would have beaten Mr. Lincoln's army long ago."

Spotting the maid in the doorway, Clarisa

swallowed her admonishment. It was too hot to fuss. Besides, Eugenia was correct about her friends' penchant for exaggeration. "There you are, Kathleen. We're parched dry out here, and I had to ring for you twice." Clarisa dropped her sewing into the basket for the last time that day.

Kathleen carried a pitcher to the table at the only speed she knew — turtle slow. "Had to squeeze more fresh lemons. No lemonade left after lunch." She wiped her hands down her apron.

Clarisa saw nothing on the tray but a small bowl of sugar and two spoons. "Were there no tea cakes with the apricot jam left?"

"No, ma'am. Et at breakfast."

"*Eaten* at breakfast. What about those shortbreads? I know some remained in the tin."

She shrugged her shoulders. "Esther packed the last ones for Mr. Duncan to have for lunch with two measly boiled eggs."

The two women locked gazes. Clarisa experienced a surge of anger that a maid would comment on the quality of lunches the household provided. "Refill our glasses and that will be all, Kathleen."

Eugenia waited until they were alone to speak. "Don't you think Cousin Maddy should have returned by now? The vendors pack up their wares and leave by this hour."

"Micah plans to pick up your father on their way home. No sense in making two trips." Clarisa added plenty of sugar to her lemonade and drank half the glass for fortification. "While Madeline is out, there is something I must discuss with you, daughter."

Eugenia sat up in her chair. "I didn't eat the last apricot tea cake, Mama, on my honor."

She sighed wearily. "I'm referring to your frequently correcting your cousin's manners and habits. I know you don't mean to be rude, but you are. You're constantly pointing out Madeline's differences to what you consider proper etiquette, regardless of who might be within earshot."

"I only meant to be helpful. How will she ever learn if no one tells her?" Eugenia's eyes glazed with moisture. "At mass last Sunday, she didn't know when to stand, when to sit, or when to kneel. And she started reciting the Lord's Prayer when only the priest is supposed to talk. One would think she'd never been to church before." A large tear ran down her pale cheek.

Clarisa reached for her daughter's hand. "Come sit with me." She patted the foot of her chaise.

Eugenia complied, but soon her face streamed with tears. "I tried to explain because Maddy said she didn't understand a word of Latin."

"Madeline goes to a Christian church, but it's not Catholic. Similar, but not exact. They have ministers, not priests; English and not Latin; and they seldom kneel. And it wasn't just this past Sunday that I noticed this. You are quick to correct her at table too. Country folk don't use a separate fork for oysters, salads, entrees, and desserts. They often use one fork throughout the entire meal." Clarisa stroked the girl's back.

Eugenia peered up with a streaky face. "Are you teasing me?"

"I am not. A well-bred lady never points out someone's shortcomings in the company of others. I heard told that at Queen Victoria's court, a visiting foreign dignitary picked up his finger bowl and drank the contents."

Eugenia's delicate hand flew to her throat. "Oh, my. What did the queen do?"

"She picked up her finger bowl and drank as well. Then everyone at table followed her lead. Do you understand why the queen would do such a thing?" Clarisa lifted her daughter's chin with one finger.

"Because she didn't wish the foreigner to

feel like a ninny?"

"Exactly. Victoria wanted all to take comfort at her table, and not just from the delicious food she provided."

Eugenia's tears returned in earnest. "I am a dreadful person. No wonder Cousin Maddy went to the market alone. Who needs the constant assault of my wickedness?"

Clarisa gently shook her daughter to get her attention. "You're not wicked, my love. We just need to remember that someday this horrible war will be over, and our Maddy will return to her friends up north, but she will always be our blood kin. We want her to take home fond memories of her days in Richmond, along with a desire to visit often."

"I promise to do better, Mama," Eugenia said, laying her head on her mother's shoulder.

"I have no doubt you will." Clarisa kissed her smooth, unlined forehead. "Let's go inside. I hear the carriage. Your father and cousin have come home, and I have a matter to discuss with Micah."

Clarisa watched her daughter scamper off with the energy and exuberance of a child. The admonishment already forgotten, Eugenia was eager to hear about any market day escapades she had missed. Clarisa sent up a quiet prayer that Eugenia would meet and fall in love with a patient man — a man who would overlook her shortcomings and recognize her true nature — a simple, gentle soul in a world that grew frightfully more complex each day.

"Micah, a word with you, please." Clarisa waited until her husband and niece had entered the house, wishing no one to know her intentions until it was too late to change her mind.

Micah halted on the path to the stable and tightened his grip on the horse's bridle. "Yes, madam?"

"The first chance you get, I would like you to dig up those roses on the side of the house."

"Which bush, Mrs. Duncan?"

"All of them. I want them dug out and heaped into the refuse pile to be burned."

If he hadn't been better trained, his jaw would have dropped open several inches. "Your rose garden, madam? The prize roses your guests fuss over all the time?"

"Those are the ones. Impressing my garden club is of little importance to me now. I read in the newspaper that food shortages are imminent all the way down to Wilmington. I won't have people in my house going hungry while I cultivate varietals of fancy thorn bushes."

Micah scratched a stubbly chin. "What are you going plant there, if I may ask? You won't have room for corn or cotton, and the soil's too dry to plant rice."

"Don't be silly. I want to plant food we can eat, such as carrots, potatoes, beans, and squash. I'll see if my neighbors can spare their gardeners for few hours tomorrow to give you a hand."

"It's too late in the season for a garden." He took a step toward the stable.

"Maybe not for root vegetables if we have a mild winter. I wish to try, at least."

"Digging up your roses for potatoes?" Micah shook his head like a stubborn mule. "What is Master Duncan going to say about this idea, madam?"

With waning patience, Clarisa crossed her arms. "Have you been spending your free time chatting with Kathleen? If so I'll take this matter up with Esther."

"I'll start digging soon as I return from driving Master Duncan to work in the morning, madam. There is no need to take this up with my wife." Micah bit down on his lower lip, but his twinkling eyes gave him away.

"Thank you, Micah. I will discuss the

garden with Mr. Duncan when I deem the time is right. If you have no other questions regarding tomorrow, you may see to the horse."

"Yes, madam." He tipped his cap and led the horse into the stable.

Clarisa took a few moments to collect her thoughts. John wouldn't like another reminder of the sorry state of affairs in his beloved city, but a woman had to do what she had to do.

NINE

Madeline couldn't sleep Tuesday night. Tomorrow she and Eugenia would head to the market after breakfast. She was as giddy as her young cousin, but not with the prospect of eating sweet callas or bowls of steamed shrimp and grits. It had been a week since her visit to the *Bonnie Bess.* Had James received her letter? Would he have replied back by now? It was doubtful, to be sure, but possible nonetheless. She needed to force romantic notions from her mind or dawn would find her still staring at the rosettes in the plaster ceiling. Just as Madeline began to doze off, she heard a faint rapping on her door.

"Come in, Genie. The door isn't locked." She'd spoken loud enough to be heard, but a second knock ensued. Madeline reached for her long wrapper and headed for the door, mildly annoyed.

"I said come in —" Seeing the face in her

doorway, she abruptly halted midsentence. Her late night caller wasn't her cousin, but the Duncans' imposing butler.

"I beg your pardon, Mrs. Howard." Looking very uncomfortable, Micah spoke in a whisper. "But I was sent to fetch you."

Madeline tightened the cloth cord around her waist. "Who sent you? Is Esther ill?" For a moment she feared that false notoriety of her nursing abilities had spread.

Micah's discomfort increased by leaps and bounds. "No, ma'am. A gentleman is outside in the garden. He said I was to fetch you and no one else. He said it was a matter of utmost urgency — could be life or death." The butler met her gaze for a brief moment.

Madeline thought she might melt into a puddle on the polished cherry wood floor, to be mopped up by the maid tomorrow. "Very well. I'll come at once." Closing the door behind her, she followed the butler to the back staircase — the servant's staircase which led directly to the terraced garden below. With a pounding heart and damp palms, she feared at any moment bedroom doors would open and a resounding, "Where are you going, Madeline?" would echo through the house.

Will it be James waiting in the jasmine and

bougainvillea? Will he sweep me into his arms and pledge lifelong devotion?

Unfortunately, the officer hidden by potted plants was not General Downing but Major Lewis. His face looked pinched and drawn, as though his sleep had been as troubled as hers.

"Mrs. Howard, thank you for seeing me at this indecent hour." Instead of stepping into the pool of moonlight, he gestured for her to move deeper into the shadows.

With little recourse, she complied. "What is it, Major, that couldn't wait until morning?"

"That will be all," Lewis hissed to the butler.

Micah still lingered at her heels, not pleased by the midnight rendezvous.

"It's all right, Micah," she said. "Please wait for me at the foot of the steps to the gallery."

"Yes, ma'am." He vanished into the darkness.

"That's the trouble with *former* slaves. They act as though they rule the comings and goings of the household." Lewis tugged up his jacket collar despite the evening's warmth.

"Please state your business, sir. I would like to return to the house before my absence is noted. I wouldn't wish to explain meeting a man in the garden at this hour."

"No, that would not do for my plans . . . our plans, Mrs. Howard." Smiling with disturbing familiarity, Lewis pulled something from his pocket and held it out in his open palm.

Madeline stared at a leather-bound book, smaller than a deck of playing cards. "What is that?"

"Take it, please. It might prove useful to you."

With her curiosity aroused, she thumbed through the small volume.

"It's a code book, known only to one or two Union officers. Those officers would appreciate any information you might become privy to." His gaze drifted toward the mansion's soaring roofline illuminated in the moonlight.

Madeline practically dropped the book into the dirt. "I have no use for such a thing. I'm not part of your web of secret intrigue. I'm a farmer's widow living temporarily south of the Mason-Dixon Line." She felt a chill run up her spine into her scalp.

"I know exactly who you are." Smelling of stale tobacco and dried sweat, Lewis took a step closer. "You sent a letter to General Downing of the Fourth Corps. Your lover,

194

perhaps? Don't you think he could use some assistance, holed up in unfamiliar territory? He's cut off from the bulk of General Meade's army. Or would you prefer him to blindly blunder into battle?"

"What makes you think I could help . . . the Union? What we overhead at that dinner party was a coincidence, a one-time occurrence. My uncle doesn't make a habit of sitting around the house and discussing General Lee's plans for attack." Madeline's anxiety was rapidly changing to anger. *How dare this man make such allegations and assumptions?*

Major Lewis lifted both palms. "I don't mean to upset you, Mrs. Howard. Just consider the possibility that you *may* hear something useful in the future — something that could aid General Downing's infantry corps. Maybe save the lives of his men . . . or him."

Madeline wanted to run from the pompous man, but she couldn't dismiss his suggestion cavalierly.

"After I leave you tonight, you won't see me." He glanced around the encroaching shrubbery. "I hope to never again set foot on Virginia soil. Keep the book in a safe place. If you wish to convey information, use the code to compose your message. If your message falls into the wrong hands, no one can use it as evidence against you."

Evidence? Just the word intimidated Madeline. She knew about foaling pregnant mares, not about passing military secrets. "I will accept the code book, Major, but I make no promises." She slipped it into the pocket of her robe.

"Nor would I expect any. Take any messages to Captain George of the *Bonnie Bess.* He'll see that they get into the right hands."

Madeline gasped with the mention of the friendly boat captain's name, but Major Lewis had already disappeared into the shadows. She ran to the bottom of the steps, where the sight of Micah leaning against a post nearly brought her to tears with relief.

"Is everything all right, Mrs. Howard?"

"Yes, thank you, but I would appreciate your not mentioning this visit . . . by an old friend."

"I assumed as much, ma'am." He offered his elbow as they ascended the stairs.

Madeline couldn't wait to reach her room and close the door behind her. Yet her heart rate had barely returned to normal when she heard a second scratching at the wood panel.

"Maddy, may I come in, please?" Eugenia didn't wait for a reply. She opened the door and walked in. "I stopped by a few minutes ago, but your room was empty."

"I took a few turns around the garden. I was restless and tried to tire myself out."

"I couldn't sleep, either. That's why I hoped we could talk for a bit." Dropping onto the settee, Eugenia lowered her face into her hands and began to weep.

Madeline exhaled with relief as she hurried to comfort her young cousin. "What is it, dear heart? Surely your burdens will seem lighter come the dawn. Mine usually do."

"My troubles continue to grow worse. Have you heard the recent casualty numbers? Young men keep dying every day. By the end of the war, there won't be a single eligible bachelor left in Richmond."

Madeline placed a hand on her shoulder. "We must think of the sorrows suffered by their mothers and sisters instead of our reduced prospects for courting."

"I know that's what I should do, but I fear I'll spend the rest of my life sipping tea with Mama in the parlor."

"You're barely nineteen, Genie. You have plenty of time to find your perfect match."

"Not if every man under forty is dead. I just heard that Major Penrod might be sent to the battlefield to replace fallen officers."

"But his leg hasn't properly healed yet."

"That's what I told Papa. Do you think you might speak to Colonel Haywood? I so wish Joseph to remain in town, especially with the social season drawing near. My debut last winter was less than eventful." Eugenia trained plaintive blue eyes on Madeline.

"Colonel Haywood? What influence would I have on him? And I don't know when I'll see him next."

"In case you do? I believe he's been smitten with you ever since you saved his life."

"I did not —" Madeline paused as the girl's face crumpled. "All right. If I'm given the right opportunity, I will speak to the colonel on Major Penrod's behalf."

"That's all I ask. Thank you so much, cousin. I thank God each night that you moved to Richmond." Eugenia kissed both of Madeline's cheeks and squeezed her hard.

November 1863
Colonel Elliott Haywood dressed carefully in the better of his two uniforms. He had been given the second uniform when assigned to Richmond's beleaguered home guard. The new government expanded Richmond's local militia after the capital had been moved from Montgomery in the

early months of the war. The home guard protected not only President Davis and his family, but the entire war department staff, the Confederate Treasury, and the state department, besides the ordnance and munitions depots. The number of men under Elliott's command had fluctuated greatly during the past few months. Enlisted men and officers had been called away to support other campaigns due to a chronic shortage of both, but as federal troops advanced closer to Richmond, men were quickly recruited to swell the home guard's ranks. His office also directed the tide of dispatches flowing between Richmond and Fredericksburg. Elliott often made the trip himself because many under his command were unable to ride due to wounds or other infirmities. Determined to still be of service, these loyal soldiers stood guard at various offices and processed the endless blizzard of military paperwork. Able-bodied staff members not needed for courier duty acted as President Davis's personal bodyguards.

Elliott was considered accomplished among his peers, even though his education consisted only of one local grammar school and brief terms with a tutor. As the fourth of five children and the youngest son of a cotton planter, his father had little regard for higher education. He sent his eldest two sons north to college, yet neither of Elliott's brothers had distinguished himself in the academic world. When he came of age, a career in the military appeared his best option. Years of poor harvests, low prices for cotton, and general mismanagement had sent their plantation into a downward spiral. The Haywood family's once impressive fortune had dwindled well before the onset of war.

Charles Haywood, never much of a businessman, invested what he had left in Confederate bonds, staking everything on the Confederacy. Elliott's father had already turned the day-to-day operations over to his third son, a dissipated man unfit for military duty. Robert's physical condition proved to be a blessing when the eldest sons were killed days apart at the battles of Frazier's Farm and Malvern Hill. When his father received the letters, unfortunately arriving the same day, his interest in the plantation ceased and he remained mildly drunk from then on.

Elliott's mother died of yellow fever when he was ten years old, along with his four-year-old sister. He could remember his mother walking the length of the second-floor gallery in the morning, her skirts billowing behind her. Whenever she spotted him playing in the garden, she would wave her lace-gloved hand. His mother, never a strong woman, had spent most days in her room, venturing downstairs only for dinner. Elliott and his sister had been fed in the kitchen by their nanny. His faded memory of the woman who bore him was a wren-like creature with fair hair and tiny hands. She addressed her husband as Mr. Haywood, instead of Charles. Elliott had never once heard her raise her voice.

By contrast, his baby sister was a bumblebee who ran as soon as she learned to walk and knocked over anything in her path whenever she was out of her nurse's eye. Elliott had grieved when his father carried down the tiny, linen-wrapped bundle for the funeral wake. His father looked as though his heart would break. Two days later, his mother was gone too.

Colonel Haywood squeezed his eyes shut to force away painful memories. He was a grown man. All of that was long past. Before Elliott's enlistment, his father secured a position for him as an apprentice to a cotton factor. Having no sons of his own, the elderly gentleman took Elliott under his wing and trained him in the savvy business. Mr. Lowe invited Elliott to live above the carriage house behind his opulent Savannah townhouse, treating him like family. In Savannah, Elliott learned to broker commodities with finesse, and more importantly, he established the necessary connections to conduct business in the old South. Elliott seldom went home to the plantation in the years preceding the war, vastly preferring the lifestyle offered by Mr. Lowe.

Now that life was behind him as well. Since enlisting in the Confederate Army more than two years ago, he'd heard nothing from Mr. and Mrs. Lowe of Savannah. The federal blockade along the coast prevented cotton from leaving eastern seaports. With farmers fighting for the Cause and the slaves run off, almost no cotton grew in Georgia anymore. What kind of job — what kind of world — would be left when the war finally ended?

The only thing intriguing Elliott these days was a tall, lovely Yankee, unlike any woman he had ever known. Forthright and direct, Mrs. Howard thought logically and spoke her mind without affectation or pretense. Unafraid of hard work, she demonstrated more courage than any delicate Southern belle. Society ladies were accustomed to being taken care of. They had done little for themselves before the war and resented having their luxuries taken from them now. Mrs. Howard's independent spirit appealed to him more than false graciousness and social artifice.

Elliott adjusted his tie, took a final look in the mirror, and hurried downstairs, grabbing his hat on his way out the door. As commander of the Richmond home guard, the Confederacy paid for his suite of rooms in a fashionable but shabby hotel on the west side of town, although actual pay envelopes were few and far between these days. It had been weeks since he had dined with the Duncans, yet he hadn't forgotten his offer to accompany Mrs. Howard to church. Today he wouldn't allow war business to interfere with his well-laid plans. Stopping in the hotel kitchen to pick up the hamper he ordered, Elliott set off toward Forsythia Lane. He had borrowed a carriage from a merchant and would reward him for his generosity with free labor, courtesy of the guards. Everything had its price in wartime Richmond.

Mrs. Howard was descending the steps of the Duncan mansion as he reached the carriage block. "Good morning, Mrs. Howard. What a coincidence. I'm on my way to St. Paul's Episcopal for services. Would you care to join me?" He offered her his best smile.

"I'm not sure that this is a coincidence, Colonel. However, I won't question your word on the Sabbath." A smile lifted the corners of her mouth. "I have a feeling my aunt had a hand in this."

"She may have suggested the possibility to me." He extended his hand to her.

Mrs. Howard swayed as though in mental turmoil. "I'm not sure I should cram into your family's pew and make others uncomfortable. Perhaps I'll enter the sanctuary alone and sit in the back."

"Nonsense. You will crowd no one. My grandparents have passed on and my father and brother no longer drive in from the country for the weekend. You would make a lonely man less so for a brief interval because I usually sit by myself."

After reflecting a moment more, Mrs. Howard took his hand and climbed up beside him. "Very well, I shall ride with you. My uncle described the length of the walk, and I feared these slippers wouldn't hold up well." She lifted her skirt an inch to reveal her footwear — something no Southern lady would ever do.

Elliott bit back his impulse to laugh. "Those won't be suitable for our sloppy winters. You and Miss Duncan will need to go shopping."

Mrs. Howard chose to ignore his advice and made polite conversation about the weather and changes to the Duncan garden along the way. When they arrived in front of the church, her banter stopped. "Goodness, I hadn't expected so grand a cathedral. I'm used to small country churches that also serve as the schoolhouse and town hall."

"I hope you'll find the message as inspiring as the edifice," Elliott said, offering her his elbow as they climbed the long flight of stone steps.

One and half hours later, if her grin and the volume of her singing were any indication, Mrs. Howard had enjoyed the service immensely. After they paused to greet the pastor on the way out, she practically skipped down the steps.

"That was lovely," she said. "Although my aunt's church is beautiful beyond description, I can't understand a word of their Mass in Latin. Thank you, sir, for inviting me."

"I apologize for our minister's plea to be generous to the Cause in the offering plate. Funds are short, I daresay."

"No apology necessary, Colonel. I dropped what few coins I could spare in the poor box by the door."

"Resourcefulness, thy name is woman." Elliott took her arm on their way to the hired carriage.

"I'm determined to let nothing dampen my good mood on such a glorious day."

For several minutes they rode along in companionable silence, enjoying the warm sun on their back and the cool breeze on their face. Suddenly, she swiveled on the seat. "Shouldn't we have taken Grace Street to return to my uncle's, or am I confused? The houses are becoming sparser instead of more closely spaced."

"You're very observant, Mrs. Howard. If your uncle's home was our intended destination, we are indeed going in the wrong direction." He shook the reins to hasten their progress.

"I'd prefer you take me home, Colonel. I don't wish to worry the Duncans regarding my whereabouts."

"We're merely taking a short drive. There's something I wish you to see. Your uncle and aunt won't worry for your safety in my company."

"May I at least know where we are headed?" She turned her neck in both directions.

"To the prettiest view in Richmond, my

favorite spot. It's not far, I assure you." After another mile, they turned off Idlewood Drive onto Cherry Street and rattled over rough stones through an open gate. A carved wooden sign indicated they entered the hallowed grounds of Hollywood Cemetery.

"You've brought me to a cemetery? Do you have relatives you wish to pay your respects to?" She lowered her voice to a whisper.

"I do have relatives buried here, but they are not why we've come. I want you to see a place that holds much of Richmond's history since the Revolutionary War."

Cobblestone paths had been laid out just wide enough for a carriage to pass in between stately old trees. Massive oaks, walnuts, and sycamores provided ample shade, while holly trees were massed with plump red berries. Verdant rhododendrons, mountain laurel, and crabapple had set their buds for the first warm days of spring months away. Acres of rolling hills had been divided into private family plots by low stone walls. Graves were well spaced and well marked.

"It is beautiful here." She peered from side to side at the impressive grounds. "I'm sure it would be lovely in winter."

Elliott chose the narrow lane that followed

a cliff-like ridge of land, stopping the horse in front of a large crypt. "Our first stop," he announced. "President James Monroe, our fifth president and last president who was a founding father of the United States. He was a planter born in Westmoreland County, Virginia, and died on Independence Day in 1831. Ironic, no?"

"Truly, but at least he was laid to rest in a beautiful place. Look, someone recently visited his grave." Mrs. Howard pointed at a wreath of red flowers. White pearly seeds still clung to the dried boughs.

"There is plenty of history here — Virginia's history." With a click of his tongue, the carriage began to roll. Elliott halted a second time before a vast expanse of wind-blown acreage at the extreme end of the property. "Up on that hill they plan to rebury our boys who died at Gettysburg. So many young men on both sides. They intend to dig up the bodies and bring them home to Virginia soil. Your government doesn't want Rebs in their new cemetery, and the families don't want their sons spending eternity up North."

Mrs. Howard stared into the distance, her words floating on the breeze. "Where they spend eternity is up to their Maker."

"Well said, madam. We just left church,

and I had already forgotten myself."

"I didn't know that about the new Gettysburg cemetery, Colonel. I'm saddened and a little ashamed that the gray-clad soldiers who died wouldn't be welcomed in hallowed ground. In death, our earthly battles are over."

"Ah, it's nasty business on both sides. Let's move on. I have one more site to show you." Elliott chewed the inside of his mouth in frustration. Why had he brought up the subject of Gettysburg with the woman who had saved his life? He released the brake and the carriage continued along the narrow road.

"Oh, my! Please stop." Mrs. Howard hopped out before the carriage came to a halt. She ran to the precipice and peered over the edge where a wide valley had been cut by the shallow but turbulent river. "This must be the view you spoke of."

Elliott lifted the hamper and folded quilt from the back before joining her side. "It is. Look down there." He pointed with a gloved finger. "We have a canal next to the river, dug by immigrants, to move goods when the river is too low to navigate."

"Ingenious. They built such a canal in Pennsylvania too."

While they watched, canopied flatboats

pulled by mules on the towpath made slow progress along the narrow canal. A row of trees separated the two waterways, while jasmine, honeysuckle, and blackberry bushes covered the embankment down to the water. Flowering vines and shrubbery had managed to gain foothold on the cliffs.

"I can see the white columns of your capitol building." Mrs. Howard stood on tiptoes as she tried to discern other landmarks. "Yet here we stand in a pastoral Eden — such a contrast within the city."

"I thought you would like my favorite spot in Richmond." Elliott stepped closer to savor the view — both of the river and his companion. "Shall we sit and share a meal? It won't be as elegant as the repast provided by your aunt and uncle, but it's edible to be sure." He held out the willow basket.

Her pleasant expression slipped a notch. "I wish you hadn't troubled yourself, Colonel."

"It was no trouble, I assure you. This is the advantage of living in a hotel and flirting shamelessly with the proprietress."

Her eyes flashed with annoyance. "And what advantage do you hope to gain by flirting shamelessly with me?"

"I was teasing, Mrs. Howard. My landlady is a widow well into her seventies. I paid a dear price for this hamper of food." Elliott placed a hand over his heart. "That is the honest truth. An hour of your company is the only advantage I seek."

"In that case, I beg your pardon." She dropped down to her knees on the quilt. "What did she pack for us? Your minister's long sermon has left me ravenous."

"Let's see," he said, pulling out items wrapped in white paper. "Cold sandwiches, apples, and some type of cake. What do you suppose this could be?" Elliott held up a lidded container to the sunlight, swirling the dark, murky contents. "A mysterious jar of something to drink."

"It looks . . . dangerous." Laughing, she studied the tiny leaves and other foreign matter swimming around the brew.

Uncapping it carefully, the colonel brought the jar to his nose for a cautious sniff. "Mmm, it smells much better than it looks. Shall we be brave?" He pulled two chipped mugs from the hamper and poured a bit into each.

She accepted one mug and gingerly sniffed.

"To your health, madam." Elliott clinked her cup with his and downed his portion in one large gulp. "Delicious. It's sassafras tea. Don't be frightened; drink up."

211

She swallowed a mouthful and grimaced. "I wasn't aware sassafras *tea* could ferment, Colonel. This concoction contains something spirituous." She set her cup in the tall grass.

"I believe it's my proprietress's special blend." Elliott refilled his cup and then divided their lunch onto china plates. "Looks like the sandwiches are ham and the cake is chocolate. But dessert is only for those who eat their healthy apple first."

"Bounteous fare during wartime." Gazing over the broad river valley, Mrs. Howard took a small bite of her sandwich. "How fortunate to have a day so mild this late in the fall."

"Fortunate, yes," he agreed, studying her every move.

His rapt attention hadn't gone unnoticed. "Is my hat on backward, sir? Or perhaps I have mustard on my nose?" She swiveled to face him. "Why exactly are you staring at me?"

"Forgive me, Mrs. Howard, but I can't seem to take my eyes off you." He placed his gloved hand over hers.

She yanked her hand back as though stung by a bee, spilling the contents of her forgotten mug. "Colonel Haywood, I have done you a disservice if I've given an incorrect impression. I accepted your invitation today based on friendship, nothing more." Rising gracefully to her feet, she peered down at him. "My heart already belongs to another. You've made me uncomfortable, sir, and I wish to be taken home."

"Forgive me, Mrs. Howard. I'd been led to believe you were a widow, recently released from the restrictions of mourning." He also scrambled to his feet. "Another man has already claimed your affections?"

Lifting her chin, she crossed her arms over her bodice. "I left the constraints of mourning this past spring and met someone in July."

"The same month one of God's most divine angels saved my life? What bitter irony that it was not me who caught your eye." He pressed his hat to his chest.

"You have a rare gift for words, Colonel, along with a flair for the dramatic. I daresay a panoply of belles await your attention in Richmond with myself removed from the mix." She strode purposefully toward the carriage.

Haywood hastily packed their lunch back into the hamper, grabbed the quilt, and sprinted to catch up with her. "You have resoundingly won this skirmish, madam, but I pray not the entire war. Allow me to parlay

213

again another day . . . as a cherished friend, if nothing else."

"I will attend services with you on Sundays because your church is much to my liking. And because I have few other friends in your fair city." She halted at the carriage steps and faced him like a feral cat. "But I grant you no other liberties than that."

"I have tried every tactic and maneuver my military career taught me, but I have been bested . . . and by a Yankee, no less." Elliott bowed from the waist and offered his hand.

Accepting his help into the carriage, she replied with indignation. "It's not a case of being bested, Colonel. Love is neither a game nor some type of competition."

"That's where you are wrong, Mrs. Howard. Love is most certainly that and more." He placed the hamper between them as a fortress and clucked to the horses.

The ride back to Forsythia Lane was long that afternoon.

■ ■ ■ ■

TEN

■ ■ ■ ■

Tuesday

Madeline could get no respite from her monthly cramps, no matter how many cups of Esther's willow bark tea she drank. She had declined Aunt Clarisa's invitation to join her on the afternoon round of social calls. Sipping weak coffee and eating sweets still required a smile and polite responses to conversation — two things Madeline felt incapable of in her current state. She tried walking in the garden, recently replanted with tiny seedlings, but a cold rain had begun to fall. Then she tried to stretch out in her room, but could find no comfort there, either. Dampness drifted through the ill-fitting glass panes.

Alone in the house except for the servants, Madeline reclined on the parlor sofa and covered her legs with a shawl. The fire in the hearth, along with the soft patter of rain on the window, brought relief at last. She fell asleep within minutes and slept soundly for hours. When she awoke, she felt momentarily discombobulated.

Stretching like a cat, Madeline heard the sound of conversation coming from the next room. Deep male voices easily carried through a silent house. Lethargic from the warmth and with no place to go, she listened to their discussion with growing interest.

"Would it be wise to move the army this late in the year? We've had so much rain lately, and heavy clouds show no indication of letting up soon."

Madeline recognized the speaker as Colonel Haywood, whom she'd grown fonder of after each Sunday service. Not the way she felt toward General Downing, but like an old childhood friend — one you wished life had treated better. Eugenia had explained the unpleasant situation on the Haywood plantation — his father and surviving sibling both drunkards. It was no wonder Elliott lived in rented rooms in a poor section of town and worshipped alone Sunday mornings. Madeline vowed to show him nothing but kindness during her remaining time in Virginia.

"Haywood's right. Artillery caissons will mire down in the muck, allowing them to fall into enemy hands should our troops retreat in haste." Her uncle's deep baritone voice was also easily recognizable.

"There will be no retreat this time and no artillery," declared a third man. "Cannons will remain positioned where they are. We'll use cavalry with one division of infantry and strike swiftly. We can surprise their position along the Rapidan and drive them east, straight into Longstreet's corps positioned along the Rappahannock. We'll trounce the Yankees in one more decisive battle before the snow flies. If we can reduce their numbers, we can begin the spring offensive more evenly matched."

"They can outnumber us two to one and we would still have the advantage."

Madeline thought she recognized the nasally tone of Major Penrod — the man who had captured Eugenia's young heart.

"I don't disagree, but we need time to re-outfit with guns and ammunition. And over the winter months we *must* convince England to take a stand. We need the ordnance their foundries produce."

Madeline heard a murmur of agreement in the dining room and the clink of brandy snifters.

"If England joins our side, we can lick those Yanks that much sooner," Major Penrod blustered.

"Has General Lee approved this plan, General Stuart?" asked Colonel Haywood.

"Of course he has, or I wouldn't be here in Richmond. We'll use Ewell's corps of infantry, commanded by General Early."

The unfamiliar voice now had a name — the illustrious James Ewell Brown Stuart, commonly called "Jeb" Stuart. Madeline had read about his exploits prior to the battle of Gettysburg.

"In that case, prepare your dispatches, sir, and I'll see that they reach the necessary commanders."

Madeline bolted upright on the couch while her heart slammed against her chest wall. Was this the type of information Major Lewis had alluded to? But she had no date for the Confederate movement of troops against Union forces. With a queasy feeling in her gut, Madeline knew General Downing's soldiers were camped west of Fredericksburg. Would General Stuart's cavalry sound the death knell for her beloved?

This information had come by way of her dear uncle — a man who provided shelter when no one else could. And from Colonel Haywood — a man she considered her friend, who had shown her nothing but kindness since Aunt Clarisa's dinner party. On shaky legs, Madeline climbed the ornate flying staircase to her room. For the next hour she prayed at her window, which had once overlooked row after row of beautiful roses. Their scent had drifted in on summer nights when sleep refused to come.

At long last, when no divine insight arrived, Madeline pulled out a sheet of paper and the code book from its hiding place. She painstakingly translated the meager details she heard into a bizarre language of letters and symbols. It took her more than two hours to relate five lines of information, omitting the nuances of Queen's English she'd learned in school.

Although her cramps had abated, a headache now plagued her composure. Creeping to the top of the stairs, Madeline strained to listen but heard no voices coming from the dining room. Eugenia was in the parlor, chattering about the afternoon's social calls. Interrupting her, Aunt Clarisa gave supper orders to the sluggish Kathleen — never one to anticipate chores on her own. Madeline peeked out the front window, but the horses that had been tied to the hitching rail were gone, the afternoon's war council on Forsythia Lane apparently concluded.

The distinguished Southern officers would return to their offices, homes, or hotel rooms unaware that a spy lurked among them. As Madeline folded the sheet of paper into a small square, she realized with clarity that that was what she had become. That night during supper, she could barely look at her uncle. Fortunately, Eugenia shared enough gossip during the meal that no one noticed Madeline's lack of conversation. Micah, assisted by Kathleen, served roast chicken, buttered yams, and yellow beans, with pickled cucumbers as a relish. Madeline had noticed only two chickens being plucked and prepared for supper. Esther had become an expert at stretching a meager amount to feed three Duncans, their houseguest, and three staff members. Feast or famine ruled in Aunt Clarisa's house. Provisions were reserved for when they entertained guests, and everyone went to bed slightly hungry whenever they didn't. Aunt Clarisa treated Madeline as family, not a guest, which pleased her. Yet at the same time, Madeline suffered a guilty conscience with her newfound role.

"If the weather is mild tomorrow, shall we venture to the market?" Madeline posed her question over coffee and a sliver of pound cake, once Genie had exhausted her stream of gossip.

"Oh, yes indeed! I need a day away from the auxiliary ladies." Her cousin practically levitated from her chair.

"We have nothing to spare for frivolity this week. Not even callas, unless you can buy broken ones for a penny." Aunt Clarisa spoke with her usual dignity and grace. "If they have a good price on corn, bring home two bushels." She directed this to Madeline, not her daughter. "Corn should have come down by now. We can put up jars for winter, grind some into meal, and dry a few cobs to pop over the hearth. In the meantime, Esther can make batches of cornbread and corn fritters."

"Micah, I'll take a brandy in the parlor with my pipe," Uncle John said before brushing a kiss across his wife's head as he left the dining room. "For Christmas you can whittle me a new pipe from a corn cob, dear heart."

"Good night, Uncle," murmured Madeline.

"Good night, Madeline, Eugenia. Sleep with sweet dreams of fair skies for your outing."

The next day dawned cool and bleak with low clouds threatening to open at any moment into torrents of rain. Yet the two young women didn't cancel their trip to the docks. Eugenia eagerly anticipated market day as a break to her *ennui,* and Madeline couldn't

223

wait to transfer the note, tucked in the inner flap of her reticule, into the callused hands of Captain George of the *Bonnie Bess*.

Elliott glanced at his pocket watch for the third time, but not because he was in a hurry to confer with Jefferson Davis. With no good news to present, he didn't care if their meeting was postponed indefinitely. He stared out the window at a dismal city. Rain continued to fall, dampening spirits as well as Richmond's already muddy streets.

The paneled door of the executive office swung open, and John Duncan greeted him with a smile. "Good morning, Colonel Haywood. President Davis will see you now."

"Thank you, sir." With hat in hand, Elliott entered the elegant, high-ceilinged domain of the president of the Confederate States of America. Duncan's tiredness paled in comparison to Davis's. The man's face had sunk beneath his cheekbones, causing his sharp nose to stand in sharp relief. He'd gained a hawkish appearance after losing at least thirty pounds since the start of the war.

"Thank you for waiting, Colonel. Please have a seat." Davis pointed to a leather chair in front of his desk.

Elliott scanned the room. Two aides stood against the wall, their side arms unstrapped. Davis's staff members served as bodyguards in addition to the protection Elliott kept posted. Maps, dispatches, and handwritten rosters covered every inch of the desk. Clutched between his fingers were more papers to add to the clutter. "Thank you, sir."

President Davis tossed the sheet he'd been reading onto the desk. "I hope you have better news for me, Colonel."

Lowering himself to the edge of the chair, Elliott chose not to answer the question directly. "General Lee has withdrawn his troops south of the Rapidan River, while Meade's army is encamped close to the town of Brandy Station. For the past week, Meade tried to push our boys back. Apparently, a ford of the Germanna River changed hands five times. It is once again ours, sir."

The president gritted his teeth. "Seven days of fighting and yet we gained nothing."

"True, but we haven't lost ground, sir. By all reports the campaign around the town of Mine Run has been declared a stalemate."

"The Yanks have no trouble replacing the soldiers they lose. I, on the other hand, have no more men to send General Lee. Our efforts to recruit in Georgia and the Carolinas have yielded either men too old to march or boys too young to shoot straight."

Elliott merely cleared his throat. He had nothing positive to add.

"Give me the casualty report from the hospital." Davis stood and walked to his window, clasping his hands behind his back.

"I have it here, sir." After shuffling through the stack for the correct piece of paper, Elliott conveyed the statistics of the dead, amputees discharged from service, and wounded returned to their regiments to serve out enlistments.

Midway through the report, Davis turned and slapped an open palm down on the desk. "Unacceptable! What are those surgeons doing? They kill more than they save. Are they all blind or drunk?"

"According to the chief surgeon of Chimborazo, more are dying in the wards from typhus than the festering of wounds."

The color rose in Davis's usually pale complexion. "I shall direct General Lee not to attempt additional engagements this year. He must establish a suitable winter camp and restore his men. In the spring we will attack Meade's rabble with a renewed army."

"I will personally deliver dispatches to the

commanders, sir," Elliott said as he scrambled to his feet.

"The first one I need sent is a request for another prisoner exchange. My officers are languishing on Johnson's Island in Ohio. Who knows if they can survive a winter on Lake Erie? Some of those boys never saw snow before."

"I will deliver your request, sir, but rumor has it that Lincoln would refuse any future officer exchange. He knows our need is greater than theirs."

Considering Davis's facial expression, Elliott regretted sharing this information even though it surely wasn't gossip. He'd seen it printed in a Baltimore newspaper.

The president pinched the bridge of his nose as though another headache had arrived. "That will be all for now, Colonel. Thank you for your patience this morning. You may return to your duties until I complete my directives."

Elliott saluted and left the executive suite with a sour taste in his mouth. He wished the news had been better, but boasting and overwrought arrogance hadn't served the Confederacy thus far. If they were to win this war, they must recognize their weaknesses as well as their strengths.

The guard posted at the office of the home

guard was asleep at his post, his head lolling against the doorjamb. Based on his ghastly pallor, Elliott suspected the soldier still suffered blood poisoning from his arm amputation. "Look sharp there!" he ordered on his way past.

Once he had returned to his office, he stared out the window at the street below. How he'd loved coming to the city from the plantation as a child. While his grandparents had been alive, his family home had been a happy place, filled with good things to eat and the sounds of children at play. Now Elliott could barely stand the sight of his broken father or godless brother. Only the thought of seeing Mrs. Howard Sunday mornings kept him from slipping into despondency. Pulling his map of Northern Virginia closer, he studied the approximate location of General Meade's encampment. One of his aides interrupted him before he could plot the best way to approach the camp.

"Excuse me, Colonel, but a Mr. Jonas Weems wishes to see you."

"I don't know any Mr. Weems. Send him away." Elliott scraped his hand down his face.

"He's a newspaper man for the *Richmond Times Dispatch* and says the matter is of the utmost importance."

Isn't every matter these days? Elliott's eyes rolled back for a moment. "Send him in, Lieutenant."

A few moments later a rotund, middle-aged man pulled off kid gloves and extended a hand. "Colonel Haywood, a pleasure to make your acquaintance, sir. I believe our fathers belonged to the same club in town. But that club is no more, I'm afraid."

Elliott half rose to shake hands. "A pleasure, but I'm afraid I can grant you only five minutes, sir. I'm awaiting urgent dispatches from President Davis."

"Five minutes will be more than ample. I come with concerns of a rather personal and delicate nature." Weems lowered his voice despite the fact the aide had left the office.

Elliott pushed his map aside. "What personal matter do we have to discuss? I've never laid eyes on you before today."

"A tall, blond woman has been seen Sunday mornings in your family's pew." Weems consulted a small book that had gone unnoticed thus far. "A Mrs. Madeline Howard."

"You feel whom I sit with in church is your business, Mr. Weems, or worthy of the *Richmond Times'* attention?" Elliott didn't hide his irritation.

"Certainly not, sir. I'm a journalist, not a gossipmonger. But I've learned on good authority that Mrs. Howard hails from Pennsylvania and was briefly associated with a Yankee hospital up north."

"She does and yes, she worked in a humanitarian capacity for which I will always be grateful. Mrs. Howard saved my life, sir."

Weems blinked several times. "Astonishing, Colonel. The coincidences in life must truly give one pause. Then was it her humanitarian nature that brought Mrs. Howard to our city? Perhaps to assist at Chimborazo Hospital? I visited there recently, and the need for nurses is great."

"I don't believe so, sir. Please speak your business frankly. I have no time for innuendo."

"Innuendo? I'm here with nothing but respect for your service to the Confederacy, but I must beg you to consider a possibility. The enemy often sends the fairer sex to trick those with a trusting nature — a Trojan horse, if you will. This wouldn't be the first time an officer divulged military information. From one gentleman to another, a pretty face and comely figure can often mask a devious heart."

"Mrs. Howard is no Delilah. And I will thank you to keep your baseless opinions to yourself." Elliott pushed back from the desk.

"In October someone conveyed information regarding Lee's planned assault near the town of Bristow. Division commanders insist their maneuver came as no surprise to the Yankees. A houseguest of the Duncans would have access to sensitive details." His aspersion hung in the air like the stink of rotted meat.

"I don't discuss military matters between hymns at St. Paul's Church, and neither does John Duncan at his dinner table." Elliott stood so that he towered over the short journalist, but then he leaned precariously close so there would be no misunderstanding. "I suggest you obtain proof before you smear the good name of a gentlewoman such as Mrs. Howard."

Mr. Weems turned pale as though finally aware he'd overstepped whatever good intentions he had. "I beg your pardon, sir, for giving offense. I will leave you with a humble word of caution, nothing more." He bowed low from the waist, plopped his hat on his head, and hurried from the room, leaving Elliott both furious and confused.

ELEVEN

December

From her bedroom window, Madeline watched snow falling on a bleak city. It offered no blanketing, softening effect as it did up north. Instead, the snow quickly melted, creating a slushy mess in the streets.

"Maddy, breakfast!"

Eugenia's call pierced her reverie. Since moving in with the Duncans, Madeline felt her social position diminish. She was treated more like an older sibling rather than a widowed matron accustomed to answering to no one.

"I'll be down shortly," she hollered, falling easily into the role. She wrapped a shawl around her shoulders. The mansion was drafty and under heated due to the high price of both coal and firewood.

"Think warm thoughts and go to bed early." Aunt Clarisa's often-repeated advice to Eugenia made Madeline smile. She'd grown up believing the South to always be warm. With a final glance out her bedroom window, Madeline caught a glimpse of a soldier in a plumed hat making his way down the flagstone sidewalk of Forsythia Lane. With his head bent against the wind, the man tried to dodge puddles along the way. Even at this distance, she could see that his coat was too threadbare to provide much protection.

Where was James on this sunless Monday? Had the Union Army built quarters or commandeered abandoned farmhouses to house their officers? Or did a general sleep in a canvas tent with damp grass beneath his bedroll? Madeline shook away thoughts of a man whose face grew more obscure with each passing day.

Worry not about what you cannot change, but endeavor righteously with what you can. Her grandmother's favorite saying had been stitched onto a scrap of muslin cloth. Madeline had framed the sampler and hung it in her living room . . . in a house that existed now solely in her memory.

"Good morning, my dear," Aunt Clarisa said the moment she entered the dining room. "I trust you slept well."

Smiling, Madeline slipped onto a dining room chair. "Yes, ma'am, I did."

"There's an extra quilt in the trunk at the foot of your bed," Aunt Clarisa said as she held up a porcelain cup to the butler.

"I found it, thank you. Just one egg and toast, please, Micah. No sausage gravy today."

"You need to eat enough to maintain your strength. The ladies' auxiliary needs both you and Eugenia every day this week." Aunt Clarisa scooped a mound of fried potatoes onto everyone's plates.

Eugenia's head snapped up. "All five days? I will never survive the stultifying boredom of sewing that long. I shall fall into a mortal faint from which there will be no recovery." She dropped her fork into her poached egg.

"Very well, daughter. I will tell the guild you care not for our soldiers in the field, who don't have enough socks, mittens, or wool hats to prevent their freezing to death. The girls with compassionate hearts will be the ones planning this season's teas, soirees, and parties." Aunt Clarisa sipped her coffee, never lifting her hawk-like gaze.

Madeline almost choked on laughter, while Eugenia's lips formed a perfect letter *O*. "I'm sorry, Mama, I spoke without thinking. Forgive me. I would be happy to sew with the ladies all week." She swabbed egg yolk with her toast crust for a few moments, and then she asked, "Do you think we could host a ball over the holidays? It's been so long since anyone has had one."

Her father cleared his throat from behind a copy of the *Richmond Times Dispatch*. He'd been so quiet that Madeline had forgotten he was there. "I think a ball would be inappropriate, daughter, considering how many of our friends are in deep mourning."

"But life goes on, Papa. We must hold up our heads and survive. That's what Father Michael said during Mass this past week."

Uncle John turned his patient brown eyes on his only child. "You've taken his words out of context, my dear. The priest meant we're not to wallow in despair or self-pity over our plight, but continue on the Christian path. Father Michael cares little about balls and cotillions."

"But he didn't say we must stop living for the rest of the war." Eugenia's tone turned desperate.

"Calm yourself, my dear," said Aunt Clarisa. "Perhaps we could hold a low-key dance for the New Year. A few string musicians with Miss Graham at the piano. Nothing too showy or expensive."

"Inexpensive would be a wise choice, wife." Uncle John slanted a wry glance at her over his newspaper.

"Is there bad news in the *Times*?" she asked.

"Washington has declared the battles in October and November to be Union victories. I cannot see how that could be true if both armies hold the same ground as before the skirmishes. They are trying to tweak our noses to incite another rash move by General Lee."

Madeline glanced around the table. In light of her recent activities, any war talk made her nervous. "Surely with the Advent season upon us there will be no further fighting." She forced herself to eat a few bites of egg, wondering, as she had several times, whether the success of the Union forces was due to Lewis's information or hers. She felt heat climbing her neck and filling her face despite the meager fire in the hearth.

"Are you all right, Madeline? You look flushed."

"I'm fine, Aunt. Perhaps I can assist Esther with the baking today. I would love to make oatmeal cookies to take to the guild."

"With your sewing and baking talents, you are a godsend to our family. Have Eugenia join you in the kitchen. Perhaps one day she will need to do more than just give orders to staff."

That afternoon, Madeline knitted and sewed until her fingers stiffened into claw-like positions. She sipped endless cups of weak tea, while elderly women bemoaned life without slaves, middle-aged women spread gossip about the unfortunate ladies unable to be there with them, and young women planned a Christmastide with as much social interaction as limited means would allow.

Pity the remaining bachelors in Richmond. If their battlefield wounds didn't kill them, surely the aggressive belles vying for their attention would.

Aunt Clarisa must have noticed her niece's waning interest in the conversation. "Lest you think all our activities are self-serving, Madeline, this Friday and every Friday until Christmas Eve we will be caroling on city streets. Each church along our route will pass out cups of cocoa. Will you come along? Some of the men of the home guard usually join the fun."

Madeline nodded. "I haven't caroled in years. That would be lovely. Thank you."

"Splendid! If the home guard is invited, then Papa's staff will be there too." Eugenia clapped her hands, drawing a frown from the guild's matriarch.

"We also pack food baskets with whatever

can be spared," continued Aunt Clarisa. "And distribute them to the poor on Christmas Day."

"Our baskets grow ever leaner, but those in need become ever more abundant." This sour observation was offered by a thin woman in unrelenting black.

Madeline smiled politely at the widow — a smile that would be repeated many times during the next four days of sewing.

By Friday she couldn't wait to go caroling. Walking the streets in the brisk air and raising her voice in songs of goodwill raised Madeline's spirits, as did the prospect of seeing Colonel Haywood. She'd grown fond of the man. His quick wit usually offset his somber demeanor. The Duncans were fond of him as well. According to her uncle, no other man connected to the war department worked more diligently. So it came as no surprise when her aunt announced that Colonel Haywood would join them for dinner before the Christmas outing.

Madeline was startled, however, to spot him in the dining room doorway while her aunt already had on her long fur wrapper and Uncle John wore his wool overcoat and top hat. "Has something happened?" she asked, midway down the stairs.

"Nothing to worry about, dear niece," said

Aunt Clarisa. "Father Michael invited us to dine at the rectory. He has parish business to discuss. I hope you don't mind serving as hostess tonight."

"Not at all. Welcome, Colonel. I hope you've brought your singing voice as well as your appetite. Will any of the other guards be joining Eugenia and me for dinner?"

"Good evening, Mrs. Howard. No, I believe you're stuck listening solely to my tiresome repartee."

Madeline offered him a gracious smile as she stepped off the staircase, but then she stopped short in the dining room doorway. Only two places had been set at the elegantly appointed table, the chairs intimately close. With only half the normal number of candles burning, the illumination reflected off the crystal goblets was downright sparse. Inhaling deeply, Madeline turned to her aunt. "Why has no place been set for Eugenia? Surely Father Michael doesn't require her input on parish matters."

Clarisa put an outrageously feathered hat atop her head. "Goodness, no. Major Penrod came by earlier to take Eugenia to supper at his private club. I believe she'll have a chance to meet the major's parents before they join the caroling at the Methodist church."

"Perhaps you can post Micah as sentry if Mrs. Howard is uncomfortable dining alone," Colonel Haywood said to Uncle John.

"That won't be necessary. I live in fear of no man. We'll see you at the Saint Patrick stop." Madeline half curtsied to the Duncans and marched into the dining room.

"Good luck to you, sir," said Uncle John. "Perhaps you'll be the one needing a sentry before the meal concludes." Laughter followed him out the door.

Madeline waited for the Colonel to pull out her chair — a new habit she'd learned from her aunt. If she counted the times Tobias had helped her sit down, she would have all ten fingers left. "Considering the kindness you've shown me, I hope you'll forgive my confusion about tonight. I'm not very good with last-minute changes of plans." She sat down primly.

"No apology necessary. Most ladies would be disconcerted to find themselves in a new role." Haywood spread the linen napkin across his lap.

Madeline leaned back as Micah filled her goblet with lemonade. "Would you like a brandy, Colonel, or some other aperitif? I'm sure Micah knows where Uncle John keeps his spirits."

"Brandies are for *after* a meal, and aperitifs, as the name implies, decidedly before. One drinks wine with the meal, madam." He softened his lecture with a magnanimous smile.

Still, her cheeks tingled with embarrassment. "So it's a glass of wine you wish?"

"No, thank you. I prefer lemonade, the same as you."

Madeline bit the inside of her cheeks until Micah finished filling the colonel's goblet. Once the butler retreated from the room, she swiveled around to face him. "If you wanted lemonade, why not just say so? And what did you mean by *most* ladies? Are you implying I'm not like the rest of my gender?"

"Absolutely that was my implication, but it was intended as a compliment."

Madeline swallowed and dabbed her lips. "Why would it be flattering to be told I'm odd?"

Colonel Haywood leaned back in his chair to study her. "Because most females live by an unwritten code that makes them complacent, predictable, and as intriguing as a herd of sheep. You, on the other hand, appear to follow no rules other than your own common sense. I find that laudable."

"I hope I live by God's rules, sir."

"Indeed, those happen to be the hardest to uphold." He lifted his goblet in toast.

Suppressing a giggle, she clinked glasses with him.

"What has amused you, Mrs. Howard?"

She rang the bell for the butler, who appeared instantly. "Please bring all of the courses as soon as possible, Micah. We have no time to dillydally with supper. I don't wish to miss a minute of caroling."

"Yes, ma'am."

Madeline waited until he left before answering the colonel's question. "Cows congregate in herds, sir. Sheep can be found in flocks. I'm amused you did not know that. For a man raised on a plantation, you know pitifully little about livestock." She lifted her napkin to her mouth and laughed without restraint.

Being an oddity in society did have its advantages.

James was not a happy man. He surveyed the former cow pasture his soldiers were rapidly turning into a camp. Another winter spent in the field, his corps' third since their debacle at First Manassas. It would be another Christmas spent away from home, apart from their wives and children, sweethearts and parents. Americans had spent three bloody years trying to kill one another — fathers against sons, sons against brothers. The state of Virginia was split in two because of opposing viewpoints. But each time James bowed his head in prayer, he no longer asked to prevail on the battlefield or that his men would vanquish their foes with swift precision.

Those fighting in butternut and gray seemed less like the enemy and more like scared young men with little keeping them warm and without enough to eat. Much like his own new recruits. Lately, James prayed for fair weather, meat free of maggots, bread without weevils, and a swift resolution to the conflict in the spring. Yet he would lead his men to the bitter end. Never one to issue orders from the rear, James knew any battle might be his last. Soldiering had been his life from his early days at West Point, to the Mexican War, to the territorial conflict with the Indians out West. That night, as his men lifted a scrap tin roof over the crude cabin that would be his home for the next five months, James sent up a second silent prayer — this one for Madeline.

His spies had told him she left Cashtown and traveled to Washington by train. At the war department she obtained a pass and crossed into Arlington County. As far as anyone could deduce, she'd reached the home of John Duncan, a well-regarded member of Jefferson Davis's administrative staff.

Great Scott, why couldn't her uncle be an ordinary farmer, eking out a living on thirty hardscrabble acres? What danger would Madeline's political stance place her in? James hoped she would remain meek and submissive to her aunt, but considering how she'd ridden to his headquarters and demanded her horse back, he thought meekness from her was highly unlikely.

He had written her at least a dozen letters following the Gettysburg victory. Each letter had been painstakingly composed to avoid his illegible scrawl and then given to his adjutant to post in a variety of Maryland and Virginia towns. He instructed Major Henry to bribe postmasters if necessary to increase the likelihood of delivery. Yet he hadn't received a single letter in return. Not so much as *I must insist, sir, that you stop badgering me with your continual and unwelcome sentiments.*

Had their brief acquaintance in Pennsylvania been sufficient to endear him to her? Certainly, it had been so for him, but James had little experience with matters of the heart. A brief engagement back home had ended when a case of typhus took the young woman to heaven's gate. Mrs. Howard might be more knowledgeable about courting, but one thing was certain: Only death would keep him from finding her.

"The men are ready to lay slats for the floor, sir."

James became vaguely aware someone was speaking. His head swiveled around to his chief of staff. "What did you say, Major? My mind was elsewhere."

"Understandable, sir." Major Henry saluted and offered a cup of cold coffee. "I said the men have cut slats for a wooden floor in the officer quarters. At least we'll be dry even if we have to spend several months in this forsaken land." He stared bleakly at the tree-covered hills beyond the rocky pasture.

James returned the salute. "Very good. See that they cut slats for their tents too. Succumbing to influenza would not be a hero's death for my brave men."

"Yes, sir." His adjutant began moving away.

"One more thing, Major. Have my horse saddled and a saddlebag filled with food." James downed the bitter coffee in two swallows and tossed the grounds onto the grass.

"I will be gone several days on a short trip. Send word to the other commanders."

The major looked as though he'd seen a ghost. "Where to, sir, if I may ask? This isn't exactly friendly territory for soldiers wearing our color of uniform."

"I know exactly where we are. I've studied the maps for days. We're in the county of Culpeper, west and north of Fredericksburg. I need to travel through Spotsylvania County, and then through Hanover and into Richmond. I may be gone a week."

Major Henry's mouth pulled into a tight line. "May I know the reason for your errand, sir?"

"You may not," the general said dismissively as he strode away.

The major followed him. "Sir, if this has anything to do with the widow Howard, wouldn't it be more prudent to renew your acquaintance after the war?"

"Your orders are to continue establishing the winter camp, Major. This matter does not concern you."

"I strongly advise against this idea, sir. To reach Richmond you must cross enemy lines. You could ride straight into Lee's encampment."

Outside his cabin door, James turned to face him. "With my maps and reports from the scouts and cavalry, I believe I'm capable of circumventing Rebel troops." He enunciated each word through gritted teeth.

"General, please reconsider." Major Henry opened his palms and dropped his voice. "You would need to cross the Rapidan, both the North and South Anna Rivers, and depending on Mrs. Howard's address in Richmond, perhaps even the James. The men you took along would be in danger every step of the way."

His patience at an end, James grabbed hold of the major's lapels. "I have no intention of risking soldiers for personal reasons. They will accompany me only through this valley, and I'll send them back before first light. You, sir, have overstepped your bounds as my chief of staff." James released his grip on the man's coat. "I'll ride into Richmond alone wearing civilian clothes purchased in Maryland. My uniform will stay in my saddlebag."

The major shook his head mulishly. "Sir, you can court-martial me tomorrow, but tonight I will speak my mind. Just the fact you ride so fine a horse would make you suspect in the enemy's capital. Please mull this over one more night. Tomorrow the moon will be full — better to light your way. I beseech you to consider our corps. We are woefully short of officers, sir, certainly those possessing your fearlessness in battle. We can't afford to lose you."

Though James glared at his aide, he couldn't argue the logic of waiting another night. Perhaps the infernal drizzle would dissipate by then. "Very well. I'll postpone my errand until tomorrow. But in the future, Major, I suggest you confine your advice to war maneuvers." He stomped inside on the new slat floor, the sound alien beneath his boot heels.

Unfortunately, the drizzle hadn't let up by the following night, and a heavy bank of clouds obscured the full moon. His entourage bogged down on the trail long before they crossed the Rapidan River. And his impressive gelding? The horse threw a shoe before midnight, forcing James to turn around with his men. He fumed all the way back to the Army of the Potomac's winter camp.

If one considered the vastness of the planet, Mrs. Howard was so close. Yet considering his luck lately, she might as well live on the plains of Persia.

■ ■ ■ ■

TWELVE

■ ■ ■ ■

Madeline climbed the steps of the Duncans' home that evening exhausted but filled with the Christmas spirit. Who could have imagined there were so many churches close to the center of town? She had never drunk so many cups of cocoa in her life and couldn't eat another cookie after the first stop. At St. Paul's Episcopal, she had been greeted graciously by the pastor and his wife as though a longtime member. Being the friend of Colonel Haywood was not without unique rewards. Mrs. Price invited her to the ladies' tea the following weekend, along with a food drive for the poor. Madeline declined both, explaining that she was already participating in similar activities at her aunt's parish.

"If you change your mind, the door of the ladies' auxiliary at St. Paul's is always open." The pastor's wife couldn't have been more effusive with her invitation.

And the enigmatic Colonel Haywood? He never was more than a step away no matter where Madeline wandered among the revelers. When she sang alongside Aunt Clarisa, he boomed his off-key baritone over her left shoulder. When she joined Eugenia and the stoic Major Penrod, the colonel managed to squeeze his way to her side. He knew the words only to the first stanza of most carols, and then he proceeded to hum along instead of using the songbook. She seemed to be the reason for his distraction, something she didn't feel particularly proud of.

Throughout the remainder of their dinner he'd shared tales of childhood Christmases over roast beef, boiled potatoes, and creamed corn. What a different life he had led compared to hers. As the son of a wealthy tobacco planter, he'd traveled abroad, met foreign dignitaries, and had dozens of slaves at his beck and call. The colonel expressed little shame over his family's penchant for owning human beings. The Emancipation Proclamation came as a great relief to his father in that "he would no longer be responsible for so many mouths to feed."

On that topic, Madeline offered only one comment. "Most men would prefer to go hungry in freedom than have a full belly while living in bondage."

The colonel reflected on that for several moments and then concluded, "By the grace of God that point of argument is now and forevermore moot."

Madeline didn't understand him. He seemed to be intrigued by their differences in philosophies and cultural upbringings. Most men preferred women to think like them, if they bothered to think at all. Five minutes spent with Eugenia and Major Penrod provided a perfect example. Perhaps Colonel Haywood saw her as a sparring partner, an intellectual challenge who kept conversations from turning dull. Yet something lurked beneath his clever repartee and witty jests . . . something that cautioned her to tread wisely.

Opening her bedroom door, Madeline gasped when she saw the cook asleep in the hearthside chair. She shook the older woman gently. "Esther? Were you waiting to speak to me?"

Esther's coal black eyes shot open. "Yes, ma'am, I was. Beggin' your pardon, I must have dosed off waitin' for you to come home. How much singin' can one pack of folks do?" She moaned a little as she straightened stiffly to her feet.

"There was as much socializing in church

257

vestibules as caroling, I'm afraid. I couldn't eat or drink another drop," Madeline said as she hung her cloak and bonnet on a wall peg.

"I kept your fire stoked so you'd be warm if you ever got back."

"Thank you, Esther." Madeline cocked her head to one side, knowing Kathleen laid the evening fires, not the cook. "Was there another reason you waited for me?"

Grunting, the woman pulled a tattered envelope from her apron. "Hope this don't cause no trouble, but Micah went to the market two days ago while you and Miss Eugenia were sewing."

Madeline's breath caught in her chest.

"Miz Duncan sent him to buy all the corn that was left. This family gonna turn yellow before spring comes." Esther clucked her tongue and pressed the envelope to her ample bosom.

"What happened at the market?" Madeline moved closer and dropped her voice.

"This fishmonger come up to Micah. He says he knows Micah works for Mr. Duncan and that Micah knows you." The cook's dark face wrinkled with anxiety.

"All true enough. Go on."

"This fishmonger asked Micah if he be trusted, and he says as good as another man." The furrows in her forehead deepened.

Madeline thought she might scream but inhaled a calming breath instead.

"He gave this letter to Micah to give to you and not nobody else in the meantime. Just *you*," she emphasized. At long last, Esther handed her the envelope.

Madeline ran her fingers over the watermarked handwriting. The return address read *Major General James Downing, 4th Corps Infantry, Army of the Potomac* in neat script in the left-hand corner. "Thank you, Esther. This means the world to me. My . . . friend is a soldier."

"On the Yankee side?"

Madeline nodded. "Yes. I'm from Pennsylvania."

"Then why are you trifling with that nice Colonel Haywood?" The words were barely spoken before Esther covered her mouth with her hand. "Begging your pardon, Miz Howard."

"I'm not trifling with Colonel Haywood. He is my friend." Madeline ran a fingernail beneath the flap to loosen the seal.

"I 'spose it's none of my concern." Esther limped to the door, still stiff from her nap. "But here in the South, ladies only make friends with the female half the population.

Beggin' your pardon again. Good night, Miz Howard." She softly shut the door behind her.

Madeline had nothing to say anyway. *That's what they do up North too.* With trembling fingers she extracted the single sheet and held it near the candle.

My dearest Madeline,

I hope you don't mind my being so bold as to address you by your given name. It is with fond regards that I think back to those dark days in July. You were the sole beacon shining in the night. That we should meet under such circumstances underscores the complexity of God's handiwork. Who could imagine that our paths would cross in such a fashion? I have thought of you often these past months and written a shameless number of letters. I instructed my adjutant to mail them in a variety of locations in Maryland and Virginia, but I posted this one myself in a small burg called Culpeper. With much to recommend it, it is my hope we visit the quaint town someday. I pray each night for your safety inside the Confederate capital. If God's grace allows, I shall endeavor a brief visit. Until then, I pray you will not forget me or my fond hope for a shared future.

With deep respect and affection,

James

Madeline thought she might drop into the type of mortal faint Genie so frequently spoke of. *With deep affection? A shared future? A shameless number of letters?* She hadn't been just a pleasant distraction in a world gone mad.

Swallowing hard, she read the words a second time and focused on his other promise: *I shall endeavor a brief visit.* Here at Uncle John's on Forsythia Lane? With the home guard and cavalry officers coming and going at all hours? Madeline grasped the edge of the mantel for support. A visit to her could prove deadly.

Nevertheless, she couldn't help but draw one, significant conclusion. Only a man in love would take such a risk.

Elliott returned to the office of the home guard not in the best of moods. His visit to Chimborazo Hospital didn't supply the good news he had hoped for. Confederate soldiers still trying to recover from battle wounds were dying at a frightening rate from blood poisoning and influenza. The army would need to seek recruits from Florida or perhaps the western territories if they wished to swell their ranks by the spring campaign.

At least that night he would see Mrs. Howard and forget the war for a few hours. He would also forget that she was in love with another man. Each of his thinly veiled questions regarding the man's name or nature had been rebuffed with polite determination. She reacted to his inquiries about her beau as though he'd asked her weight or age. "Dear me, Colonel, I don't feel comfortable discussing such things with you."

Doubtlessly the man was a Yankee soldier, but in whose division or corps? John Duncan relayed that her husband had been killed in the opening battle at Manassas, but he provided no information about her current paramour. Elliott only knew for certain that it wasn't him. Despite his attempts to charm and ingratiate himself, Mrs. Howard managed to stay at arm's length. Other than the dinner party prior to the first night of caroling, they were never alone. The intimate supper *coincidence* had required thoughtful planning by Mrs. Duncan. Afterward, Madeline invited a neighbor to join them in the carriage to church, and she even invited the elderly widow to the Haywood pew on Sunday mornings.

Subsequent suppers before caroling were potluck as dozens of guests milled around the table or balanced plates on their laps on the terrace. Because neighbors brought bowls or baskets of their favorite food, the meal had become a festive hodgepodge. Considering that the meal lasted an hour and a half, followed by socializing at each church, Elliott would have grown weary of celebrants if not for Mrs. Howard. The belles and matrons, on behalf of their daughters, parried like artillerymen on the battlefield, lobbing salvos in an attempt to score victory over the other women. Because ladies weren't supposed to discuss politics or religion, or inquire about a man's financial position, the women chattered endlessly about topics of no interest. Heaven forbid they be deemed schemers searching for a suitable mate.

Mrs. Howard, however, yearned to know everything about Richmond society, and she had few qualms about someone's impression of her. She had asked him once if he found her curiosity vulgar. He assured her he did not. Instead, he found her fascination with his town a step in the right direction.

Elliott was packing his papers into his worn leather satchel when a knock at this office door commanded his attention.

"Excuse me, sir. I know you're eager to leave this afternoon, this being the last Friday before Christmas . . ." his aide paused, looking nervous.

"What is it, Lieutenant? I'm still here, aren't I?"

"A woman is here to see you. She wouldn't give me her name, but she talks rather strangely."

Elliott's head snapped up. *A woman — has Mrs. Howard decided to pay me a call?* "I wouldn't describe the lack of an affected drawl as strange, Lieutenant," he said. "You may show her in." He slicked a hand through his hair and buttoned his uniform up to his throat. When the woman entered his office, Elliott was wearing his widest smile.

But she was not Madeline Howard.

"Good afternoon, Colonel, sir. I don't 'spose you remember me. I'm Kathleen O'Toole. I work for Mr. Duncan over on Forsythia?" She blinked several times while fidgeting with her bonnet ribbons. The brim was so wide she had to turn her head to look left or right.

Elliott tried not to show his disappointment. "What can I do for you, Mrs. O'Toole? Would you like to have a seat?" He gestured toward the chair opposite his desk.

"It's Miss, and I'd best not sit." The woman slid her palms down her skirt, drawing attention to two dark stains on the fabric. "Seeing that the Duncans don't know I'm here." She giggled as though amused by her comment.

Elliott found nothing funny as he sat down. "Perhaps you should explain the reason for your visit. I have a pressing engagement later this evening."

Miss O'Toole's grin faded. "I'm the maid. I knows all 'bout the suppers before singing Christmas songs. The three of us got a devil of a time figuring out who owns those bowls they leave behind to wash."

Elliott merely stared silently at her. Any comments from him would only delay whatever business this woman felt she had.

"But I seen a couple things since you started calling on a regular basis. You and that nice Major Penrod. He seems quite smitten by Miss Eugenia, don't he?" Miss O'Toole arched her spine, pleased with her observation.

Elliott's jaw dropped open. *This maid dares to comment about Miss Duncan and a respected member of Jefferson Davis's elite staff?* "I have accepted Mr. Duncan's gracious invitations to dine, but I fail to understand what concern that is of yours, Miss O'Toole."

Paling to the color of watered milk, the scrawny maid shifted her weight to the other hip. "I'm not stupid, Colonel. I got eyes in me head, the same as anybody. I see you might be a wee bit smitten with that Yankee, Miz Howard. Thought you better have a look-see at this letter I found." She withdrew a wrinkled envelope from under her frayed shawl and held it out to him.

"What have you done?" For several moments, Elliott sat stunned by the woman's boldness. No servant of the Haywoods — neither slave nor free — would ever overstep common decency in such a way.

When he made no move to accept her offering, she laid it on top of his scattered papers. "Somethin' I thought I needed to."

Helpless to stop himself, Elliott peered at the water-stained handwriting. The letter was addressed to Mrs. Madeline Howard in care of the Duncan residence with a return address of only two lines: Major General James Downing, Army of the Potomac —

Fourth Corps. *A major general, while I'm only a brevetted colonel?* "Where did you get this?" he asked, finally rousing from his stupor.

"From Miz Howard's room." The maid's lower lip began to tremble, evidence her bravado was slipping. "You should read it, sir. That there's a love letter. I might not be long off the boat, but I'm a Southerner. She's not playing you right. That man says he loves her and countin' the days till the war's over. What she doin' here in Richmond if she got some Yankee general sweet on her?"

The colonel didn't know what to say, where to begin. His life thus far hadn't prepared him for this. Because she was an employee of John Duncan's, throttling her would be inappropriate. Slapping the presumptuous, ill-bred woman across the mouth was also out of the question. His sweet mother would turn over in her grave. Yet on the other hand, this sort of behavior could not be tolerated or Miss O'Toole would take encouragement from his inaction.

Pushing himself up from the desk, Elliott stood and straightened to his full height of six feet in an attempt to intimidate her. "You have made a grievous error if you assumed

267

I would welcome an act of thievery by a maid. If I make your actions known to Mr. Duncan, you would be immediately turned out into the streets. I would imagine plenty of freed slaves seek domestic positions in the city."

His comment released the wind from the woman's sails. Her eyes turned moist and glassy.

"I will assume you were motivated by loyalty and patriotism to the Confederacy, and so I will overlook this travesty this one time. But any further intrusion into Mrs. Howard's private life will not be tolerated. I will insist the Duncans fire you on the spot."

Kathleen's hands bunched into fists, but she kept her voice controlled. "I understand, sir."

"Even though it's none of your concern, Miss O'Toole, Mrs. Howard has already told me of her affection for someone else. As friends, she and I are respectful of each other's political opinions and well aware that they differ. Furthermore, Mrs. Howard is Mrs. Duncan's niece — blood kin. I suggest you return her personal property posthaste and don't ever overstep your bounds like this again." Narrowing his eyes into a glare, he pushed the envelope to the edge of the desk.

Miss O'Toole hesitated only for a moment. "All right, I'll put it back where I found it." She grabbed the letter, jammed it into a pocket, and ran out the door.

It took a while before Elliott's heart stopped pounding and murderous thoughts no longer filled his mind. How he'd yearned to read the contents, to determine whether Madeline's paramour was truly a man of flesh and blood. Until now, he'd deluded himself that her mystery beau was nothing but a coquettish ploy. But in the end, he behaved as a gentleman because she had behaved honorably. She hadn't deceived him. She'd said from the beginning that her heart belonged to another man.

Although not personally acquainted with General Downing, Elliott had heard about the commander of the Union Army's Fourth Corps. His valor on the battlefield, including a penchant for leading instead of ordering troops to the front, was legendary. *Of course, a general becomes an easy target for artillery or a sharpshooter's bullet while sitting on his horse.* Elliott immediately shook off the cruel, un-Christian notion. He wouldn't wish another man dead merely because he desired a woman.

A second, more helpful thought came to mind. This Kathleen O'Toole might be the reason that pompous newspaperman had cast aspersions on Mrs. Howard. Yet for now, Elliott would do nothing about the audacious maid. The last thing he wanted was to seriously upset John Duncan or Mrs. Howard with Christmas less than a week away.

Madeline searched through her bureau for the third time. In exasperation, she overturned the drawer onto her bed and dug through her camisoles, bloomers, and chemises, but still couldn't find it.

She'd tucked the letter from General Downing under her underpinnings after rereading it a half dozen times. How could it disappear into thin air? She planned to dash off a reply and then head down to the neighborhood supper before caroling. With the Duncans out for the evening, perhaps Micah would have a chance to check the docks for the *Bonnie Bess.* With the recent spate of rain, perhaps Captain George hadn't made his usual run up the Chesapeake Bay and back.

Hope sprang eternal for women in love.

Madeline sprawled across the bed amid the assortment of clothing and tried to think. Her aunt and uncle had never ventured into her room since she'd taken up residence. As far as she knew, Esther had entered only once. But the cook would have no reason to remove the letter because she had been the one to deliver it. That left Eugenia or Kathleen. And one of the two suspects just strolled into her bedroom.

"Goodness, what on earth are you doing? You're already dressed for the evening. Why are you looking for more . . . underpinnings?" Eugenia giggled behind her hand.

Madeline rolled her eyes. "I'm searching for something that was hidden underneath them. By any chance have you seen a letter addressed to me?"

"A letter from a secret admirer?" Eugenia fluttered her lashes. "Who from?"

"If I told you, it would no longer be a secret. And a lady never tells." Madeline pressed an index finger to her lips.

"Oh, what great fun. No, I didn't rummage through your bureau, but I will help you look." Eugenia unceremoniously picked up fistfuls of dainties, shook them, and tossed them back into the drawer.

Madeline stopped her with a gentle hand. "I didn't think you would do something like that, but I had to ask. I'm certain where I put the letter and now it's gone."

Eugenia needed less time to guess than it took to put the drawer back in place. "I imagine it was that loathsome Kathleen. I've caught her pulling faces behind Mama's back. And she's always creeping silently around the house as though trying to catch me . . . or you . . . in some naughty act. What does she think we do when no one's watching?"

"Kathleen was my choice too." Madeline perched on the blanket chest. "But I dare not accuse her with not a shred of proof. She wouldn't find another service position without Aunt Clarisa's recommendation."

"You can't ask Kathleen now because nobody knows where she is. Mama is fit to be tied. Neighbors and ladies from her guild will arrive within the hour, along with several members of the home guard, and our maid isn't here to help Esther and Micah."

Madeline felt a frisson of anxiety for no reason. "Where do you suppose she went?"

"She told Mama she had a personal errand that couldn't wait until her day off, but she would be back shortly." Eugenia leaned close to whisper. "Perhaps 'shortly' has a different meaning in Dublin than it does in America."

"Don't be unkind." Madeline scolded with little enthusiasm. "She still struggles with the English language."

"Let's worry about Kathleen later. Come help me pick out my jewelry for tonight. Major Penrod has already seen this piece twice." She fingered the broach on her bodice.

"You look beautiful, Genie. If your mother is worried about tonight, why don't we go downstairs and lend a hand?"

Eugenia slipped an arm around her waist. "You're so considerate, Maddy. That's why Mama hopes you'll stay in Richmond after the war is over."

Madeline returned her hug. "Thank you, but my home is in Pennsylvania. I plan to return there someday."

"What about Colonel Haywood? He hovers by your side each Friday evening."

"I value his friendship, but he will not change the future."

"But surely the missing letter was from Colonel Haywood." Eugenia's brows knit together above the bridge of her nose.

Madeline weighed several responses within the span of a few seconds. James risked his life on a daily basis to lead his troops and serve his country. Although she wouldn't purposely mislead the colonel to gain information, she shouldn't burn her bridges too soon. "As I said, we won't discuss the letter, and let's not put the cart before the horse regarding Colonel Haywood." Flashing a grin, she hurried out her bedroom door.

Downstairs, Esther and Micah were buzzing between kitchen and dining room like bees before the first frost, while Aunt Clarisa wrung her hands and paced the long center hall. Madeline entered the kitchen just as the elusive maid slipped through the back door, less than ten minutes before the first guests were to arrive. Kathleen's hands and face were wet from washing up at the pump, and her long red braid hung limply down her back.

Madeline stepped into the maid's path. "I would like to speak with you for a moment."

"You'll have to excuse me, Miz Howard, but I need a fresh cap and apron, and then I need to get to the front door. Miz Duncan will skin me alive if I'm not there to greet folks bringing in bowls of food," Kathleen said as she tried to step around her.

"Then you should have better planned your outing. This is important, and it will only take a minute of your time." Madeline crossed her arms.

Kathleen's eyes flashed with an evil glint, but she quickly composed her bland face. "What do you want to ask me?"

"I had a letter in my drawer. It's no longer there. Have you seen it? Perhaps you misplaced it while you were cleaning?"

"I didn't take your letter. You probably dropped it in the garden. You're always walking outside all hours of the day or night." She sniffed as though personally affronted by Madeline's behavior. "Or maybe you left it in the pocket of your day dress when it went to the laundry. It's probably dissolved in the bottom of the washtub." She tried again to circumvent her tormentor, but Madeline grabbed the girl's wrist.

"I didn't take it from my room or leave it in any pocket. It was hidden, and now it's gone."

Kathleen tugged her arm back. "Maybe a widow-woman shouldn't be getting love letters from Yankee generals. Maybe she should keep her mind on sewing and packing up food for the poor."

"How would you know the letter came from a Yankee if you never saw it?"

Her voice faltered as she realized her mistake. "I-I saw the envelope when puttin' away your clothes, but I didn't take it. Don't be accusing me falsely, Miz Howard. I'll help you look once I'm done in the dining room, but let me pass now." Her plea sounded desperate.

"All right, we'll search together when I return from caroling." Pivoting on her heel,

Madeline preceded the maid from the kitchen. She felt mildly sick to her stomach, but with her aunt and cousin waiting in the parlor, she plastered a pleasant expression on her face. When she reached her cousin's side, she gasped. In Madeline's estimation, the neckline of Eugenia's gown grazed the bounds of decency.

Is this a ball or a troupe of Christmas carolers spreading good cheer through the streets?

Aunt Clarisa noticed her reaction. "Kathleen, fetch a shawl for Miss Eugenia. I feel a chill in the house, and I don't want her to catch cold."

Oblivious to her mother, Eugenia peeked between the curtains at the sound of the first carriage. "Oh, my. It's Major Penrod and Colonel Haywood. Joseph said he would bring the carriage so we could ride to the first church." Her young face glowed with anticipation.

"I thought the whole point was to sing down the streets and lift people's spirits during this holy season," Madeline said, looking over the girl's shoulder toward the hitching post.

"That's true, but Major Penrod's parents will be at the first stop." Aunt Clarisa tucked a stray lock of hair into her bun. "A lady shouldn't become perspired or be spattered with mud if she wishes to make a good impression."

Madeline nodded with agreement as she hurried into the foyer to greet their guests. As usual, Colonel Haywood was first across the threshold.

"Mrs. Howard, may I say you're looking lovely this evening." He swept off his plumed hat and bowed low.

"I suppose you may, Colonel, since you have already uttered the words." Stifling her laughter, Madeline offered a small curtsey. The colonel gazed at her as though stymied, while those within earshot chuckled. If she stayed in Richmond another ten years, she would never understand these Southerners.

■ ■ ■ ■

THIRTEEN

■ ■ ■ ■

Sunday

Clarisa waited until she climbed into the coach and they were headed home after Mass. Then she broached the delicate topic she'd been stewing about with her husband. Eugenia had attended the Methodist Church with Major Penrod, and Madeline had accompanied Colonel Haywood to the Episcopal cathedral. With Micah topside driving the conveyance, John and Clarisa had a rare moment alone.

"I'm troubled," she stated abruptly, having no time to dance around her dilemma.

"What about, my dear?" Her husband placed a gloved hand atop hers. "Christmas is mere days away. I'm sure Saint Nicholas hasn't forgotten sweet little Clarisa."

"Oh, John, really." She squeezed his fingers. "How like you to cheer me up, but I have no need of possessions I don't already own. I'm worried about the girls, both Eugenia and Madeline."

"What about? They both seemed to be enjoying the season. We haven't had as many festive parties as in years gone by, but I thought the Jacob suppers have worked out splendidly. So much good cheer without families emptying their larders of the last crust of bread. Our ensemble has gained additional carolers each week." Without warning, the carriage hit a pothole so deep they both slid toward the floor. "Great Scott! Is there no man left in town to patch these craters? We'll break an axle before spring if this keeps up!"

"Calm yourself, husband. We just came from Father Michael's inspiring words at Mass." Clarisa patted his arm with affection. "And I agree the Advent events have been a blessing for Eugenia. Without the caroling and the New Year's Eve ball to look forward to, she would simply 'expire from boredom.' Those were her exact words." Clarisa drew back the carriage curtain to peer at the shuttered homes they passed. Many plantation owners who also owned houses in town apparently would be spending the holidays in the country.

"What do you mean by 'ball'? I agreed to a dance, nothing more. Despite my daughter's fondness for excess, anything extravagant would be deemed tasteless by our friends."

"Only by those who have become too poor to throw a ball themselves," she muttered. Clarisa smoothed the creases from her best Sunday dress, noticing for the first time how frayed the cuffs were.

"Clarisa Endicott Duncan, I've never heard such words come from your lips." John feigned an expression of indignation.

"I don't wish to be unkind, merely honest. Suddenly, everything that was fashionable before the war no longer is because of the infernal blockade. Eugenia isn't the only one who has grown weary of the somber mood this Christmas."

"Parents have lost sons, dear heart. Perhaps having one daughter was a blessing in disguise." John's mouth pulled into a frown as he slipped an arm around her. "Richmond isn't the only place feeling the pinch from the Yankee navy. Gunboats are blocking ports all along the seacoast."

"President Davis instructed those at home to be strong and carry on while our boys fight valiantly. He and Varina will still throw their January ball. I do hope you'll allow us to attend."

"You're that certain of an invitation?" He laughed with amusement.

"Yes, I am. Varina remarked about the good work the auxiliary at Saint Patrick's has been doing for the Cause."

"This is what you wished to discuss with me — the social season of our once vibrant city?"

Grinning, she leaned back against the supple leather cushions. "Goodness, I sidetracked myself. No, I wished to discuss something to keep Eugenia and Madeline busy during the winter months. They have endured sewing for weeks with the ladies, but they both abhor it and frankly neither is very good. They only come to be of service."

"I would say that's true of Madeline, but our daughter is worried someone will think poorly of her character if she were to stay away."

"True enough, but Madeline would like to call on Chimborazo Hospital. She believes she can be useful there, and I think Eugenia should go with her. The experience will help our girl mature into a woman."

"Have you lost your mind, dear wife?" John pivoted on the seat until he faced her.

"Not that I'm aware of." She cocked her head to one side to look at her husband.

"Then perhaps you haven't read the newspaper accounts or listened to the conversations of the home guards before dinner.

Those wards are teeming with disease. Soldiers are dying from typhus, pneumonia, and influenza more often than from their wounds. Chimborazo isn't a safe place for anyone, let alone two gently raised young ladies."

"Madeline saved the life of Colonel Haywood up North."

"I am well aware of that. He has mentioned it several times." Loosening his collar with a finger, John growled, "This weather won't make up its mind what it wants to do. A person soon becomes uncomfortable no matter what they choose to wear."

"So Madeline has been in military hospitals before."

John released a weary sigh. "She spent one day in a temporary field hospital immediately after a battle, not days on end in a huge hospital filled with men languishing from a variety of dreadful ailments. I heard that the beds have lice, and vermin scuttle down the corridors at night."

"Oh, John, please." Clarisa pressed a handkerchief to her nose, mildly nauseated.

"Forgive me, my dear, but I don't know how else to impress upon you the unsuitability of Chimborazo for either Eugenia or Madeline."

"Of course I respect your decision regarding our daughter," Clarisa said as she gathered her cape in preparation to step out. "But I insist you be the one to tell Madeline. She has her heart set on this idea." She quickly stepped onto the carriage block the moment Micah opened the door to prevent further discussion. Clarisa knew her husband, and she knew her niece. Better to let those two discuss the matter while she and Eugenia stood back out of harm's way.

Within the hour three members of the household sat down to Sunday dinner of creamed corn, stewed chicken, and some kind of mysterious wilted greens that tasted suspiciously like dandelions.

"Is Eugenia dining with the Penrods?" asked Madeline, opening her napkin.

"I imagine so, or she would have been home by now with tales of woe to share." Clarisa rang the silver bell next to her place setting. "Let's say grace so we can begin. Would you honor us, my dear?"

Madeline uttered a simple, childlike prayer of thanksgiving and then reached for her water goblet. "The chicken smells delicious — a hint of rosemary, I believe."

"Esther works magic with old hens well past their laying days. She adds a pinch of this and a spoonful of that until they taste divine." Clarisa leaned back in her chair, confident fireworks were about to begin.

Madeline selected a chicken breast from the bowl Micah was offering her. "I will remember that when I have my own kitchen again. Have you had a chance to speak to Uncle John yet, ma'am?"

"Yes, I broached the subject on our way home from Mass." Clarisa turned her focus on her husband with great animation.

Glancing from one to the other, Madeline scooped up a hearty portion of corn. "May I borrow the carriage to drive to the hospital while you're at Confederate headquarters, sir?"

John cleared his throat. "No, you may not. I'm sorry, but Richmond is filled with rabble off the plantations and deserters from both armies. The streets aren't safe."

"Then perhaps Micah can accompany me, providing he's back in plenty of time to pick you up." She leaned forward in her chair to gaze seriously at her uncle.

John flashed Clarisa a brief but pointed frown before turning back to Madeline. "I'm sorry, but having a chauffeur along won't help once you're inside Chimborazo. I have been there myself, and I can assure you that it's no place for a lady." He ate a forkful of wilted greens, usually not one of his favorite side dishes. "Ah, Micah, give my compliments to Esther. Only she can make weeds taste this delicious."

Stifling a smile, Micah bowed his gray head. "I shall tell her, sir. Thank you."

Madeline waited until the butler had returned to his post at the door. "Do you think it's untoward of me to be concerned with suffering soldiers, those with no loved ones nearby to offer comfort?"

Clarisa hid her grin behind her coffee cup.

"Not untoward, Madeline, but dangerous and impractical. Those wards are filled with disease. Many a brave nurse has caught whatever miasma lingers in the air. Then they suffer the same plight as those they sought to help."

"But Jesus walked among the lepers to heal bodies and save souls."

John's mouth dropped open as he stared at their niece speechlessly. After a moment, he managed to find his voice, and his tone was rebuking. "As the Son of God, our Lord was able to do many things that would cause certain death among us mortals."

Madeline flushed the color of ripe tomatoes. "Forgive me, sir. I didn't express myself well. I only meant we are to reach out to the less fortunate and provide aid without thought to our own selfish needs."

"I was under the distinct impression from Colonel Haywood that you didn't care for nursing up North."

Madeline's blush deepened. "That is true. I don't wish to care for patients' wounds, only to tend their broken spirits. I thought I could read to them or write a few letters home for those unable to hold a pen. If Chimborazo has no need for me in that capacity, then perhaps in the laundry or kitchen. I was a housewife without servants back home."

John sighed deeply in surrender. "Very well, my dear. I can't very well forbid a grown woman from volunteering, but my daughter may *not* join you. And you may not go alone. I insist you either accompany Father Michael or your Episcopal pastor. Those are my terms."

Madeline lowered her gaze and nodded her head. "I accept your terms, Uncle John, and thank you."

"Just don't touch those sick men. And be sure to pray for your own health as often as you pray for theirs."

"I promise." Madeline lifted the bowl of wilted greens and passed it to him. "More dandelions, sir?"

"Splendid!" Clarisa clapped her hands. "A successful parlay. Now let's finish eating so Kathleen can serve the apple pie. I'm craving a bite of something sweet."

December 23

Madeline began lifting corn muffins from the baking pan the moment the cook removed them from the oven.

"Mind you don't burn yourself, Miz Howard. Those are mighty hot." Esther hovered nervously behind her, shaking her head.

"I'm eager to leave before Eugenia comes down for breakfast. She might ask to go with me." Madeline laid a third layer of muffins in her basket with the latest batch. "Genie wants to be helpful to the Cause as long as it doesn't involve sewing or knitting, but Mr. Duncan won't let her go to the hospital."

Esther carried the empty muffin tin to the washtub near the door. "He should have put his foot down with you too," she said, under her breath.

"I beg your pardon, Esther?"

"I said I don't know why you want to go near those sick men. They got crippled soldiers to take care of them, Miz Howard. It's not safe for a lady in that place."

"Sounds as though you've been listening in on Uncle John and Aunt Clarisa's conversations."

"Right is right, but I wasn't eavesdropping. They don't hide their worries from me."

Madeline slipped her arm around the woman's waist. "It's almost Christmas. I wish to read the blessed story to the soldiers from the book of Luke. It must be sad to spend Christmas in a dreary hospital."

"You got a kind heart, but make sure you sit a good distance away and read loud." Esther covered the muffins with a clean linen cloth and closed the hamper. "Go on now, before Miss Eugenia gets hungry. Micah got the carriage ready. You fetching Colonel Haywood's preacher on your way?"

"No, his preacher is too busy this week with baskets for the poor. He said perhaps in January I can accompany him during his round of calls."

"You going alone?" Esther wrinkled her nose.

"No, Father Michael from Aunt Clarisa's parish said he would accompany me. He goes three times a week to deliver last rites to the dying." Madeline exchanged a sorrowful look with the cook, grabbed the handles of the hamper, and hurried outside before her courage waned.

Along the way, she viewed a town preparing for the holiest night of the year: Hitching posts were wrapped with red ribbons, and entrance gates and front doors were festooned with garlands of holly and fresh-cut pine boughs. But black crepe covered the doors of some homes, indicating the recent loss of a family member.

At the Catholic church, Micah turned the coach around in the cobblestone courtyard. The priest exiting the rectory wore a long brown cassock with a length of rope tied around his waist. Thick black socks covered his feet, along with leather sandals. If they had walked instead of using the Duncan carriage, his feet would have quickly become wet and cold. Without the grand vestments worn during Mass, the priest looked small and humble.

"Good morning, Mrs. Howard. Looks like we have a fine day for our outing," Father Michael said as he climbed in and took the seat opposite from her.

Madeline peered out the window at heavy, low clouds and drizzle, without a patch of blue sky to be found. "I love your attitude, Father. It promises a successful day for us."

"This rain will wash the city clean of its layer of dust. Tomorrow evening we celebrate the birth of our Savior. Despite our earthly cares and woes, we have much to be joyous about." Deep creases encircled his mouth as he smiled.

Madeline snuggled into her woolen cloak for the short ride. Once they reached the sprawling grounds of Chimborazo, she found little to smile about. Perched on the western outskirts of Richmond, the goliath of a hospital sprawled before her like a city unto itself. Any foolish notion she had that she could make a difference here vanished. Dozens of white-washed, one-story buildings lay in rows as far as the eye could see, while a steady stream of ambulances, wagons, riders, and pedestrians approached from the north and east.

Once they had entered a building marked Hospital Number Three, Father Michael instructed her to wait on a bench next to the door. He headed down the corridor to an office at the far end. From her vantage point, Madeline witnessed a stream of surgeons, stewards, orderlies, ambulance drivers, and men of the cloth all in a hurry. The temporary hospital in Gettysburg where she had nursed one fateful day was downright primitive by comparison.

"All right, Mrs. Howard, you may follow me."

Trying not to breathe too deeply, Madeline followed the priest through the doorway into a ward. The mingled odors of beef stock, smoky whale oil lamps, and inadequately washed bodies didn't bode well for her breakfast. Two corn muffins and a cup of chicory coffee roiled in her gut like a ship at sea. She pressed the handkerchief usually tucked up her sleeve to her nose.

Dr. Raymond, the hospital's chief surgeon, met them in the main aisle. "We have no cases of influenza in his ward, Father, so Mrs. Howard may join you at bedside. I'm needed elsewhere, but you may send the ward sergeant for anything you require." His voice was modulated and cultured, with vowels rolling off his tongue as though each word was part of some enchanted melody. Dr. Raymond turned his attention from the priest to her. "The men in the beds along the windows won't live to see the new year." He spoke in a soft whisper. "There isn't a man over twenty in that group. Some Union, some Confederate, but each one has been away from home for two years. Any kindness you can show them will be appreciated more than you'll ever know." He nodded and then walked away, his focus already on the chart he carried in his hand.

The bottom fell from Madeline's queasy stomach. She glanced at the entrance behind them. Beyond the solid oak door were fresh air, a brisk breeze from the river, and a town joyously preparing for Christmas. Inside Chimborazo were young men, desperate to see mothers or sweethearts, waiting solely to die.

"Would you like to stay with me, Mrs. Howard? We could take turns reading about Christ's birth, switching between Saint Luke's and Saint Matthew's accounts." The priest's question pulled Madeline from her woolgathering. "Or you could start at the opposite end to see if anyone wishes to convey a last message home in a letter."

With her opportunity to flee gone, Madeline pulled a worn testament from her bag. "I believe I'll start with the beds by the window. I've brought my own Bible."

"Very well. Mr. Duncan asked me to remind you not to touch any of the patients." Father Michael smiled encouragingly at her and then moved away.

Madeline marched to the end of the row of men, perched on a bedside stool, and inhaled a breath. "Good day, sir, and a merry Christmas to you. I'm Mrs. Howard. I would be happy to write a letter on your behalf, or read from Scripture, or simply listen while you speak of home." She delivered her rehearsed speech without looking at the boy lying on the cot. Once she did, though, she saw that heavy bandages obscured most of his face and head. From the sunken contour of his right cheek, part of the bone must be missing. His mouth, wrapped with strips of cloth, wouldn't utter messages anytime soon.

"Forgive me, soldier," she murmured inadequately, trying to repress a shudder.

His soft brown eye filled with moisture.

"Why don't I read you the Christmas story from one of the Gospels?" With trembling fingers, Madeline struggled to find the correct page. *How could I have been so insensitive?*

As she silently chastised herself, the young man reached out to pat her hand. His touch sent a shiver throughout her body. When Madeline found the beginning of the book of Luke, she closed her fingers around his as tightly as she dared. She read the Gentile physician's words, which offered hope to the living and the dying, in a clear voice until the soldier drifted to sleep. Then she finished the chapter for those listening in nearby beds.

"Sit with me a spell, ma'am," said another patient down the row.

Madeline let her gaze drift from the foot of the bed to the man's face. Noticing a perfectly flat blanket where his legs should be, she tried to keep her expression benign. "What can I do for you, soldier?" She settled primly on the stool, her Bible clutched between her hands.

"I would like to get a word home to my wife." He sucked in a painful breath. "Doc had to cut off both legs below the knees. Then he had to take 'em off higher 'cause the rot keeps spreadin'." He paused, wheezing for air. "Doc can't stop the rot, so I'm just about done for. Those bullets might have kilt me quick and spared all the trouble." The soldier coughed into a bloody rag.

When Madeline averted her gaze, she spotted a blue uniform jacket folded atop the small trunk next to the bed. "I see you fought for the Republic, sir," she whispered.

"Don't make much difference now when you're facing the pearly gates, but yes, ma'am. Fought with the Fourth Corps in General Birney's division. Got shot outside a little town called Remington while ridin' cavalry scout."

Madeline placed her hand on his shoulder. "The Fourth Corps — commanded by General James Downing?"

It took him several moments to respond. "Yes, ma'am. The general took a bullet in the shoulder just 'bout the time I got hit."

"He's been shot?" Madeline's voice sounded like a rusty door hinge. "How is he?"

The soldier trained his watery gaze on her. "Can't say, ma'am. The Rebs brought me here when I didn't die like they thought I would. But I imagine if General Downing was dead, you would have read 'bout it in the newspapers. Him being a general and all. He kinfolk to you?"

"Yes," Madeline answered without thinking. "I mean no, not yet." She glanced away to hide her embarrassment. "Shall I write down that letter you want to send to your wife?"

"Yes, ma'am. I would be mighty grateful if you would do that."

■ ■ ■ ■

FOURTEEN

■ ■ ■ ■

On Christmas Eve, Elliott and Mrs. Howard delivered food baskets to the refugees living on the edge of town. They chatted and sang and listened to the repartee between Eugenia and Major Penrod. That night, neither poverty nor the war intruded on the promise and hope of Christmas.

Elliott spent Christmas Day at home with his father, brother, and a few elderly slaves too old to leave when Lincoln issued his proclamation. Elliott's home more closely resembled a backwoods farm than the impressive plantation it once had been. But he cared naught about the broken fences, fallow fields, dying apple trees, and empty tobacco curing barns. Huge hogsheads once lined the wharf, awaiting shipment overseas or to other parts of the country. Flavored with sugar, cinnamon, nutmeg, or honey, Haywood tobacco plugs were the best in the county. A soldier could cut a slice from his plug, rub it to loosen the delicate leaves, and fill his pipe. Considering the quality of army rations, the evening smoke became a man's sole pleasure.

The Haywood holiday dinner consisted of several rabbits Robert snared along the river, with stringy sweet potatoes, and unpalatable baked apples. But Elliott cared little about food during his three days at home. He dutifully listened to his father's reminiscences about the past and mediated squabbles between his father and brother. When Elliott returned to Richmond, he felt ambivalent about the family left behind.

Tonight, New Year's Eve, he would dine and dance at the Duncan mansion, and he would see Mrs. Howard — something that made him happy indeed.

Elliott climbed into the Penrod carriage for the ride to the Duncans' in a far better mood than he'd been in for days. During the short drive to Forsythia Lane, Joseph entertained him with amusing stories. Apparently, Miss Duncan had made quite an impression on the elder Penrods, and not all of it was beneficial. Yet Joseph was utterly enchanted with the woman. Elliott knew all about attraction exceeding the bounds of practicality or common sense.

The Duncans' butler, dressed in full

livery, met them at the front door. "Good evening, sirs. The family awaits you in the parlor." Micah bowed and then accepted their overcoats.

"Thank you, my good man." Major Penrod placed his top hat atop the pile on Micah's arm and strode through the open double doors.

Elliott paused a moment to take in the scene and was rewarded for his patience. Mrs. Howard stood at the top landing wearing a long gown that accentuated curves only alluded to until now. "By my word," he said.

"Oh, dear, I told Aunt Clarisa this dress was too much, but she insisted I wear it." Mrs. Howard came down the stairs resembling a doe ready to bolt at the first sound of gunfire.

Elliott stared with blatant admiration. "You are unquestionably the most beautiful woman in the world."

She burst out laughing, an unanticipated reaction. "Goodness, Colonel Haywood. If you mean that sincerely, you *must* broaden your scope of acquaintances." She accepted his outstretched gloved hand for the final two steps.

"I stand by my opinion, and I'll have you know I've traveled on three continents." He kissed the back of her gloved fingers.

"But what of Miss Duncan?" Mrs. Howard turned to watch Eugenia descend the staircase. "I think she's never looked lovelier."

"Well, Colonel Haywood, what say you?" Eugenia paused dramatically on the steps to giggle behind her fan.

"I beg your pardon, Miss Duncan. You look equally stunning. Will you favor me with a waltz tonight?"

"A waltz you shall have, as long as Major Penrod can bear my absence for so long a time." Eugenia dropped into a curtsey as Penrod materialized next to Elliott.

"Perhaps a reel, but not a waltz. Haywood might turn scoundrel and try to win your heart." Placing Eugenia's hand on his arm, Penrod led her into the drawing room, where the orchestra's first strains could be heard.

Elliott faced Mrs. Howard. "Whew, that was close. I feared Penrod might challenge me to a duel."

"You recovered nicely, Colonel, but would you have accepted his challenge?"

"Certainly not. Dueling has been outlawed. The Confederacy can't afford to lose a single man. Shall we, Mrs. Howard?"

When she took his arm, Elliott led her into

the unrecognizable parlor. Most of the furniture had been removed, the rugs rolled up, and the floors polished to a high gloss. Dozens of tapers burned from window sills and two crystal chandeliers, lending the effect of dancing light and shadow. Cut pine boughs and garlands of holly berries added a festive feel.

"Lovely, isn't it? Aunt Clarisa borrowed every maid in the neighborhood to help decorate and serve. People were more than willing to share members of their household staff in exchange for an invitation." Mrs. Howard leaned close to his ear. "I hope we don't run out of food. Let's wander through the crowd and check the buffet on the far side."

Her whisper in his ear buoyed his confidence like a tonic. Elliott smelled the lemon verbena on her skin and thought he might swoon. "As you wish," he said.

They worked their way around the edge of the dance floor, where officers and ladies flirted in small clusters. Couples shared secrets at tables along the wall as though they were alone in the room. Elderly ladies gossiped behind upraised fans, while white-gloved maids carried trays with flutes of champagne and glasses of punch. Elliott lifted two of the latter as a tray passed by.

"Punch, Mrs. Howard?"

"Thank you," she said, accepting a cup. "The buffet looks ample even if everyone brought hearty appetites." Before them was a spread of sliced ham, cold roast beef, and bowls of cold salads. "Uncle John refused a formal dinner beforehand because of the number of guests. I suppose people can find places to carry their plates throughout the house and garden. At least the evening is mild for the end of December."

"Everything looks perfect. You may stop fretting now," he said with a laugh.

"Fussing over details is the only way I can earn my keep, sir." Mrs. Howard hid her blush behind her fan.

Elliott turned her face up to his with a finger. "You are not hired help, Mrs. Howard. You are a guest. And I'm sure Mrs. Duncan wants you to enjoy yourself."

"Then why don't we dance, Colonel," she said as the fiddler plucked the first notes of a reel. "After all, isn't that the point of the evening?" Without waiting for an answer, she set down her cup and then walked to the end of the line.

They danced not one, but two reels and two waltzes in a row. The entire room moved in harmony to the lively music, insulated from the world outside. People smiled and chatted as though Richmond were a carefree place once again. This one night everyone seemed to possess all they needed for happiness.

When he was finally breathless, Elliott pulled Mrs. Howard from the crowd to an open window. "You dance well," he said, handing her a fresh cup of punch. "I wouldn't think your small town held many balls."

"It did not, but my mother insisted I learn the social graces. I was taught to dance by a neighbor's wife who'd been educated in Boston. I must admit this is my first fancy ball."

"The woman's tutelage has paid off handsomely."

Mrs. Howard's lips pulled into a grin, as though at a secret jest. She softly waved her fan in front of her heated face.

"You found what I said funny, Mrs. Howard?"

"Yes. I find most of what you say amusing." She studied him over the edge of her fan.

Elliott wasn't sure how to respond. "If I can do no more than amuse you, then I will content myself with that. Excuse me while I refill our cups." He strode across the dance floor toward the refreshment table, hoping to find something stronger than punch. With each encounter, he grew more infatuated with the woman, and she found him merely amusing? *Like a playful kitten or a toddler fresh from his nap?* But with Methodists and Presbyterians in attendance, there were no hard spirits on the table. Elliott selected a long flute of champagne and tried to rein in his disappointment as the bubbles tickled their way down his throat.

"How does a Pennsylvania woman become belle of the ball?" Mr. Duncan asked over his shoulder.

Elliott turned his attention to his host. "Your niece would take exception to your assessment, sir."

"Probably so, but I couldn't help but notice Madeline receiving more than her fair share of appreciative glances from the bachelors. If my daughter wasn't already smitten with Major Penrod, I would fear hair-pulling before the dance concluded."

Elliott cleared his throat. "Mrs. Howard is an attractive woman indeed, but I believe her magnetism lies in the singular ability to perplex and confound."

Mr. Duncan released a bark of a laugh. Elliott sighed. Apparently, he was amusing everyone he came in contact with tonight. But before he could request an explanation, they were interrupted by General Rhodes.

"May I have a word with you, Colonel? And would you join us, Mr. Duncan?"

Elliott pivoted on his boot heel to face his superior. "Of course, sir." Mr. Duncan nodded with a pinched expression on his face. The mood of cheerful conviviality was gone. "Shall I collect Major Penrod and the other staff members?"

"No, that won't be necessary." The heavyset general leaned precariously on his walking stick.

Elliott set his empty flute on a tray and followed his elders down the hall. Inside the library, the air smelled stale and musty, but the room was blissfully quiet without the ceaseless chatter of young belles.

"Would you care for a brandy, gentlemen?" asked their host.

"Very good, sir. If I drink another mouthful of punch, I'll float away." General Rhodes accepted the first snifter of amber liquid.

"No, thank you, sir." Elliott's desire for spirits vanished with his growing sense of doom. "How can I be of service?"

The general's bulbous nose reddened. "I want you to find out who has been leaking sensitive information to the Yankees."

Elliott's spine stiffened. "Are you implying I have a traitor among those of the home guard? With all due respect, sir, upon what do you base such an allegation?"

"That bloody travesty at Bristow Station. That was no lucky guess on the part of the Union Army." Rhodes downed his brandy and then held out his glass to be refilled.

"Our sentries are constantly picking off their scouts all the time. A Yankee scout could have spotted our movement."

"I'm not talking about just the October skirmish. The November debacle was more of the same. We can't seem to tie our shoes without that devil Meade anticipating every move. There are too many coincidences for it to be anything other than a spy in our midst."

Mr. Duncan rubbed his hand across his jaw. "It's not just military maneuvers they're finding out about. Last Wednesday a dozen Southern sympathizers were detained in the Yankee capital. Two were arrested, while the others were ordered out of Washington with barely the clothes on their backs. They were given no warning and little time to pack. They were told they would be shot if they returned to the city. Who knows what will remain of their homes by the time the war is over?" He shook his head in dismay.

General Rhodes just as swiftly downed the

second snifter. "Someone familiar with Richmond's wealthiest families supplied that list of names to the Yankee war department. Someone connected to President Davis's staff might be a Judas. I entrust the responsibility of finding out their identity to you two."

Elliott saluted. "We are at your service, sir. I've heard rumors about this Mrs. Van Lew and others. I intend to investigate."

The general scowled over his empty glass. "See that you look into *all* unsubstantiated rumors, Colonel. We need to nip this flow of information in the bud."

Elliott returned to the dance floor feeling chastised for no apparent reason. He had never discussed military matters with civilians. And adding insult to injury, the fascinating Mrs. Howard was nowhere to be found.

January 1864
Madeline slipped into her usual chair at breakfast, grateful that her cousin still chattered endlessly about the ball nearly two weeks ago. Sweet Joseph did this, and then he said that . . . it was apparent to anyone within a five-block radius that Eugenia was in love.

Fortuitously, Colonel Haywood had found

a permanent staff position for the major so he would not be returning to the battlefront. Not that the men of the home guard didn't encounter their own brand of danger. They were expected to sacrifice their lives to protect Jefferson Davis, his family, and the war department of the Confederacy.

"Joseph intends to take me to Varina's ball if it is still held as planned." Eugenia's wide smiled revealed almost every tooth in her mouth.

Aunt Clarisa arched an eyebrow. "Her name is Mrs. Davis, young lady. As an unmarried woman, you are not her social equal and thus not entitled to such familiarity."

"Yes, ma'am." Eugenia took dainty bites of scrambled eggs. Since she met a beau, her appetite had diminished to that of a sparrow. "Mother Penrod said she will teach me to play the harp. We shall begin the lessons on Sunday after church."

Clarisa blew out a breath of exasperation. "Please refer to her as *Mrs.* Penrod, Eugenia. You're becoming too bold at this stage of courtship. You musn't allow your behavior to become a black mark against your suitability as a wife."

"Yes, ma'am," Eugenia said again, dropping her focus to the tablecloth as she reined in her carefree ebullience.

"Perish the thought of a black mark," Uncle John said sardonically. "Explain to me why you've stopped attending Sunday Mass with us." He scowled over his half-moon reading glasses.

Eugenia's smile reappeared. "That's easy, Papa. Now I go to Joseph's — I mean, Major Penrod's church. We sing more hymns than at our service."

"Kathleen!" Uncle John thundered. "Bring us more coffee." He lowered his tone to address his daughter. "When and *if* you and the major wed, then you may change to your husband's denomination. Until then I expect you to attend church with us."

"But I've been going to the Methodist Church for weeks. Neither you nor Mama has said a word." Her luminous blue eyes filled with tears.

"I was tolerant during the holiday season. You would appear ill-bred if you so quickly dismissed the faith of your father and grandfather."

Madeline thought Eugenia would slip from her chair into a pile of starched skirts and petticoats. She began whimpering like a hungry mongrel at the back door.

Aunt Clarisa inserted a measure of compromise into the stalemate. "Perhaps Eugenia could attend early Mass with us and then the later service with the Penrods. I've never known Alma to be an early riser. Would that be all right with you, dear?"

Folding his newspaper, Uncle John dropped it on the table. "Very well. We'll see how long two services per Sunday last with someone so fond of her goose down pillow and thick quilts."

Madeline cleared her throat. "If you've finished the *Richmond Times Dispatch,* may I take it with me to read?" She extended a hand toward her uncle as she spoke.

"Of course. There's no good news anyway. Shortages of this, shortages of that, and that blackheart Jonas Weems pointing fingers at anyone not born and raised in Richmond. He's on a witch hunt to catch traitors, but I think it's just a ploy to sell newspapers. Weems considers any single female from the North a seductress or a courtesan here to ply information from unsuspecting men. What rubbish. Better to hide under a rock until this whole nasty business is finished."

Madeline glanced nervously at her aunt and cousin, but they were planning their next trap for the hapless Major Penrod and not paying attention to her. Madeline finished her eggs quickly, grabbed the paper, and refilled her coffee cup in the kitchen.

"Where you going?" asked Esther, stopping Madeline in her tracks.

Her entire breakfast felt like a boulder in her gut. "I thought I would read in the garden and enjoy another cup of coffee."

"Where do you come from, Miz Howard? It's January. This ain't some island in the South Seas like in those yellow-backed stories Miss Eugenia reads." The cook wrapped a heavy woolen cloak around her as though she were a child and buttoned it to her chin.

"Thank you, Esther. I'll come in the moment I get cold."

In the privacy of the backyard, Madeline scanned each page for news of her beloved James, as she had every day since hearing the gruesome news in the hospital. The paper contained a chilling account of parents still claiming bodies in Pennsylvania for reburial in Virginia. She found a list of soldiers who had recently died at Chimborazo from wounds or disease. There was a desperate plea from Mr. Davis for silver, gold, or Yankee greenbacks to buy munitions for the Cause. But the small amount of war news had to do with the exploits of Ulysses S. Grant out west, near a town called Knoxville.

There was no mention of any Union corps commanders succumbing to a shoulder wound.

"Thank You, Lord," she whispered. Refolding the newspaper, Madeline slipped inside the warm kitchen unnoticed except by Esther.

"Done with your reading so soon, Miz Howard?" The cook's hands were coated with flour.

"Yes, all finished." Madeline set the paper on a counter. "Please tell Mrs. Duncan that I went to St. Patrick's."

"What for? It ain't Sunday, and you ain't Catholic."

"Correct on both counts, but Father Michael said I could accompany him on his rounds again today."

"You're going back to that hospital? Mr. Duncan ain't gonna like it." Esther stopped kneading dough and fixed a frown on her creased face.

"Then you needn't worry because Chimborazo isn't where we're headed." She grabbed the basket she'd packed earlier and hurried out the door before Esther could ask more questions. Madeline didn't wish to explain she was on her way to Libby Prison — not to her aunt, and certainly not to her uncle.

She walked to the rectory, not daring to involve Micah or borrow the carriage. Once she was there, Father Michael hailed a passing coach to take them to the facility that held captured Union officers. Climbing into the carriage, she set her basket on the leather seat.

"What have you brought for the prisoners, Mrs. Howard? I do love Esther's apple-cornmeal muffins, in case there's a broken one." The priest rubbed his hands together with anticipation.

"Sorry, Father. I just have leftovers from meals from the last few days: a few slices of ham, four sugared yams, and some plum jam with toast squares. No muffins today. I saved uneaten food so as not to create additional expense for my uncle and aunt. I daresay the dance to celebrate the New Year crimped their budget."

The priest sighed. " 'Tis a sad day when my wealthiest parishioners feel the pinch of this extended conflict. I pray each night for the Union soldiers to simply go home and leave Virginia in peace."

Madeline smiled at him. She felt ill equipped to discuss with a man of the cloth why the Union couldn't simply "go home." She doubted God looked favorably on either side after so much bloodshed and cruelty.

Libby Prison was a long, brick warehouse standing four stories tall with a tin roof and tall windows. A sign still hung at its post on the corner angle: Libby & Sons, Ship Chandlers and Grocers, but inside provisions were in short supply. Formerly filled with barrels and boxes, the building was now overflowing with Union officers. Libby stood beside the Lynchburg Canal with a good view of the James River. Three long, white bridges spanned the waterway, their supports hidden by thick, entwining foliage. On a clear day Belle Isle could be seen downstream, its white tents flapping in the breeze. The charming name belied the wartime prison home for thousands of enlisted men without solid walls to offer protection from the elements. Directly across the James from Libby were a row of factories and the small village of Manchester.

Because Libby housed officers and not enlisted soldiers, Father Michael was permitted inside a common area where he said Mass and provided communion to Roman Catholics once a week. Madeline was also admitted after signing a roster at the front desk. Relatively unfamiliar with the liturgy, she stood clutching her basket against the wall with other non-Catholics.

When Father Michael paused to hear the private confessions of several prisoners, Madeline approached a spectator standing near the barred windows. "Would you care for something to eat, sir? It's not much. Just a few leftovers from home."

"Thank you, ma'am. Whatever you got has to be better than what's served in here." The man reached into the hamper, grabbed a cold yam, and ate it ravenously. "I taste brown sugar or maybe honey on this?"

Before she could answer, the metal door they had entered through banged open. In marched an officious-looking man flanked by two armed guards and the soldier who manned the front desk.

"That's her, Colonel." The soldier who had previously paid her little attention pointed a crooked finger.

"Seize that basket and that prisoner!" The colonel gestured toward the yam-eater.

When the Confederate guards reached where Madeline stood, the officer glared down at her. "You will come with us, Mrs. Howard."

"Of course, sir," she replied graciously, not in keeping with her inner turmoil or the woeful surroundings.

On her way from the common room, Madeline cast a sidelong glance at Father Michael. From his expression, the priest was surprised and concerned. With each step down the long hallway, Madeline's courage flagged. When they reached a heavy iron door, a guard pulled the basket from her hands, along with her reticule, and herded her into a windowless room with a table, several chairs, and a cot.

A cot? Surely they aren't going to arrest me and keep me in this loathsome place.

Her fear must have been palpable, because the colonel's features softened slightly. "You are not under arrest, Mrs. Howard. Not at this time, anyway. Sit." He pointed at a chair. "A matron will go through your basket and bag for any messages or contraband goods. The Yankee officer you were talking to instead of worshipping will also be searched, along with those sweet potatoes."

"I carried no messages inside Libby, only food." Madeline forced herself to speak clearly. "And I didn't participate in the service because I'm not Catholic." She swallowed down the sour taste of bile.

"Then the question begging to be asked is why would you come today?" The colonel's steel gray eyes practically bored holes through her forehead.

"I felt sorry for your prisoners and brought them some food."

His face registered surprise. "Then you don't deny being a Union sympathizer?"

Madeline was unsure how to respond, but she could think of nothing other than the truth. "I don't deny it, but I also aided Rebel soldiers when I lived in Pennsylvania after the battle of Gettysburg."

The colonel's expression changed to contempt. "Your one-woman humanitarian league isn't welcome in Libby. You are neither a nurse nor a person of the cloth. Wait here. A matron will come to search your person. If we find nothing suspect, you will be free to leave." Tugging on his gloves, he said sternly, "But I strongly advise you never to return. Union sympathizers have no place in Libby or anywhere else in Richmond, for that matter."

The metal door clanged shut behind him. Madeline was left alone to shiver and fret until a distasteful woman showed up some time later. Never before in her life had she been forced to strip down to bloomers, chemise, and bare feet in front of a stranger in a cold room. She could remember nothing said during the carriage ride back to St. Patrick's. Gratefully, Father Michael insisted on seeing her home. She would remember little of her explanation to Aunt Clarisa or Eugenia when she entered the house, pale and wan. All she recalled after her ordeal was scrubbing in a tub until the water turned cold and still not feeling clean.

Later, she ate a meager supper in the kitchen and then crawled under the quilt in her room. Yet no matter how she tossed and turned, Madeline couldn't sleep.

The man she'd spoken to in Chimborazo kept running through her mind. The soldier had said James had been shot while scouting around the town of Remington.

Remington. Repeating the name over and over didn't lull her into slumber. Instead, she was galvanized to action in the dead of night. Lowering the wick of her oil lamp, Madeline crept downstairs and through the house, certain she would be discovered at any moment. In her uncle's library hung a framed map of Virginia. Madeline had remarked several times about it, marveling at the details included by the mapmaker.

Once she reached the cluttered room and closed the door, she exhaled with relief. Turning up the wick of her lamp, she studied the towns west of Richmond in a methodical radius. Finally her fingers landed on the black dot of Remington and then the name Culpeper drew her like a beacon. Uncle John had complained several times that his brother's home now lay under Yankee control.

Could I possibly leave Richmond and reach Culpeper? What excuse would I have to make such a trip?

With her blood throbbing at her temples, Madeline blew out the lamp and then walked soundlessly back to her room. She had the flame of love illuminating her path. Because no matter what the risk, she knew she must try. Withdrawing a sheet of paper and a bottle of ink from her drawer, she penned a long-overdue answer to his letter — the one she still hadn't found.

Dear James,

I pray this finds you well, if it finds you at all. I received your letter last month and have been remiss in replying. Uncertainty had stayed my hand — uncertainty and cowardice. But I will be a coward no longer.

My heartfelt desire is to see you. I believe I could safely reach the town of Culpeper. I will meet you for an overdue reunion the first Saturday in February.

I'm unsure of the details, only certain of my intentions. I cannot remain in Richmond while you may be languishing from your wound, unknowledgeable of my affection for you. Do not chance a return response. Simply come to Culpeper on the appointed day.

I shall be the one wearing her heart on her sleeve.

With fond regards,
Madeline

Adding a final flourish to her signature, Madeline sealed the single sheet inside an envelope and tucked it in her apron pocket. Tomorrow was market day. She would find an excuse to visit the docks with Micah even if Aunt Clarisa had no money for fresh seafood. Tonight she would pray for the *Bonnie Bess* to be moored at its usual dock, that Captain George would deliver her message to General Downing wherever he might be, and finally that neither his wound nor anything else would keep him from their rendezvous in two weeks.

FIFTEEN

February 6, 1864

"Are you saying you refuse to take me, Uncle John?" Madeline tried her best to control her temper.

"No, I'm not refusing, but I believe I have a right to know why you wish to go to the station."

"With all due respect, Uncle, I wish to catch a train." She stared stubbornly at him from a spot just in front of the dining room windows. He was standing on the other side of the room, his movement to the table interrupted by a sudden request of a ride to the depot from her.

"Madeline, have you no concept —"

"John, perhaps you and our favorite niece could continue the argument like civilized people, seated at the breakfast table." Aunt Clarisa bustled into the dining room with a flurry of lace and a wry smile. "Isn't it a tad early for either of you to be up on a Saturday?" She sat down and waited for Kathleen to bring her first cup of coffee.

"I'm sorry, Aunt. I hope we didn't disturb you, but I have no time for breakfast this morning."

"Sit and eat something," Aunt Clarisa ordered. "Then Micah will drive you to the station."

"Yes, ma'am." Madeline walked over to the table, sat, and reached for a piece of toast.

"Where is it you wish to go?"

"Now, Clarisa, don't encourage Madeline's foolish notions. It's not safe for a lady to travel these days, least of all by herself." Uncle John huffed out his breath like an angry bull as he sat in his place.

"Shouldn't we at least inquire about her foolish notions? After all, Madeline is a grown woman." Aunt Clarisa offered her husband a gracious smile.

Madeline washed down the dry toast with a gulp of coffee. She should have left the house unseen and walked to the depot, no matter the distance. However, considering how kind her aunt and uncle had been for the past six months, she couldn't leave without saying goodbye. "I'm on my way to Hanover Junction, where I'll transfer to the Virginia Central Railroad. I plan to ride that train to Gordonsville."

Looking perplexed, Aunt Clarisa leaned back in her chair. "What on earth for?"

Uncle John shook his head. "Impossible. We have no way of knowing if the tracks are intact between here and there. One army tears up entire sections, only to be replaced when the battle lines change. You could end up in the middle of nowhere and be forced to turn back."

Her aunt sipped her coffee and then returned the cup to the saucer. "Do you know someone in Gordonsville, my dear?"

Madeline swallowed another bite of toast. "No, ma'am. I intend to transfer to the Orange and Alexandria railroad and head toward Culpeper. That will be my final destination."

You could have heard a pin drop in the room for several moments. Her uncle's face turned very pale. "How did you learn of these rail lines, Madeline?"

"I studied the map on the wall of your library after deciding to make this trip," she said as she dabbed her mouth with her napkin.

"Ladies don't usually venture into my library." His statement hung in the air as Kathleen carried in a platter of pancakes.

"Forgive my intrusion, sir. I meant no

disrespect, but this journey is of the upmost importance." Madeline focused her eyes on an artfully sewn patch in the tablecloth rather than her uncle's unhappy face.

"Culpeper is firmly entrenched in enemy territory. Are you aware of that fact?"

"That it is held by the Union Army? Yes, sir." Now she met her uncle's gaze without blinking.

"Then I strongly advise against traveling there. Any soldier I send to accompany you would be in grave danger."

"There is no need for someone to accompany me, Uncle. I will travel alone. The only thing I do need is a ride to the station." Madeline waved off Kathleen's attempt to slide pancakes onto her plate.

Aunt Clarisa spoke before her husband gathered his wits. "May we know the reason for your trip?"

Madeline considered for a moment. "I heard that a dear friend of mine from Pennsylvania has been wounded. So I wish to go at once."

Uncle John gripped his fork ever tighter, his lips thinning into a harsh line. "A friend from Pennsylvania in Culpeper?"

"How on earth could one of your lady friends become wounded in Virginia?" Her aunt couldn't have sounded more confused.

"I didn't say my friend was female. I intend to visit a gentleman."

"Oh, dear me." Aunt Clarisa pressed a hand to her bosom.

"And Colonel Haywood? What shall I tell your *Richmond* gentleman friend?" Uncle John's tone dripped with scorn.

"I know you're disappointed in me, sir, but I have never deluded Colonel Haywood. He has been aware of my affection for someone else from the beginning of our acquaintance." Madeline refilled her cup and drank it down. She would need all the coffee she could stomach today.

Uncle John blushed to the roots of his silver hair, finally realizing the inappropriateness of their discussion. "You're a grown woman. I'll have Micah drive you to the train station. We shall pray for your safe passage into enemy —" he cleared his throat. "Into Union territory." Then, with great dignity, he rose from his chair and left the room.

"Oh, Madeline, I'm very worried about this. Surely your friend will heal without placing yourself in danger." Aunt Clarisa suddenly looked older than her years.

"Perhaps so, but I won't be able to rest until I know for certain." As Madeline rose from the table, tears filled her eyes. "Thank you for all you've done for me, Aunt Clarisa. You've been as kind to me as my own mother, and I will be forever indebted."

"This sounds so dire, so final. Won't you return to us after seeing your friend? I thought you planned to remain here for the duration of the war."

A single tear slipped from her eye. "With the difficulty in crossing lines even one way, I don't know if I'll be allowed to return. My love for you hasn't changed. If I can come back, I will. Now please let me go before I lose my nerve."

Fifteen minutes later, Madeline appeared in the foyer dressed in her traveling cloak and heavy bonnet. Her aunt waited by the front door. "I had Esther pack a lunch for you."

Madeline lifted the basket's lid. "There is enough here to feed four people."

"Perhaps you'll make friends on the train." Her aunt attempted a cheerful smile and pressed several folded greenbacks into Madeline's hand. "Take this without argument. You can repay me with a new filly someday. I won't have you sleeping in some dirty railway depot. My sister would turn over in her grave."

"I don't know what to say."

"Say you'll come back to us. You've been

a fine influence on Eugenia." Aunt Clarisa winked impishly.

"I will see you again." Madeline kissed her aunt's cheek and then hurried from the house on Forsythia Lane. She couldn't look back for fear of changing her mind. Since joining the world of Richmond society, she'd grown indolent and pampered. All the way to the station, she tried to picture James's handsome face but couldn't. *Have I lost my mind? I have no way of knowing whether he will be waiting in Culpeper even if I'm able to reach it.*

"This is a mistake, Mrs. Howard." Micah's honest observation as she stepped down from the carriage at the train depot didn't surprise her. "I'm sorry I helped you with your mischief. You could end up dead."

"I don't think I will, whether or not my journey turns out to be a mistake." Grabbing his large hand, Madeline pumped it like a handle. "Thank you for your kindness, Micah. Please say goodbye to Esther for me. Now go straight home. A train station is no place for a free person of color."

Once inside the depot, it took only one quick glance to conclude it wasn't a place for a woman, either. Soldiers and rough-looking men were everywhere, some in a hurry, some lounging as though they had nothing better to do. But at least she didn't have long to wait. The train going north to Hanover Junction, where she would change lines and head west to Trevilian, left in twenty minutes. She bought her ticket and concentrated on trying to attract no attention from passing guards.

However, once she reached Gordonsville, the conductor explained that the tracks had been torn up in several places. Everyone had to get off, walk two miles to the other side of town, and then board the Orange and Alexandria rail line toward Culpeper Courthouse. Prudently, Madeline changed her explanation as to where she was headed and the reason for her trip. The soldiers perusing passengers and randomly searching valises were decidedly Yankee. When one young private inspected her hamper, Madeline suspected his motivation was hunger. After sharing her lunch with him and two other soldiers, she settled back for the rest of the journey. By the time the train finally chugged into the Culpeper station with a whistle blast, she was too tired to feel much of anything.

But that was about to change. General James Downing was waiting on the wooden platform with his hat in hand. He looked taller than she remembered and very handsome in his starched uniform and neatly trimmed beard.

"Mrs. Howard." He stepped forward and offered his gloved hand. "I've been meeting trains for hours, unsure how long the trip would take."

Madeline accepted his assistance, mildly embarrassed. Her gloves were buried beneath her spare clothes. "I had no knowledge of schedules when I penned my letter. The rail line is broken in several places, but the conductor herded us to the next set of tracks." She tucked a stray lock of hair beneath her bonnet, feeling covered in dust and perspiration, even though the winter day was quite cold.

"I intended no complaint by my comment, only that I was eager for your arrival. I would have waited until dark and then through the night if necessary. It was by God's grace your message reached me across enemy lines. When business took me to Culpeper, I inquired at the post office and found your letter waiting." He took several deep breaths as other travelers jostled them from both sides.

Once they reached a quiet spot beyond the station, she turned to face him, oblivious of the other travelers passing on both sides. "I traveled from the capital of the

Confederacy to meet you, General Downing, based on our brief acquaintance in Cashtown and one letter hence, a letter which mysteriously disappeared shortly after it arrived. Don't you think you could call me Madeline and, perhaps, I may call you James? At least when no one else is within earshot?"

He locked gazes with her. "Little would give me more pleasure than that . . . *Madeline.*" Her name seemed to roll off his tongue like warm honey.

"Thank you, James." She smiled as she handed him her valise. "Do you know of someplace we might find a meal? I'm famished."

He grinned. "I've made arrangements at Culpeper's finest establishment for your accommodations. The innkeeper's wife promised to draw you a bath upon arrival and will serve dinner by the fire. We shall be her only guests."

"We?" she asked, with a flutter of nerves.

"I booked rooms for privacy — one for you, one for me, and a third for your chaperone, if you chose to travel with one."

"My uncle tried to send someone along, but I wouldn't permit a . . . chaperone." Madeline blushed, knowing Uncle John had intended Elliott Haywood to ensure her safety. How would she have been able to explain his role in her life?

Madeline took James's elbow as they set off down the raised wooden sidewalk through town. But with each step, the confidence she had felt in Richmond flagged. *Renting a room, arranging for my bath, and an intimate dinner by the fire — what expectations does he have?* "I hope my bold decision to visit hasn't given you an incorrect impression of me." She tried to sound composed and not like a frightened child.

"I expect nothing other than to spend a few hours with you. If you're hungry, we shall eat. If you feel talkative, I can listen for hours. If you're neither, I will be content to simply remain in your presence for as long as you deem fit."

"You talk like a scholar. Did you study rhetoric at West Point?" She tried unsuccessfully not to laugh.

Without warning, he clasped her wrist. "I talk like a man in love. You may not share my sentiments right now, but I came here to make my intentions clear. Upon receiving your letter, I became the happiest man on earth. I don't plan to waste a single moment of our time together." He released her as they stopped in front of a large, clapboard house.

"Is this where I'm staying tonight?" she asked, dazed by his confession. Her skin tingled where his hand had been.

"Yes. Go on inside, Madeline. Mrs. Lang is expecting you. I will join you for dinner in an hour. I have business to attend to at the telegraph office." He handed her the valise, bowed, and turned on his heel.

As she climbed the steps to the boarding house, she couldn't help feeling a thrill of excitement and a spike of trepidation.

James strode back to the center of town at a lively pace. He knew that General Meade could court-martial him for his actions. He had been given no authority to ride away from the Union winter camp after placing his chief of staff in charge. Though engagement with the enemy was highly unlikely, even a corps commander needed permission to leave his post. But sometimes a man had to risk his career for something . . . or someone . . . this important. He never would have believed it before, but meeting Madeline had changed everything for him. Now he had but a few short hours to change everything for her.

In Culpeper he sent telegraph dispatches

to General Meade and two other corps commanders sharing the same valley less than twenty miles away: *An urgent, unavoidable family emergency has occurred.* A stretch of the truth, if not an outright lie, but James couldn't dwell on his false witness at the moment. He needed to purchase flowers, a bottle of wine, another of cider, and perhaps a gift for his dinner guest. What did a man buy for the love of his life after she had traveled more than eighty miles, crossed enemy lines, and most likely severed relationships with her family to visit him?

Both the wine and cider were local brews. Regarding appropriate gifts for a lady, the shopkeeper who sold him the wine had only fabric and notions for sale. "I'm afraid there's not much call for fans, combs, or fancy baubles in these parts, sir."

When James inquired about flowers for sale, she stared at him. "In February? Come back in April and I'll have my daughter pick you a handful."

"Thank you, madam." James paid the woman for the beverages and left quickly. He couldn't wait to return to the inn and change his shirt. This one was sticking to his back despite the frigid temperatures.

Half an hour later he headed downstairs to the parlor, where he hoped a delicious supper awaited them. He imagined long tapers casting a soft glow, a roaring fire on the hearth, and an elegantly appointed table with silver and china. What he found instead was a rickety table without a covering, a few stubby tallow candles, and mismatched plates and cups. But at least a fire had been lit and the room was warm. James had little time to bemoan the arrangements.

Madeline came down the stairs and into the room a few moments later. "Oh, good, you're here. I feared I would be first to arrive. The innkeeper keeps watching me from the corner of her eye as though unsure of me. What exactly did you tell her?" She spoke in a soft whisper.

James felt heat rise into his face. "That you were my sister from the South, and that arranging a wartime visit had been difficult."

"Your *sister*?" she asked, lifting an eyebrow.

"I dared not make the presumption of calling you my betrothed, yet I didn't wish her to think poorly of your reputation."

"I have no reputation in Culpeper, and I don't plan to establish one." She settled gracefully on one of the wooden chairs and smiled up at him. "What are you hiding behind your back?"

James set the two homemade concoctions on the table. "A bottle of local wine and another of apple cider. You may have your choice." Tugging down his waistcoat, he settled across from her. The table had a definite tilt to one side.

"You should know, brother dear, that I don't imbibe." Madeline winked while fluffing out a patched cotton napkin.

"Of course, dear sister, but I thought you may have picked up a few bad habits in Richmond."

Suddenly, the innkeeper marched in as though she had two flat feet, interrupting their repartee. "Here's your supper, General Downing, Miss Downing." She angled a brief nod in Madeline's direction. "Hope it suits since food ain't exactly gourmet in these parts." The woman set down a kettle of food all of the same shade of brownish red.

"What have we here, Mrs. Lang?" James peered at the dish with little enthusiasm.

"That there's beef, slowed-cooked with beets, tomatoes, and onions. All ends up the same color." Mrs. Lang pulled a jar of green vegetables from her apron pocket. "These here are Brussels sprouts I pickled. Came out right fine, even if I do say so myself."

James thanked her and then waited until she left before rolling his eyes. "I'm sorry, Madeline. I'd hoped for something a bit more . . . distinctive."

Smiling, she ladled some of the concoction onto both plates. "Please don't worry about it. I'm a country girl. I used to cook stews like this all the time. However, I would have pickled the beets with the sprouts and not simmered them with shanks of beef." She spooned the vegetables into small bowls and popped one miniature cabbage into her mouth.

"How is it?" he asked, picking up a fork.

"Delicious. Be not afraid." Madeline sampled a bite of meat. "Even the beef is good, tender and well-seasoned."

"Perhaps you're just hungry. As for me, I'm grateful the food is edible, but I had wanted to make this night memorable."

"I didn't travel to Culpeper for the cuisine, James." She looked him in the eye without hesitation.

Her comment stopped his nervous chatter. For several minutes they simply enjoyed Mrs. Lang's stew and pickled Brussels sprouts. After he got past the strange color, the taste wasn't bad. "Shall we try some cider then, dear sister?" He uncorked the odd-shaped bottle and filled both cups.

Madeline took a hearty swallow, and then her eyes grew round as an owl's. "Goodness! That cider has fermented into applejack." She pressed her napkin to her mouth.

James hastily pulled the offensive bottle from the table. "Forgive me. I had no idea what she was selling me."

Madeline moved her glass out of reach and folded her hands in her lap. "Of course you didn't. Seeing your uniform, she probably assumed you wished something stronger. I suggest you stop fretting and enjoy your supper. We can drink the well water Mrs. Lang provided and be grateful." Unexpectedly, she reached for his hand. Her touch was electric beyond words.

"A wonderful idea. Beef with beets is starting to grow on me. Perhaps you could obtain the recipe before we leave." James would have held hands throughout the meal, but she squeezed his fingers and then withdrew her hand and resumed eating. When they finished, they sat like old friends savoring a moment of tranquility. Outside a cold February wind blew and rain pelted the windowpane, but next to the fire they were warm and utterly content.

"Thank you for arranging the meal. That was very thoughtful of you," she said, finally breaking the silence in the room.

"We have no music to dance to and I don't wish to read, despite the Langs' decent library." He gestured toward a wall of books.

"What then do you have in mind, sir?"

Swallowing down what he truly wished to do, he pointed at a round table near the window. "I noticed the game had been set up when I arrived."

Madeline pivoted around in her chair. "A chess board? But I don't know how to play."

"All the better, because then I have all night to teach you."

The next morning dawned sunny and clear. The rain was gone and a brisk breeze smelled of spring still weeks away. James washed and dressed in an austere guest room, eager to see Madeline. He hoped she wouldn't sleep too late. Last night's chess game hadn't yielded any new devotees, but it had provided hours to gaze on her lovely face and listen to the sound of her voice. Their time together was dwindling. Loping down the steps, he found the object of his affection calmly sipping coffee in the parlor.

"You're finally up," she said. "I feared you would sleep all day."

"*What?* Forgive me for keeping you waiting. You should have sent the innkeeper to knock on my door." The more excuses he made, the more flustered he became.

She smiled like a naughty child. "I'm teasing you, James. I arrived mere moments before you."

He crossed the room to the coffeepot on the table. "Your sense of humor will require a brief period of adjustment."

"I read in one of Eugenia's periodicals that gentlemen prefer ladies who are unpredictable."

"Then you, Mrs. Howard, will make me infinitely joyous."

She blushed and pointed at the table. "Mrs. Lang put out corn muffins and fresh butter. And there's a bowl of what looks like corn chutney. I'm feeling as though I never left Aunt Clarisa's — corn, corn, and more corn."

He lowered himself to a chair. "I assure you this feels nothing like winter camp for the Union Army."

Madeline slathered a muffin with butter. "What plans do you have for us today?"

"How about a ride in the country? Not too far away. I don't want to run into my own pickets."

"On horseback? It's still February."

"The sun is shining and the day is mild. Besides, I have a surprise for you. Did you bring a riding habit?"

"I did."

"Then finish eating and change your clothes. We'll see what kind of horseflesh awaits us in the barn, sister dear."

Madeline finished her muffin in two bites, downed her coffee, and rose to her feet.

"But you didn't try Mrs. Lang's corn relish." James lifted the glass jar.

"I'll save that pleasure for another time." With a wink, she hurried from the room in a rustle of silk.

James stood at the mounting block holding the reins of his horse and a sleek mare when she appeared twenty minutes later. Madeline wore leather boots beneath her long skirt and a broad brimmed hat. Her hair hung in a single plait down her back. Although James expected her to be surprised, he didn't expect a flood of tears.

"Bo!" She threw her arms around the mare's neck. "Wherever did you find her, and what is she doing in Culpeper?"

"The cavalry quartermaster acquired her in Pennsylvania and recognized her as the same horse I came seeking after the first day's battle. He gave her to me for my personal mount, but I only allow trusted staff to ride her on short errands."

Madeline lifted her foot into the stirrup

and mounted with ease and grace. "Thank you, James. I won't ever forget this." Grinning impishly, she shook the reins and took off down the street.

"But you so easily forget *me*?" he called after her. He swung up into the saddle, happy to finally return a jest in good measure.

When the road from Culpeper eventually turned into a narrow country lane, they headed across a meadow and then followed a rushing stream. Madeline, an accomplished equestrienne, had no trouble traversing the unfamiliar terrain. While they rode, the sun warmed their skin and not a cloud marred the crystalline blue sky. James couldn't imagine a ride more singularly pleasurable.

"See that pine forest on the hill? I'll race you to the top." Madeline pointed one gloved finger. Without waiting for a response, she gave Bo a light kick and took off like a flash of lightning.

Although mounted on a larger, faster horse, James stayed behind her, content to watch her braid bouncing against her wool jacket. Once they reached the summit, a sunlit patch on the forest floor beckoned invitingly. "Shall we stop a moment?" he called.

Breathless, Madeline brought Bo to a halt. After slipping from the saddle, she tied her reins to a low branch. "I beat you, sir, fair and square."

"To the victor go the spoils." James dismounted and then pulled a wrapped parcel from his saddlebag.

Madeline was already reposing on her elbows in the clearing. "We're in luck. These pine needles are dry. What have you brought me?"

"Apples and cheese." He tossed her the parcel.

She set it aside. "Along with corn, that's the usual fare in Richmond. What I wouldn't give for a slice of strawberry pie."

"Far better than hardtack and dried jerky."

"Forgive me. I didn't mean to sound ungrateful for Mrs. Lang's or my aunt's hospitality."

"You didn't. In fact, I doubt that you could." He tugged off his gloves to feel the thick needles between his fingers.

"You flatter me, dear brother, but your praise has no basis." Madeline laid back and focused to the patch of sky overhead. "It's beautiful here. I may be tempted to linger for some time."

Stretching out beside her, James savored the sun on his face after weeks of cloudy days. "If I didn't long so much for home, this part of Virginia might appeal to me."

Cupping her hands behind her head, she closed her eyes. "Let's enjoy the peace and quiet for a while. It has been in short supply for both of us."

But she didn't remain mute for long. Sitting up abruptly, she pawed through the pine needles where she'd lain. "I felt something hard beneath my head. Here. What do you suppose this is?" She held up a silver medallion at the end of a long chain.

James examined the necklace in the dappled light. "It's a Saint Christopher medal. Our Irish housekeeper had one just like it when I was growing up."

"Beautiful, isn't it? I'm not familiar with Saint Christopher."

"He is the patron saint of travelers. Our housekeeper believed wearing one offered protection on long journeys." James deftly slipped the heavy chain over her head, letting it fall against her dress. "There, my dear, now the good saint will keep you safe."

"Do you think it will work for Episcopalians?"

"Only those as God-fearing and gentle as you." Impetuously, he placed a chaste kiss on her forehead.

"I wonder about the health of the person

who lost it here." His kiss, no different than one bestowed by her grandmother, sent shivers up her spine. Flustered, Madeline pressed the metal to her lips. "Goodness, James, the day grows colder by the minute. Since neither of us is hungry, let's be off." She scrambled to her feet and started back to where he'd tied the horses.

He grabbed the wrapped parcel of food and followed her. When he reached her side, he took off his frock coat and wrapped it around her shoulders. "Wear this for the ride back to town. I'm far more accustomed to the cold than you are."

"Thank you. And thank you for recovering my horse, but I'm not sure what to do with her." She mounted Bo as easily as she'd slipped off.

"Have no worries about her. I'll keep her safe in camp with me."

They set off in the direction they had come in a full gallop. Neither reined in their horse until reaching the inn in Culpeper. While they rode, Madeline slipped the new-found medallion into the breast pocket of his coat, buttoning it securely.

At the inn, he reached for her reins and dismounted his gelding. "When I return to our winter camp, where will you go? It's not safe to stay here. There are too many battles, too many skirmishes in this part of Virginia. Shall I arrange transportation for you to Philadelphia to the home of my parents?"

"No. I've decided to return to Richmond. It wasn't my intention when I left, but I've changed my mind."

"What on earth for? It's even less safe there."

"I can be of service in the Confederate capital." Her voice dropped to a whisper.

"But the Duncans won't trust you after coming here. They might assume you carried military information and have you arrested." James took hold of her chin. "I cannot allow such dangerous behavior."

Madeline jerked away from him. "You have no say-so in the matter, any more than my Uncle John. And goodness knows, he tried to prevent my trip here. In fact, you're starting to remind me of Uncle John more and more."

"Surely you have other relatives or friends up North. If not, why don't you return to Cashtown? I can pay Reverend Bennett and his wife for your expenses until the war is over."

She shook her head. "Certainly not, sir. I will not be kept by a man, whether in a preacher's house or not."

"Be reasonable, Madeline." James gripped

his hat between his fingers, the brim paying a dear price for his anxiety.

Her expression softened. "You risk your life every day to serve the Republic. A cavalry scout in Chimborazo Hospital told me you were shot near Remington. How is your wound?"

"My shoulder is just fine. It's nothing for you to be concerned about."

"Only by the grace of God was your life spared. The citizens of Richmond won't hang me for visiting a beau in Culpeper."

"What if I send for my adjutants and have you incarcerated? I would do almost anything to keep you safe."

"I'll be gone before your soldiers arrive." She reached for his hand. "Try to understand, James. I'm not the same peevish woman you first met who fumed about horses trampling her hollyhocks. I'm loyal to the Union, and I have a right to help my country."

Words escaped him — the irrefutable logic, the convincing argument that would change her mind. Wearily he hung his head.

"If it's our destiny to be together, God will make it so. But if not, then it matters little if I die in Richmond, or in Cashtown, or in a train wreck somewhere between here and Gordonsville."

He met her gaze. "Please don't say such things."

She stretched up on her tiptoes to kiss his cheek. "Please don't go to the station with me. A long goodbye on the platform will make parting that much harder." She hugged him gently and then pulled away.

But in one reckless maneuver James pulled her into his arms and kissed her squarely on the mouth.

When their lips parted at last, she fluttered her lashes. "Goodness, General Downing. Now you will be impossible to forget."

"That's what I had in mind."

"And you know I'm awfully fond of that horse. I plan on seeing you both again." With that, she ran up the steps of the boarding house, retrieved her bag, and left for the station without another word. She hurried away from Mrs. Lang's, and Culpeper, and the protection of the Union Army.

And there wasn't a thing James could do to stop her.

■ ■ ■ ■

SIXTEEN

■ ■ ■ ■

Richmond, Virginia

Madeline stepped off the train late in the afternoon on Monday. Having slept the previous night in her clothes and without a bath since Mrs. Lang's inn, she felt miserable. A hard bench in the Gordonsville station had been her sole option for Sunday night. Every boarding house was either filled or closed for repairs due to damage from recent battles. The packet of apples and cheese James forced her to take had provided her only sustenance.

How foolish she had been to leave on a Sunday.

How foolish she had been to leave Richmond at all. What had she expected from James? Did she wish him to abandon his sworn duty to the Union and whisk her away to the Western territories? As a man in command, he could no more change his fate than she could. But at least she'd seen for herself that he was well and that his wound had healed. And she'd heard his sweet pledges of fidelity. Yet his words and promises had little place in a world gone mad.

Monday morning the soldiers at the Gordonsville station finally permitted her to board an eastbound train. But she'd been forced to utter a passel of lies.

She had been tending a dying relative in Culpeper.

She needed to travel to Richmond to see a relative who was lingering at death's door.

Falsehoods and fabrication came easier these days than the truth, adding to her already heavy burden of shame, but if she could help James it would be worth it. The Union Army must prevail. The Republic must be restored and slavery abolished. Then the country could finally fulfill the rights and freedoms promised in the Constitution.

Yet her lofty ideals provided little comfort during the long walk from the train station to Forsythia Lane. Staggering from hunger and fatigue, Madeline opened the front door without waiting for someone to answer her knock. Inside the mansion's ornate center hall, she was instantly filled with a sense of relief. At least for the foreseeable future, she was home.

"Mrs. Howard!" Micah exclaimed. Spotting her from the drawing room doorway, the butler hurried to take her valise. "Mrs. Duncan has been so afraid you weren't coming back because you would marry your Yankee beau. She's been moping around the house, and Miss Eugenia has been crying and fussing for two days."

"As you can see, I have returned a single woman." Madeline forced a smile for him. "Things between my beau and I didn't turn out well, so there will be no elopement anytime soon. I hope Aunt Clarisa is willing to take me back."

"Don't you worry about that, ma'am." Micah gave her a bright smile. "I'll send Kathleen to get your room ready. You go on to the kitchen. Esther has some soup and cornbread leftover from supper."

Madeline held out her hands for inspection. "What I really need is to scrub for an hour. Trains and depots are not very tidy places."

"You can wash your face and hands at Esther's kitchen tub. I know you must be a tad hungry, ma'am. So you go on now." He started up the stairs with her bag.

A tad hungry? That was the understatement of the day. James's apples and cheese seemed a distant memory, as though eaten

359

days ago. Shuffling into the kitchen, Madeline let Esther question, scold, and chatter while she stuck her face and arms into a bucket of fresh well water. However, Madeline had less than five minutes for her *toilette* before Aunt Clarisa and Eugenia bustled into the room. Both were wearing belted silk robes indicating they had already retired for the evening.

"Is it really you or am I seeing a ghost?" Eugenia exclaimed as she flung herself at Madeline and enveloped her in a hug.

"I'm not fit to embrace at the moment, but yes, it is I. I'm not sure if I should launder this garment or burn it."

The cook shook a finger at her. "I'll take care of that dress, Miz Howard. Sit down and eat. You can talk to your family in between bites. I think you're skinnier than before you left."

"I couldn't have lost weight in two days, Esther." Madeline managed to extract herself from Eugenia and slipped onto a kitchen chair. The bowl of onion soup the cook set before her smelled wonderful. Ladling up a spoonful, she felt her aunt's eyes boring into her forehead. "I've taken great liberty assuming your home would remain open to me, Aunt. If you wish me to leave, I will. My behavior has been erratic, to be sure." With her soup spoon held aloft, Madeline locked gazes with the older woman.

"Of course you're still welcome here, my dear. You're my sister's only child. My home will always be open to you." She issued a dismissive snort. "Although I must admit I didn't think you would return in two days' time."

"Did he jilt you, cousin?" asked Eugenia. "Did you discover him in the arms of another woman when you arrived? Or perhaps the gentleman had a wife he neglected to mention until now." Her eyes grew rounder with each new possibility.

Aunt Clarisa's interruption precluded Madeline from responding. "Then he would be no gentleman! I forbid you from reading anymore of those sensational novels, Eugenia. I don't know why you read such rubbish when we have a library filled with good books."

"Eat, Miz Howard," Esther said softly, placing one of her large hands on Madeline's shoulder.

Madeline complied, peering from one Duncan woman to the other.

"How else would a girl learn about the devious minds of men?" Eugenia asked. "Now that I'm courting, I must be prepared for any mischief Joseph may try behind my back. Those comportment classes only taught me silly rules and manners. If not for books, I would know nothing about the game called love."

Aunt Clarisa pointed one delicate finger at her daughter. "If I don't see you feeding those novels into Esther's cook stove tomorrow, I shall tell your father about your tawdry collection. Then you will read a few choice passages for his entertainment over teatime."

Paling, Eugenia folded her hands in her lap. "Very well, Mama. I prefer we not involve Papa in this matter." She turned toward Madeline. "But that doesn't mean my cousin can't bring us up to date with her news."

Even Esther stopped washing the dishes to listen.

Madeline concentrated on her soup until she'd swabbed the sides of her bowl with her bread crust. "There's not much to tell really. He has no wife, but I made too much of a brief encounter in Pennsylvania. I blew things out of proportion in my mind. A Union general helped me during the difficult days following the July battle. Then he saved my life when my house was burning down around me and provided shelter when

I had nowhere else to go." She paused in her tale to reach for another slice of bread. "Like a character in Genie's novels, I saw love where none existed, misinterpreting simple kindness for commitment and devotion."

Amazing how the lies rolled off her tongue once she started the ball rolling.

"Oh, you poor dear." Eugenia hugged her again. "At least there was no other woman to rub salt into your wounds."

Esther hovered behind her chair. "Eat more soup, ma'am. Food will make you feel better."

"Women often fall victim to their own imaginations. You're not the first, dear niece, and you won't be the last." Aunt Clarisa's sympathetic words soothed her like a warm quilt.

"Was it terribly humiliating for you?" Eugenia scooted her chair closer. "Was there a great scene in a restaurant or a hotel lobby?"

"That's enough, young lady," said Aunt Clarisa sternly. "Go to bed. And I forbid you from deviling Madeline with your impertinent nonsense."

"Yes, ma'am. I'm sorry, Maddy. I truly feel awful about your mortification. That Yankee was just another snake in the grass —" The girl stopped talking and swiftly left the room as her mother's expression went from stern to furious.

"I feel foolish, but not mortified. Better to find out now that my affections weren't returned than to pine for the rest of the war. I'm grateful you're not angry with me." Madeline ate a few more spoonfuls and then dug the remaining greenbacks from her purse. "I still have most of your traveling money. The general insisted on paying for my one night's lodging. The second night I dozed fitfully in the train depot."

Aunt Clarisa let the bills remain where Madeline laid them. "I'm not angry with you, my dear. Although it has been a while, I do remember being young and impetuous once." A smile removed years from her aunt's face. "But I fear that your reentry into Richmond may not be easy." She and Esther exchanged a glance as the cook stashed the bills in a canister labeled "Oats."

"Better have another slice of bread, Miz Howard." The cook pushed the plate closer.

"I was only gone two days. I doubt my absence in church yesterday would have caused much of a stir. No one knew where I was headed."

Aunt Clarisa shook her head at that and then sighed. Slowly she said, "I'm afraid that isn't exactly true. On Saturday Eugenia prattled on to Kathleen a sensational story of romance with the enemy and stealing away to a secret rendezvous. I didn't know about it in time to stop her."

Madeline swallowed. "I doubt the opinion of one maid will make much difference in my future." Though her words were brave, she spoke them without an ounce of real conviction.

"Our maid gossiped to the neighbor's maid, who then repeated the story until every household on the street knew your business. Unfortunately, each subsequent retelling added another bit of spice until you were practically courting the entire Army of the Potomac."

"That Kathleen is a thorn in this family's foot. I said it before and I'll say it again," Esther muttered angrily as she hung two iron pots on their ceiling hooks with a clang.

The mistress of the house ignored her opinion. "I'm hoping the ladies of your acquaintance will dismiss the gossip as baseless."

Madeline pushed herself up from the table and swayed a little. "Thank you for the meal, Aunt, but if you'll excuse me, I-I need to bathe and retire. I can barely hold open my eyes."

"Off with you then. Kathleen should have

drawn your tub by now. Sleep late in the morning. I'll send your breakfast up on a tray." Her aunt started for the door and hesitated. "Allow me to break the news of your return to your uncle. Then you can see him at dinner. Tomorrow afternoon, plan to accompany Eugenia and me on our round of calls. You may as well nip the story in the bud before the rumor mill spreads it any further." With that she left the kitchen, heading for the main staircase.

Madeline climbed the back steps to her room. Indeed, a tub of water awaited her in the bathing chamber, along with two fresh towels. Yet heating the water first hadn't occurred to the troublesome maid. Lowering herself into the tub, Madeline scrubbed her skin and washed her hair quickly before she turned into an icicle. At least under the heavy quilt, she fell asleep within minutes. But phantoms with flashing angry eyes and rabid, jeering crowds tormented her dreams.

With the light of day, her anxieties seemed foolish. Madeline enjoyed a lunch of ham croquettes with the Duncan women, relishing the normal, everyday routine. When Aunt Clarisa complained of a headache, Madeline and Eugenia set off down the street to pay their first of three anticipated visits. The Emersons, three doors to the east on Forsythia, curtailed Madeline's hopes for a smooth reentry into Richmond life. The butler greeted them at the door and ushered them into the foyer. He smiled graciously at Eugenia. "Mrs. and Miss Emerson will receive you in the morning room, Miss Duncan, but I'm afraid Mrs. Howard may only leave her calling card." He formally held out a silver tray toward Madeline.

"There must be some mistake, Amos. Mrs. Howard is my cousin and Miss Justine is my dearest friend. Kindly show us both to the ladies at once." Eugenia utilized her most imperious tone of voice.

"Begging your pardon, Miss Duncan, but Madame Emerson was quite specific this morning. Mrs. Madeline Howard is no longer to be received in this house. I'm very sorry." He bowed deeply from the waist.

Eugenia's healthy glow faded. "In that case I shan't stay for tea either. You may present both cards with our sincere regrets." She dug in her bag and dropped her elegantly engraved card on the salver. "Good day to you, Amos."

"Good day to you, Miss Duncan. Mrs. Howard."

Madeline followed her young cousin out the door, feeling diminished physically as well as socially. The unfortunate performance was repeated at the second house as well. The dialogue was so eerily similar, Madeline suspected the ladies had discussed and rehearsed their reactions after church on Sunday.

What a poor use of time on the Sabbath.

However, when she reflected upon her schemes to continue deceiving the Duncans, Madeline immediately stopped judging the neighborhood ladies for *their* shortcomings. This treatment was what she rightly deserved.

Kathleen nervously glanced over her shoulder for the third time. She had told Esther she was headed to the privy. No one would miss her for at least ten minutes. Still, Mr. Duncan wouldn't look kindly on her meeting a strange man, especially a newspaper man in the back alley at night.

At last she heard a rustle of dead leaves and a snap of a twig, and then a short, rotund man stepped out of the shadows. "Miss O'Toole?"

"Yeah, I'm Kathleen O'Toole. You Jonas Weems?"

He curled his upper lip. "I am Mr. Weems of the *Richmond Times Dispatch*. You sent word that you wished to speak with me in private?" He moved closer, allowing her to smell the cigar smoke that clung to his heavy wool coat.

"The maid at Dr. Emerson's house said you pay good money for information. How much you pay? I don't take no Confederate script. I want gold or greenbacks so it be good anywhere." Kathleen glanced at the looming mansion behind her. The last candle in an upstairs window flickered out.

"Let's not get ahead of ourselves, miss. I pay money for *useful* information. If all you have is the usual servant gossip, I'll thank you not to waste my time." Weems took a step back.

"I got me a letter sent to Miz Howard. She's that Yankee who got Miz Duncan wrapped round her finger." Kathleen began withdrawing the envelope from her sleeve, but then she hesitated. "You willing to give gold for this?"

"If it proves worthy of the time it took to come to you in the middle of the night, then yes. Show me what you have or be gone with you. I have no time for —"

Kathleen cut him off by thrusting it toward his chest. "This here's a love letter from a Yankee general name Downing to that troublesome Miz Howard. If you wanna keep it, you gotta pay me. I need to look out for myself. If the Duncans keep trying to impress their friends, their help ain't gonna get enough to eat. I ain't stickin' around with a half-empty belly."

Frowning, Weems carried the letter deep into the alley and struck a match. He had to light three in succession before he could finish reading. Then he stuffed the wrinkled piece of paper in the envelope and handed it back to her. "All this proves is that Madeline Howard has a Yankee lover, and everyone already knows that. Or they will soon, thanks to the rumor mill in this town. I'll pay nothing for old news." Weems pulled on his waxed goatee. "But I am interested in Mrs. Howard. I believe her to be a jezebel, a courtesan of the worst kind. Unfortunately, she still has powerful friends who wear Confederate uniforms as well as Yankee blue."

"You're talkin' 'bout Colonel Haywood," hissed Kathleen. "That woman's playing him for a fool."

"I agree, but I suggest you not voice that opinion within Haywood's earshot. He'll make your life more miserable than it already is," Weems said curtly, staring down his hooked nose at her clothing.

Why is this pompous man speaking to me like this? "I'm tryin' to help you, Mr.

Weems, and help the Cause at the same time. I saw Miz Howard sneak outta the house to meet another soldier in the garden right under the Duncans' nose."

"A Union soldier, here in Richmond?"

"No, he was one of us. His last name was Lewis. Came to one of them fancy parties the Duncans love to throw."

Even in the thin light, Kathleen saw his face contort with rage. "Major Lewis, formerly of Colonel Haywood's staff?"

"Yeah, that was him. He was a friend of Major Penrod — Miss Eugenia's beau."

"That turncoat disappeared on his way to the battlefront, taking several documents about artillery and ordnance shipments from New Orleans with him. The home guard plans to hang that scoundrel if he ever sets foot in Virginia again."

"What do you suppose Miz Howard wanted with him?" Kathleen rocked back on her heels.

"What, indeed, but I have only your word they met in the garden. Mrs. Howard could say he was one of her many paramours."

"Her *what*?"

"Never mind, Miss O'Toole. Did anyone else in the family witness her with this known traitor to the Confederacy?"

"Not that I know of. I saw the butler waiting for her by the steps. I 'spose he knew who that jezebel was meetin'." Speaking such a word aloud sent a thrill of excitement up Kathleen's spine.

"Is the Duncan butler a slave?"

"Not no more. He's a free man."

Weems shook his head. "I would need more than the word of a black man and a maid who hasn't been in this country for long. Especially if I'm to pay greenbacks or gold coin."

Kathleen was ready to stomp inside the house. She'd had enough of his insults and looking down his crooked nose at her. But the mention of money kept her tongue in her head. "How much? A gal gotta take care of herself. This country ain't no different than my old one in that regard."

"I'll pay you fifty dollars, but you must catch Mrs. Howard in the act of snooping through Mr. Duncan's important papers with someone else to corroborate . . . back up your story. A witness who's not a slave or a former slave. Another maid at the very least. Or get your hands on her letters to Yankee officers. I would wager my eyeteeth she's saying plenty more than sweet words of love."

"Fifty dollars gold? I'm not risking a job for Confederate script. Some shops don't want to take it anymore, and it don't buy very much."

"Yes, gold, but come to my office at the newspaper with your information. I don't like walking these streets late at night. Too much riffraff lurk in the alleys. They would cut a man's throat for the coins in his pocket."

"I'll get you proof Miz Howard ain't the sweet little gal these folks think she be. You make sure you got my money. I gotta hankering to move down to Georgia. I hear Savannah treats Irish folk better than these Redcoats."

"Redcoats? What on earth are you talking about? The citizens of Richmond are loyal to the Confederate States of America."

"Everybody who comes to the house has kinfolk in England. That means they were once Redcoats."

Weems rolled his eyes. "Just get me what I need, Miss O'Toole. Then you can head to Savannah or even back to Dublin for all I care."

Kathleen hurried toward the house as the newspaperman disappeared into the shadows. She could almost feel the gold jingling in her pockets.

■ ■ ■ ■

SEVENTEEN

■ ■ ■ ■

Elliott stopped in front of the Duncan house forty minutes prior to the start of the Sunday morning service. In this weather, driving an open carriage didn't make for an enjoyable experience, but without a chauffeur at his disposal, he couldn't very well borrow a friend's box coach. At least Micah kept the walkway clear of ice and snow. After his second knock, the tall, imposing butler swept open the door.

Micah bowed and stepped to one side. "Good morning, Colonel. Are Mr. and Mrs. Duncan expecting you?"

"No, they are not. I'm here to take Mrs. Duncan's niece to church." Elliott strode through the door and removed his hat.

"Is Mrs. Howard expecting you, sir?"

Elliott frowned pointedly. "No, she is not, but you can inform Mrs. Howard that I'm not leaving until she speaks to me. I shall wait for her in the parlor."

With a respectful inclination of his head, Micah turned and vanished down the hall.

It was a breach of manners for him to enter the Duncan parlor uninvited and without his host's knowledge, but Elliott had waited long enough for the elusive Mrs. Howard to emerge from her shell. He paced the floor for ten minutes before his Northern friend and one-time savior entered the room.

She wore a scratchy-looking gray dress more suited to a New England schoolmarm than Richmond's latest seductress of innocent soldiers. The garment hung in a straight line to the floor without benefit of hoop or stiff crinolines. Her blond hair had been braided and coiled at the back of her head without a wisp or tendril to soften the effect.

"My word, dear woman, two days away from our civilized culture and your appearance has altered dramatically." Elliott bit the inside of his cheek to keep from grinning.

"You have me at a disadvantage, Colonel Haywood. I didn't send word that I would attend church today. How did you even know I had returned to town?" She walked past him to the windows, which overlooked the street.

"Come now. Everyone in this part of Richmond knows of your ill-fated trip to Culpeper, thanks to Kathleen. Your uncle should fire that viper and send her back to the wharves."

With her back to him, she stood motionless as a statue. "Then you must also have heard that I was rebuffed. Have you come to gloat over my misfortune?"

Elliott clucked his tongue. "Goodness, your opinion of me has fallen significantly in so short a time. What have I done to deserve your contempt?" He approached the windows and paused when he stood a foot away from her.

"Nothing. Forgive me, Colonel." She turned to face him, her expression registering surprise at his proximity. "I shouldn't take my bad temper or my shame out on you. I have no one to blame except myself."

"Maybe no one is to blame. You were following your heart to see where it would lead. When people are old and gray, rocking on their front porches, then they can behave with predictability."

"So you encourage women to make fools of themselves in such a way? And in the process lose the respect of family and friends alike?"

"You haven't lost my respect. I'm overjoyed you won't pine over this unworthy General Downing for the rest of the war. His loss is . . . the Duncans' gain."

"If not to gloat, then why have you come, Colonel? I don't wish to discuss this personal matter with you or anyone else."

"I thought my motives would be obvious." Elliott let a moment pass as she watched him curiously. "I'm here to take you to church, which begins in less than thirty minutes."

She crossed her arms. "You're not serious. I can't walk into St. Paul's."

"Why not? Surely you're not mad at God because you had a lapse of judgment. Look at the mercy He showed Eve after she disobeyed a direct order."

"Of course not, but I'm no longer received by the good people of Richmond. I was dismissed at the doors of two different homes, leaving Eugenia humiliated. What a poor way to return my family's kindness," she added, more to herself than him. "The highest echelons of Richmond society attend the Episcopal church. Perhaps by spring I could slip in the back of my aunt's Catholic church and sit in the balcony with the free blacks and slaves."

"I'm pleased you haven't lost your keen wit." Chuckling, Elliott placed his hand on her shoulder. "But church is the one place you can't be turned away. Even the unwashed beggars, the fallen dissipates, and the most loathsome criminals are welcome in the house of the Lord."

"Thank you for your accurate analogy, Colonel." A tiny dimple appeared in her cheek. "I will send word to you next Sunday should my courage rise to the necessary level."

"Nonsense. I thought you were a horse-woman back in Pennsylvania. Didn't you climb back on the beast after each time you were thrown? The longer we wait, the more terrifying the prospect grows in our minds. To stop the gossip, you must appear on my uniformed arm. That should quiet most of the wagging tongues."

"Or their gossip will include *you* in nasty speculations." She arched an eyebrow.

Elliott stiffened. "Do you think I care what those pretentious dowagers say about me?" He pulled out his pocket watch. "Go get your wrap and bonnet. Unfortunately, there's no time to change out of that morbid dress. I suppose one can say it's your sackcloth and ashes. Go, Mrs. Howard. If you want to remain in Richmond, you must hold your head up high and act as though you've done nothing wrong."

"Other than ride the westbound train to see my Yankee general at the army's winter camp?"

"We can discuss your ill-fated journey another time or not at all, however you prefer." Elliott snapped his watch case shut. "How brave are you now?"

She bit her lip and then suddenly seemed to make up her mind. She turned, went swiftly up the steps, and then reappeared a few minutes later with her cloak and an atrocious bonnet.

"A perfect choice of millinery with that particular dress. The younger ladies will *never* believe you're a siren among Confederate officers."

She tied the ribbons into a ridiculous bow. "And the elderly matrons?"

"They'll be pleased as punch you now dress like them."

Despite her burst of bravery, his companion said little on the way to St. Paul's. Devout parishioners were flowing into the cathedral from both directions. "Could we wait until they ring the bells and then find seats in the back?" She sounded like a little girl asking favors from a stern grandmother.

"Absolutely not. We're walking up the center aisle to the Haywood family pew. If we don't claim our rightful place, some ruffians will sneak in as squatters."

When several heads on the street swiveled in their direction, Madeline kneaded her hands like bread dough. "You're making a horrible mistake, Colonel, if you insist on remaining my friend."

"Step out of the carriage, Mrs. Howard, or I'll drag you by your arm. You saved my life once, and I must return the gesture. At least I'll save your social life during this dreary season."

She scowled but climbed down to the sidewalk. When he offered an elbow, she locked her fingers around his arm as though she were in danger of drowning in a swift river. He heard a deep intake of breath, which she appeared to hold all the way to the front of the church. As she expected, quite a few fans opened to hide a lady's snide remarks, while more than one elderly gentleman frowned. The younger men smiled with interest, as well as the unmarried girls. When they were seated, a widower in the adjacent pew turned to speak.

"See here, sir. What is the meaning of you bringing this Yankee-lover to the service? Don't you have a scrap of common sense?" His question could be heard by several others in the vicinity.

Elliott bent toward the man with a warm

smile. "Worry not, Mr. Chester. It's all been sorted out with Mrs. Howard. She had the courage to confront her former beau and tell him in person they had no future together. Clearing the way, I might add, for worthier candidates to vie for her attention."

Mr. Chester's face flushed hotly. "Just that simple, eh? You think she's suddenly changed sides in this conflict as well?"

"Goodness, no. She's still a Yankee. But like proper ladies everywhere, she doesn't hold political affiliation over a divine authority." With the preacher staring at him, Elliott cast a meaningful gaze toward the pulpit and altar.

Mr. Chester considered and nodded, mollified for the moment.

Elliott faced front and pulled the hymnal from the bracket. Flipping to the indicated page, he held the book where Mrs. Howard could also view it. "I hope you brought your vocal cords," he whispered. "This is one of my favorites. I expect you to sing."

She joined in meekly, but by the third stanza her volume had increased substantially. After the two-hour service, they walked out side by side, making eye contact with no one other than the priest on the front steps.

"Blessings on you, Mrs. Howard," greeted Father Daniel.

"And you also," she said.

Elliott champed her hand onto his arm for the stroll to the street. Other parishioners continued to stare, but the first step had been taken. "Well done. You survived the initial skirmish with barely a scratch from that dodgy Mr. Chester."

"Not all wounds are visible, sir," she said with a sigh as she climbed into the carriage.

"True enough." Elliott shook the reins over the horse's back. "Where to? Shall we take a ride out to Hollywood Cemetery?"

"Have you lost your mind? It's too cold for an open buggy in the first place, let alone for a leisurely Sunday excursion." Her wry grin contained a bit of the old spark.

"That's the friend I remember. Unafraid to accuse me of lunacy. Care to share your travel saga on the way home? I refuse to listen to gossip."

"It's hard to believe news on my fall from grace even reached you. You live blocks from the Duncans."

"I heard about it only because I share an office with other members of the home guard. They are aware of my high regard for John Duncan's niece."

She turned to face the passing houses.

"There isn't much to tell. I took the train to see an old beau in hopes of reconciliation. It was a foolish mistake. Soon after my arrival, we discovered we had little in common and no passion for each other. I'm not sure what I had hoped for. I had become tired of months of ignorance and needed to see him face-to-face."

Elliott said nothing for several moments. Then he said, "A clean slate?"

"What do you mean?"

"Have you have wiped your romantic slate clean?"

"I suppose that's one way to put it."

"Very well. Because you intend to remain in Richmond, I suggest you appear often in my company, even if you barely tolerate my bad humor and foul breath. Only a Southern gentleman of my standing will keep the angry mob from roasting you like a Salem witch."

Mrs. Howard hesitated before replying. "Your sense of humor is your best attribute, Colonel. And your breath — foul or sweet as honey — won't be an issue as long as we remain at a respectable distance."

"A bargain has been struck. Splendid!" He pulled the horse to a stop at the carriage block in front of the Duncans' home. "Here you are, safe and sound."

"Thank you, Colonel. I'm grateful for your thoughtful gesture today. You are a rare man of courage and integrity. A kind man." She stepped out and started up the walkway. "Please call for me next Sunday," she said over her shoulder.

Elliott watched until she disappeared inside the house. "If you would allow me, Madeline, I yearn to be much more than a *kind man.*" He'd spoken the words aloud with only the sharp February wind for an audience.

March 1864

"My dear, may I speak with you?"

Madeline, startled from her woolgathering, poked her finger with her needle. "Yes, please come in, Aunt." She rose stiffly to her feet.

Aunt Clarisa bustled into the her niece's room and threw back every curtain and drapery. "I don't know why you insist on sewing and reading up here alone. The light and heat are so much better in the parlor." She poked ineffectively at the charred coals in the fireplace grate.

"Eugenia needs time to discuss things with her mother without outsiders constantly interfering."

Aunt Clarisa dropped the poker into the

387

bucket. "You're not an outsider, my dear. Genie loves you and misses your company. At meals you barely utter a word."

"I love her too, which is why I don't want to impede her social season."

"Don't be ridiculous. Justine Emerson was horrified to see you leaving that day. She insists it was a horrible misunderstanding by their butler."

"We both know that's not the case."

"That may be true, but most of the horrible gossip has died down, partly due to Colonel Haywood's threat to cut out the tongue of any man who repeats slander against you."

"He has become my protector and avenger, yet I have no need of such services. I'm quite content to remain here on my window seat, sewing for soldiers and reading from Uncle John's library of books."

"Cloistered like a nun? You're not Roman Catholic, dear niece. This is totally inappropriate for an Episcopalian." Aunt Clarisa winked over her shoulder as she opened the doors to the armoire.

"Solitude provides opportunity for contemplation of one's errors."

"My, you have been reading your uncle's tomes instead of your cousin's yellow-back novels. But I would say your self-flagellation has been sufficient. John received an invitation to a dance that General and Mrs. Rhodes are throwing, and you are included. So it's time to venture out beyond church on Sundays."

"He didn't," said Madeline in disbelief.

"He did. Your name — Mrs. M. Howard — is printed on the outer envelope beneath ours." Clarisa pulled out a dark green gown from the wardrobe, along with matching dancing slippers.

"Did Uncle John approach General Rhodes about my inclusion? He has barely spoken a dozen sentences to me since my disastrous trip. Why would he do this?"

Clarisa laid the garments across the bed. "He was rather piqued with you — I won't lie. Running to the arms of some Yankee when the utterly perfect Colonel Haywood would camp in our back garden if we allowed it? But your uncle decided your penance has been sufficient. Coercing an invite was his idea."

"Poor Mrs. Rhodes, betwixt and between two mighty forces — the ladies of society and her husband." Madeline laughed despite herself.

"I was told to not take no for an answer. You've been holed up more than a month. You must be ready to talk to people other than your family." She pointed at the silk gown on the bed. "Wear the green so you won't look so pale. You've never worn it once."

Madeline forced a smile for her aunt. "I am facing a worthier opponent than Mrs. Rhodes."

"Yes, you are. Don't tarry in your bath because I don't wish to be late to the final ball of the season." Her aunt waltzed from the room as though the dancing had already begun.

The palatial home of General and Mrs. Rhodes stood at the edge of town. Surrounded by tall boxwood hedges and manicured gardens, the residence commanded an impressive view of the James River. Despite her beautiful gown and cascade of golden curls fixed by Eugenia, Madeline moved through the convivial guests like a specter on All Hallows Eve. Heads turned, but not in her direction. Madeline refused to cling to her aunt or cousin because both women had spent as monastic a winter as she. At least Eugenia had the devoted Major Penrod. The two of them were determined to dance every number together.

Madeline stood at the windows overlooking steep cliffs and a rocky riverbed. Lush green pastures in the distance promised an early spring. As she passed each small cluster of guests, conversation intensified. Female listeners became fascinated with their partner to avoid eye contact with the local pariah. Madeline was ignored more effectively than the liveried servants collecting discarded punch cups.

Or perhaps it was just her imagination.

Wherever the truth lay, Madeline wasn't enjoying the evening. On her way to the refreshment table, Justine Emerson pulled her partner from the circle of dancers.

"Ah, Mrs. Howard," she said. "So nice to see you this evening. Be sure to try some of the shrimp paste. I gave Mrs. Rhodes the recipe our new cook brought from New Orleans. It is truly divine." After a sugary smile, Miss Emerson whirled back into the throng in the arms of her admirer.

A friend . . . at long last. Madeline felt temporarily back on the schoolyard when a girl said her shoes smelled like horse manure. But her relief was short lived. As she placed a few sweets on her dessert plate, she spotted the tray of cookies she had baked for the occasion. Someone had pushed them to the back of the table. Her cookies — the same ones the auxiliary ladies adored at sewing. December seemed like a lifetime ago. Madeline practically choked on a dry toast point she had just taken a bite of. She hurried through the French doors to the verandah, not slowing down until far from the revelers. She was about to dump her plate of snacks into the shrubbery when a familiar voice called out.

"Stop! Don't you dare squander food when shortages abound throughout the city."

Embarrassed, Madeline watched Colonel Haywood stride toward her. "Forgive me, sir, but I have lost my appetite, and I didn't think anyone would eat food touched by my fingers." She set the plate on the balustrade.

"I'm not just anyone." He peered at her selections and then popped a pecan tartlet into his mouth. "Superb," he declared around the mouthful. "Doesn't taste the least bit tainted."

Even though she realized he was jesting, she burst into tears — the exact same reaction as when told her shoes smelled.

The colonel set the plate on the railing and put his arm around her shoulders. "Here, here, Mrs. Howard. Tell me who made you cry. I shall cut out their tongue with my saber — whether man or fair damsel."

Covering her face with her hands, Madeline leaned into his tender embrace. "No one *said* anything, but no one will eat the cookies I baked from my . . . my mother's recipe." She sobbed against his shoulder, helpless to stop.

"Is that all? The dowagers didn't point fingers and shout, 'Fallen woman. Lock her in the town pillory so we might pelt her with those dastardly cookies'?"

Madeline slapped her palms against his chest and pushed him away. "Oh, Colonel, you mock my humiliation." She struggled not to laugh but failed with the mental picture of old-fashioned stocks on Church Hill.

"I mock only their juvenile behavior, not your pain, so dry your tears." He handed her a handkerchief. "I feared your reentry into society would be much worse."

"Did you?" Regaining her composure, she dabbed at her eyes.

"Truly, I've been watching you when not smoothing the feathers of my fellow officers. I believe you're well on your way back to those insufferable teas with the matriarchs each afternoon." He resumed devouring the snacks.

Madeline sucked in a breath. "Suddenly, their approval sounds less appealing." She took a cookie from the plate.

"Every rose has its thorns." He popped

the last sweet into his mouth. "I believe you owe me a token of your gratitude — a kiss is in order." He tapped the side of his face with a finger. "On my cheek if it's all you can stomach."

"Oh, I truly am grateful." Madeline stretched up to kiss his clean-shaven face.

"You need to take one last step to be trusted and respected again." He extended his elbow and gestured with his head toward the house.

"What would that be?" Her forehead furrowed suspiciously.

"General Rhodes hired a photographer for the evening. A displaced New Yorker has set up his tripod and equipment in the library. He wants to capture images of every happy couple in attendance tonight."

"A daguerreotype with you?"

"No, these are the newfangled tintypes, no longer produced on a piece of glass. Quite the rage up north, I understand."

A frisson of panic spiked up her spine. On the one hand, she needed to continue her subterfuge if she wished to be useful, but what if James saw her on the arm of another man? He might judge her faithless and debase. "As long as you understand we are not courting, sir. I wish to make that clear to you."

"Indeed, you have many, many times. The photographer creates two plates, one for you and one for me. It will be nothing more than a reminder of a lovely evening, despite the unfortunate cookie incident. What say you, Mrs. Howard? If you stand beside me, no one will ever gossip about you again."

She swallowed hard. "I doubt that, Colonel, but very well. Let's get in line to be captured forever on a metal plate."

Yet with each step across the Rhodes' wide verandah, the notion she was making a terrible mistake took root and began to grow.

■ ■ ■ ■

EIGHTEEN

■ ■ ■ ■

Frankly, Clarisa didn't know what else to do. With mounting nervous energy, she paced the floor for more than an hour — from the back conservatory, down the portrait-lined hallway, into the parlor, and out the door to the terrace. She repeated the circuit until her legs ached from exertion and the dampness in the spring air. She perched on the settee until the ticking of the clock threatened to drive her mad. Would John never get home from the war department? Why must the president keep his staff late every night this week? There had been no engagements since November, and none could possibly be planned until the infernal rain stopped.

"Tea, Miz Duncan?" Kathleen asked from the doorway.

"No, thank you. You already asked me that twice in the last hour." Clarisa fought to control her temper.

"Thought maybe you changed your mind." The maid stood with a tray of china cups and a steaming teapot.

"Put it there for Miss Eugenia. She should return soon from her calls." Clarisa pointed at the marble-topped table.

Kathleen set the tray down with a loud clatter. Before Clarisa could scold the girl, she heard the distinctive sound of hooves on cobblestones beyond the window. "Oh, thank goodness!" She ran to the front door, cutting off the maid in midstride. "I'll get the door for Mr. Duncan. You see if Esther needs help with dinner."

With her usual sour expression, the maid remained rooted in place as though unsure how to react to such a breech in normal behavior.

"Go, Kathleen. I'm capable of opening a front door, and I'm anxious to speak to my husband alone."

"Yes, ma'am." Kathleen retreated down the hall with her signature sluggishness.

Clarisa opened the door the moment she heard John's boots on the steps. "Oh, my love, I've never been so happy to see you." She practically swooned into his arms.

Her husband's haggard face brightened. "You haven't greeted me with such enthusiasm in years. To what do I owe my good fortune?" After a brief embrace, he removed his gloves and hat and handed them to her.

Clarisa tossed them onto a chair. "Let's leave your things for Micah to put away later. It's urgent that we speak before Eugenia and Madeline return home."

"What is it, Clarisa?" He added his overcoat to the heap and followed her into the parlor, his smile fading.

"It is not good news, I assure you." Clarisa forced herself to take several deep breaths before reaching for the *Richmond Times Dispatch* from the mantel. She'd read and refolded the newspaper not less than six times. "That horrible Jonas Weems has printed an editorial in the paper. That boorish man had the audacity to return after receiving no polite welcome during his first visit." She held out the paper with shaking fingers.

But instead of taking it, John walked to the sideboard. "Jonas Weems, here in our home without my knowledge? Why wasn't I informed?" He poured two snifters of brandy and drank the first with barely a grimace.

"You have so much on your mind outfitting the troops for the spring campaign. I didn't want to burden you with such nonsense."

"But considering your present state of mind, his nonsense appears to have enormous importance." He handed her the other glass. "Drink, Clarisa, and then tell me about Weems's initial call."

She took a tiny sip, letting the burning liquid trickle down her throat. "He came around a week ago asking to speak to Madeline. When I said that she wasn't in, he seemed to not believe me. He said he wants answers from her, and that the Confederacy would be better served if we didn't coddle and protect a known Yankee-lover." Clarisa took another swallow of brandy. "I told him I would coddle whomever I chose, and that the Confederacy would be better served if he reported military matters instead of idle gossip."

"Good show, my dear." John refilled his glass from the decanter.

Clarisa sighed wearily. "The insufferable man returned yesterday morning when Madeline and Eugenia were at the market with Esther. I tried explaining again that Madeline wasn't home, but the oaf stepped inside the foyer anyway." She stamped her foot with sheer indignation.

"I'll speak to the publisher of the *Times*. Such effrontery will not be tolerated in my home." John sipped his drink without taking his eyes off her.

"He said he wished to talk to *me*. I neither showed him into the parlor nor offered refreshment. Because he was acting impolitely, I returned the behavior." She set down the glass and smoothed her palms down her skirt. "He asked me if it was true that Madeline had visited Union Army camps. Because it was common knowledge that she went to Culpeper to end a relationship, I couldn't deny it. Then he asked if she had visited Chimborazo Hospital and spoke to wounded Yankees." Clarisa picked up the glass for another sip, coughing from the fiery liquid.

"What did you tell him, my dear?" John crossed the room in a few strides.

"I explained that she had accompanied our priest during his rounds and read Scripture to men from both armies. It was Christmas, and many patients wouldn't live to see the New Year. Then Weems asked if I knew Madeline had been caught attempting to speak to Yankee officers at Libby Prison, that she had been searched and escorted off the grounds with the order not to return." Clarisa pressed a fist to her bosom, willing herself not to cry. "I knew Madeline's visit with our priest had distressed her, so I never pressed for details. She never went back to the hospital or to Libby."

"You should have demanded that he leave the house at once." John took her by the forearms. "Please try to calm yourself. It's over, and I'll see to it he never returns."

"But that's not all," she cried, her composure slipping. "Today in the newspaper he printed a . . . a scathing editorial on how pillars of society have chosen to harbor Yankee sympathizers in our midst. And that no matter how well-meaning their initial intentions, their complacency threatens the safety of everyone in Richmond. Read it for yourself." Clarisa thrust the paper toward her husband.

With his face flushing hotly, John unfolded the paper and quickly scanned the contents. He huffed out a breath with Weems's allegations and read, "Who knows what information finds its way to Secretary Seddon's ears due to the inexhaustible Southern hospitality of some scions of society?" John stopped for a moment, gripping the paper so tightly his knuckles were white. Then he continued. "A certain *guest* in our city has taken advantage of her hosts' benevolence and repaid their kindness by entertaining gentleman callers — known traitors to the Confederacy — in the middle of the night. One former major has left the South and is purportedly on his way to Canada to wreak his havoc beyond the reach of our dedicated men."

He stopped reading and threw the paper onto the fire, where it quickly turned to smoke and ash. "Lies and innuendos. I'll speak to President Davis about this Jonas Weems." He made an effort to be calm and then took his wife's hands. "But in the meantime, do not distress yourself, my love. Say nothing of this to Eugenia or Madeline. Wartime creates thugs who willingly sacrifice a lady's reputation to sell newspapers or further their own agendas. If that man comes here again, I'll order him arrested as a trespasser. It's over, so don't give this trash another thought."

Clarisa allowed herself to be folded in his embrace, accepting his tender placation willingly. Yet deep in her gut, she knew Jonas Weems was far from finished wreaking havoc on the Duncan household.

April 1864

James stood in the doorway of this field office, staring at a lush but soggy world. The breeze carried the sweet smell of apple and pear blossoms along with dogwood, honeysuckle, and forsythia.

Forsythia — the name of the Richmond

street where his heart resided. It had been two months since he'd heard a word from Madeline. Each time he handed a letter to his chief of staff, Major Henry assured him it would be mailed at a post office inside Confederate lines. And yet he had no idea if any found their way to her. The sooner they defeated the Rebels, the sooner the Republic could be united again and they could pick up the pieces of their lives. How he yearned for a future with her. Once peace was restored, he would let nothing stand in his way.

At least spring had brought welcome change. Ulysses S. Grant, the newly appointed commander of all Union forces, planned to initiate an offensive against Robert E. Lee in Virginia. Utilizing Meade from the Fredericksburg area and Ben Butler from south of the James River, Grant set his sights on Richmond as their ultimate objective. William T. Sherman, commander of the western troops, would take on Joe Johnston in Georgia. President Lincoln canceled future prisoner exchanges, depriving the Confederacy of desperately needed officers. Grant dispatched cavalry to destroy rail lines in West Virginia, which would cut off a significant source of food and munitions from the Gulf of Mexico. Only a concerted effort would bring the lumbering beast to its knees.

James watched his adjutant make his way through the regiments as the sergeants led morning drills — endless activity was needed to keep soldiers from falling into mental and physical decay.

"General Downing, sir. I have dispatches from the war department in Washington." Snapping a salute, Major Henry handed him a sheaf of rolled papers.

"At ease, Major. Let's take a look at these inside." James went to his desk and slouched into a wooden chair as he thumbed through inspection reports, ordnance requisitions, and quartermaster accounts.

"I'll be glad to strike this loathsome camp and never see this part of the world again." Major Henry frowned at the rolling hills beyond their city of huts and dirty white tents.

"You're tired of Virginia?" James asked, not looking up.

"Down to the soles of my boots, sir. I can't wait to return to Philadelphia, where people carry on intelligent conversation without interjecting colloquial nonsense. And why do Southerners insist on adding extra syllables to words?"

James had no answer as he searched the

stack of correspondence from last night's train. "Is this everything from the Culpeper post office?"

"Yes, sir. The train tracks from Lynchburg to Charlottesville are still torn up, so there's no mail from the west."

"General Sherman has his work cut out now that Sam Grant has taken over for Meade." James sipped the dregs of his cold coffee, the Army of the Tennessee not foremost on his mind.

"If we would have dogged Lee out of Pennsylvania, we could have ended this war then and there. His whipped army had their throat laid bare, poised for slaughter. But instead we let them limp back to Virginia. Now those Rebs have had nine months to lick their wounds." The major spat into the spittoon by the door.

When did my aide take up the enlisted man's habit of chewing navy? James glared at his adjutant. It was one thing for soldiers to utilize every opportunity to prevail on the battlefield, but it was quite another to hear one of his officers speaking without a shred of compassion. "Some sentiments are best left unspoken, Major, lest the victorious army be branded as a band of ruthless dissipates. Besides, Lincoln didn't appoint General Grant commander because he wished more of the same. If it be God's will, this will be the final spring of this war."

"We're ready, sir. The men are itchin' for a fight. They've cleaned their muskets so many times they could do it in their sleep."

"Spirits are high?"

"I would say so, sir."

"Good to hear. See that rations are increased. I won't have them starting the campaign with empty bellies."

The major looked surprised. "At the risk of depleting our storehouses? We have no idea when more food can be shipped from Ohio or from Kentucky and points west."

"The almanac predicts this will be a good year for crops. Let's trust in Providence and not let our flour and cornmeal molder. Has the packet of mail been distributed to the men?" James tried his best to sound disinterested.

"It will be later. The company sergeants hand it out after they finish morning drills. We don't need Billy Yank wondering whether Betsy Lou still pines for him in Peoria." The adjutant snorted with derision. "These recruits don't need any more distractions."

Unfortunately, the corps' general had his own distraction on his mind. "Was there any personal correspondence in the mailbag for me?" Helpless to stop himself from asking, James summoned his most imperious expression.

"There was not, sir. There haven't been letters for you for several weeks." Major Henry made little effort to hide his contempt.

"Mail delivery in this part of the Virginia is less than reliable. Who's to say which singular piece will find its way to the intended recipient?" James kicked a log that rolled onto the hearth back into the fire.

"May I speak for a moment as your friend, sir, instead of an officer under your command?"

James ground his teeth but nodded permission.

"Could Mrs. Howard have had a change of heart since her visit in February? Indeed, she stayed less than twenty-four hours in Culpeper. What woman could so easily be torn from the arms of the man she loved? Her silence might be a gentle way of revealing the truth about her affection."

"There could be a dozen reasons for a lack of correspondence or the brevity of her visit. Only a madwoman would feel at ease in the midst of a war. Who knows what dreadful sights she encountered along the way?"

"You may need to consider another possibility — one less complimentary to the elusive Mrs. Howard." Wisely, the major hesitated before he continued.

"Go on, but I assure you this will be the last time we will discuss this particular topic."

The major lifted his chin. "Perhaps Mrs. Howard is playing you for a fool, sir. I have eyes and ears in Richmond. It's my job as your chief of staff. Apparently, she has been seen on the arm of Colonel Elliott Haywood of Jefferson Davis's home guard. Rumor has it that they are a courting couple."

Although unspoken, the words *he and not you* resonated in the room louder than a cannon shot. "I prefer to deal with truth and not speculation, Major. There could be any number of reasons why she'd been with Haywood, so don't spread idle gossip. And if you ever demean Mrs. Howard in such a fashion again, I will have you brought up on charges of insubordination."

Major Henry straightened to attention. "Begging your pardon, sir!"

"There is a list of infractions in these inspection reports. I suggest you see to their correction immediately." James pulled a paper from the stack and thrust it toward his aide.

"At your service, sir." The major took the

list and marched from headquarters without bothering to salute.

But James was so eager to be rid of the noxious man he let the incident of disrespect pass without correction.

Madeline stretched and tossed her book on the chaise. She was so weary of reading and sewing and knitting socks that she could scream. Listlessly, she rubbed the small of her back and decided upon a stroll in the garden. Longer, warmer days had filled the air with the scent of gardenia and magnolia, and the overhead arbors were lush with wisteria. Apple, pear, and cherry trees blossomed gloriously, promising an abundant harvest of fruit this summer. But despite the beauty of spring in Virginia, Madeline couldn't be more miserable. It had been weeks since her return to Richmond, and what had she accomplished? The entire point of leaving James was to be of use to his cause . . . her cause. Yet she'd done nothing except drink tea, read sonnets, and wear out the soles of her slippers. Despite the Duncans' social standing and Colonel Haywood's subterfuge, her opportunities to garner military information had been sorely curtailed. There were no more parties or balls where ladies might converse with

Confederate officers. Even though every indication pointed to a renewed Rebel initiative, she was privy to none of it. Uncle John didn't discuss even the most innocuous of military matters within her presence.

Some residue of the rumors regarding her motives obviously remained with her uncle. Who could blame him? And why did Colonel Haywood wish to convince people they were a courting couple? She'd made her feelings known to him on several occasions. The minds of men would forevermore remain a mystery to her.

"Hello, Esther," she said. "Can I help you with that?" Madeline stood above the cook, who was up to her elbows in rich, dark earth.

"Goodness, Miz Howard, you scared the wits out of me." Esther peered up only long enough to scowl. "I'm getting these seeds in early. Soil's warm enough, and we need potatoes and carrots we don't have to pay for. The prices they're charging at the market should make those thieves red faced with shame." She chopped at a clod of clay with the trowel as though it were one of those market vendors.

"I take it Mrs. Duncan decided to replace these flower beds with vegetables too," Madeline said mildly as she tightened the bonnet ribbons beneath her chin.

"Yes, ma'am. First the rose garden, now the herb patch and cutting beds. Miz Duncan said a body can't eat gladiolas and peonies, plus folks can live without chives and parsley." Esther carefully pulled a rather long worm from the loam and tossed it into a coffee can.

"Why don't I dig up the row from the other end?" asked Madeline. "Then we could meet in the middle."

"Kneel down in the dirt in your pretty dress?" Esther's expression questioned her sanity. "No, Miz Howard. If you want to help, read aloud from that book of yours. I like hearing 'bout that little Copperfield boy."

"I could change my clothes. Back home I planted a big garden and did all the hoeing and weeding myself." She picked up a spade.

The cook pushed herself to her feet. "This ain't Pennsylvania. What if the neighbors saw you? You barely got yourself invited back to the sewing parties. Miz Duncan would have my hide." Esther yanked the spade from Madeline's grasp. "Why didn't you go with Miss Eugenia?"

"Because she accompanied Father Michael to a place I have been asked not to return to." Though the words were painful, Madeline forced a smile.

The news didn't sit well with Esther. "That don't sound right."

"Aunt Clarisa prefers I not go near Libby Prison, or Chimborazo Hospital, or Uncle John's office, or even the post office. I feel like a prisoner in Richmond." Madeline regretted the words as soon as she spoke. "Not that I'm ungrateful for having a home, but I do get bored. That's why I hope you'll let me help with chores." She smiled sweetly at the older woman.

Esther shook her head in defeat and said, "Just this one time you can peel those potatoes in the kitchen sink, but don't let nobody see you, 'specially not that Kathleen. She'll make trouble for me. I want to get these seeds planted and this can full of worms and slugs. Tomorrow Micah's going to the docks and tradin' bait for fish, if there's any fish to be had."

Madeline felt a thrill of excitement. "May I go with him to the market? It's been so long since I've been there."

"Why you askin' me permission? There's nothing down there you can afford, Miz Howard. Best to steer clear of those stalls. Plenty of folks up to no-good near those docks." Esther thrust her spade into a new section.

"We might have enough money for some fruit or fresh vegetables. I've been known to bargain with the best of them."

Esther shrugged. "Ain't up to me. If it's all right with Miz Duncan, Micah won't mind the company."

"Thank you, Esther. I'll check with my aunt this evening. Right now, I'll go tackle those potatoes." Turning on her heel, Madeline ran toward the house. *A trip to the docks?* It had been ages since she and Eugenia had combed the aisles on market day. Esther was right about everything becoming expensive. Even the deep pockets of the Duncans had their limits. And her small cache of money had been exhausted long ago. But Madeline wasn't interested in pralines or other sweets. With a trip to the river tomorrow, this might be her best chance to help the Union Army.

She checked to see who might have come home while she was in the garden and then peeled the potatoes quickly. Aunt Clarisa was still on her afternoon calls. Her destinations today wouldn't welcome Madeline, so she had happily stayed home. Kathleen was at the home of the neighborhood laundress, and Uncle John was at the Confederate offices.

Mustering her courage, Madeline crept into her uncle's private domain and closed the door behind her. After ten minutes of snooping, the room revealed nothing helpful to the Army of the Potomac. Log books of past requisitions for supplies, munitions, and armaments would be of little use to present campaigns. With the blockade growing more effective each week, little of what was ordered abroad would arrive at Richmond's harbors. Lists of recently brevetted officers wouldn't make much difference unless they also indicated where they would be transferred. Just as she backed away from the organized clutter, her focus landed on something curious. A heavy parchment had been mostly hidden by the desk blotter, yet bold lines and artistic embellishments on one corner caught her eye.

Carefully, Madeline extracted a hand-drawn map of the city of Richmond, detailing the banks of the James River as it snaked its way from the bluffs of Hollywood to Libby Hill down to the Rockets Landing and beyond. Her fingertips ran lightly over the hallowed ground of the cemetery, a mournful yet beautiful place. Memories of her picnic with Colonel Haywood soon after her arrival returned, bringing a fresh wave of shame and regret. As fond as she was of the colonel, his persistent attentions made her feel guilty whenever she thought of James.

Could the Union commanders make use of such a map? Each approach to the city was marked, every shallow spot in the river notated. Because the James River was tidal, both low water and high water levels had been indicated, along with bridge and roadway accesses. If nothing else, they would know how to impede couriers between the Confederate war department and Rebel officers in the field. Madeline folded the parchment where it had been creased and slipped it under her voluminous skirt. It only took a moment to secure it beneath one of her lacy garters. She would chance a baggy stocking to remove the document from Uncle John's study without being seen. Once in the privacy of her room, she copied over the map onto two sheets of foolscap. Although possessed of none of the creator's artistry, Madeline duplicated the details to the best of her ability.

Throughout dinner, followed by an interminable evening by the fire with the ladies, Madeline waited for her larceny to be discovered, but Uncle John left the house

418

immediately after supper and hadn't returned by the time the ladies retired to bed. She had no recourse but to hide her copy of the map until the morrow, when she hoped she could transfer it into the hands of Captain George of the *Bonnie Bess.*

Nightmares plagued her sleep — guards from Libby Prison appeared at the door to demand her arrest; specters of dead soldiers from the blood-soaked fields of Gettysburg followed her as she attempted to flee pursuers. Madeline awoke with a start, damp with perspiration despite the coolness of the night. She would find no more rest that night, and had little appetite for the grits and cheese Esther set on the table at breakfast.

"Madeline, do plan to accompany us during our calls. We'll be spending the afternoon at the Emersons, and you know Justine is quite fond of you." Aunt Clarisa could utter little white lies without batting an eyelash.

"Thank you, ma'am. Perhaps the next time I shall." Madeline smiled graciously at her aunt. "But I already promised Esther I would go with Micah to the market."

"Whatever for? The family coffers are depleted for the week. We must make do with our pantry and whatever's left in the cellar until your uncle receives his next pay envelope." Clarisa daintily sipped her weak chicory coffee.

"Yes, ma'am, but Micah has fishing bait to trade. I'm an accomplished barterer. It's a talent taught by all Pennsylvania mothers. Some merchants may try to take advantage of a former slave, so I thought I could go along to assist the transactions."

Aunt Clarisa blinked her eyes, speechless. "Bartering? My sister taught you that?"

"Yes, ma'am."

"I'm not sure if your uncle would approve. Perhaps next week." Clarisa reached for a piece of toast, believing the conversation was at an end.

"But Esther has a full can of worms and slugs today. They'll die by next week."

Her aunt pulled a face in annoyance, but then said, "All right, Madeline. Go if you insist, but let's not discuss the particulars of your bartering when you return."

"I promise I won't." Madeline drained her cup and rose from the table, trying not to appear overly eager. *What woman in her right mind would find such an errand exciting?*

"You're leaving already?" Aunt Clarisa's forehead furrowed.

"Soon, yes. The early bird catches the —" Madeline shook her head. "Excuse me. I

420

almost broke my promise already." Brushing a kiss across her aunt's cheek, she dashed upstairs.

From her window she saw Micah talking with Esther near the well pump. The horse, already harnessed to the open carriage, stomped his hooves in the dirt impatiently. Madeline donned her plainest bonnet so as to attract the least amount of attention, wrapped a shawl around her shoulders to counter the cool breeze, and rummaged in the bottom of her trunk. Hidden inside her old boots, now appropriate solely for walking in the garden, she pulled out her reproduction of the James River landings and crossings. She'd already returned the original while Uncle John snored loudly and the rest of the family slumbered.

Suddenly, a frisson of something amiss chilled her blood. Moving next to her drawer of lacy camisoles and delicate chemises, her fingers sought her most prized possessions — her grandmother's cameo broach and a framed daguerreotype taken on her wedding day to Tobias so many years ago. They were there, and every one of her silk dainties seemed to be in place, yet with growing trepidation Madeline realized exactly what was not — the tintype taken at General Rhodes' ball last month. She hadn't particularly cared for the likeness and thus hadn't selected a better hiding place. The photographer's demand that she smile had left an artificial expression on her face.

Colonel Haywood declared the souvenir a masterpiece of ingenuity and had both copies framed, delivering hers within the week. With no desire to be reminded of her ruse with the kindhearted colonel, she'd tucked the tintype away and not thought of it again . . . until its absence dulled her earlier exuberance. First James's letter and now this trinket created by a Northern entrepreneur trying to earn a dollar? She hadn't dropped it in the garden or accidentally sent it to the laundress in the pocket of a dress. Someone in this household was obviously her enemy, and Madeline had a fairly good idea who that person might be. Thank goodness her map and codebook were still safe.

At the fishing docks, Micah sold his bait for a fair price. After she had helped secure the best deal, Madeline took a few minutes to slip down to the berth of the *Bonnie Bess* while Micah studied the smoked meats and fresh fruit. Captain George was only too happy to carry her document downriver to the fort, where it could transfer into appropriate hands. He insisted she take several pounds of bass he had caught that morning. With fish for supper for several days, Micah bought root vegetables and a bag of oranges with his proceeds.

She should have been overjoyed at their good fortune, yet a dull sense of dread settled in Madeline's gut, refusing to budge. Somehow the missing tintype would lead to her undoing. She just knew it.

■ ■ ■ ■

NINETEEN

■ ■ ■ ■

Colonel Haywood knocked on the door at the Duncan residence far too early in the morning to expect to be received. However, Micah barely lifted one bushy white eyebrow when he opened the door.

"Good morning, sir." The butler bowed, welcoming the colonel in, and reached for his hat. "Is Mrs. Howard expecting you? I'm afraid Mr. Duncan has already left for the office. He chose to walk on such a lovely day."

"No one is expecting me, but I happened upon a stunning bouquet and thought immediately of Mrs. Duncan. Perhaps you can see if she'll receive me at this hour." From behind his back, Elliott produced a large bunch of flowers he'd cut from a neighborhood garden in the middle of the night. He was lucky he hadn't received a backside full of buckshot for his efforts.

"Did you say Mrs. Duncan, sir, and not

Mrs. Howard?"

"You heard correctly, my good man."

"I'll see if madam is still breakfasting, sir." Chuckling, Micah marched off with military erectness.

Elliott leaned against the center hall pillar, praying his idea would work. Another minute later, Mrs. Duncan strolled from the dining room with the grace of a queen.

"Colonel Haywood, Micah said you came bearing irises and lilies and asked for me, not my niece." Her smile erased a dozen years from her face.

"It is the truth, madam." Bowing, he held out his bribe. "I offer these in hopes you'll invite me in to breakfast."

"They are lovely, thank you." Mrs. Duncan accepted the armful and handed them to the maid, who was lurking behind a potted plant. "Put these in water, Kathleen. Then place the vase on the sideboard in the dining room." To him she said, "Of course, you may join Eugenia and me. Had I known your intentions, I would have requested something heartier than grits with strawberries and melon from Florida. Madeline and Micah performed some kind of magic yesterday and managed to acquire fruit and a basket of fish in exchange for a can of night crawlers."

Elliott followed her into the lavish room. "Are you referring to *worms,* madam?"

"I am, but I'm so pleased to taste fresh berries again that I didn't ask too many questions. Please be seated, sir."

"Colonel Haywood, what a pleasure. Is Major Penrod with you?" Eugenia asked, grinning from ear to ear.

"I'm afraid not, Miss Duncan. I'm on my way to Fredericksburg on errands, but I allowed myself a short wayside stop."

She made a noble effort to hide her disappointment. "Joseph has been keeping such long hours. I barely see the man anymore. I can't wait for this dreadful war to be over. I know he wants to propose, but won't until our victory is in sight."

"If it's the major's desire for his intentions to remain private, then I suggest you not speak on the matter," Mrs. Duncan said softly to her daughter.

"My lips are sealed, ladies. And I agree with you, Miss Duncan. I long for a cessation of hostilities for more reasons than I can count." Elliott leaned back as Kathleen set a plate before him. Despite the absence of any type of meat, the food looked delicious.

"Coffee, Colonel?" Mrs. Duncan asked.

"I would love a cup." Elliott gazed around

the room as though counting the occupants. "I see Mrs. Howard has not come downstairs. I hope she hasn't fallen ill."

"I had a feeling there was method to your madness, Colonel." Laughing from deep in her belly, Mrs. Duncan passed him the coffee carafe. "Madeline sent word with Kathleen that she hadn't slept well and thus would skip our morning meal. However, I feel her presence is an absolute necessity. She has remained cloistered in her room long enough, always reading or sewing."

"Attending church with me has been her sole outings since the ball?"

"Yes, other than shopping with our butler yesterday. Eugenia, please ask Madeline to join us. Tell her I request her appearance and mention nothing about our guest."

The young woman sprang from her chair. "Mama, it would be my pleasure."

Elliott nodded his gratitude. "I would have thought negative sentiments would have ended by now, but no matter. I have news that should lift her spirits." He patted the pocket of his frock coat.

"Splendid. And do encourage her to eat. I fear she worries about the servants' meals unnecessarily. I assure you, I make sure Micah and Esther never go hungry."

Elliott noticed an omission of Kathleen's

name as one of Mrs. Duncan's concerns. During the time it took Mrs. Howard to arrive, he finished his plate of grits even though he ate at a snail's pace.

When she walked into the dining room in a frumpy frock and her hair plaited down her back, her expression was incredulous. "Colonel Haywood, what are you doing here on a Thursday?" Her mouth dropped wide enough to reveal a lower row of perfect teeth.

"I'm well aware of the day, madam. Mrs. Duncan graciously invited me to breakfast before my trip south."

The niece and aunt exchanged a speaking glance. "How thoughtful of her. Welcome," she added, as an afterthought.

"Sit and eat, Madeline. I'm already finished, and I require Eugenia's opinion in the garden on a botanical matter."

The young woman peered up from her grits and mashed berries. "Of course, Mama. I'll finish this on the terrace." She carried her bowl outdoors through the double doors, something cultured people seldom did.

Mrs. Howard filled her cup with coffee. "You have apparently cleared the room, Colonel. I trust that was your objective."

"It was, because I preferred privacy while

showing you this." He extracted a folded newspaper from his coat and passed it across the table. "Your aunt probably hasn't seen the *Richmond Times Dispatch* yet. I wished you to be made aware first." He watched her visibly blanch at the mention of the newspaper's name.

"Is it another vindictive editorial from that loathsome reporter?" Her fingers trembled as she brought her cup to her lips.

"No. I will demand that man choose his second if he ever prints such scandalous editorials again. This article is on the newly resurrected society pages of the *Times*."

"Society news? How can people be concerned with debutant parties and recent betrothals in the midst of a war?" She clucked her tongue. "The roster of names of those succumbing to illness in the hospital is still a page long. Celebrations seem tasteless."

"I agree with you, Mrs. Howard, but under the current circumstances I thought a bit of publicity might help your reputation in town."

Her spoon clattered in the bowl. "What on earth are you talking about?" She grabbed the paper that had remained where he dropped it. Her gaze flickered between him and the several pages of articles she scanned.

Elliott kept his features composed and benign.

When her focus finally locked on the intended target, her grip tightened until her knuckles turned white. " 'Miss Henrietta's Around Town Happenings'? It that what you're referring to?"

"It is. Please continue. I love hearing the sound of your voice, even if you're merely reading local gossip."

At first she didn't oblige him as she scanned the column, her lips moving as she read the fodder. Then with a gasp, she began to read aloud. "Certain couples photographed last month at the luxurious home of General and Mrs. Rhodes continue to be seen around town now that spring has arrived in our beloved city. Last month the renowned photographer Alexei Gardenier from New York provided honored guests with tintype mementos of the lavish affair. Many long-wedded spouses, the recently betrothed, and a few new couples were captured forever at this special moment in history." She lifted her chin and scowled.

"Go on," he encouraged. "It gets even better."

"Miss Eugenia Duncan and Major Joseph Penrod, Miss Justine Emerson and Colonel

William Grayson, Mr. and Mrs. Robert Forsythe of Five Forks . . ." Her voice trailed off as she skimmed over several unfamiliar names. "At least thirty couples waited in an hour-long queue to be photographed. Mrs. Madeline Howard, formerly of Pennsylvania and now a resident of Richmond, stood proudly with the illustrious commander of the home guard, Colonel Elliott Haywood. This particular columnist hopes to see more of Mrs. Howard at St. Paul's charity functions and St. Patrick's sewing guild. Doesn't everyone deserve a fresh start?"

The newspaper slipped from Mrs. Howard's fingers. "I can't believe she printed such nonsense. I can count the homes that receive me on one hand! Why would this . . ." she hunted for the byline, "Henrietta Wyatt invent such a story? I don't believe I've ever met the woman."

"You haven't, and to answer your question — money." Elliott leaned forward in his chair. "Just about anything and everyone can be purchased in Richmond these days."

"You *paid* her to print a complete fabrication? Why would you do such a thing, Colonel Haywood?"

"I hope it wasn't a total fabrication. You danced with me half a dozen times and made polite social conversation for the entire time we waited for Mr. Gardenier." Elliott contorted his face to feign confusion. "Is it the 'illustrious' description you object to? I swear I had nothing to do with her grandiose adjectives."

She exhaled in exasperation. "No, Colonel. You know very well that what I object to is her insinuation we are courting. Tell me why you paid for this . . . news."

"Because I'm fond of you, Mrs. Howard, whether you like it or not. I don't like you hiding in your room except on Sundays. Even in church, you scurry up the aisle like a mouse and then remain as meek as one. I wish to remove the last vestige of suspicion so you can resume a normal life."

"I don't scurry." She crossed her arms. "I have never *scurried* in my life."

"I stand corrected." He nodded his acquiescence. "But I also had a hidden motive for paying someone to spread rumors about us."

"And what would that be?"

"I hope to make the rumors come true. That can't possibly surprise you."

Madeline pushed up from the table. "From the beginning of our acquaintance, I've been honest with you, Colonel, regarding my affections."

"Yes, but all that was before the rude turn of events in February. Life is short, Mrs. Howard. Battles will resume within a week or two. I would like to go forth with your smile branded in my memory." He spoke with a calmness he didn't feel.

"I can't control the images in your head, but I don't plan to remarry or ever let my heart become vulnerable again. Good day to you, sir." Madeline stalked out the French doors into the garden without offering him as much as a backward glance.

Late May 1864

Madeline paced the upstairs hallway like a madwoman. She could neither read nor sew, nor perform any other normal activity that had filled her days of late. She'd heard nothing from Colonel Haywood since that uncomfortable breakfast in the Duncan dining room. He hadn't been happy with her answer, but what did he expect? She couldn't in good faith pledge a fidelity or affection she didn't feel. She had a limit to the number of lies she was willing to tell.

Her life had become a ruse, a sham in which she cloaked activities that didn't feel very Christian to her. She'd heard nothing from James since their parting in February. The colonel had begged her to be practical.

Where did practically or even reality lie? For several weeks they had heard gunfire in the distance, but lately the shots sounded frightfully close to their refuge on Forsythia Lane. The war had come to Richmond, bringing a nervous tension to Aunt Clarisa and Eugenia that Madeline had never witnessed before.

Uncle John had ordered the women to remain indoors for the past week — no more sewing guild, afternoon social calls, or even working in the new vegetable garden. Except for church on Sundays when the world remained blissfully quiet, her uncle was the only one to leave the house. Diligently, Uncle John trudged toward the war department soon after sunrise and didn't return home until dark. He insisted Micah not endanger the horse and carriage with the Yankee cavalry just beyond the James River.

"I refuse to surrender my favorite gelding to that devil Sheridan," he blustered in a fit of temper. "And that carriage belonged to my father."

But General Philip Sheridan wasn't a devil to Madeline, nor was he the enemy. In her heart she considered the potential restorer of the American states a hero. Here in her uncle and aunt's home, Micah and Esther had been freed from slavery long ago. They received compensation for their work, albeit a small sum. But elsewhere in the capital of the Confederacy, household servants were still in bondage, including many on Forsythia Lane. Several of Aunt Clarisa's friends refused to give up personal maids as though it were their birthright to be waited on by people of color. Madeline despised their arrogance, selfishness, and lack of compassion for their fellow man. These same women raised their voices in hymns of praise Sunday mornings and yet found nothing wrong with the institution of slavery. Madeline had had enough of their double standards.

She decided to stop her pacing in order to seek out Esther. Perhaps chores would keep her better occupied. Walking down the front staircase, Madeline froze at the sound of an angry voice. She lowered herself to the polished step and strained to hear the conversation taking place in the parlor.

"John, I won't permit you to pack a bag and dash off without telling me what's going on. Something dreadful must have happened if you're home at midday. How could you possibly take a journey with the Yankees practically at our back door?" Aunt Clarisa's cultured, musical voice had grown shrill. "I will throw myself prostrate at your feet and block your path if need be."

"Dear me, please don't become overly dramatic like our daughter, Clarisa. I don't think my sanity could take it." Uncle John tried to sound amused but failed.

"I'm quite serious. As your wife I have a right to know what is happening!"

"Sit down, my dear, and stop pacing. I have but little time." He spoke so softly his words became incomprehensible.

Praying no one would witness her shameful eavesdropping, Madeline crept to the doorway and plastered herself against the wall.

"Grant sent his Fourth Corps of infantry to attack our troops west of Fredericksburg in Orange County. There were heavy losses on both sides. Then he engaged Lee again in Spotsylvania County a few days later. According to reports, the Yankees lost more than thirty-five thousand men and yet continue to fight. Grant cares not a whit as to how many men die."

"Lord, have mercy on their souls."

"That's not the worst of it. When General Stuart heard that the Yankee cavalry crossed the South Anna River, he decided to circle around Yellow Tavern and cut them off from the rest of the army."

"Yellow Tavern? That's barely ten miles from here."

"Yes, such was the reason for Stuart's hasty action. His cavalry turned the Yankees back. Our boys had them on the run, but a sharpshooter — or scalawag straggler by some accounts — pulled a pistol and shot General Stuart off of his horse."

Madeline could hear the pain in her uncle's voice. J.E.B. Stuart was one of Robert E. Lee's favorites, along with the rest of the Confederate Army.

"They took him to Chimborazo. President Davis is on his way there right now with several guards. I must join them there to bring the president back to Richmond. The men from the home guard may be needed at the garrison to shore up the city's defenses. General Beauregard has been placed in charge of protecting the capital. That devil, Sheridan, has torn up railroad lines and destroyed several bridges. We can't get the wounded — ours or theirs — back to the hospital to be treated. This war is no longer fought by civilized gentlemen with a code of honor."

"Has it ever been?"

If Uncle John answered his wife, Madeline couldn't hear his response.

"But why are you packing if you're merely

bringing President Davis back from the hospital?"

"I don't know where he'll send me afterward. Don't you see, Clarisa? If those Yankees break through our line, the capital could be lost, and with it goes all hope for a new South."

"Richmond in the hands of Yankees? God would never allow it."

Madeline peeked around the door frame to get a glimpse of her uncle's face.

"God turned His back on both sides long ago. This is man's war, and the outcome will not have His grace no matter which side wins."

Aunt Clarisa staggered to her feet. "I'll send Esther up to pack your valise. You'll come with me to the kitchen —"

"I have no time," he interrupted. "I need to get to —"

Aunt Clarisa interrupted her husband with equal vehemence. "Esther can pack faster than you, so you'll have a chance to drink a cup of milk and eat a sandwich. We'll wrap the leftover bread and cheese to take with you. Who knows what difficult situation you'll ride into?"

Madeline scampered up the stairs so not to be discovered. From the landing, she watched her aunt and uncle head down the hall toward the kitchen, both seeming older than their years. But at the moment the Duncans' premature aging wasn't foremost on her mind.

Grant had send his *Fourth Corps* to fight west of Fredericksburg — James's corps. He could be lying dead in a farm field while she eavesdropped in the comfort of a mansion. Or he could be lying on a filthy cot awaiting his turn with a surgeon's bloody blade.

He might be dying alone without the one who loved him at his side.

■ ■ ■ ■

TWENTY

■ ■ ■ ■

Early June 1864

Clarisa waited at the parlor window as the church bells chimed nine and then ten o'clock. She refused to retire to her bedroom until her husband arrived safely home. Surely he wouldn't spend another night at the war department. With the Yankee cavalry and their sharpshooters so near Richmond, President Davis wanted his staff close so they could be protected. If John didn't come home tonight, she would send Micah to his office in the morning with a fresh change of clothes. Just when she had begun to doze in her chair, a clatter of carriage wheels on cobblestones roused her senses. A conveyance was stopping in front of their house. Clarisa strode into the foyer as quickly as a dignified matron was permitted. Pulling open the door, she watched her beloved husband climb down from an unfamiliar carriage. Illuminated by the faint glow of gas lamps, John approached with a hitch in his step. Though he looked as though the weight of the world was on his shoulders, he smiled when he spotted her in the doorway.

"Why on earth are you still up, wife? You know I would have woken you when I got home." His gait was that of an old man.

"How could I sleep not knowing if you were alive or dead?" Clarisa met him halfway down the walk, not caring if passersby saw her in her dressing gown.

"Still among the living, I'm grateful to say." He slipped an arm around her waist. "You shouldn't fret so much, my love. The job of the Confederate treasurer isn't the same as a captain or lieutenant leading his valiant regiment into battle. I'm in little personal danger."

Together they climbed the steps, and after they had entered the foyer, Clarisa closed and locked the door quietly behind them. "Plenty of civilians have died, so please don't take chances. Who brought you home tonight — Colonel Haywood or one of the other members of the home guard? I didn't recognize the crest on the carriage door."

John hung his coat and hat on the hall tree where Micah would see them in the morning. "One of the war correspondents for the newspaper. The man sells stories to anyone with coin. Apparently, I was on the way to his hotel." In the parlor, he poured a brandy at the sideboard.

"Spirits on an empty stomach, John? I'll bet you haven't eaten in hours. Bring your snifter along, and I'll slice some bread and cheese."

He complied without argument. In the kitchen he slumped onto a chair used by Esther when peeling potatoes or making pie crusts. "Whatever you have handy, Clarisa. I won't have you fussing over me in the middle of the night."

"It's a wife's prerogative to fuss." She sliced fresh bread from dark, coarsely-ground wheat and then cut into a wedge of soft farmers' cheese Madeline had bargained for at the market. "I hope it wasn't that horrible Jonas Weems. Why didn't one of the home guards accompany you? One of those Yankee deserters or vagrant riffraff could have accosted you. Our streets aren't safe at night."

John pressed the thick slice of cheese between two slices of bread and took a bite. "Of course not Weems. I would be more likely to shoot that man on sight than to climb into his carriage. As for Colonel Haywood, he has been reassigned to a field commission, along with most of the other guards. General Lee needs every able-bodied officer on the battlefield." He swallowed a mouthful as though savoring a rare piece of steak.

"Including Joseph Penrod?"

"Yes, dear heart, including Major Penrod. He's been sent to join General Beauregard's corps."

Clarisa lowered herself to the other kitchen chair. "What shall I tell Eugenia? She was hoping to see her beau more since there's been a break in the weather."

John chewed another bite of sandwich before meeting her eye. "A break in the weather means a resumption of the war. Tell our daughter the truth. Eugenia isn't a child anymore, and I don't want you treating her like one, despite whatever . . . limitations you believe she possesses. This is war, and Eugenia should be aware. She cannot cling to the memory of old Richmond any longer."

Clarisa nodded but averted her gaze. She had insulated their daughter as much as she could in the vain hope all would be well one day. After the death of "Jeb" Stuart earlier that month, Richmond's favorite son, her illusions of a Confederate victory had diminished. "Who is left to protect the president, his family, and members of his staff?"

John patted her hand. "Rest easy. Plenty of invalid soldiers surround the Davis home and the war department offices. They might not be fit to march in their regiments, but they are willing to give their lives for the Cause. Sentinels are posted everywhere in town, more plentiful than ever. These good men will be loyal until their last breath."

Clarisa felt little relief. From what she heard at sewing guild, much treachery was afoot in the city. "How goes the fighting? You've said little since the death of General Stuart. Surely that ghastly battle must have concluded."

John finished his sandwich with two bites and wiped his mouth. "While Stuart was fighting Sheridan's cavalry north of town, General Lee trounced Grant in the area the Yankees call the Wilderness. Their losses were almost eighteen thousand, while we lost but eight thousand. Yet despite our victory, Grant didn't retreat as expected. Instead, he dogged Lee's army and attacked a few days later west of Fredericksburg. Is there no limit to the number of Union recruits? How can Lincoln replace his soldiers so easily?" He took a long swallow of brandy.

"Perhaps the men are new immigrants." Clarisa refilled his snifter with cool water from the pitcher.

John drank deeply and cleared his throat. "After eleven days of fighting, Washington newspapers described the Spotsylvania Courthouse battle as inconclusive — no clear victor determined. We lost *half* the number of men they did. How can that not be a Confederate victory except for the fact a madman refused to retreat? I heard the commander of the sixth corps was killed. Generals John Sedgwick and James Downing are Grant's key officers. I wish no ill will on my fellow man, not even in wartime, but could the loss of Sedgwick finally turn Grant back to lick his wounds?"

Clarisa had no answer. Military matters never held any interest for her, but the name James Downing grabbed her attention. "Let's pray that General Grant comes to his senses and goes home." She stood and held out her hand. "Let's go to bed, John. You must be exhausted. I'll bring up a cup of chamomile tea to help you relax."

"I'll have no trouble sleeping. Thank you for the sandwich. It tasted finer than a fancy meal served to our most esteemed guests." He drained his glass of water and climbed the back staircase reserved for servants. On a night such as this, he was probably too tired to walk to the front hall.

And she was too tired to take exception to his breech of etiquette. As Clarisa waited for the water to heat, she tried to absorb all he had said. Although it hardly seemed possible, the terrible loss of life would continue into summer. Until when? Until every able-bodied man in the South lay moldering in his grave, along with half the sons and husbands from the North? Despite the hateful rhetoric, those Yankees were nothing but farmers, shopkeepers, and boys too young to even select a vocation yet.

Carrying two cups of tea in case John changed his mind, Clarisa also wearily climbed the back stairs to the upper hallway. Like her husband, she was too tired to walk to the front of the house. What did it matter anyway? Who would see her break long-established propriety between master and servant? At any time Micah and Esther could pack their meager possessions and move north. Certainly employers in New York or Connecticut could afford to pay better wages and serve better meals than coarse bread, pickled corn, and apple preserves.

As she was about to enter her bedchamber, a light in Madeline's room caught her

451

attention. Clarisa eased open the door to find her niece sitting at the dressing table with her head in her hands. "Madeline, my dear, is something wrong?"

Closing her bottom bureau drawer, Madeline turned to face her aunt with a tear-streaked face. "Nothing of a physical nature. What ails me cannot be mended with either salve or poultice."

"Then you heard the news about Colonel Haywood?" Entering the room, Clarisa leaned wearily against a bed post.

"News? What news? I've heard nothing."

"He's been reassigned to General Lee and sent to Petersburg, where the danger is far greater than at the offices of the war department."

Madeline paled, her mouth pulling into a grimace. "In that case I truly regret my actions."

"Would you care to elaborate?" Clarisa handed her niece one of the two cups of tea, thinking she needed it more than her husband.

"Despite my efforts to discourage him, he continued to believe I might develop feelings for him. He deserves a woman who can love without reservation, with her whole heart."

"Leading on a man is playing with fire.

It's the cruelest kind of dishonesty. Why would you do such a thing?"

Madeline winced. "It hadn't been my intention, Aunt. I told him from the start I was in love with another. But when I returned in February, he thought his attention would be welcomed. I supposed I considered it harmless flattery."

"Are you saying you care nothing for him? What about the photo taken at the Rhodes' ball?" Clarisa struggled to keep her voice level. "The colonel showed the tintype to your uncle more than once."

"I feel friendship but nothing more. Having the photo taken was a mistake."

"It seems that you no longer consider deception harmless," Clarisa chided. "I would like to see the picture."

Madeline peered up at her. "It's gone. It was stolen from me weeks ago."

"Who would do such a thing?"

"I believe it was Kathleen, although I can't prove it. She all but admitted to taking a letter from my drawer."

Clarisa watched tears course down her niece's pretty face, and her heart relented. "Go to sleep, Madeline. Pray that God will protect Colonel Haywood and grant you an opportunity to make amends with him."

"Yes, ma'am." She walked toward the bed

on shaky legs.

Clarisa closed the door and went to her own room, falling asleep the moment her head hit the pillow, her tea forgotten on her nightstand. When she awoke the next morning, she slipped on her wrapper and went in search of her tiresome Irish maid. Kathleen was still asleep on the cot in her attic bedroom.

"Get up, Miss O'Toole, and get dressed."

Bolting upright, the maid's dour face flushed brightly. "I was just about to help Esther with breakfast, ma'am." She swung her legs out of bed.

"This isn't about your laziness. Collect your belongings and come to the drawing room for your final pay envelope."

"You're firing me? What lies did that Yankee tell you?" The woman's surprised expression changed to one of pure hatred.

"Why would you assume your dismissal has something to do with my niece? Pack nothing that doesn't belong to you, because I intend to inspect your bag before you leave this house. If you take even a can of peas that's not yours, I'll turn you over to the authorities."

Clarisa marched from the room and slammed the door, something she never did.

■ ■ ■ ■

June 1864

From his headquarters tent, James could see troops talking in small clusters. Tonight no noisy camaraderie was among the men, no bawdy songs sung out of key to pass the time while supper roasted over the campfire. Every man from division commanders to lowly privates was subdued by the carnage of the past several weeks.

On General Grant's orders, they had pursued the Rebels from the Wilderness into Spotsylvania County, where they fought for fourteen straight days. When their gunpowder wouldn't ignite in the incessant rain, they fought hand-to-hand. It had been the cruelest combat James had witnessed during his entire career. When the Confederate line held at Spotsylvania, Grant ordered the men to cross the North Anna River and engage Lee's army at Cold Harbor. Grant had told a newspaperman he would continue fighting if it took all summer . . . and if it cost the life of every blue-coated Union soldier.

After three intense days at Cold Harbor, followed by nine days of skirmishes, the Union Army had lost twelve thousand men.

Lee had lost a fraction of that number. Northern papers were calling their new commander "a butcher," yet General Grant refused to retreat. *This is what the president wants, no matter what the cost.*

At the sound of an approaching rider, James rose stiffly to his feet. His chief of staff beat him out the door to meet the rider.

"Let's hope this will be new orders," said Major Henry. "How long can we remain this close to Richmond without advancing to crush that arrogant aristocrat, Jeff Davis?"

Almost every chance he got, his adjutant revealed contempt for anyone wealthy, and in so doing, he also revealed the poor circumstances of his upbringing. "At ease, Major. I'll take those dispatches, Corporal." James reached up to accept the sheaf of rolled parchments.

The courier saluted and spurred his horse to deliver the next batch of orders.

As they walked back into the tent, the major tried to read over his shoulder.

"Give me room!" James snapped.

"I beg your pardon, sir." The major backed up two paces.

James scanned the document twice before addressing his aide. "You have your wish. Tomorrow we break camp and leave Lee's Army of Virginia. We're to cross the James

456

River on the twelfth and then head south."

"South — even farther away from Washington? But that will leave the nation's capital exposed to Rebel attack."

"Even General Lee can't be everywhere at once. We won't win this war with a defensive campaign. We're marching toward Petersburg, the enemy's supply center. Tomorrow the cavalry will strike railroad junctions and cut off the flow of food and munitions to Richmond. We must finish what the naval blockade started. I strongly advise you not to question our commander's directive."

"With all due respect, sir, how does General Grant plan to move thousands of infantry across the James River with all the rain we've had?"

Running out of patience, the general shot the major a look that could have curdled milk. "The Army Corps of Engineers is building a pontoon bridge as we speak. Spread the word throughout the corps. We are moving out at dawn."

James spent several minutes stacking maps and journals before he realized his adjutant hadn't left the tent. "Was something unclear about my orders, Major?"

"No, sir, but I have another matter to discuss — of a personal nature. Perhaps you can make time for me before you retire this evening."

Frowning, James stopped packing. "I have time right now. We'll check on the picket line so the aides can finish up here." Two lieutenants hovering near the door hastened to comply, much like his chief of staff.

The two soldiers walked from the temporary headquarters toward the scrub brush that separated the camp from the dense woods beyond. Smoke from dying campfires carried on the breeze, thickening the already heavy humidity. Many men were enjoying a last pipe of tobacco before spreading out their bedrolls to sleep.

"Speak your mind," James said once they were beyond earshot.

"I know you asked me to not bring up the subject of Mrs. Howard —"

"I didn't *ask* you to refrain, Major. It was a direct order." He tried to tamp down his escalating temper.

"Yes, sir, an order I wish to obey. But in good faith I feel I have little choice." Major Henry rocked back on his heels with his chin lifted, as though taking some moral high ground.

"Then by all means proceed at your own risk." James clenched down on his back teeth.

His adjutant's confidence seemed to falter.

"I have in my possession one of those newfangled tintypes. Apparently, a traveling photographer from New York stopped in Richmond this past February and attended a party given by General Rhodes."

"Rhodes — of which corps? I've never heard of a Rebel general by that name."

"Nor had I until I questioned my informant. The man is well into his seventies and rather doddering. But Bobbie Lee is so desperate for officers that he'll take anyone still breathing that possesses a smidgen of military knowledge." Henry released an unpleasant laugh. "Rhodes is a consultant to Jeff Davis."

James sighed. "It's late and I have much to do. I take it this photo involves Mrs. Howard or you wouldn't be bothering me with trivial matters, such as Richmond social events." As soon as he voiced the words, he knew the answer as assuredly as day follows night.

The major pulled a small frame from his pocket, which he gazed upon with ill-concealed delight. "Yes, it is indeed Mrs. Howard, and she is on the arm of a Rebel colonel. My informant tells me that he's Elliott Haywood, commander of the Richmond home guard. Although I doubt he's still in the city now, considering how many officers Lee lost at Cold Harbor."

"His losses were not more grievous than our own." James held out an open palm.

"True enough." Major Henry handed him the tintype and stepped back in case the messenger paid a dire price due to the content of his report.

James studied the rather clear image of his beloved Madeline in a low-cut, extravagant ball gown, the likes of which he couldn't imagine a Pennsylvania farmer's widow ever owning. Her waist-length blond hair had been swept into a cascade of curls from the crown of her head down to her shoulders. Madeline's hand was hooked through the crook of the man's elbow. The pompous colonel wore a dimpled smile as ostentatious as her dress. Haywood appeared strong and self-assured, if not smug. Certainly not doddering and elderly like his host, General Rhodes.

There was no doubt that the woman was his Madeline. But obviously she wasn't *his* at all.

"You would agree the tintype is of Mrs. Howard?"

The general nodded. "Where did you get this? Usually those vagabonds make two copies from each sitting of those involved."

"My contact in Richmond procured it

from a newspaperman, one who's eager to oust Mrs. Howard from their city. Many don't trust her since her visit to Culpeper. This journalist doesn't like her latest liaison any more than you do, General."

"I suggest you hold your tongue."

"Come now, sir." Henry grasped his arm with undue familiarity. "Surely now you don't believe her to be anything other than an opportunistic mercenary. She probably sells secrets to both sides with plans to emerge from this war a wealthy woman. That photo doesn't lie. Mrs. Howard isn't being held against her will by this colonel."

James shrugged off his hand. "I will consider Mrs. Howard's true nature in private rather than debating it with you, but I am curious how this newspaperman came by this . . . evidence of her duplicity." His fingers balled into fists.

The question wasn't one his adjutant had expected. "I understand that the maid at the home where she's staying procured it. Apparently, the woman would steal the spectacles off a man's nose if the price were right." Henry sneered, the sound becoming the straw that broke the camel's back.

James drew back his arm and let his fist fly, connecting with the major's nose with malicious intent. His reaction, although forbidden by an officer's code of conduct, was profoundly satisfying. "I warned you to proceed at your own peril, Major. If you *ever* bring up Mrs. Howard to me again or initiate *any* action against her, you'll get more of the same." He shook the picture in Henry's face. "Then I'll have you court-martialed for disobeying a direct order, or at the very least have you reassigned to lead a brigade into battle."

The major yanked a handkerchief from his pocket to swab at the blood on his face. His broken nose was already starting to swell. "That was wholly unnecessary, sir. My intention wasn't to offend you."

James gazed at the happy couple, who smiled back at him. The sight of the arrogant Rebel holding Madeline's arm closely to his side soured his stomach worse than that shipment of rancid beef. Seeing her sweet, innocent face, despite the hardships she'd endured, made him want to weep. "Is this mine to keep?"

"Of course it is." The major pressed a handkerchief tightly to his nostril. "I have no use for it. If you'll excuse me, sir, I wish to get a cold compress from the medic." He stomped off with his head at an odd tilt.

James felt a modicum of remorse as he tucked the tintype into his frock coat. When he returned to headquarters, he found a flurry of activity and no opportunity to collect his thoughts. With his corps moving south tomorrow, they all had plenty to do. But before he stretched out for a few hours rest, he penned a letter to the woman he had planned his entire future around. After expressing himself to the best of his abilities, James slipped the sheet into an envelope and scribbled the address he knew by heart.

The next morning he assembled his men into companies. Then, one by one, they marched in formation from their protected valley. They would take everything with them, leaving nothing behind the enemy might find useful. Artillery caissons, ammunition wagons, and the stream of sutlers followed the divisions like an itinerant carnival. All was in order except his emotions. James's mind parried back and forth attempting to find explanation for the tintype other than the obvious one. Madeline had fallen in love with someone else — a rakish fop with thick hair and a sly smile. Or perhaps he was merely jealous.

With the relocation of his corps underway under a blistering Virginia sun, James motioned for his chief of staff to ride at his side. Major Henry, his nose still red and swollen, had thus far kept his distance that morning.

James pivoted in his saddle and experienced a pang of guilt about the man's nose. "First, I would like to apologize for striking you, Major. Considering your insistence that you acted in my best interest, my reaction was unprofessional and uncalled for."

Henry nodded, but kept his eyes focused on the dusty road ahead.

"I hope you'll accept my apology so we can put this unpleasantness behind us." James extended a gloved hand.

The adjutant shook halfheartedly, meeting his gaze with heavy lidded eyes. "The subject will not be brought up again, sir."

"Thank you. Later today the road will take us near the town of New Market. Please see that this gets posted." James handed over the letter penned the previous evening. "This will put an end to my distraction with Mrs. Howard."

The major glanced at the address and tucked it inside his coat. "Of course, sir, I'll see to it myself." Snapping a salute, he spurred his horse and rode off to the head of the column.

This will be one letter that won't land in the campfire tonight.

TWENTY-ONE

July 1864

Madeline enjoyed the warm sun on her back as she hoed weeds from between rows of potatoes, carrots, and beans. Aunt Clarisa had finally stopped insisting she not work in the garden like a field hand. The family needed to eat, and Esther and Micah could only do so much. Kathleen had been easily replaced with an emancipated slave who had come east from the Lynchburg area. The young woman's husband had died during the winter from pneumonia, along with her son. But she'd given birth to a baby girl in March and desperately needed work to support the two of them.

Aunt Clarisa said the sound of a baby would do them all good, even if she cried during the night. There had been too much death, too much misery for so long.

But Patsy's daughter, Abigail, almost never cried. And Eugenia happily stepped in as nanny when their maid needed a moment in the privy. Eugenia asked Patsy a bushel load of questions as though eager to learn the secrets of motherhood. Blessedly, Major Penrod received a staff position with General Beauregard. Although his letters were few and far between, Eugenia lit a candle at Saint Patrick's each week and prayed for his protection not less than a dozen times a day.

From Uncle John, Madeline learned that a fierce three-day battle was fought in June for control of Petersburg. The Yankees broke through Confederate trenches and might have taken the city if fighting hadn't inexplicably stopped for the day. By morning Lee arrived with reinforcements and prevented disaster for his army.

Instead, "disaster" continued in the form of a siege, with constant sharpshooter sniping and frequent skirmishes at the fieldworks surrounding the city. The prolonged siege cost lives on a daily basis and emptied the vast storehouses in Richmond. With disruption in the rail lines from the Carolinas and Georgia, the citizens of Richmond began to suffer. Any available food cost dearly.

And so Madeline hoed, weeded, and plucked bugs from cabbage leaves. Later, she and Aunt Clarisa would pick apples and pears to bake or can, reserving the seeds to be planted where roses once grew. Those with the ability to grow food wouldn't starve. The family wasted nothing and never complained if their diet contained creamed corn or tart applesauce every day. Madeline's heart broke for those in refugee camps beyond the city, displaced whites and freed blacks seeking jobs from people with few resources to pay salaries.

That afternoon, Micah entered the kitchen as Madeline, Patsy, and Esther were pitting sour cherries to make into jam. Because Uncle John had sold his horse and carriage to a visiting banker from Canada, both men walked everywhere they needed to go. Uncle John had mourned the loss of his favorite gelding, but the proceeds would keep the family in cheese, eggs, and milk, with occasional meat or fish, for at least six months.

"Where on earth have you been with that?" Esther pointed at the large basket that Micah returned to the ceiling hook.

"To the market, of course. I wanted to see if anything had been left when folks packed up. Sometimes they leave behind bruised fruits and vegetables free for the taking." He rolled up his sleeves to wash at the hand pump.

"And was there?" asked Esther.

"No, not so much as a moldy grape." The butler cast Madeline an odd look despite the fact she hadn't been the one asking the question.

Esther snorted. "I could have told you it would be a waste of time. You went too late in the afternoon."

"With less produce, the merchants sell out and pack up earlier these days," Eugenia added, using her newly acquired habit of observation.

"Yes, ma'am." Micah nodded at Eugenia, but focused on Madeline as he dried his hands.

That evening, after they had eaten and washed the supper dishes, Madeline went in search of the enigmatic butler. Micah usually was as straightforward as a judge, so his strange behavior earlier had unnerved her. She found him in the garden whittling sharp points on several long sticks.

"Good evening, Mrs. Howard. I thought I would go fishing in the river shallows tomorrow. Maybe I can spear some shad or trout if I don't catch anything with my hook and line."

"You found no fish today down on the docks?"

Again Micah angled an expression supposed to mean something, but Madeline had no idea what that was.

"I heard they sold their catch to the army sutlers. All Captain George had left was some shrimp not fit to use for bait. And I have been able to dig up night crawlers now that Mrs. Duncan keeps ripping out flower gardens to plant vegetables." Micah folded his pocketknife and tucked it into his pocket.

"You saw Captain George?" Unable to control her excitement, Madeline glanced over her shoulder at the door.

"I did. I tried selling him some bait, but he had all he needed."

"What a shame. I'm sure you and Esther are trying to put aside a little money for the future with life so uncertain in Richmond." Madeline tightened the shawl around her shoulders, the breeze cool with the sun having set.

Micah straightened to his feet and stood less than a foot away. "Captain George sends his regards to you, Mrs. Howard. He asked me to give you this." He withdrew a folded envelope. "He said no charge for delivery and that you two are even."

Madeline quickly hid the letter under her shawl. "Thank you. I'm grateful for your discretion."

"I don't know what you're up to, ma'am, but this is the last time I want to be involved."

"I understand." Madeline reached for his hand. "I'm indebted to you, Micah."

He stared at her for a moment and then clasped her fingers between his. "I suppose you are. Let's hope something's biting in the shallows tomorrow. I have a taste for fresh fish dipped in egg and cornmeal and fried up in hot bacon fat." He was already on his way to the carriage house.

Despite how delicious that sounded, Madeline couldn't think about food as she climbed the back steps two at a time. Once she was within the private confines of her room, she extracted the sheet filled with James's slanted script. Holding the paper close to her nose, she inhaled the quintessentially male scent of shaving balm and tobacco as her heart pounded with anticipation.

Dear Mrs. Howard,

With his salutation Madeline's exuberance slipped a notch.

Recently I was shown a photograph of a Confederate colonel, Elliott Haywood, and yourself taken at a Richmond social event not long after your return from Culpeper. Although I was reluctant to believe your affections could have changed in so short an interval, I held proof of your newfound joy in my own hand.

I must surmise this infatuation began prior to your trip to my winter camp. Could this Elliott Haywood be the reason you stayed such a short time? Although I feel foolish over my relentless pursuit of you, I regret nothing I said or did during our acquaintance. You possess a gentle soul with a resilient spirit. I had so yearned to spend my life with you. Because your heart belongs to another, I pray Colonel Haywood keeps you safe and far removed from the horrible privations that war brings.

I respectfully withdraw my petition and wish you much happiness in life.

James A. Downing

September 1864

Madeline applied the fan so vigorously that the stiff paper novelty snapped in half. Festooned with bizarre Chinese symbols, the gift from Justine Emerson was no match for the stifling heat of late summer. If only a breeze picked up or a thunderstorm blew in from the ocean — anything that would break the city's relentless humidity. Just as Madeline was about to stick her head in the horse trough, her cousin skipped into the garden wearing a fresh cotton dress and broad smile.

"Good afternoon, Maddy." Eugenia chirped like a sparrow.

"Good afternoon, although I find little good about it. It must be one hundred degrees even in the shade." After Madeline had slumped against the chaise, Eugenia planted a kiss on her forehead.

"Don't be cross, dear cousin. Why don't you help plan my spring wedding? That should help pass the afternoon until supper." She perched on the edge of her chair.

Madeline bolted upright. "Did Major Penrod propose in a letter? He hasn't been here in weeks."

Eugenia glanced around the courtyard for eavesdroppers. "No, he hasn't, but I have a feeling he'll be home soon. And the first words out of his mouth will be: 'Miss Eugenia, will you honor me by becoming my bride?'" She spoke in a deep baritone voice with her hand positioned over her heart.

Madeline chuckled despite her bad mood. "You truly do sound like him. But Joseph coming home soon may be wishful thinking by a woman in love."

"*Au contraire, m'petite.*" Eugenia offered one of the few French phrases she learned in finishing school. "I heard Papa tell Mama the war will soon be over. It's practically a foregone conclusion."

Madeline stopped tearing the broken fan into shreds. "A victory for which side?"

"For the Confederacy, of course, with all due respect to your late husband's memory." Lowering her eyelashes, Eugenia patted Madeline's hand.

"Thank you, sweet girl, but perhaps Uncle John was expressing his hopefulness. Surely morale must be low at the war department." Madeline resumed mutilating the paper fan.

"I don't think so. Papa read in a Washington newspaper that Northern sentiments have turned against General Grant. People are fed up with their boys dying for no good reason."

"What *people,* Genie? There always will be pacifists against war, no matter what principles are involved."

"I'm not talking about Quakers and such. These rabble-rousers are called Copperheads — what an odd name. According to the report, they are rioting in the streets in New York and Ohio. The Copperheads demand that Lincoln recognize the Confederacy and schedule peace talks. If your president refuses, they're encouraging Union soldiers to desert." Eugenia plucked a flower off the bougainvillea bush. "That isn't wishful thinking if it was in a *Yankee* newspaper."

Madeline stared speechlessly at her cousin for several moments before gathering herself and saying, "That will never happen, Genie. President Lincoln promoted General Grant over other commanders and gave him full control."

"Then Lincoln will lose the election in November most assuredly. A democrat in the White House will bring this nasty business to a swift close." Eugenia smiled politely to soften her words.

"Uncle John actually said this to your mother?" Madeline had never heard Eugenia talk about anything other than ball gowns and local gossip.

"Indeed he did. Maybe Joseph will be home by Thanksgiving, Mr. Lincoln's new federal holiday. I'm certain Mama will throw a grand Christmas party so we can announce our engagement. Then we can be married in the spring." Eugenia began waltzing around the courtyard as though at a ball. "I do hope babies arrive right away, because I've absolutely fallen in love with little Abigail."

So like Eugenia to turn the conversation back to herself within five minutes, Madeline thought uncharitably. "Will you please sit down? How can you dance when I can barely breathe in this heat?"

The girl ceased celebrating an assured Confederate victory, along with her promising future. "I beg your pardon, Maddy. Since you came home, I've been hoping you would remain with us forever."

Home? Remain with us? How can I possibly forfeit a lifetime commitment to freedom without slavery or repression? "The fact my former beau and I parted ways doesn't mean I won't return north after the war. Pennsylvania will always be my home, Genie."

"I understand that your friends are there, but promise me you'll at least stay for my wedding."

Her annoyance faded, leaving Madeline with nothing but pity for her cousin. "Of course I'll be here for that."

Eugenia perched on the edge of Madeline's chaise. "Will you stand by my side as matron of honor?"

"What about Justine? Don't you think you should ask her?"

"I want you both — maid and matron." Without warning, large tears flooded Eugenia's eyes and streamed down her face. Her emotions had swung like a pendulum to the other side.

Madeline pulled her into her arms and patted her back. "I would be honored to stand up with you. You have my word I'll be here, but please don't get too far ahead of yourself. The siege drags on at Petersburg. General Grant hasn't surrendered yet."

"He must give up soon because he won't have any soldiers left. Didn't you hear about the crater? Yankees built a tunnel under our trenches, and filled it with gunpowder to blow a hole in our line. Grant ordered his troops to charge. They jumped into the hole but couldn't get out the other side. Papa said it was like shooting fish in a barrel —"

"Enough, Eugenia!" Madeline stood up so fast her cousin landed in a heap of petticoats on the flagstones. "I don't care if your precious army wins tomorrow, but I don't want to hear another word about it. You should be ashamed of yourself. Gloating over boys suffering and dying isn't very Christian." Her breath came in gasps even as she tried to rein in her own emotions.

"You should light a candle at Saint Patrick's in petition to be delivered from your bloodlust."

Eugenia gazed up from her undignified position in shock at her cousin's vehemence, her hoop askew.

In a fit of rage from months of wanting to serve her country but not being able to do so, fueled by the dismissal from the man she loved, Madeline ran down the path toward the street. Heedless as to her destination, she kept going until she doubled over with a painful side stitch. Cobblestones pressed through the thin soles of her slippers to bruise her feet. But who remembered to wear sensible boots when they stormed away from everything despised and loved at the same time? Her life had become a quagmire of deception with no one to blame but herself.

Lately, during weak moments, she had actually entertained thoughts of Colonel Haywood. He would return from the battlefront — either victorious or conquered — to rescue her from her Richmond existence. He would take her to his country estate, where she could plant a garden and raise horses again. Not as the indolent mistress of a vast plantation surrounded by servants, but as a simple farmer's wife. Then she would forget holding the hands of wounded men with the coppery stench of death filling her nostrils. Colonel Haywood had been the only soldier she saved in Gettysburg. The hopelessness and futility of war would continue to haunt her forever.

But moments of imagining a future with Colonel Haywood would soon pass, replaced by the visage of James. A man not quite as handsome . . . an officer nowhere near as polished or cultured . . . yet infinitely more appealing to her. She couldn't stop thinking about him, yet she'd destroyed his passion by pretending to be someone she was not.

Eventually, Madeline slowed her pace but kept walking. Her anger with Eugenia had already evaporated. How could she blame her cousin for the way she had been raised? Everything she'd been taught and the future she yearned for was dependent on a Southern victory. Madeline was sick of it all — both sides eager to kill each other in cruel ways; both armies praying for God to grant them victory. Both sides discovering God seldom takes sides in a war.

With her dress sodden with sweat and her feet cut and dirty, Madeline arrived at the gates of the city market. No vendors displayed vegetables or smoked hams today.

With food tightly rationed, produce booths were set up only three times per week. Fishmongers appeared seldom more than every other Wednesday due to the naval blockade. Nevertheless, something she couldn't name drew her like a siren's call. Madeline crawled under the gate, tearing her hem on a sharp stone, and headed straight for the wharf, where boats bobbed in shallow water. With the tide out, she descended a ladder to reach the dock. Blessedly, the *Bonnie Bess* had sailed into the Richmond harbor.

"Captain George," she called, fearful of being heard by other boatmen. "May I come aboard? It's Mrs. Howard."

The grizzled sea captain stuck his white pate out a porthole. "Madeline, my girl. What a lovely surprise. Climb down, but mind your step." His head disappeared briefly and then reappeared in the hatch of the freshly scrubbed deck.

Madeline lifted her skirt with one hand while holding the ladder with the other.

"To what do I owe this rare pleasure? If it be seafood you're after, I'm afraid I'm plum out. The fish managed to stay away from me nets and lines this week." The captain's pleasant expression vanished when he noticed her deplorable appearance. "Come now, what befell ya on the way to the docks?" George steered her to a bench in the stern. "Did you have to outrun one of those thievin' scalawags? That sort would steal gold from a dead man's teeth if the undertaker turned his back long enough."

Madeline grimaced at the mental image. "No, sir. I ran pell-mell solely from myself."

"Ahhh. That can be the trickiest to outmaneuver. Care for a nip?" He pulled a silver flask from his pocket. "It's rum from the West Indies, the finest available in this hemisphere. After one or two swigs you'll forget your woes."

She sniffed the bottle and handed it back. The vapors alone could inebriate the unsuspecting. "A couple of swigs and I wouldn't find my way home."

"Would that be so bad? Why not stow away on the *Bonnie Bess* down to Fort Monroe? You could catch a passenger transport headed up the Chesapeake and spend the rest of the war in Annapolis or Baltimore. Make a fresh start."

Madeline laughed without humor. "I don't know anyone in Maryland, and I have no money and few useful skills other than breeding and raising horses."

"Perhaps you could nurse in Washington — either Armory Square or Campbell

Hospital on Seventh Street."

She covered her face with her hands. "No, Captain. I have no stomach for blood."

"That would present a problem. Maybe a cook then. Those fancy hotels are filled with speculators and journalists circling around like buzzards."

"I was a wife who prepared simple country meals without a shred of culinary training." Madeline shook her head and sighed deeply. "I have no choice but to return to my uncle's home."

Captain George placed his callused hand on her shoulder. "At least you can sleep knowing you served your country well."

Madeline's head snapped up, her self-pity momentarily forgotten. "What do you mean?"

"General Meade was very grateful of that map you drew of the James River landings in Richmond. He passed it along to General Grant and his navy admiral." The captain took a stout swig from his flask before replacing the cork.

"But General Sheridan gave up his idea to take Richmond. I heard talk that his cavalry followed Jubal Early into the Shenandoah Valley."

"I see you're still eavesdropping, Madeline, my girl." Captain George's smile revealed his gold tooth. "The cavalry may have given up, but your map will help to position artillery."

For a moment the boat seemed to sway as though tossed on high seas. "Cannons aimed at Richmond — is that what you mean?" Madeline felt as though her throat was starting to swell shut.

George stroked his beard. "Aye, artillery usually precedes an infantry assault. There's no better way to breech a line, storm a fort, or in this case, take the capital of the Confederacy." The captain no longer looked like a happy-go-lucky seafarer who made his living selling fish along the coastline. His eyes gleamed with the same bloodlust as Eugenia's had earlier that afternoon. The lingering war fanned hatred in people's hearts.

"I didn't think my map would be used to place cannons to destroy the city."

"What did you think? Our boys needed a sandy shoal to tie up their rowboat for a picnic lunch?" The captain walked to where his lines looped around cleats to keep the boat in place, his eyes narrowing into a glare.

"Of course not, but I assumed it would be used for our army to fight *an army,* not make war on innocent people!"

"Keep your voice down, or we'll both face a military tribunal. No one is innocent anymore. When a war lasts this long, even 'innocent people' end up helping one side or the other. Trouble is, you need to decide which side you're on." He stared down at her without a hint of merriment remaining in his watery blue eyes.

"How dare you, sir. I know *exactly* where my loyalty lies. But that doesn't mean I want my aunt and uncle's home, their church, or my church destroyed by cannon fire."

"Nothing will happen for a spell, not with our boys chasing Rebs in the Shenandoah and Grant latched onto Petersburg like a dog with a bone. But the day is coming, so I suggest you leave Richmond." He walked to where a thick rope was tied to the dock post. "I can offer you passage on the *Bonnie Bess,* but I'm leaving tonight as soon as the moon rises. I don't know when I'll be back. My friends don't like me selling fish to these townsfolk anymore." He angled his head toward the market above the wharf.

Madeline tightened the thin shawl around her shoulders, her damp dress growing chilly against her skin. "Thank you, Captain, but I couldn't leave my family without saying goodbye. Not after all their kindness toward me."

"Suit yourself, but I advise you not to tarry in the city too long." Doffing his soiled cap, he offered her his hand to climb the ladder.

She fled the fishing boat and outdoor market as fast as her legs would carry her. With a gut churning with anxiety, she ran all the way to the Duncans', heedless of people's stares or how much her feet ached. Captain George was right. No one was innocent anymore — not Elliott or James or her. They all had blood on their hands. And someday they would answer to a power higher than Lee or Grant, Davis or Lincoln.

TWENTY-TWO

Kathleen shrank back into the shadows along the riverfront. Lately, it hadn't been hard for her to blend into the grimy back alleys of a city she'd thought would be home for the rest of her life. She hadn't expected Richmond streets to be paved with gold, but she had expected to be treated better than she had back in Dublin.

All these prissy ladies counting their silver each morning as though a missing teaspoon would change the fate of their lives. Just like in Ireland, the rich only looked out for themselves and each other, not caring whether the salaries they paid would be enough to survive on. And ex-slaves were no better than their former masters. They wanted to order her around simply because they had worked longer in the house.

Kathleen had had a bellyful of Virginia. She planned to get one more pouch of gold from Jonas Weems and then book passage on a steamer. She would head up the coast, maybe as far as New York City, where plenty of her people had landed. With any luck she might convince some foolish couple she was their long-lost niece or cousin from home. And with what she'd seen and heard this afternoon, that newspaperman should pay enough for her to leave the refugee camps forever. Between squalling babies, arguing couples, and drunks fighting over the last sip of whiskey, Kathleen barely slept a wink most nights.

The next morning she stuffed her meager belongings into a tattered valise, washed her hands and face in a rain barrel, and left the crude tent city behind. She said no good-byes because she'd made few friends since getting fired. Mrs. Duncan refused to supply a reference after finding a stashed gravy boat among her clothes. At least she hadn't been beaten the way she had in her last position. But without a recommendation, no family would hire her, despite her mournful tale about dead children and a missing husband.

Kathleen hurried inside the offices of the *Richmond Times Dispatch* as soon as the doors opened. Without hesitation she approached a clerk and demanded to see Mr. Jonas Weems. The skinny, pinched-faced girl pressed a hanky to her nose, insisting she wait out in the hallway. Kathleen knew she couldn't smell bad after bathing in the James River just two days ago. Besides, why should she worry about her clothes needing to be laundered when the entire hallway reeked of tobacco smoke?

She was finally shown to a paneled office after a purposefully rude amount of time.

"Mr. Weems?" The clerk barely lifted the linen from her face. "This is the woman who insists she has business with you."

"Thank you, Miss Fletcher. That will be all." After the clerk skittered away, Weems motioned Kathleen into his office. "Come in, Miss O'Toole, and close the door behind you. I hope you brought information worthy of the interruption. I'm a very busy man." Adding to the haze already in the air, Weems lit a fresh cigar.

"Indeed I have, sir." Kathleen eyed a soft leather chair, hoping she would be invited to sit. "Mind if I rest me legs a spell? I walked quite a distance to come here."

Nodding his consent, Weems folded his arms across his chest.

"And a wee spot of tea would soothe the pipes, so it would," Kathleen murmured as she settled on the soft upholstery.

Weems opened the door a crack and

barked, "Miss Fletcher, please bring Miss O'Toole some tea." Turning back to his guest, he said, "Now if you would be so kind to get on with it."

Kathleen arched her spine. "Yesterday I saw that Miz Howard running down the street like the devil himself was chasing her. I happened to be checking folks' backyards at the time. So I followed her to the docks behind the market."

Weems frowned. "So what? Maybe the cook didn't have enough for supper that night and Mrs. Duncan sent the Howard woman on an errand."

"All the booths were closed and everybody was gone for the day. Same with the fish-mongers." Smiling, Kathleen allowed the newspaperman to mull this over. "I kept out of sight but stayed close enough to watch her climb aboard one of them fishing trawl-ers. Pretty as you please, just like she knew the captain in a personal sort of way."

Weems's brows knit together above the bridge of his nose. "Are you implying a romantic rendezvous?"

Kathleen figured out the meaning of the unfamiliar word. "No, I'm not. She was in an untidy state if I do say so, with her hair all loose and tangled down her back. And her dress —"

"I don't wish a fashion commentary from you, Miss O'Toole. What did you see aboard the trawler?"

Kathleen paused while the sour Miss Fletcher carried in a cup of tea. But instead of handing it to her, she set the cup on the edge of the desk. "I watched her chitchat friendly-like with a codger old enough to be her granddaddy. How would some Yankee even know a Virginny sea captain? That Howard woman wasn't there to buy fish." Kathleen picked up the cup and drank the weak tea in a few long swallows. "Then she rushed off his boat and back to the Duncan house in the same all-fired hurry."

Weems stroked his clipped beard. "Why, indeed? It would be easy for a fishing trawler to run up and down the coast well inside the naval blockade." His comment was more to himself than her. "Did you observe Mrs. Howard give the captain documents or a letter? Anything?"

"No, but I had to hide behind the dust bins for a spell while the guards patrolled the wharf. They are always on the lookout as though Yanks might swim up the river for a surprise attack." Noticing a dirty stain on her dress, Kathleen tried to hide it within the folds of her skirt. "Now, I just told you Miz Howard is working her Yankee mischief.

Where's my payment? A gal needs traveling money to leave this horrible city."

Weems studied her curiously while opening his desk drawer. "What happened to your job at John Duncan's?"

"I was fired due to a bit of misunderstandin'."

His nostrils flared. "Then you won't be much assistance to me in the future, will you, Miss O'Toole?" He counted coins from a leather purse and slapped them down on the desk. "I'll pay you twenty-five dollars now, and another twenty-five if this information proves useful. You did get the name of the boat, didn't you?"

"The *Bonnie Bess*. What do you mean useful?" Kathleen grabbed the gold before he changed his mind.

"For all we know, that man could be her grandfather who moved south years ago. I'll have a military detail detain his trawler in one of the other Southern ports. If they find anything treasonous during their search, he will be arrested. Then you'll receive the rest of your payment." Weems's expression curtailed negotiation on the amount. "Check back with my clerk in a few weeks for an envelope." Withdrawing a handkerchief, he pressed it to his bulbous nose. He opened the door and with a flourish of his hand dismissed her. "And Miss O'Toole? Don't barge into my office demanding to see me again. Our . . . association has run its course."

"I'll be checking with Miss Fletcher. Don't you be forgettin' your promise." Kathleen stomped out, her fingers caressing the gold coins deep in her pocket.

With the reelection of President Lincoln in November, a somber mood descended on the inhabitants of Forsythia Lane that would last the winter. Madeline's spat with her cousin was quickly patched up. Eugenia and Aunt Clarisa had been desperately worried for her safety after she ran away. Their hometown had grown unpredictably violent in the past few months. Eugenia had begged for forgiveness, declaring she would never gloat about the Confederacy's imminent victory again.

It was a pledge easily kept, as the Rebel triumph at the "crater," along with Jubal Early's success in reaching the outskirts of Washington, were quickly reversed. Sheridan's cavalry pursued Early's corps relentlessly, finally defeating him in the Shenandoah Valley in October. With the fall of Atlanta and victory in the Mobile Bay, President Lincoln returned to the White

House. Both armies realized the siege at Petersburg wouldn't end anytime soon. Major Penrod hadn't visited Eugenia in weeks, but at least Uncle John kept regular hours now that the war department had fewer requisitions to prepare. Not many outstanding orders were being filled.

One cold morning Madeline joined the three Duncans at the breakfast table. Whatever Esther fixed for the meal would be welcome. She was hungry. Last night's dinner seemed ages ago. "Good morning." She greeted each one with a smile and received a pleasant response in return.

"There's no coffee left, but we have tea with sweet cream," said Aunt Clarisa.

"Tea will be fine." Slipping into her chair, Madeline bowed her head for a quick prayer. Gratitude had been in short supply lately.

"I can't believe my eyes," Uncle John groused as he read the paper. "I assumed the rumors had been exaggerated at best. Were any of you about town yesterday?" He peered at his wife, daughter, and niece in succession.

"I stayed indoors all day. What troubles you, John?" Aunt Clarisa nibbled her toast.

"Esther and I canned the last of the apples," said Madeline.

"I walked only as far as Justine's." Eugenia's expression turned fearful.

Her father pivoted in his chair. "Did you see any of these marauding females? I certainly cannot call them 'ladies.' " He thumped his fist on the newspaper next to his plate.

Eugenia shrank smaller behind her breakfast. "I saw only Mrs. Pinckney returning home after Mass. She walked normally, in no way . . . marauding."

Madeline was certain her cousin had no idea what the term meant. "Were there more bread riots?" she asked softly. Several times during the past year, displaced women from the refugee camps marched through Richmond streets demanding food for their children. Occasionally they converged on bakeries, picked the shelves bare, and ran out without paying.

"These weren't homeless farm widows trying to feed their families. They were an organized mob wielding hatchets and knives."

"Oh my word." Aunt Clarisa pressed a fist to her bosom. "What is happening to this town?"

"Close to a hundred women broke the windows of jewelry and clothing stores. They were after baubles and fancy dresses, shoes, and expensive leather. They behaved like a lawless pack of rabble."

"Where did they come from?" Eugenia sounded utterly perplexed.

"From those festering camps outside the city. No doubt that viper, Kathleen O'Toole, was among them. They weren't interested in bakeries or greengrocers this time, but merchandise they could stuff into their bags and resell elsewhere. What they couldn't haul off they destroyed without a care about the livelihood of shopkeepers."

"What happened to them?" asked Madeline, feeling a little queasy.

"The mayor attempted to quell the melee. Even the governor was telegraphed. But the mob refused to disperse until the militia fired shots above their heads with threats to kill."

"Oh, John, shooting women? Speak no more about this." Aunt Clarisa looked ready to faint.

"The truth must be told. I don't want any of you leaving this house without a male escort. Is that clear?" Uncle John flushed to a dangerous hue as he glanced around the table.

One by one Madeline, Eugenia, and Clarisa nodded in agreement. Thus began Madeline's imposed confinement inside the mansion or within the high stone wall of the gardens. Not that she had many places to go. Invitations over the holiday season had been few, and none of them included her name on the outer envelope. She was allowed to attend church, but without the companionship of Colonel Haywood, Catholic Mass with the family became her sole option. Her understanding of Latin had improved little, so instead she often chose to stay home and read her Bible by the fire.

On Christmas Day, the brave Major Penrod slipped through enemy lines to pay a brief but poignant call on his beloved. After greeting him warmly, Eugenia chastised him for putting his life in peril. In the not too distant past, she might have whined that his gift hadn't been adequate or his visit was too short in duration. But the war had matured her cousin. Major Penrod's Christmas gift was his grandmother's sapphire ring, a pledge of his troth, and an assurance he would love her until he drew his final breath. "That's long enough for me!" Eugenia had declared. "My answer is yes." Then she shooed him out the door with a rucksack filled with sandwiches following the longest kiss Madeline had ever witnessed.

No one had had any doubts as to what

her answer would be. Madeline now included Joseph's name in her long list of nightly prayers. However, by late January she spent most of her contemplation time pleading for forgiveness. Her actions since her arrival in Richmond had been anything but humanitarian. Although motivated by fierce patriotism for her country, Madeline realized that sin committed for noble reasons was sin nonetheless. One cannot serve two masters.

Suddenly, an insistent knock at the front door interrupted her regrets and misgivings. With the household, including the staff, at Mass, Madeline hurried to see who would call so early on a Sunday morning. She opened the door on the last person she expected to see.

"Colonel Haywood! What on earth are you doing here?" She glanced left and right in case a cadre of officers accompanied him.

With his plumed hat in hand, he flashed a smile. "I've come to take you to church. Don't tell me they suspended services at Saint Paul's. Surely *everyone* hasn't left town yet." His uniform appeared more tattered than it had the last time she had seen him, but it was clean and pressed.

For several moments Madeline stood in the doorway just staring at him.

"Goodness, Mrs. Howard. Either invite me inside or send me on my way. With the price of coal and firewood, I'm sure the Duncans wouldn't wish to heat the great outdoors."

Stepping to the side, she allowed him to pass and closed the door. Indeed, the air in the foyer was cold enough to see one's breath. "Is it stalemate over at Petersburg?" she asked, the question sounding ridiculous. She would have heard about any cessation of fighting or withdrawal of Union troops surrounding the city.

"No, the seige is not over, but I chose to take care of an errand today and pay you a call." He bowed dramatically, his hair falling across his brow.

"You left your command, just like that?"

His confident demeanor slipped a notch. "For a few more weeks, little will be happening on the battlefield. I really did have military business in Richmond, so I obtained permission for two additional stops before returning to my post. Do you fear a court-martial and firing squad awaits me? My heart swells at your concern." He winked at her in wry mockery.

"I'll get my cloak and hat so we can be off. We'll have plenty of icy sidewalks to contend with along the way."

The condition of frozen sidewalks didn't end up being an issue because at the end of the walkway waited a faded but serviceable carriage. The horse stamped and snorted with impatience, while the colonel's usual mount had been tied to the back. Madeline climbed up and settled against the upholstery, noticing an unpleasant odor — like a guest who lingers after a party. *Like I am becoming at the Duncans.*

"Where did you find a carriage for hire? Most were sold off to speculators long ago."

He waited to reply until they were comfortably settled and headed toward Church Hill at a brisk trot. "My first errand was to visit the family plantation, although the term hardly describes a rundown house and untended fields. More fences were broken down than upright." A slight tick in his cheek appeared.

"I trust your brother and father are in good health." Madeline gripped the seat as they bounced over ruts in the street.

"I'm afraid not. My father died shortly before Christmas of an unknown ailment. My brother buried him without a physician's examination, or notifying the authorities, or bothering to inform me."

Though the colonel focused on the road, Madeline saw a muscle jump in his neck.

"I'm sorry for your loss," she murmured inadequately.

He nodded, turning his head to meet her gaze briefly. "My brother was drunk when I arrived. It's his usual state, according to an elderly slave couple who remain when the others have run off. I couldn't fathom how Robert manages to buy whiskey until I talked to his servant in private. The two of them distill it from corn mash and then sell the rotgut to any passing fool with coin to spend."

Madeline had trouble thinking of an appropriate response. "At least they're still planting corn," she said after an uncomfortable pause.

His harsh laugh set her nerves on edge. "Not exactly, Mrs. Howard. Robert and Otis roam far and wide to steal corn during the night. But when I tried to discuss the subject, he resented my interference. He demanded I take whatever I like from the house and get out before Yankees burned the place to the ground." He ran his hand over the worn leather seat. "So I took my father's old carriage and his favorite Morgan."

"An odd remembrance of home. Were there no portraits or family heirlooms to recall happier days?" Madeline asked as they stopped in front of the cathedral. Most attendees arrived on foot these days.

Elliott offered his hand to help her step down. "I have no use for sentimentality and no place to store mementoes. My accommodations are far from luxurious these days."

Madeline took his elbow as they joined the last parishioners trailing inside. She didn't understand his complacency or his resignation over the loss. It was as though Colonel Haywood *expected* nothing good to ever happen again. "I hope I don't attract undue attention to add to your woes."

"I assure you, the opinions of others couldn't diminish the pleasure of your company."

Once she was seated in the Haywood pew, she stopped worrying and concentrated on the priest's sermon. It seemed that each of his Scripture readings had been intended for her:

"Let nothing be done through strife or vainglory," Father Daniel read from the book of Philippians, "but in lowliness of mind let each esteem other better than themselves. Look not every man on his own things, but every man also on the things of others." He closed his Bible. "Don't allow yourselves to be consumed by hatred, greed, or corruption. Someday these difficulties will be over, yet we can never hide our black hearts from the Lord. Beware."

Madeline was unable to look away as his eyes seemed to be solely fastened on hers. It was as though the priest knew exactly what she'd done, along with everyone else in town . . . everyone except for Colonel Haywood.

After the final hymn, Madeline wanted to run from the friend she had lied to and defrauded. Believing all women kind and virtuous, the colonel would never see her for what she really was. But instead she climbed into his dead father's coach like a coward.

"How about a drive along the river?" he asked as he spread a blanket across their laps and gave the reins a shake. "No sharpshooter would dare to take aim on the Sabbath."

"No, sir. Please take me to the Duncans'."

"Then we'll take the long way back. Surely you'll grant me that much time. Tonight I return to my post and soon the winter hiatus will end. This could be the last chance I get."

She peeked at him from the corner of her eye. "For what?"

"To win your heart, of course."

Madeline's composure crumbled as tears streamed down her face. Her emotions welled up like a fountain and refused to be contained. "Please, Colonel Haywood. You must stop. I have deceived you in order to advance my personal agenda. Although he turned me away, I'm still in love with General Downing. I have played both you and my family falsely. After everything Uncle John did for me, I stole a map from his desk and eavesdropped on his conversations." With the words strangling in her throat, Madeline gasped and hiccupped like a child.

"Stop, Mrs. Howard! I do not want to hear this —"

"But you *must* hear me and realize that your infatuation has been misguided. I have repaid kindness and friendship with deceit and dishonesty. Arrest me if you will, because that is what I deserve. People may die because of my trickery."

"Are you still up to your . . . trickery?"

Miserably, she shook her head. "No."

"Then we shall never speak of this again." Though his words were gracious, his normal ruddy complexion had faded to an unhealthy pallor.

For the duration of the drive, Madeline sniffled and sobbed with her gaze straight ahead. Along Broad Street the imposing homes were shuttered against the stiff winter wind. When they reached the Duncan mansion, Colonel Haywood drove down the lane behind the house. When they reached the stables, he pivoted toward her on the seat. "This will be my gift to the Duncans. Your uncle will need a rig sooner than he thinks." The colonel jumped down and began to unhitch the horse.

Madeline climbed down after him. "Why would Uncle John need a horse and carriage? He can walk almost everywhere in town." She wiped her wet face with her handkerchief.

"He will need to move his family and household staff, along with any possessions he doesn't wish to lose. I've spoken to him before, but he refuses to accept the dire situation." With Madeline at his heels, he led the horse to a stall, hung the harness on a peg, and returned to the carriage. Pulling the reins of his gelding free, he mounted in one smooth motion. "You must convince your family to leave Richmond. Soon it will not be safe here."

"Because of *my* doing?" she asked, swallowing the bitter taste of regret.

Sighing wearily, he plucked a burr from his horse's mane. "No, Mrs. Howard, not due to your mischief. And to offer salve for your conscience, you never fooled me for a moment. I knew you were still in love with General Downing, but I refused to believe I couldn't change your mind." Running a hand through his hair, he gazed at a row of dead cornstalks in Aunt Clarisa's garden. "Nothing you have done will change the inevitable outcome of this war. The conclusion has been predetermined by the amount of food, men, weapons, horseflesh — unfortunately, the Southern well has run dry."

Madeline touched his sleeve. "Then don't return to the battlefield. There's no reason for you to die, Colonel. Haven't both sides lost enough men already?"

He patted her hand and mustered a smile for her. "There is every reason. Even if the Cause is lost, I must do my duty or I will never be able to hold up my head."

"Thank you for your kindness to my family. I will pray for you, Colonel Haywood, in case God listens to the pleas of shameful liars."

"I believe He does, Mrs. Howard, and so I'm confident I will survive." He tipped his hat, and with a spur to his horse's flank, he rode away.

■ ■ ■ ■

TWENTY-THREE

■ ■ ■ ■

March 1865

Madeline sat in the parlor reading one of Uncle John's many leather-bound books. Yet try as she might, she couldn't keep her mind on the story of a brave white settler, raised by an Indian chief, during the war between France and England over Canada. When she had read the same page for the third time, she set the book on the end table next to her with a moan.

"What ails you, niece? You've been listless for days." Aunt Clarisa studied her over her half-moon spectacles.

"Not anything to worry about, but I can't seem to concentrate today." Madeline forced a smile.

"I'll tell you what's the matter," said Eugenia crossly. "It's too bloody cold in here. My fingers are so stiff I can barely embroider a simple rosebud on this pillowcase."

"Young lady, I'll thank you not to use

vulgarity in my parlor," Aunt Clarisa admonished, not raising her voice.

"The word 'bloody' is vulgar? The Emerson's new English maid uses that word all the time."

"It most certainly is. I will speak to Prudence regarding Bertha's language."

"But why can't we add more coal to the fire? It's still chilly outside."

"It's nearly spring, so let's think sunny thoughts. Besides, there's no more coal or wood to add. Or coffee or sugar either in this week's ration for that matter. Shall I continue listing what we don't have, or do you have sufficient items to pout about until supper?" Aunt Clarisa arched one dark eyebrow at her daughter.

"Sorry, Mama."

"You've sewn enough for one day, my dear. Why don't you visit Justine for the afternoon? Perhaps the Emerson parlor will be warmer."

Eugenia paled to the shade of the pillow slip. "Please don't send me away. I promise not to pout or say another disagreeable word until tomorrow."

"Tomorrow would be soon enough, but I'm not sending you off because of your grousing, my love," Aunt Clarisa said, laughing good-naturedly. "I wish to speak to your cousin and prefer to do so in private."

Madeline, who had been silently listening to the mother-daughter tête-à-tête, felt a chill descend on her that had nothing to do with a dearth of coal.

Eugenia dropped her embroidery in her basket, rose, and hugged her cousin around the shoulders. As she did so, she whispered in her ear, "Better keep quiet if the lemonade is sour. Remember, we have no sugar left." Then the young woman scampered into the foyer to retrieve her cloak.

Aunt Clarisa wasted no time once they heard the front door close. "I will ask you again, Madeline, what ails you? And I know it's something more serious than the wordiness of James Fenimore Cooper's masterpiece, or a frigid parlor, or the fact that our lemonade can pucker a pair of lips with one sip." She chuckled merrily over her jest.

Madeline gazed at the sweet, gentle soul who had fed her, clothed her, and taken her in when she had nowhere to go — the same woman she had lied to and deceived many times. She could no longer sit in the woman's presence when artillery shells might reduce this house and everything the Duncans held dear into a pile of rubble. Filled with shame and revulsion, Madeline burst into tears.

"Goodness, child, what is it?" Jumping to her feet, Aunt Clarisa sat next to her on the settee. "Are you ill? Should I send for the doctor?"

For several minutes, Madeline cried uncontrollably, soaking her blouse with tears. Never in her life had she felt so wretched, so utterly corrupt.

When she finally stopped sobbing, Aunt Clarisa asked, "Does this have something to do with Colonel Haywood? Your unhappiness began after his last visit. Are you frightened that something dreadful will befall him in Petersburg?" She rotated between rubbing Madeline's back and patting her head like a young child. "You must care deeply for him."

Her undeserved solace only made Madeline feel worse. "I do care for him, but not in the way you assume. He has proven himself loyal, but I have returned his friendship with manipulation, his affection with deception. During his last visit, I . . . I confessed that I had been false. I never stopped . . . loving . . . General Downing from Pennsylvania." Madeline's words came in fits and starts. "I had planned to manipulate him to gain information for the Union Army."

Her aunt stared at her, dumbfounded. "Why would you do such a thing? How could you behave in so un-Christian a fashion?"

The question hung in the air while Madeline moistened her dry lips. "Because the war took my husband, my horses, and my farm, and then burned my house to the ground with everything inside. I feared if the Confederacy won, my Tobias would . . . would have died in vain." Her tears began anew, but Madeline kept her focus on her aunt's face. "I never thought I would grow so fond of you, Uncle John, and Genie. I have paid back your charity by biting your hand. If I live to be a very old woman, I will forever regret betraying your trust." Madeline dabbed her nose with a sodden handkerchief.

Both women sat silent, with only the tick of the mantle clock marking time.

"Did you relay information you obtained from your uncle?" asked Aunt Clarisa.

Madeline nodded. "Yes. Once I listened in on his conversation, and once I copied a map of landings along the James River. I sent the map upriver into the hands of the Union Army."

"Oh, dear me, those are treasonous acts! You could hang for what you've done."

"Then so be it." Straightening, Madeline forced herself to stop crying. "I jeopardized my family, along with Colonel Haywood, who didn't deserve my treachery. People may die if the Union Army aims their cannons at Richmond. For that I should be executed."

Clarisa's head snapped back. "No one shall hang my sister's only daughter, not if I can help it. Speak of this matter to no one. You were foolish not to realize that your actions would come with consequences, but what's done is done." She dusted off her palms like a schoolmarm after a lesson.

Madeline shifted nervously. "Do you mean you can forgive me?"

"Of course I forgive you, but now we must make plans. What if Colonel Haywood rallies the home guard against you? A scorned man, rejected by the woman he loves, may behave in a less than gentlemanly way."

"Loves?" asked Madeline, cringing at the word.

"Yes, loves. Elliott admitted his feelings to your uncle on several occasions. He planned to ask for your hand after the war."

Madeline shrank against the cushions and buried her face in her hands. "It's his prerogative to alert the guards if he chooses. Please don't fret about me. I'm not worthy of your concern."

Aunt Clarisa wrapped her arm around her. "You lost your parents, your husband, your home, even your favorite horse. No woman should suffer that kind of sorrow. I believe you're repentant and worthy of a second chance — a new beginning up north."

Madeline returned her embrace. "Colonel Haywood probably won't retaliate, but he insisted we all leave Richmond as soon as possible. I spoke to my uncle about this to no avail."

"I'm well aware why Elliott gave John his father's horse and carriage. But as I told my husband, this is my home." Clarisa flourished her hand around the room. "I don't fear if the Yankees take Richmond, not if it means an end to the fighting. Come, Madeline, we'll talk no more of this. I know where Esther hid some ginger root for medicinal purposes. Let's brew a pot of tea to toast your fresh start as an honest woman."

Early April 1865

Clarisa paced from one end of the hallway to the other. Even after a sleepless night, she wouldn't be able to get a daytime nap due to the chaos in the streets. The constant

517

movement of soldiers in and out and around Richmond created a din of confusion.

"Please sit down, Mama," Eugenia called from her position on the stairs. She and Madeline sat on treads halfway up, as though uncertain which direction to go. "I fear you will faint from exhaustion."

"I'm fine, daughter. Or at least I will be once your father comes home."

"There have been train whistles throughout the night and all morning," said Eugenia. "With so many soldiers marching in formation, do you suppose the army is leaving?"

"Of course not. Without General Lee's troops to protect the city, Richmond would soon fall into Yankee hands."

"Shouldn't we start packing, just in case?" asked Madeline.

Clarisa turned to meet her niece's gaze. "Yes, I suppose the time has come, but only one small trunk each. No more, daughter, or we won't have room in the buggy for the food left in the pantry."

"What about my *trousseau*?" cried Eugenia.

"You may take your new clothes."

"And Grandmama's silver and the crystal vases? I must have them for my wedding chest. And what about the linens I've embroidered?" Eugenia sounded near hysteria.

"Fine. I will walk *beside* the carriage so you and Joseph can furnish your new home." The sharp words were accompanied by a smile. Clarisa loved her daughter, regardless of how shortsighted she was being.

"What about Micah, Esther, and Patsy?" Madeline's question was barely a whisper. "We can't leave them behind. What if the Union artillery shells the city?"

"Of course they can come along if they choose. They can walk next to me. Now go pack. When you're finished, please help Esther in the kitchen."

Madeline pulled her cousin to her feet. "Come, Genie. You can fill my trunk with your things. I'll have no need for fancy ball gowns once I'm home. All I need is one change of clothes."

"Thank you, Madeline. I'll never forget this." Soon the young women's voices trailed off as they reached the upper hallway.

None of us will forget today, Clarisa thought. As her pacing brought her past the front window again, she spotted a courier heading up the flagstones. Steeling herself for dreadful news, she swept open the heavy oak door.

A sallow-faced teenager doffed his crumpled cap. "Mrs. Duncan? A message for you from President Davis's office, ma'am." He thrust a thrice-folded sheet into her hand and hastened back down the walk.

Unfolding the sheet, Clarisa tried to decipher her husband's scribble: *We are engaged at Five Forks. General Lee requested all troops posthaste. Richmond is to be evacuated tomorrow. We will leave in the morning at first light. I'll be home soon as I can. Your loving husband, John*

Clutching her husband's note to her bodice, Clarisa closed her eyes and swayed on her feet. "He's coming home. We'll leave Richmond together. Thank You, Lord."

Within several hours, the women and household staff finished packing. Only essentials necessary for survival would be taken, such as cooking pots, warm blankets, and food. Clarisa and Madeline packed small valises to allow Eugenia the extra space. Esther, Micah, and Patsy filled pillowcases with their belongings to string over their backs. That night, everyone ate a hearty supper in the kitchen and went to bed early, except for Clarisa.

She waited up for her husband in the parlor, finally dozing off after midnight. When she awoke, she saw John's lined face looming above her. "I'm so relieved to see you!" she said, pulling him down beside her to hug him with all of her might.

"Take care, dear wife. I have thus far escaped injury." John hugged her fiercely in return.

"Should I awaken the household?" She buried her teary face against his jacket.

"No, let everyone sleep. We'll leave shortly after dawn." John drew back the curtain to reveal darkness beyond the window.

"Then you should rest. Come upstairs."

"If you will indulge me another minute, we need to talk."

"What has happened?" she asked softly, her gut tightening with anxiety.

"I heard today that the militia arrested a Chesapeake fisherman. Apparently, the man had been passing documents to Yankees up the coastline."

His grim expression turned her mouth dry. "Go on," she prodded.

"This sea captain had on his person a letter from our niece addressed to that Union general she went to see. I'm afraid the letter incriminates Madeline." John reached for Clarisa's hand. "I fear for her, my love. Tempers are short. Everyone in the war department is looking for someone to blame."

She gripped the back of a chair. "She's my niece, John. I must protect her at all costs. I won't have her sacrificed for a stupid mistake — one she deeply regrets."

The lines in her husband's forehead and around his mouth deepened. "There is truth to the allegations?"

She nodded. "Some truth, I'm afraid."

"Then I made the right decision."

"What have you done?" Clarisa's knees threatened to buckle beneath her.

John offered a supporting arm. "I sent word to Colonel Haywood in Petersburg. Grant has broken through their lines and General Hill has been killed." His voice cracked with emotion. "With Union artillery firing on Petersburg, our soldiers are in a westward rout. President Davis has ordered Petersburg evacuated, as well as Richmond. Anyone not wishing to live under the thumb of the federal army must leave. We packed up critical government documents and took them to the station. Invalid soldiers will work through the night destroying documents we don't want to fall into Yankee hands."

"But what can Colonel Haywood do for Madeline with the army in retreat?" Clarisa lowered her voice to whisper as though reluctant to utter such words aloud.

"Perhaps nothing, but I told him where we'll head tomorrow. If there's anything he can do to help Madeline, I believe he will." John led her toward the door with a supportive arm. "Now we must rest, my love. Our future is in God's hands."

The next morning the Duncans awoke to a world gone mad. Civilians loaded down with everything they could carry crowded the streets. No one seemed to know the safest route or where they would go once they were beyond the city. Most headed to the depot, where every available train car had been brought south from Fredericksburg. Doors to the quartermaster and commissary storehouses had been thrown open. The half-starved people of Richmond rushed in and hauled away whole hams, along with sacks of coffee, sugar, and flour — items meant to be rationed for months. If a storekeeper no longer guarded his door, men and women broke in and looted whatever they could carry. Bolts of fabric, piles of dresses, and stacks of hat boxes filled a parade of passing wagons.

The Duncan family and their employees flanked the carriage as John fought to control the skittish horse down Forsythia Lane. Only Patsy and Abigail rode next to him. Clarisa insisted on walking with Eugenia and Madeline for as long as possible.

"Where are we going, Papa?" asked Eugenia, unusually subdued.

"We shall head east toward the naval yard and Rocketts Landing, and then follow New Market Road. Everyone else will head south along the Richmond and Danville rail line. Our boys have been ordered to set fire to the bridges, so other routes will soon be blocked."

"East? Won't that be where the fighting will commence?" Clarisa couldn't help but ask. "We don't want to blunder onto a battlefield."

"Rest easy, my love. The bulk of both armies is well south of Richmond, so there'll be no fighting today. Besides, it's not Yankees we need to fear." Though both of John's hands were occupied with the reins, his sidearm was visible and close by. Micah, armed with a shotgun, followed behind the group, vigilant for approaching threats from the rear.

"Then who?"

"Deserters from either side, profiteers who came south to pick our bones, or those hatchet-wielding trollops — a full assortment of ruffians who would love a horse and carriage to carry their bounty."

Clarisa shivered, unaccustomed to such

bluntness. John normally tried to shield her as much as possible from anything unpleasant. For several hours she plodded along the streets toward one of the bridges across the James River. This would be their best and perhaps only means of escape. Esther and Patsy gathered discarded items along the way from those lightening their loads. Clarisa clung tightly to the tarnished brass rail of the carriage like a frightened child. Only Madeline kept pace without complaint, always within reach of the horse's bridle. When they reached the river, she clambered down the hillside for a bucket of water for the horse, a chore repeated at each stream they crossed.

While the thirsty mare drank, the sudden sound of explosions louder than any clap of thunder froze them in their tracks. Everyone turned back toward Richmond to watch a red glow spread like a stain across the horizon.

"Is that artillery fire?" asked Madeline, staggering against the buggy wheel. "Are the Yankees firing on the city?"

"No, dear niece." John patted her shoulder. "That is the Confederate Army setting fire to the munitions and tobacco warehouses. The Yankees don't need cannons to take Richmond, not anymore. They know our troops have abandoned the capital."

Horrified, Clarisa watched flames leap ever higher against the darkening sky. Fire spread from building to building along the riverfront. Thick, billowing smoke filled the air and drifted on the breeze, reaching them within minutes. "Will the whole city burn, including our home?" she asked, choking down the taste of bile.

John shook his head. "I don't know, but we are alive and safe. Climb up here, dear heart. Patsy insists on walking."

Clarisa did as instructed, grateful for his suggestion. Her flimsy boots hadn't been designed for long treks. For hours the carriage rolled along the rutted turnpike, encountering fewer pedestrians the farther they journeyed.

Finally, John brought the carriage to a stop and set the brake. Handing his wife the reins, he climbed down and said, "Micah, I want you to stay with the carriage and guard the women. Madeline, I would like you to come with me. We need to find a dry place to spend the night."

"Where are we?" She peered up at the bronze cross atop a wooden steeple.

John gazed skyward too. "We've reached Laurel Hill Church. With the grace of God, Colonel Haywood will find us here."

"Colonel Haywood?" said Madeline. "Why on earth would he come here?"

"As a member of President Davis's staff, I cannot take you closer to Union lines than this. If anyone can deliver you safely to General Downing's protection, it would be Colonel Haywood."

"Oh, Uncle, I am grateful, but your idea is hopeless. You have done enough. I will set off alone at first light so I don't endanger your family."

John put his arm around her and drew her tightly against his side. "For now, let's select seven pews for our beds for the night. Then we shall see what the morrow brings."

TWENTY-FOUR

Colonel Haywood gazed down on seven sleeping people in the plain, country church. With only moonlight shining through high clerestory windows, it was difficult to ascertain who was who. Silently, he crept up the aisle, finally stopping at one particularly rounded form. Without a doubt, beneath the tattered quilt lay Mrs. Howard, a woman he'd hoped to spend the rest of his life with. Her signature scent of lemon verbena still clung to her clothes and hair despite an arduous trip from the capital.

Elliott settled on the adjacent pew, rested his head on his folded arms, and watched her sleep. Dozing off and on, he would wake with a start unsure of where he was or what he was doing. Then he remembered why he was outside of New Market, within a few miles of the Union Army. He was preparing to deliver the woman he loved into the arms of the enemy. Elliott forced away the end

result and concentrated on his motivation
— a life for a life, along with the request by
a man he respected — John Duncan.

*I am a fool, or perhaps addled by too little
food, too little sleep, and too much killing.*
Soon all that bloodshed would be for
naught. With a sigh Elliott closed his eyes
against images that would remain etched in
his brain for the rest of his life.

"Colonel Haywood?" A soft voice roused
him from his reverie.

"Ah, Mrs. Howard, you're awake." He
scrubbed his face with his hands to banish
the last of his drowsiness.

"What on earth are you doing here?" she
whispered.

"Isn't it obvious? I've ridden to your
rescue — your knight in shining armor.
Alas, my steed is dark brown instead of pure
white," he also whispered as he offered her
his most sincere smile.

She glanced around the church interior.
"You've come alone? Have you lost your
mind?"

"Affirmative, on both counts. I've just
drawn the same conclusion." Elliott rubbed
the small of his back, which ached from the
position he had slept in. Then he stood and
gestured to the back of the church, where

they could speak quietly without waking the others.

"I don't need to be rescued. You must return to your division at once." Her eyes filled with pity. "I'm fine with my aunt and uncle."

"Your bravery is commendable, but if Confederate authorities catch up with your troupe, you will be in grave danger. And if Mr. Duncan attempts to deliver you closer to Union lines, he would be in danger."

"I don't understand," Madeline said softly as she swung her legs off the pew and straightened her skirt to cover her ankles.

He sighed and then whispered, "Captain George has been arrested, and the *Bonnie Bess* was confiscated by our navy. Apparently, he was carrying a letter from you to the commander of the fourth corps. However, your letter to him discovered on a known Yankee spy places you in a precarious position."

"Lord, have mercy." Madeline scrambled to her feet, staggering a step. "I must leave the Duncans right away so they aren't implicated."

"Easy, Mrs. Howard." He tried steadying her with a firm grip.

She shrugged off his hand and moved as quietly as she could to the back of the church before speaking again. "Why are you here? To deliver me to the war department to answer for my crimes?"

"You think I would betray the woman who saved my life? I don't care if you were on a mission to steal gold from the Richmond Treasury."

Her eyes grew round as an owl's. "You will help me after I treated you cruelly?"

"A life for a life, but there is no time to discuss sentimental gestures. We have a long ride ahead of us if I'm to get you away." He handed her one of his saddle bags. "Inside are some clothes. Take off your skirt and hoop and put them on. They should fit over your other . . . garments."

She withdrew the butternut jacket, trousers, and cap. "The uniform of a Confederate soldier?"

"How better to blend in? I'm hopeful that neither side will shoot at the insignia of the medical corps. You'll have to hide your hair under the cap."

Madeline fingered the red crossed lines that had been painted boldly on the fabric.

"If we're stopped along the road, let me do the talking. I'll say I'm delivering my mute cousin to the nearest field hospital. Your accent may give us away. I would hate to end an illustrious career in so inglorious a fashion," he smiled ruefully at her as he tugged on his gloves.

"Thank you for your gallantry and fore-thought." Madeline began unfastening the row of buttons on her bodice and then hesitated.

When she stood motionlessly, Elliott's patience waned. "Be quick, Mrs. Howard. We have a long ride to get you out of harm's way."

"Could you turn your back, sir?" she asked shyly.

"Oh. Of course. I'll wait outside. You may have a few minutes to say goodbye." He felt a blush climb up his neck as he strode from the dark church. Outside, the first pink streaks of dawn appeared.

Just as his patience ran out, the entire entourage of Duncans and longtime staff emerged from the sanctuary. A scrawny youth walked with Eugenia, his trousers held up with a length of twine. With a jolt, Elliott recognized Mrs. Howard. All of her thick blond hair had been tucked under the cap. "Step lively, soldier, and I expect a duti-ful salute."

"Wearing this scratchy wool will prove hardship enough, Colonel. Please don't expect much military precision." Madeline glanced around the churchyard while her family closed in, each one silent and morose. "Did you bring only one horse, sir?"

"No others could be spared. But he's a sturdy beast, capable of carrying both our substantial weights."

Madeline angled a wry frown at him, tied her cloth valise to the saddle, and turned to her family.

"I shall miss you, Maddy." Eugenia hurried forward, despite the prancing hooves of the horse.

"And I, you. I will make every human effort to return for your wedding," Madeline said as she hugged her cousin and then kissed her cheek. "Goodbye, dear aunt and uncle. I am in your debt." Her luminous blue eyes were shiny with tears as her aunt enveloped her in a last embrace.

"And my wife and I are in yours, Colonel Haywood. Thank you." Mr. Duncan reached out his hand.

Elliott shook and then tipped his hat to Mrs. Duncan. "Someday I'll collect my reward at your dinner table, ma'am. Goodbye." Swinging up into the saddle, he held out his hand to assist Mrs. Howard up behind him. He was immediately assaulted by her lemony scent, while her soft curves beneath the private's uniform pressed against his back.

"Goodbye," she called as the horse trotted down the trail. "I'll never forget all that you've done."

Elliott knew the back roads west of Richmond and thus avoided the thoroughfares where Confederate pickets might be posted or Union detachments of cavalry might patrol. He stayed on farm traces and trails that connected towns too small to appear on Virginia maps. While they rode he tried concentrating on the scenery — rich fields ready for planting, the canopy of new green leaves, and the cacophony of birds singing in the trees. But try as he might, he couldn't keep his mind off the woman clinging to his midsection. A wisp of her hair across his neck, the press of her leg next to his, her warmth radiating through the threadbare jacket — all conspired to entice him like a moth to a flame.

It will be a long ride, indeed.

When they paused beside a shallow stream around midday, Madeline pulled bread, a block of cheese, and two shriveled apples from her valise. "My aunt insisted I take some food." She offered half the provender in her outstretched hand.

Elliott gazed at her slender fingers and delicate wrist, the curve of her hips beneath trousers, and felt palpable desire. He stood motionless, paralyzed by the forbidden fruit.

"What are you staring at, Colonel?"

Elliott grabbed an apple from her palm. "Seeing you without one of those ridiculous hoops. It's been a long time. I'll bet you welcome your release from bondage."

"I do, but it's unusual for a man to recognize those uncomfortable tormentors for what they are."

"I'm not like most men." The statement hung in the warm spring air.

"I've recently discovered that." With a blush she averted her gaze.

"Yes, well, thank you for lunch, however, this might be the last grass not ravaged by the cavalry — one or the other." Taking a large bite of apple, Elliott led his horse to a thick patch. But when he turned around the object of his affection stood behind him.

"May I know where we're going?" She peered up at him through impossibly thick eyelashes.

"We're headed to the Namozine church. It should be south of the Confederate exodus from Richmond and with any luck, north of the Yankees reconnoitering from Petersburg. But we must reach the rendezvous point by nightfall, so eat up."

For hours they rode at a gentle pace so as to not overtire the horse. Just when he sensed she might fall from the saddle from exhaustion, Elliott spotted a familiar landmark in the distance. "Wake up, Mrs. Howard. We had better walk from here."

She slipped from the saddle clumsily. Getting used to being on her feet again, she peered around the scrub brush and briar patches as though expecting recognition. "Have we reached our mysterious destination?" she whispered.

"We have. Keep quiet and remain behind me. If anyone shoots first, perhaps you'll live long enough to answer their questions." Elliott stumbled along the rutted path but kept a tight grip on the reins and her small hand.

The trail led down to a well-hidden river ford, used primarily by local farmers to move livestock to pastures downstream. He had known of this crossing for some time and expected it to be unguarded. The far bank, shrouded by thick foliage and vines, looked steeper than the one in front of them. Pulling Madeline behind a mountain laurel bush, he issued a mediocre imitation of a hoot owl.

"What on earth?" she whispered.

"Hush and stay down." Elliott repeated his bird call.

For several moments they listened to

silence and then heard an equally poor imitation of an owl's cry.

Inhaling a deep breath, Elliott stepped into the circle of moonlight.

"Colonel Haywood, I presume?" A deep voice resonated from the shadows.

"Show yourself, General Downing. Have you come alone?"

"What?" Though she burst from the shrubbery, the colonel held on to her tightly.

James Downing stepped from the shadows twenty paces away. Taller than Elliott had imagined, the general looked powerful as a bull with a chest almost as wide. "I have two lieutenants tending the horses, but I approach you unarmed." He slowly lifted his hands, revealing an empty scabbard and holster.

"James, is it really you? I can't believe my eyes." Madeline broke free and closed the distance in a few long strides.

The poignant reunion of two people separated so long nearly ripped Elliott's soul in half. Downing enveloped Mrs. Howard in his arms, knocking off her cap and releasing her mane of golden hair. He planted a string of kisses across her forehead. Her response was no less enthusiastic. She transformed in the Yankee's presence. She'd spoken of her feelings for him, but until

Elliott witnessed for himself he'd refused to believe. Their affection — their passion — was punishment to watch. He'd been deluded, not by her but by himself, his male ego tricking him into believing he could capture a heart that belonged to another. Clearing his throat, Elliott approached the pair unconcerned who might be hiding in the trees.

"Excuse me, sir." General Downing swept his wide-brimmed hat from his head, pulled off his gloves, and extended his hand. Madeline shrank back in embarrassment. "I would like to thank you —"

"Save your words, General. I didn't do this for you." His voice was little more than a growl. "I owed Mrs. Howard a debt from Gettysburg. Now she and I are square."

Withdrawing his hand, the general nodded with mute understanding. He knew Elliott's motivation went beyond the ageless code of honor among enemies. "I will see that she safely reaches Pennsylvania soil. You have my word."

"How on earth did you know where we would be?" asked Madeline.

"Colonel Haywood sent his aide directly from Petersburg under a white flag of truce. He said he would bring you to this river ford and described its location perfectly."

Madeline turned toward him with a tender smile. "Thank you, Colonel. Your debt has been repaid many times over."

Elliott felt weak in the knees. Filled with envy for the general's happiness, he looked away. "You should get moving. Resume your belated reunion once you are on Northern soil. I have no desire to be hanged on your behalf, General Downing, should *my* pickets find us first."

Downing whistled into the darkness. Almost immediately, two grimfaced soldiers appeared, holding the reins of four saddled horses.

"Bo! You still have her." Mrs. Howard threw her arms around her horse's neck. She pulled the reins from the lieutenant's hands and swung up into the saddle as effortlessly as any cavalry soldier. But instead of joining the general's side, she nudged her horse in Elliott's direction. "I will continue to pray for your safety, Colonel." She extended her hand.

Instead of shaking, Elliott kissed the backs of her slender fingers. "You will want to change out of that Confederate uniform as soon as possible." He pulled her valise off of his shoulder and tied it to her saddle horn.

Downing cleared his throat and met

Elliott's gaze. "I suggest you ride due north and avoid roads south of here. Our normal logistics have been reversed — my army is south of yours." With a tip of his hat, the general kicked his horse's flanks. In an instant, the four riders crossed the river and disappeared into the woods, leaving Elliott staring into the dark for a long while.

Although he was now alone, he could still hear her infectious laughter and smell her lemon verbena. Four years' worth of anger and frustration, along with something far more personal, rose from deep in his gut and threatened to explode. Finally, when his rage subsided, Elliott walked back to where he'd left his horse, thankful for the long ride ahead of him to find his division. He needed time to dwell on the sweet hours they had spent together and consider what he might have done differently.

Because once he returned to Richmond, he vowed never to think about Madeline Howard again.

Judging by the sun's last glow against a dark sky, the well-packed trail ran true west. The four riders put less than five miles between themselves and whatever troops the Confederate colonel had hidden in the woods. Unfamiliar with the territory, General

Downing selected a spot he hoped was beyond the usual radius of a picket line. "We'll make camp here for the night," he announced, reining to a stop. "The horses have ridden hard and will be no use to us if they go lame."

Madeline reined to a stop and peered around the small clearing. Trees and scrub loomed menacingly on all sides. "Where are we?"

"In my estimation, we're smack in the middle of nowhere, but that should make us difficult to find by the Rebs." James reached up to help her off the horse.

"This doesn't appear too loathsome a place." Madeline slid effortlessly into his arms and then turned to unbuckle the straps on Bo's saddle.

"My aides will see to that." James took her by the hand. "Lieutenant Jeffries, please feed and water the horses. Then you men open your haversacks and find a soft spot for bedrolls." The soldiers snapped salutes and saw to his orders, astute enough to stand watch without intruding on his privacy.

"Come, Madeline, have something to eat and then rest. You must be starving." James led her to a massive oak tree and spread out the wool blanket on a thick patch of moss.

"What do we have for supper?" she asked, dropping to her knees.

He opened the parcel procured from an Army sutler. "Smoked turkey, bread, cheese, raisins, and dried currants."

Her eyes widened with the array. "That's more food than I've seen in a long time. Thank you." She picked up the canteen and drank half the contents before selecting a piece of bread and cheese.

While she ate he built a small fire to keep the mosquitos at bay. "Don't be shy. We've had plenty to eat lately."

"Won't the fire draw attention to our location?"

"It shouldn't as long as we keep it small. The wind is from the west." James added dry sticks and fanned the flame into a small blaze.

"Aren't you having something to eat?" Madeline handed him a turkey leg.

James took it to put her at ease. "If you insist, but I would much rather just watch you."

"To evaluate my table manners on the trail?" Her eyes twinkled with mischief.

"To study every detail of a face I've dreamed about for months."

Madeline paused between bites. "I have missed you too, James."

He waited to speak until she'd eaten a few more bites. "Colonel Haywood grew rather fond of you during your stay in Richmond." It wasn't a question.

Madeline swallowed and met his gaze. "Yes, he did — a fact that causes me no small measure of shame."

"What do you have to be ashamed of?" James felt his back stiffen.

"Believing the end justified the means, I used our friendship to mask my subterfuge." Madeline placed the piece of meat down on the wrapper. "But I don't feel that Christians should lie, manipulate, or steal — not even for noble purposes. Colonel Haywood and my uncle risked their lives for me after I betrayed their trust. I'm sorry I returned to Richmond and foolishly assumed I was cut out for this . . . espionage business."

"I never should have let you leave Culpeper in February."

"You couldn't have stopped me, James." A grin played at the corners of her mouth. "I've never been one to listen to common sense."

"We have brigs and stockades for those who refuse to follow orders."

Madeline winked at him. "Never underestimate the power of a willful woman. I would have bribed your guards into releasing me."

He laughed, feeling the knots in his stomach loosen. "Don't think me ungrateful for what Colonel Haywood did tonight, or for the protection he provided in Richmond."

"That's a relief to hear. For a moment there, I thought you might be jealous." Madeline reached out and touched his face, her fingers tracing the line of his jaw.

The sensation caused his heart to miss several beats. "Is this the face you remember?" Emotion turned his voice hoarse.

"It's very much as I recall." Her hand paused on his lips.

James kissed her fingertips, wrapped an arm around her waist, and leaned against the tree.

"This looks like a comfortable spot to pass the night," Madeline said softly, nestling into his shoulder.

James shuddered in pain. "Can we try the other side?"

"What's wrong?" she asked, pulling away.

"A minor wound, nothing to worry about," he said through gritted teeth.

"You were shot?" Her eyes grew round.

"Yes, but I'm fine —"

"I will check your wound once we get where we're going. After all, I had a whole day of nurse's training," Madeline said, smiling as he directed her to his other side and nestled her into the crook of that arm.

"Only one day, yet you managed to save Colonel Haywood's life." He hoped that didn't sound as petty to her ears as it did to his.

"Please don't worry about him, James. You have my heart."

He withdrew the tintype taken at the ball from his pocket. "You have no idea how happy that makes me."

Pulling the frame from his fingers, she stared in abject shock. "Is this why you wrote that letter? I can't imagine how this picture found its way to you, but the colonel was never more to me than a friend."

"Thank goodness. I feared calling out an aristocrat at dawn wouldn't go well for me, but for you I would risk far more than dueling pistols." He kissed the top of her head. "I regretted writing that letter as soon as it was posted. Then when I discovered my chief of staff's trickery, my regret increased ten-fold. Justin Henry was badly wounded at Fort Stedman, but before he died, he confessed to burning my letters to you, along with yours to me. And for obtaining the picture so he could end our relationship."

"We have no need of letters or subterfuge, and certainly no dueling pistols at dawn. Nothing will separate us ever again." Madeline tossed the framed tintype into the fire.

For several minutes they watched the metal warp and distort from the heat. Once it was beyond recognition, he said, "Tomorrow we ride due west along the rail line until we reach Farmville. At the station I'll put you on the train to Lynchburg, where you can catch the train to Culpeper. I'll make arrangements for you at the inn."

"Absolutely not. I won't be separated from you —"

"Please do this for me, Madeline. I must rejoin my men and fight until this blasted war is finished. We must ensure that the Rebs don't slip through our fingers and join Joe Johnston in North Carolina. Without reinforcements, Lee will have no choice but to surrender."

"As you wish," she said, though not without reluctance. Then she sighed. "My willfulness hasn't served me very well."

"I will come for you. You have my word."

Madeline leaned back to see his face. "What about my horse? Now that I have Bo, I don't relish letting her go either."

"I'll keep your horse safe until she can be returned to Pennsylvania."

"In that case, why don't we rest for a few minutes?" Madeline nestled again into his good shoulder.

"An excellent idea." Tightening his embrace, James heard the rhythm of steady breathing within moments. Madeline had fallen asleep in his arms.

For several hours he stared into the fire, enjoying the warmth of her body and the sweet smell of her hair. Tomorrow they would set off at first light. As they had since leaving Petersburg, they would ride past plenty of pretty farms. But a closer inspection revealed peeling paint, missing shutters, and broken fences. Pastures would be overrun with sumac and hawthorn, with grapevines covering every upright fencepost. Only women and children would be tilling and hoeing the fields, as though not a single man were left in a country devoured by two rampaging beasts.

When James finally fell asleep, dead soldiers marched through his dreams in a ghastly parade. Many dead Confederates also paid him a call that night. He would see their young faces when he closed his eyes for the rest of his life. Off in the distance lightning flashed, followed by the low rumble of thunder a few moments later.

A storm was coming . . . or perhaps the maelstrom was finally moving out to sea.

■ ■ ■ ■

TWENTY-FIVE

■ ■ ■ ■

Culpeper, Virginia
April 10, 1865

"Hold your horses! I'm coming." The inn-keeper's irate voice permeated the thick oak wood.

James pulled off his hat and swept a hand through his tangled hair. When she had opened the door, he said, "Begging your pardon, madam, but four years has made me a tad impatient."

"General Downing! Come in, sir. I had no idea it would be you."

"Is Mrs. Howard here?" he asked, attempting to smooth the wrinkles from his shirt.

"Of course she is. I received your letter explaining that Mrs. Howard is not actually your sister and the wire transfer of gold. I must say you were more than generous for a week's room and board for one skinny gal."

"Did you follow my instructions?"

"Yes, sir. I took her to my personal dress-maker. But Mrs. Howard bought only two day dresses, walking shoes, and one rather plain hat. Oh, and some new unmention-ables. Nothing fancy, I assure you. She said she has no need of —"

"Thank you, Mrs. Lang, for your dili-gence. Now if I might have a word with Mrs. Howard." James scuffed his boots on the porch boards.

"Of course, sir. Will you be staying the night?" Her dark eyes blinked several times.

"If you have an available room." James's impatience began to simmer like a teakettle.

"Oh, I have lots of space. Few folks are traveling these days. At least none with money to spend. I expect you and Mrs. Howard would like dinner tonight."

"Yes, ma'am. Now, if you would be kind enough —"

"How about a nice pot roast with boiled peas served by the fire?"

"Fine. I honestly don't care if it's horse-meat with pickled turnips! May I *please* see Mrs. Howard?"

Mrs. Lang lifted her chin indignantly. "No call to get all prickly, sir. I'll fetch her to the parlor." Stomping up the steps, she left him standing in the open doorway.

James walked into the parlor, where dust motes floated in the slanted light from the west windows. He had thought about their February dinner so many times that he had memorized every detail of the room. After a few minutes he heard a clatter of feet on the steps. Then the love of his life burst through the doorway. A thin ribbon held back her long blond curls, while being away from the city had turned her complexion into a mass of freckles. The sunny glow of her flushed face intensified her blue irises. Her beauty caused his mouth to go dry and his blood to quicken in his veins.

"Is it really you?" she gasped, breathless. "I can't believe you're here! We heard rumors in town, but no one could verify if they're true."

When Madeline crossed the room to throw herself in his arms, James forgot his rehearsed speech, his promises of unending devotion. They held each other closely, silently, until he drew her to arm's length. "It's true. The war is over. General Lee surrendered his army in Appomattox Courthouse yesterday. I have tonight and tomorrow morning here in Culpeper."

Madeline stepped back from his embrace. "If the war is over, why on earth must you go back?"

"I must properly muster-out my corps or they won't receive the back pay they are due. And we need to prepare parole papers for the surrendering Confederates. If they promise to never again bear arms against the Union, they won't be imprisoned. I will face the wrath of General Grant if I'm not on the train tomorrow afternoon."

"Then why have you come?" Madeline crossed her arms with more indignation than the innkeeper. "You simply craved a pleasant jaunt through the countryside?"

His confidence slipped a notch. "I have important business here tomorrow morning — an urgent errand that won't wait. And I would like to have dinner with you tonight."

She perched her hands on her hips. "And what about right now, General Downing? Do you have something in mind for the rest of the afternoon?"

"Well . . . yes. Because we have no horses for a springtime ride, I thought a walk along the streets of Culpeper would be nice. Unless, of course, you have other plans."

She laughed despite her irritation. "Most assuredly, I do not. I'll just get my shawl."

A few minutes later she appeared on the porch wrapped in lace. "Do you have some place special in mind, or shall we walk aimlessly until our legs give out?" Linking her arm through his, she turned her face up to him.

"Anywhere, as long as the innkeeper isn't lurking behind the door. She was listening to our entire conversation in the parlor."

Madeline laughed again. "Unfortunately, I'm no stranger to eavesdropping. Ever since you sent that pouch of gold, Mrs. Lang has been fascinated by you. Nobody in Culpeper has seen that kind of money in ages."

"I'm eager to be frivolous. For four long years, I had few places to spend my army pay."

"Thank you for my accommodations and the lovely clothes, although the new shoes do pinch my toes a bit." She lifted one high-laced boot from beneath her skirt. "Didn't you wish to see me in the same two worn-out dresses? Mrs. Lang probably assumes the worst about my reputation."

"I care little about what you wear, Madeline, and even less about what Mrs. Lang thinks. Soon we'll never see that annoying woman again."

She stopped short on the sidewalk. "Why are you limping? Did you hurt your leg as well as your shoulder? You didn't have a limp a week ago."

"Nothing to worry about . . . a minor leg

wound that has healed up nicely." He snaked his good arm around her waist.

She turned her gaze skyward, where tree branches were filled with fragrant apple blossoms. "You were shot twice? I must say, my secret gift didn't live up to its reputation."

"Are you referring to this?" James withdrew the chain from beneath his shirt collar. The silver medallion discovered in the wooded glade months ago dangled from the end.

"Yes, the Saint Christopher medal. You found where I'd hidden it in your pocket?"

"I did. But you should examine it closely before pronouncing it unworthy."

Turning the medallion over between her fingers, Madeline found a smooth, dime-sized indention in the silver. "What on earth . . ."

"That medal stopped a bullet on its way to my heart. Although it was supposed to protect you, I'm grateful for your gift."

"You were shot *three* times?" Her jaw dropped in disbelief.

"Indeed, I should be set for life." On impulse, he lifted her chin and kissed her.

"That would be my fondest hope too," she said, her eyes sparkling with delight. "Shall we walk? I want to hear about Major

Henry's deathbed confession. And I have much to tell you about my dear cousin. Only Eugenia can plan a wedding in the midst of chaos."

For several hours they simply sauntered up one lane and down the next, never running out of things to say. They had two years' worth — or perhaps a lifetime — of tales to share. When Madeline's limp from her new shoes became as pronounced as his, they walked back to the inn.

"Ah, General Downing, I was wonderin' when you would be back." Mrs. Lang swept open the door before they reached the front steps. "I just set the kettle of stew on the parlor table. Didn't want it scorchin' on the stove too long. Cold is better than burnt any day."

James and Madeline sidled through the doorway, where the woman practically blocked their passage. "Thank you, Mrs. Lang. I'm sure the food will be delicious," he said graciously.

"I also put a pan of cornbread on the table, along with fresh butter. Don't have no fancy wine for your reunion, just well water. Nobody in town has spirits, except Mr. Mosley, and you don't want to drink his plum wine." She offered them an unpleasant expression.

"Water will be perfect. Thank you again, ma'am." James led Madeline to the parlor hearth, where a warm fire blazed. A jelly jar of violets sat on a table covered with starched white linen, a charming effect despite the mismatched china.

Unfortunately, their innkeeper followed them into the room. "I wanted to go over details for tomorrow, sir. Should I —"

James cut her off with a low voice. "Nothing has changed since I sent my written instructions. If you would follow them exactly and not interrupt us again tonight, I will double the fee for your services." He struggled to keep his temper.

"Fine, sir. If you wanted privacy with your lady friend, why didn't you just say so?" Mrs. Lang stalked from the room, sliding the pocket doors closed behind her.

Once they were blissfully alone, Madeline burst out laughing. "All you had to do was say so, James. I'm not sure why you can't express yourself." She fluffed her napkin over her lap and pulled off the lid to the kettle. The rich aroma of beef, onion, celery, and carrots filled the air and whetted their appetites.

"I have better luck getting soldiers to do my bidding. I have little familiarity with all of this." The tightness in his stomach had nothing to do with hunger.

Her face sobered. "Do you mean no familiarity with courting or with a world not at war?"

"Either. Both, if the truth be told." James sat clumsily on a chair too small for his size.

"Try not to fret, General. Let's eat Mrs. Lang's stew and not worry about the rest of our lives."

And so they ate two helpings each and then swabbed up the gravy with the last piece of cornbread. Although the inn's cuisine was far from gourmet, James couldn't remember a more enjoyable meal. They talked and laughed until the fire turned to cold ashes on the hearth. Yet neither wanted the evening to end.

When the mantle clock chimed eleven, Madeline pushed back her chair. "I should let you get some sleep, James," she said. "It sounds as though you have an important errand tomorrow."

"Yes, very important indeed, my dear." He studied her profile in the candlelight as though he hadn't been looking at her all evening.

"You're not going to tell me, are you?" She slanted a peevish gaze at him.

He refused to be baited. "It's a personal matter of the utmost urgency."

She rose regally to her feet and dropped her napkin on the table. "In that case, as punishment for secrecy you will get no good night kiss. Put that in your pipe and smoke it." She strode from the room with only a hint of a dimple betraying her amusement.

"Mrs. Howard . . ."

The innkeeper's voice finally penetrated her dream. Madeline bolted upright. The woman stood at the foot of her bed, holding a pale green dress she'd never seen before.

"What is it, Mrs. Lang? Is the house on fire?" She clutched the quilt beneath her chin.

"No, no. General Downing said he would like you to accompany him on a very important errand." Mrs. Lang draped the beautiful dress across a chair and then boldly pulled undergarments from her guest's bureau drawer.

"Has he indeed? And where exactly would that be?" Madeline asked, not budging from the warm, comfortable bed.

Mrs. Lang, however, wasn't one to stand on proper decorum. With a single yank she pulled the covers from the bed, leaving Madeline shivering in her thin chemise. "You'll have to ask him yourself. He's downstairs with a carriage waiting on the street. I filled you a tub in the bath down the hall. I suggest you hurry, and wear that dress there. The general ordered it special."

"I already told you I have no need of fancy gowns. I'll soon return to my farm and —" Her explanation hung unfinished in the air because the exasperating woman had already headed downstairs. Madeline had little choice but do as she was told.

She should be annoyed by James's bossy presumptuousness. She should stand her ground and assert independence before finding herself in a compromising situation. Yet something suggested patience. A small voice whispered that all would be well because she loved him and he loved her.

So Madeline bathed, brushed out her hair, and dressed in the beautiful gown that fit surprisingly well. Then she descended the steps to find her landlady gone and the general lounging on the porch.

"Ah, you're ready at last. Shall we be off?" James offered an arm.

"Very well, but I'm curious regarding your mysterious plans." She tucked her hand in the crook of his elbow.

"The sun is shining and birds are singing. I thought we could take a ride on this lovely April day."

Swallowing back her retort, Madeline took

several deep breaths. Inside the carriage she began to relax when they reached the edge of town. The air smelled clean and fresh, and the spring sun was warm on her skin. Just for a moment, she imagined she was home in Pennsylvania. When she opened her eyes, they had stopped in front of a small white church. Without stained glass windows and a soaring bell tower, it was no great cathedral like St. Paul's, yet it possessed its own beauty. "Is *this* one of your errands? Are you acquainted with this church?"

"No, I've never been here before, but why don't we go inside?" He jumped down and extended his hand.

Madeline's heart quickened, while a frisson of anxiety snaked up her spine. "What are you up to, James? Why have we come here?"

"To get married, of course. I can't take you back to headquarters and then on to Washington for the Grand Review unless we are properly wed. How would it look?" He lifted a massive bouquet of bluebells, trilliums, and purple hyacinths from behind the seat.

"Get married? In *Virginia*?" It sounded as though she were comparing the state to the deserts of Arabia. "I can't possibly marry you today."

"Why not?"

"Because . . . because we have no preacher."

"He's inside, waiting for us."

"What about a witness?"

"Mrs. Lang is also inside the chapel, doubtlessly peeking out the window."

"But you have no ring."

"Indeed, I do." James withdrew a narrow gold band from his breast pocket. "I purchased it months ago just for this propitious occasion. I ordered a wedding dress in your favorite color and spent the entire morning picking these." He held out the flowers. "Not a bad bunch, if I do say so myself. You know I love you and I suspect you love me. So, Mrs. Howard, what seems to be the problem?"

Staring at the wildflowers, Madeline smoothed her hands down the imported silk. "Green is my favorite color and the flowers are lovely, but haven't you forgotten something?" Her voice sounded small and childlike. "You haven't *asked* me yet."

James flushed to a deep shade of scarlet. "Madeline, I cannot bear another moment without you as my wife. Before another war starts, or we're captured by bandits, or lightning strikes the steeple, will you marry me?"

Her gaze turned skyward. "There's not a cloud in the sky, but very well, General Downing. I will marry you here and now. After all, Virginia is almost starting to feel like home."

Cashtown, Pennsylvania
August 1865

"Scat!" Madeline brought her broom down inches from the rodent's long, skinny tail. "I'll teach you what happens when somebody other than me naps on my new feather pillow." *Whap.* When the broom handle struck the pine floorboards with a resounding echo, the gray mouse scuttled through a hole to freedom. "And stay out!" She shouted at the top of her lungs.

With the battle temporarily stalemated, Madeline climbed down the ladder to the first floor in search of cooler air outdoors. She was greeted, however, by Reverend and Mrs. Bennett wearing expressions of shock, and her new husband, his expression mirthful.

"Mrs. Downing," said Reverend Bennett. "Have we come at a bad time?" His wife stepped closer to his side.

Madeline was flummoxed. "No, I'm always pleased to see you two. Let's go sit in the shade. I have a jug of tea cooling in the root cellar." She brushed her palms together.

Mrs. Bennett glanced toward the loft window. "Shouldn't we invite your houseguest to join us?"

"Houseguest? No one is here but James and me." She stared at the pastor's wife in confusion.

"Then who fell asleep on your bed?" Mrs. Bennett spoke softly so as not to be overheard by the intruder.

It took Madeline a few moments before comprehension dawned. "Oh, my. I beg your pardon. No one was supposed to hear my temper tantrum. A mouse has invaded our bedroom. He insists on leaving behind muddy footprints . . . or something worse."

Both Bennetts tried unsuccessfully not to laugh.

"Don't be fooled by Madeline." James stroked his beard, which he recently clipped very short. "She treats me the same way as the mouse if I roll onto her half of the bed or pull too much of the quilt to my side."

"Oh, James." Madeline blushed at his boldness in front of the preacher — a man she'd known most of her life. "Be careful or all you'll get for supper is a piece of cheese."

She linked arms with him as the foursome walked to the shade of an ancient maple.

The tree, like the horse barn, had remained untouched during the artillery shelling that destroyed her home. Thanks to the residents of Cashtown, all residue of that horrible fire was gone. Over the original root cellar — her refuge — James was building a new house atop the river rock foundation. Board by board, nail by nail, the two-story clapboard with a wide wraparound porch and tin roof would shelter their family for years to come. A family she hoped would steadily increase in number.

"The place is coming along nicely, General Downing." Reverend Bennett shaded his eyes from the sun's glare. "Astounding progress in two short months."

"James, please, sir. I resigned from the army and no longer use my military title. I have become a simple Pennsylvania farmer."

"No, sir, I don't think I could call you that, not after your exemplary years of service to our country. Why, a day doesn't go by that I don't hear about your valor on the battlefield. The men of the Fourth Corps served proudly under you and will sing your praise until their dying day."

Settling back on her elbows, Madeline stretched her legs out in the grass. James would allow the minister to ramble on about the war. He would clench his teeth but not interrupt, because it did no good whatsoever. Men loved to talk war stories . . . except for her beloved husband. James was determined to become a horse breeder and trainer as Tobias had been. His West Point education left him ill-prepared for life after the army. So when he finished working on their house for the day, he read books about horse husbandry by the fire. He vowed on their wedding day never to take up arms against his fellow man again. James didn't even like hunting deer for meat for their table. But Madeline didn't care if their diet consisted of beans, corn, and barley. His gentle heart belonged to her. And what woman in love could ask for more than that?

"Let me know when you're ready for roof rafters." Reverend Bennett finished his drink and rose to his feet. "Men from far and wide will come to help. Everyone wants you settled in the new house as soon as possible. We're all happy you decided to make Cashtown your home."

"You two need to give the barn loft back to the mice," Mrs. Bennett said as she fanned herself with her apron.

"What a splendid idea," Madeline agreed eagerly. "James promised we'll be in by the first snowfall."

"Walk me to my buggy, Madeline," said Mrs. Bennett. "I picked up your mail in town and brought lamb stew and an apple pie for supper."

"You've spoiled me so badly I won't know what to do in my new kitchen." Madeline flashed her husband a wink.

At the road James shook hands with Reverend Bennett, smiling and waving until they turned onto the road. Once the buggy disappeared, he encircled her waist with his strong arms. "Mmm. Lamb stew sounds delicious."

Laden down with the pie and a kettle of stew, Madeline was trapped in his embrace. "I think so too, and you really should let them help us beyond just bringing the occasional meal. They want to so badly, and I don't think Reverend Bennett will take no for an answer."

"They've already done plenty by organizing that party for us. People brought bedding, crockery, almost everything we'll need. The men helped me put in a late crop of hay and corn. And at least a dozen members of my former corps promised spring foals to start our breeding stock." James took the pies from her armload.

"That's what friends and neighbors do.

They help one another."

"I've never had neighbors before, only fellow officers in the military. Besides, rebuilding this house is something I wanted to do for you. A labor of love — my love."

"And I love you, but letting them help will get us under roof that much sooner."

"And curtail the romantic atmosphere of the hayloft?"

"The mice would like their domain back."

"Won't you miss cooking over an open campfire?"

"I have my eye on a new coal stove in town."

"Your pioneer ancestors would cluck their tongues," James murmured as he nuzzled her ear.

"Not the female half. They would understand. Besides, you promised me a proper honeymoon when we move your furniture from Philadelphia. I'm eager to travel east."

James kissed the bridge of her nose. "Your wish is my command."

"In that case, hold this pie and Mrs. Bennett's kettle of stew so I can open this letter. It's from my aunt in Richmond."

As they strolled up the dirt lane, Madeline's eyes skimmed over Clarisa's small, precise handwriting. "Goodness, so much news! I'll read you the whole letter at supper. But the best part is Eugenia is getting married in November. She begs me . . . us to come to her wedding. Oh, James, I do wish to honor my promise, but I don't want to travel alone. Please say you'll come with me."

He sighed wearily. "Maddy, how could a Yankee general show his face in Richmond? That town has suffered greatly."

"But it was the Fourth Corps — your men — who put out the fires or the destruction would have been so much worse."

"Few citizens will remember that detail, my love. Your family might not be able to relax if I'm there."

"My family remembers. That's why your name is also on the invitation." She showed him the envelope.

James shook his head with a slow smile. "You win, but I refuse to wear my uniform. I'll dress as a simple horse breeder or I won't go."

Madeline wrapped both arms around his waist. "I thought the Downings had sworn off lives of subterfuge."

"Hmm, why don't we implement that pledge after your cousin's wedding?"

"Very well, Mr. Downing, but don't blame me if you're mistaken for a stable boy and asked to move buggies to the back alley."

"To see you wearing one of those outra-
geous hooped gowns, Mrs. Downing, it's a
chance I'm willing to take."

DISCUSSION QUESTIONS

1. How is Madeline Howard victimized by both armies when the war comes to Cashtown, Pennsylvania?
2. Why does Richmond, Virginia — the capital of the Confederacy — seem like Madeline's only alternative when forced to relocate?
3. How does Eugenia's upbringing and home life differ from what Madeline experienced?
4. Elliott Haywood has a position of responsibility and authority in the Confederacy. Why does he assume the best about Madeline's integrity throughout the story?
5. Nothing goes right for General Downing in terms of courting Madeline. Why is it so easy for Major Henry to thwart his efforts and why would he choose to do so?
6. Madeline finds herself a spy quite

by accident. How does living with the Duncans allow access to sensitive military intelligence?

7. Despite being the enemy, Colonel Haywood is a hard man to resist. What qualities make him so appealing?

8. The upper-class citizens of Richmond attempt to carry on as normal, despite the war creating privation among the poor and working class. How is that possible?

9. Why does Madeline participate in holiday festivities if her heart is with General Downing?

10. How does having a fishing boat make Captain George effective as a spy?

11. Madeline's visit to Culpeper to see General Downing cements their relationship. Why does she choose to return to Richmond?

12. Colonel Haywood endeavors to restore Madeline's reputation even if it jeopardizes his own. Why would he go to such lengths when she's in love with someone else?

13. What makes Kathleen O'Toole so determined to undermine Madeline?

14. Why is Aunt Clarisa loyal to her niece even after learning the truth about her activities?
15. Madeline's love for James and her patriotism for her country inspire her to steal documents for the Union Army. What causes her to lose her taste for espionage work?

ABOUT THE AUTHOR

Mary Ellis and her husband, Ken, live near the Cuyahoga Valley National Recreation Area, home to the last remaining GAR Hall in Ohio, and Hale Farm and Village, home to annual encampments and reenactments of Civil War battles. She is an active member of the local historical society and Civil War Roundtable, where she served as secretary for several years. She has enjoyed a lifelong passion for American history.

Mary loves to hear from her readers at
maryeellis@yahoo.com
or
www.maryellis.net

MULTNOMAH COUNTY
LIBRARY

11 — 14

VAN READER RECORD-A

1	11	21	31	41	51	61	71	81	91	101	111	121	131	141	151	161	171	181	191
2	12	22	32	42	52	62	72	82	92	102	112	122	132	142	152	162	172	182	192
3	13	23	33	43	53	63	73	83	93	103	113	123	133	143	153	163	173	183	193
4	14	24	34	44	54	64	74	84	94	104	114	124	134	144	154	164	174	184	194
5	15	25	35	45	55	65	75	85	95	105	115	125	135	145	155	165	175	185	195
6	16	26	36	46	56	66	76	86	96	106	116	126	136	146	156	166	176	186	196
7	17	27	37	47	57	67	77	87	97	107	117	127	137	147	157	167	177	187	197
8	18	28	38	48	58	68	78	88	98	108	118	128	138	148	158	168	178	188	198
9	19	29	39	49	59	69	79	89	99	109	119	129	139	149	159	169	179	189	199
10	20	30	40	50	60	70	80	90	100	110	120	130	140	150	160	170	180	190	200

VAN READER RECORD-B

1	11	21	31	41	51	61	71	81	91	101	111	121	131	141	151	161	171	181	191
2	12	22	32	42	52	62	72	82	92	102	112	122	132	142	152	162	172	182	192
3	13	23	33	43	53	63	73	83	93	103	113	123	133	143	153	163	173	183	193
4	14	24	34	44	54	64	74	84	94	104	114	124	134	144	154	164	174	184	194
5	15	25	35	45	55	65	75	85	95	105	115	125	135	145	155	165	175	185	195
6	16	26	36	46	56	66	76	86	96	106	116	126	136	146	156	166	176	186	196
7	17	27	37	47	57	67	77	87	97	107	117	127	137	147	157	167	177	187	197
8	18	28	38	48	58	68	78	88	98	108	118	128	138	148	158	168	178	188	198
9	19	29	39	49	59	69	79	89	99	109	119	129	139	149	159	169	179	189	199
10	20	30	40	50	60	70	80	90	100	110	120	130	140	150	160	170	180	190	200

F-LOS-08
07/93